Jo

Latin Prose Composition

SALZWASSER
VERLAG

John Massie

Latin Prose Composition

Reprint of the original, first published in 1864.

1st Edition 2022 | ISBN: 978-3-75259-410-2

Verlag (Publisher): Salzwasser Verlag GmbH, Zeilweg 44, 60439 Frankfurt, Deutschland
Vertretungsberechtigt (Authorized to represent): E. Roepke, Zeilweg 44, 60439 Frankfurt, Deutschland
Druck (Print): Books on Demand GmbH, In de Tarpen 42, 22848 Norderstedt, Deutschland

LATIN PROSE COMPOSITION:

THE

CONSTRUCTION OF CLAUSES,

WITH

ILLUSTRATIONS FROM CICERO AND CÆSAR;

TOGETHER WITH

A VOCABULARY AND INDEX.

BY

JOHN MASSIE, A.M.

EDINBURGH

1864.

CONTENTS.

PREFACE.

Latin Composition, in its widest acceptation, has to do with four things,—*concord*, or the agreement of words among themselves; *government*, or the cases that adjectives, nouns, and verbs take after them; *collocation*, or the order and position of words in a sentence; and the *construction of clauses*, or the forms which subject and predicate assume. Only the last is professedly treated of here, though the others may be incidentally illustrated. It is assumed that the student has made himself familiar, through the ordinary Rudiments and Grammatical Exercises, with concord and government, and an attempt is made to place before him the forms of construction of subject and predicate in the English, with the corresponding forms in the Latin. The English form admitting of much greater variety than the Latin, the variations of which it is susceptible have been given wherever it was thought necessary. By the adoption of the English as the basis, the systematic treatment of the subject has perhaps been somewhat interfered with; but it is presumed that what has been lost to system has been more than compensated for by the greater facility of leading the student to an acquaintance with the Latin by means of the English form.

In a work on Latin Composition, it is necessary to have in view some standard, the usage of the Latin, like that of every other language, not being by any means uniform. For this reason, and not from any affectation of Ciceronianism, the illustrations have been taken from Cicero and Cæsar; and it is to be understood that the remarks in the following pages have reference to the general style of these authors. It would have been easy to have given from their writings numerous exceptions to general usage; but as it did not seem that with beginners this could serve any good purpose, it was deemed more expedient to adhere to general usage, leaving the exceptional forms to be mastered by the student when he advances to the criticism of the language.

It will be observed that most of the illustrations are in the active voice. A preference has been given to it, that the sentences, after having been rendered into English, may be again rendered into Latin in the passive voice, —an exercise that should be persevered in till every sentence can be rendered in either voice with the greatest facility. If this is done with sufficient care, the student should know not the difference of the construction of clauses in the two languages only, but also the difference of idiom,—there being scarcely an idiom of any importance that does not occur in the illustrations.

I have quoted directly from Cicero and Cæsar, and I have also freely availed myself of whatever examples occurred elsewhere in the course of my reading. I am, however, chiefly indebted, for Latin illustrations, to the Lateinische Grammatik von D. Ludwig Ramshorn, and the Lexicon Ciceronianum Marii Nizolii, and, for English-Latin examples, to my own notes of Dr. Melvin's teaching.

My best thanks are due to several friends in Aberdeen for their able assistance in revising the press, as well as for many valuable suggestions during the progress of the work.

ABERDEEN, *February* 1864.

INTRODUCTION.

Before beginning our proper work, we wish to say a few words by way of caution to the young student, which if he will but bear in mind, he will soon come to see that Latin construction is at once natural and easy.

I. *The sense governs the construction of the clauses in the Latin.*—The young student is apt to imagine that the construction depends on the verb, and when he finds that the verb is constructed in various ways, he is quite at a loss how to proceed. But it is only so far true that the verb determines the construction. Whether the *subject* shall assume a *personal* or an *impersonal* form depends entirely on the verb; but the construction of the other clauses of the sentence depends as entirely on its meaning.

Thus, in the sentence,

I repent of doing it,

the subject is personal in English, but it must be impersonal in the Latin, because the verb in Latin is impersonal. It will therefore be

Me pœnitet.

But the clause *of doing it* may be constructed in either of two ways, according to the meaning or intention of the writer or speaker. If he means to state the *doing of it* as a fact, and to lay emphasis on the fact, then the Latin will be,

Pœnitet me *quod id feci;*

but if he does not mean to make emphatic the statement *of doing it*, then the Latin will be,

Pœnitet me *id fecisse.*

The Latin *verb* thus determines the *personality* or *impersonality* of the *subject;* but the sense, idea, or conception determines the construction of the rest of the sentence. There are, indeed, some verbs and other parts of speech with peculiarities of construction, which will be noticed in their own place; but these do not affect the general rule, *that the meaning of a sentence determines the construction of its clauses.* Settle, therefore, the form of the subject, and then ascertain what is the nature of the idea intended to be conveyed to the mind of the reader or hearer by the entire predicate.

II. *The Latins have a different form for every kind of idea or conception.*—For some kinds of ideas they have more than one form, and the choice of the form is determined by circumstances noticed afterwards; but what requires to be specially remembered is, *that every idea has its form.* Existence, object, opinion, purpose or end, reason, condition, etc., etc., have each their appropriate mode of expression; and it is very seldom indeed that the form for one kind of idea is used to express another and different kind of idea. Thus,—

You may depend upon him going,

is a statement of *opinion*, and the form will be, according to Pred. III., the verb with the accusative and infinitive,

Pro certo habere potes eum iturum esse.

But,

The matter depends upon his going,

is a statement of *condition*, and the form will be, according to Pred. IV. 5., the verb followed by *si* and the subjunctive;

Res in eo nititur, si iverit.

The Latin construction thus resting on ideas, when you have determined the nature of the idea to be rendered into Latin, look for the Latin form adapted to its expression, and do not deviate from it without good reason.

It is to be observed here that the English form is rather partial to substantives, but if the Latin form require it, the substantive must be resolved into the corresponding verb; thus, the sentence,

The boy expressed his intention of going,

is a statement of opinion, which (Pred. III.) completes the predicate with the accusative and infinitive. We must therefore resolve *his intention of going* into *that he intended to go.* Then we have,

The boy expressed [said] that he intended to go.
Puer dixit se in animo habere ire.

Notice here further, that it is because the construction depends on the idea that the same *leading* verb has now one construction and now another; as,

The father *advised* the boy to do it.
Pater puero *suasit* ut* id faceret.
The father *advised* the boy what to do.
Pater puero *suasit* quid* faceret.
The father *advised* the boy before going away.
Pater puero *suasit* priusquam* abiret.

So also we may say,

The father *persuaded* the boy that it was done.
Pater puero *suasit* id factum esse.

III. *The English form is very often ambiguous.*—This ambiguity arises from its expressing very dissimilar ideas by means of the same form; as,

Be content with seeing him,

which, according to the context, may mean,

Be content to see him;
Satis habe eum videre;

or,

Be content, because you have seen him;
Satis habe, quod eum vidisti;

or,

Be content, if you see him.
Satis habe, si eum videris.

So again, in the sentences,

1. The soldiers resolved on gaining the victory;
2. The soldiers resolved on gaining the victory to spare the vanquished;

* See General Rule, foot note, p. 65.

3. The senate congratulated the general on gaining the victory;
4. The soldiers were intent on gaining the victory;

the English forms are apparently the same, but in reality very different.

In 1, *on gaining the victory* is the infinitive* of *object*, and the sentence must (Pred. II. 7.) be in Latin constructed thus:

Milites statuerunt victoriam reportare.

In 2, the expression *on gaining the victory* indicates *succession*, and the sentence must (Notes on the Construction of some Particles,—*quum*, p. 120) be made

Milites statuerunt, quum victoriam reportassent, victis parcere.

In 3, the expression assigns the *reason* of the congratulation, and is (Causal Particles, p. 122) to be made thus:

Senatus duci gratulatus est quod victoriam repor tasset (or reportaverat, if the historian does not wish to intimate that the *senate assigned* the reason for the congratulation).

In 4, the words *on gaining the victory* indicate *purpose* dependent on an adjective, and must (p. 58) be made

Milites intenti erant ad victoriam reportandam.

Care must therefore be exercised not to be misled by the mere appearance of the English form, which is so very deceptive.

* See foot note, p. 54.

IV. *The English form is often very inexact in its tenses, and even in its moods.*—The present infinitive especially is often used for the future indicative; as,

I hope to go = I hope that I shall go.
Spero me iturum esse.

So the infinitive is used for the subjunctive, as,

I know not what to do = I know not what I should do.
Nescio quid facere debeam.

Indeed, the English infinitive is used for the expression of almost every conception.

To avoid, then, falling into an error of tense or mood, resolve the English infinitive, whenever it can be resolved, into a finite mood, and the resolution will generally give the correct tense or mood.

LATIN PROSE COMPOSITION.

WHAT A SENTENCE IS.

A *Sentence is a number of words so arranged as to make sense;* or, A *Sentence is a judgment expressed in words;* or, A *Sentence is a complete proposition;** as,

1. *James is a good man.*
   Jacobus est vir bonus.
2. *James was induced to make war on Henry.*
   Jacobus adductus est ut Henrico bellum inferret.
3. *James asked them what they were doing.*
   Jacobus eos rogavit quid facerent.

In none of these examples is the word *James* what we understand by a sentence. Something must be said concerning James, and only when this is said have we a sentence. In the first example this something is, *is a good man*, which completes the sense. In the second example we have, *James was induced;* but though there is a verb here, the sense is not complete. We ask, *induced to do what?* and the answer to this question gives the complete sense, or *complement* of the predicate, *induced to make war on Henry.* In the third example, the words, *James asked them*, might in some instances form a complete sentence; but they do not

* Since the days of Aristotle there have not been wanting grammarians who have defined a sentence as a *period* or *circuit*, having beginning and end in itself. Aristotle's period, however, was not so much a sentence as a particular kind of sentence or style of writing, which is known as the *periodic* or *compact* as opposed to the *loose* style.—See *Aristotle's Rhetoric*, iii. 5.

do so here. The sense and the sentence are completed by the words, *what they were doing.*

A sentence, then, is *complete sense;* and whenever the sense intended to be conveyed by the writer or speaker is not complete, the sentence is not complete, though a few of the words taken by themselves, apart from the context, might form a sentence.

PARTS OF A SENTENCE.

In the Sentence, logically considered, there are three parts: the *Subject*, or *that of which something is said;* the *Predicate*, or *what is said of the subject;* and the *Copula*, or *that which joins the subject to the predicate;* as,

> *James* [subject] *is* [copula] *a good man* [predicate].
> *Jacobus* [subject] *est* [copula] *vir bonus* [predicate].

But it will be more convenient for the purpose of composition to regard the sentence as consisting of only two parts, *subject* and *predicate;* as,

> *Jacobus* [subject] *est vir bonus* [predicate];

or, whenever there is more than one verb in the sentence, and the second is not *directly* governed in the infinitive by the active voice of the first or leading verb, we may divide the sentence into *subject, predicate*, and *complement of the predicate*, or *subject, predicate*, and *complement;** as,

> *Orgetorix* [sub.] *was the richest of the Helvetii* [pred.].
> *Orgetorix* [sub.] *fuit ditissimus Helvetiorum* [pred.].

We have here only *one* verb, and so have only subject and predicate.

* The complement is by some called a *subordinate sentence.* Strictly speaking, it is not a sentence, but a clause of a sentence; and it were better, adopting this nomenclature, that it should be called the *subordinate clause*, and the other the *leading clause* of the predicate.

Orgetorix [sub.] *was wont to favour revolutions* [pred.].

Orgetorix [sub.] *solebat studere novis rebus* [pred.].

We have in this example *two* verbs, but the second is *directly* governed in the infinitive by the first.

Orgetorix [sub.] *persuaded them* [pred.] *to depart* [comp.].

Orgetorix [sub.] *iis persuasit* [pred.] *ut abirent* [comp.].

We have here also *two* verbs, but the second is only *indirectly* governed in the infinitive by the first. The first verb *directly* governs *them*.

Orgetorix [sub.] *said* [pred.] *that it was very easy* [comp.].

Orgetorix [sub.] *dixit* [pred.] *perfacile esse* [comp.].

Orgetorix [sub.] *asked* [pred.] *who he was* [comp.].

Orgetorix [sub.] *rogavit* [pred.] *quis esset* [comp.].

Orgetorix [sub.] *sent men* [pred.] *to tell* [comp.].

Orgetorix [sub.] *misit homines* [pred.] *qui dicerent* [comp.].

Orgetorix [sub.] *was so angry* [pred.] *that he killed himself* [comp.].

Orgetorix [sub.] *tam iratus fuit* [pred.] *ut mortem sibi conscisceret* [comp.].

Translate the following sentences, pointing out subject, predicate, and complement:

Gallia est omnis divisa in tres partes. Hi omnes lingua, institutis, legibus inter se differunt. Helvetii reliquos Gallos virtute præcedunt. Orgetorigem ex vinculis causam dicere coegerunt. Per eos, ne causam diceret, se eripuit. Persuadent Rauracis, ut, eodem usi consilio, oppidis suis vicisque exustis, una cum iis proficiscantur. Allobrogibus sese persuasuros existimabant. Helvetii legatos ad Dumnorigem Æduum mittunt, ut eo deprecatore a Sequanis hoc impetrarent. A Sequanis impetrat, ut per fines suos Helvetios ire patiantur. Ædui legatos ad Cæsarem mittunt rogatum auxilium. Allobroges demonstrant, sibi præter agri solum nihil esse reliqui. Per exploratores Cæsar certior factus est, tres jam copiarum partes Helvetios id flumen transduxisse. Ac vereor ne talium personarum imminuam gloriam. Tales enim nos esse putamus, ut jure laudemur. Non fuit tantus homo Sextus Roscius in civitate, ut de eo potissimum conqueramur. Is Stoicus esse voluit. Ego conservare coloniam populi Romani cupio; tu expugnare studes. Te rogo, ut omnes tuos nervos in eo contendas, ne quid mihi ad hanc provinciam temporis prorogetur. Nec dubito, quin Cæsar a me contendat, ut ad urbem veniam. Erubescunt pudici etiam loqui de pudicitia.

CONNEXION OF SENTENCES.

Sentences or Propositions may be connected together in three ways, viz. :—

1. By simple juxtaposition;* as,

I came, I saw, I conquered. *Veni, vidi, vici.*

Here (*Ego*) [sub.] *veni* [pred.], (*Ego*) [sub.] *vidi* [pred.], (*Ego*) [sub.] *vici* [pred.].

2. By conjunctions; as,

He slew all the armed, AND *sold the rest for slaves.*
Omnes armatos interfecit, ET *cæteros pro servis vendidit.*

Here (*Is*) [sub.] *omnes armatos interfecit* [pred.], ET (*is*) [sub.] *cæteros pro servis vendidit* [pred.].

The boy neither said it NOR *thought it.*
Puer [sub.] *id nec dixit* [pred.], NEC (*puer*) [sub.] *putavit* [pred.].

3. By relatives; as,

Crassus passed the river by a bridge, WHICH *was built by Alexander the Great.*
Crassus [sub.] *flumen ponte transiit* [pred.], QUI [sub.] *ab Alexandro magno factus est* [pred.].

* Sentences connected by juxtaposition, etc., are sometimes called *co-ordinate* propositions or sentences.

A relative may introduce *an explanatory clause* (= *an adjective*), or *a new proposition*, or a *complement of the predicate;* and you must know which of these the relative introduces before attempting to turn the sentence into Latin; as,

> *The act of* WHICH [explanatory] *we have made mention above, was passed, under* WHICH [new prop.] *there are some* WHO [comp. of pred.] *live securely.*
> *Lex,* CUJUS [explanatory] *supra mentionem fecimus, lata est,* QUÂ [new prop.] *sunt* QUI [comp. of pred.] *tutô vivant.*

Translate, distinguishing sentences, giving the connexion, and giving also the subject, pred., and comp.:

Alieno loco cum equitatu Helvetiorum prœlium committunt, et pauci de nostris cadunt. Hic pagus unus patrum nostrorum memoria L. Cassium consulem interfecerat, et ejus exercitum sub jugum miserat. Helvetii legatos ad eum mittunt; cujus legationis Divico princeps fuit, qui bello Cassiano dux Helvetiorum fuerat. Quod est bonum, omne laudabile est. Ego illi maximam gratiam habeo, qui me ea pœna mulctaverit, quam sine mutatione et sine versura possem dissolvere. Nec vero ego iis a quibus accusatus sum, aut a quibus condemnatus, habeo quod succenseam, nisi quod mihi nocere se crediderunt. Tentarem etiam summi Regis, qui maximas copias duxit ad Trojam, prudentiam. Ita, quæ mutat, ea corrumpit; quæ sequitur, sunt tota Democriti. At me, inquam, nisi te audire vellem, censes hæc dicturum fuisse? Quæ fuerit causa, mox videro. Res ipsa aut me ipsum, aut alium quempiam, aut invitabit aut dehortabitur. Crœsus hostium vim se perversurum putavit, pervertit autem suam. Animantes aluntur, augescuntque et pubescunt. Nec melior vir fuit Africano quisquam, nec clarior. Docilis est qui attente vult audire. Pugnatum est diu atque acriter, cum Sotiates, superioribus victoriis freti, in sua virtute totius Aquitaniæ salutem positam putarent; nostri autem, quid sine imperatore, et sine reliquis legionibus, adolescentulo duce, efficere possent, perspici cuperent; tandem tamen confecti vulneribus hostes terga vertêre: quorum magno numero interfecto, Crassus ex itinere oppidum Sotiatum oppugnare cœpit; quibus fortiter resistentibus, vineas turresque egit. Duces vero ii deliguntur, qui unâ cum Q. Sertorio omnes annos fuerant, summamque scientiam rei militaris habere existimabantur.

THE SUBJECT.

The Subject may be,—

1. A substantive, adjective, or pronoun.
2. An infinitive.
3. A clause of a sentence.

I. *Substantive, Adjective, or Pronoun Subject.*

1. One or more substantives in the nominative; as,

James and John were good.
Jacobus et Joannes fuerunt boni.

Copias suas Cæsar in proximum collem subducit. Helvetii impedimenta in unum locum contulerunt. Filia et unus e filiis captus est.* Secundæ res, honores, imperia, victoriæ fortuita sunt. Misericordia est ægritudo ex miseria alterius injuria laborantis. Ego et Hortensius, te hortatore, facimus. Duæ filiæ harum, altera occisa, altera capta est. Arpineius et Junius, quæ audierint,

* When the substantives are of different genders, and refer to persons, the masculine is preferred to the feminine, and the feminine to the neuter; or, the predicative adjective may agree with the nearest, and be understood to the rest. But if the substantives be names of things (not persons), the predicative adjective is generally put in the plural neuter.

ad legatos deferunt. In senatu continuo Lentulus et Lucullus de hac re faciunt mentionem.

2. One or more adjectives in the nominative; as,

The good are brave.

Boni sunt fortes.

Nonnulli inter carros rotasque mataras ac tragulas subjiciebant. Nostri eos sequi non potuerunt. Omnes magno fletu auxilium a Cæsare petere cœperunt. Sapiens nullo tempore est beatus. Stulti autem malorum memoria torquentur.

3. One or more pronouns in the nominative; as,

You and he and I are brave.

Ego et tu et ille sumus fortes.*

Ipse interim in colle medio triplicem aciem instruxit. Tu mihi etiam legis Portiæ, tu Gracchi, tu horum mentionem facis. Ego sum ille consul. Si tu et Tullia valetis, ego et Cicero valemus. Beate vivere nos in sapientia, vos in voluptate ponitis.

4. In certain circumstances, one or more substantives or pronouns, which, in Latin, must be put in the *dative;* as,

You must do this.

Tibi hoc faciendum est.

I have books.

Mihi sunt libri.

Mihi repetenda est veteris cujusdam memoriæ non sane satis explicata recordatio. Quæ quidem tibi nunc omnia belli vulnera sananda sunt. Quoniam et satis jam ambulatum est, et tibi aliud initium sumendum est. Jam tum erat honos eloquentiæ. Cæsari omnia uno

* When there are pronouns of different persons, the verb agrees with the first person in preference to the second, and with the second in preference to the third, or it may take the person of the nearest, and be understood to the rest. Observe that the Latins arrange the personal pronouns in the exact order of the persons.

tempore erant agenda; vexillum proponendum, signum tuba dandum. Exercitatio quædam suscipienda nobis est. Verbum mihi deest. De voluntate adversariorum nemini dubium esset.

5. One or more substantives or pronouns, which, with such verbs as *miseret*, *pœnitet*, etc., will, in Latin, be put in the *accusative*; as,

I pity you.
Me tui miseret.

Eorum nos magis miseret, qui nostram misericordiam non requirunt, quam qui illam efflagitant. Mea mater, tui me miseret, mei te piget. Sunt homines, quos infamiæ nec pudeat, neque tædeat.

When the subject is a pronoun in the nominative, it is not expressed, unless it is emphatic; as,

He reads.
[Is] legit.

This is called the personal subject.

Before leaving it, we may show how the subject may be amplified. To begin with this simple sentence:

James was wise.
Jacobus fuit sapiens.

We may expand the subject by

(*a*) Substantives; as,

James the son was wise.
*Jacobus filius** fuit sapiens.
James the son of George was wise.
Jacobus Georgii filius fuit sapiens.

Volusenus erat tribunus militum, vir consilii magni et virtutis. Mittitur ad eos Arpineius, eques. Deliciæ meæ, Dicæarchus, contra immortalitatem disseruit. Aristoteles,

* The words *Jacobus filius* may mean *James who is a son*, *James when a son*, *James though a son*, etc. In some positions they may mean James *as* a son = *in the capacity of* a son, though this is frequently expressed by *ut*,—Jacobus *ut* filius.

vir summo ingenio, scientiæ copia, dicere cœpit. Philippus, magno vir ingenio, inprimisque clarus, gloriari solebat. Princeps Academiæ, Philo, Mithridatico bello domo profugit, Romamque venit. Furius, noster familiaris, puer didicit quod discendum fuit.

(*b*) Adjectives; as,

James the brave, the son of George the good, was wise.

Jacobus fortis, Georgii boni filius, fuit sapiens.

Vir inprimis clarus dicere solebat. Alcidamus quidam rhetor antiquus, inprimis nobilis scripsit laudationem mortis. Neque ulla officii præcepta firma, stabilia, conjuncta naturæ tradi possunt. Demetrius Phalereus in hoc numero haberi potest, disputator subtilis, orator parum vehemens, dulcis tamen. Amicus certus in re incerta cernitur. Ipse Alexander Thebas diruit.

(*c*) Relative clauses; as,

James the brave, the son of George the good, who was dear to his father, was wise.

Jacobus fortis, Georgii boni filius, qui patri carus fuit, sapiens fuit.

Ego, qui Catilinam non laudavi, qui reo Catilinæ consul non adfui, qui testimonium de conjuratione dixi in alios, adeone vobis alienus a sanitate esse videor? Quod vitium effugere qui volet, adhibebit et tempus et diligentiam. Duces principesque Nerviorum, qui aliquem sermonis aditum, causamque amicitiæ cum Cicerone habebant, colloqui sese velle dicunt. Qui audiebant, quoad poterant, defendebant sententiam suam.

(*d*) Causal clauses;* as,

James the brave, the son of George the good, who was dear to his father, because he loved learning, was wise.

Jacobus fortis, Georgii boni filius, qui patri carus fuit, quod discere studuit, sapiens fuit.

* See Causal particles, for construction.

Stoici, quod finem bonorum in una virtute ponunt, similes sunt eorum; quod autem principium officii quæsierunt, melius [faciunt] quam Pyrrho. Ædui, cum se suaque ab iis defendere non possint, legatos ad Cæsarem mittunt. Cæsar ab Crasso certior factus, quod ipse aberat longius, naves interim longas ædificari jubet. Labienus castris hostium potitus, et ex loco superiore quæ res in nostris castris gererentur conspicatus, decimam legionem subsidio nostris misit. Nonnulli, pudore adducti, remanebant. Quorum uterque suo studio delectatus, contemsit alterum.

(*e*) Temporal clauses; as,

James the brave, the son of George the good, who was dear to his father, because he loved learning, after studying the Roman law at Rome, was wise.

Jacobus fortis, Georgii boni filius, qui patri carus fuit, quod discere studuit, postquam Romæ juri Romano studuit,* sapiens fuit.

Omne animal, simul ut ortum est, et seipsum et suas partes diligit. Postquam id animum advertit, copias suas in proximum collem subducit. Et disces, quamdiu voles. Sub vesperum Cæsar portas claudi, milites ex oppido exire jussit. Ubi [turrim] moveri et appropinquare viderunt, nova atque inusitata specie commoti, legatos ad Cæsarem de pace miserunt. Lentulus, me consule, vicit superiores.

(*f*) Concessive clauses; as,

James the brave, the son of George the good, who was dear to his father, because he loved learning, after studying the Roman law at Rome, though he was in infirm health, was wise.

Jacobus fortis, Georgii boni filius, qui patri carus fuit, quod discere studuit, postquam Romæ juri

* See Temporal particles, for construction.

Romano studuit, quamquam ægrotabat, sapiens fuit.

Quæ, quanquam * ita sunt in promptu ut res disputatione non egeat, tamen sunt a nobis alio loco disputata. Sed mehercule, ut nunc se causa habet, etsi hesterno sermone labefacta est, mihi tamen videtur verissima. Quamvis suasor non fueris profectionis meæ, approbator certe fuisti. Licet omnes in me terrores impendeant, subibo.

We might go on expanding the subject by *conditional, local, modal,* etc., *clauses,* but the above should suffice to give an idea of what the subject is, and how it may be amplified.

II. *An Infinitive Subject.*

It is not just *to make a show* [*it* here = *to make a show*] = *to make a show* is not just = *making a show* is not just = *the making of a show* is not just.

Ostentare non est justum.

It is the highest praise *to fight bravely* = *to fight bravely* is the highest praise = *fighting bravely* is the highest praise = *brave fighting* is the highest praise.

Fortiter pugnare est summa laus.

It is one thing *to speak, it* is another thing *to speak well* = *to speak* is one thing, *to speak well* is another = *speaking* is one thing, *speaking well* is another.

Dicere est aliud, *bene dicere* aliud.

It is better *to receive an injury than to inflict it* = *to receive an injury* is better *than to inflict it* = *receiving an injury* is better *than inflicting it* = *the reception of an injury* is better than *the infliction of it.*

Præstat *accipere* quam *facere injuriam.*

* See Concessive particles, for construction.

When a *substantive*, *adjective*, or *participle* is conjoined with this infinitive, the substantive, adjective, or participle, is put in the *accusative*; as,

It is a fine thing *to be made consul* = *to be made consul* is a fine thing = *being made consul* is a fine thing = *for a man to be made consul* is a fine thing = *that a man be made consul* is a fine thing.

Consulem fieri magnificum est.

This is *being cruel* = this is *to be cruel* = *this is for a man* to be cruel.

Esse crudelem hoc est.

It is certain *that they intended to do it* = *that they intended to do it* is certain = *their intending to do it* is certain.

Eos in animo habuisse id facere certum est.

Exceptions.—1. When the infinitive is an infinitive governing the *dative*, the *substantive*, etc., is put in the *dative*; as,

It is right *that the laws be obeyed* = *that the laws be obeyed* is right = *that the laws should be obeyed* is right.

Legibus pareri æquum est.

Ex. 2. When the infinitive belongs to a *substantive* verb, it has the same case *before* and *after* it; as,

It is allowed to me *to be a good citizen* = *to be a good citizen* is allowed to me.

Licet mihi *esse bono civi*.

[Here *bonum civem* would not be reckoned good Latin; but take away the *mihi*, and then, even though the *mihi* is understood, it must be *bonum civem: licet esse bonum civem.*]

The *infinitive* as *subject* occurs when the *predicate* is,

1. The verb *to be* and a *noun.*
2. The verb *to be* and a *neuter adjective* or *pronoun.*
3. The verb *to be* and a *genitive;* the verb *to be* and *two datives;* the verb *to be* and the prepositions *in, contra,* etc.
4. Any of the strictly *impersonal* verbs.
5. A personal verb used *impersonally.*

1. The infinitive as subject,—the verb *to be** and a *noun* or *infinitive* (with or without a personal dative) as predicate; as,

It was a custom *to spoil an enemy* = *to spoil an enemy* was a custom = *the spoiling of an enemy* was a custom = *the spoliation of an enemy* was a custom.
Spoliare hostem, mos † erat.

Distinguish subject and predicate, and translate, giving the variations of which the subject is susceptible:

Majestatem minuere, est de dignitate populi aliquid derogare. Hoc mihi uni dicere fas fuisset. Jus et fas est omne delere. Populi Romani laus est, urbem illam esse servatam. Hospites violare, fas non putant. Docto homini et erudito vivere est cogitare. Summum profecto malum est vivere cum dolore; cui sententiæ consentaneum est, ultimum esse bonorum cum voluptate vivere. Meum semper judicium fuit, omnia nostros aut invenisse

* The infinitive as subject with the other substantive verbs is not usual.

† With the exceptions mentioned below, the infinitive is subject whenever the predicate is the verb *to be* and a *predicative noun* or *verb;* but for the sake of the beginner, we mean to give lists of nouns, etc. Predicative nouns, then, are such as these: amentia, animus, argumentum, arrogantia, ars, calumnia, caput, conditio, consilium, dementia, dictum, experimentum, facinus, fama, fas, fatum, judicium, jus, labor, laus, liber, locus (= argumentum), ludus, malum, medicina, memoria, mos, munus, nefas, negotium, nihil, officium, onus, operæ pretium, opinio, opus, parricidium, peccatum, principium, quid, ratio, religio, res, rumor, sapientia, scelus, sententia, sermo, solatium, spes, stultitia, tempus, vinculum, vitium, voluptas.

per se sapientius, quam Græcos, aut accepta ab illis, fecisse meliora. Facinus est vinciri Romanum civem, scelus verberari, prope parricidium necari. Ut peccatum est, patriam prodere, parentes violare, fana depeculari; sic timere, sic mœrere, sic in libidine esse, peccatum est. Voluptas est, ut Epicuro placet, nihil dolere. Est enim conditio liberorum populorum, posse suffragiis vel dare vel detrahere quid velint cuique. Munus autem animi est ratione bene uti. Mihi hoc propositum est, ostendere omnia consilia P. Sextii. Si latro rursus in Italiam se recipere cœperit, Bruti erit officium occurrere ei. Dii boni! quid lucri est mori. Sed tempus est, inquit, jam hinc me abire. Magorum mos est, non humare corpora suorum nisi a feris sint ante laniata. Ad consilium autem de republica dandum, caput est, nosse rempublicam; ad dicendum vero probabiliter, nosse mores civitatis. Magna nobis pueris opinio fuit, L. Crassum non plus attigisse doctrinæ, quam quantum prima illa puerili institutione potuisset. Primum consilium est, suffocare urbem et Italiam fame; deinde, agros vastare, urere, pecuniis locupletum non abstinere. Ironiam enim alterius, perpetuam præsertim, nulla ratio fuit persequi. Erit in consolationibus prima medicina, docere aut nullum malum esse, aut admodum parvum. Magnum opus est, probare mœrenti, illum suo judicio, et quod se ita putet oportere facere, mœrere. An vitium nullum est, non parere rationi? Hoc fieri et oportet et opus est. Erat ars difficilis, recte rempublicam regere. Quid est seipsum colligere, nisi dissipatas animi partes rursum in suum locum cogere?

Exceptions.—1. Caput, causa, consuetudo, fatum, jus, mos, officium, propositum, ratio, are constructed either with the infinitive or with *ut;* as,

To show that, is the purpose of this book = *Showing that,* is the purpose of this book.

Ut id ostendat, est propositum huic libro; OR, *Ostendere id*, est propositum huic libro.

Ex. 2. Substantives of *apprehension* are constructed with *ut* or *ne;* such as cupiditas,* cura, metus, periculum, timor; as,

I am in danger of falling = *danger of falling* is to me.
Periculum est *ne cadam.*

Ex. 3. Substantives of *bargaining* and *ordering* are constructed with *ut* or *ne;* such as, conditio, fœdus, lex, mandatum, nuntius, præceptum, propositum, regula, scitum, senatus consultum, sententia, voluntas, vox; as,

The condition is *that you cease speaking.*
Conditio est *ut tu loqui desinas.*

Licinia et Ebutia lex, ne, qui fert de aliqua curatione ac potestate, ei aut suis propinquis ea potestas curatiove mandetur. Nullum est periculum, ne quid eloquare nisi prudenter. Mos est hominum, ut nolint eundem pluribus rebus excellere. Causa enim fuit huc veniendi, ut quosdam hinc libros promerem. Tua ratio est, ut mihi respondere incipias. Lex Menia, ut consules etiam ex plebe creari possent. Periculum est, ne se stuporis excusatione defendat.

2. The infinitive as subject,—the verb *to be*, and a *neuter adjective* or *pronoun*† (with or without a personal dative) as predicate; as,

* Cupiditas is constructed rather with the gerund.

† Neuter predicative adjectives are such as: Absurdum, acerbum, admirabile, æquum (æquius), agreste, alienum, aliud, apertum, aptius, bellum, caducum, calamitosum, censorium, castum, commodum, consentaneum, conveniens, credibile, curiosum, debitum, deforme, detestabile, difficile, dubium, egregium, excelsius, extremum, facile (facilius), falsum, fatale, flagitiosum, funestum, gloriosum, gratum, grave, hoc, honestum, horribile, id, imbecillum, incertum, incommodum, incredibile, indecorum, indignum, ineptum, infinitum, ingenuum, inhumanum, iniquum, injuriosum, integrum, intolerabile, inutile, invidiosum, jucundum, justum,

It is not necessary *to come in person* = *to come in person* is not necessary = *for him to come in person* is not necessary = *that he should come in person* is not necessary = *coming in person* is not necessary.

Ipsum venire necesse* non est.

Indignum est, a pari vinci, aut superiore; indignius, ab inferiore. Non enim est meum contra jus alicujus dicere. Fuit meum quidem jam pridem rempublicam regere. Acerbum est ab aliquo circumveniri, acerbius a propinquo. Esse abstinentem, continere omnes cupiditates, præclarum est. Optare hoc quidem est, non disputare. Nec enim satis est judicare quid faciendum non faciendumve sit; sed stare etiam oportet in eo quod sit judicatum. Succumbere doloribus, eosque humili animo imbecilloque ferre, miserum est. Beateque vivere nihil aliud est nisi cum voluptate vivere. Perspicuum est nihil ad jucunde vivendum reperiri posse. Aliud igitur est gaudere, aliud non dolere. Unum est sine dolore esse; alterum cum

liberum, longum, luctuosum, magnificentius, magnificum, magnum, manifestum, melius, mendosum, meum [tuum, suum, nostrum, etc.], mirum, miserum, molestum, necessarium, necesse, nefarium, notissimum, novum, obscœnum, odiosum, optabilius, optatissimum (optatius), optimum, par, pejus, perabsurdum, perarduum, perfidiosum, periculosum, perjurum, permagnum, perspicuum, persuasissimum, planum, præclarum, primum [secundum, tertium, etc.], probabile, proprium, puerile, pulchrum, quod, rectum, religiosum, ridiculum, satis (satius), senile, simile, sordidum, stultum (stultius), subitum, tolerabilius, totum, turpe, turpissimum, utile, verisimile,[1] verum, vetus, violentum, vitiosum, vulgare.

* Necesse est may have the subject in the subjunctive, but without *ut;* as,

To come in person is not necessary.

Ipse veniat non necesse est.

It must be *that he died* = *that he died* must be = he must have died.

Mortuus sit necesse est.

[1] Verisimile has rather *ut;* consentaneum, integrum, and proprium, have also *ut.*

voluptate. Hoc est non dividere, sed frangere rem. Ad te venire vix rectum erat. Verisimile est Roscios hoc fecisse. Interim eam partem nudari necesse erat, et ab latere aperto tela recipi. In vita sibi quemque petere, quod pertineat ad usum, non iniquum est; alteri deripere, jus non est. Diligi et carum esse, jucundum est. Necesse est ita feratur ut penetret et dividat omne cœlum hoc. Carum esse civem, bene de republica mereri, laudari, coli, diligi, gloriosum est. Nostrum est, ferre modice populi voluntates. Mihi integrum est facere vel non facere. Artis maxime proprium est creare et gignere. Non tam præclarum est scire Latine, quam turpe nescire. Et monere et moneri proprium est veræ amicitiæ. Dimicare melius fuit, quam deserere consentientem Græciam. Quod est convenienter naturæ vivere. Ergo credere dubium est, uter nostrum sit, leniter ut dicam, verecundior? Magnum est efficere, ut quis intelligat, quid sit illud verum et simplex bonum, quod non possit ab honestate sejungi. Facile est verbum ardens, ut ita dicam, notare, idque reprehendere. Quod non habet extremum, infinitum sit necesse est.

Exceptions.—1. Optabile, proximum, and reliquum, with *ut*. See Verbs of *remaining*.

Quæ ut concurrant omnia, optabile est. Proximum est ut doceam, deorum providentia mundum administrari.

Ex. 2. Dubium *an*, see Pred. V. 2.; non dubium *quin*, see Verbs of *doubting*.

Ex. 3. When the predicate is a *substantive* or *adjective*, and the verb *to be*:

The subject may be made by *ut*, *provided the subject is represented in the leading clause by a demonstrative pronoun* (hoc, id, etc.); as,

> *This* is a common vice in great and free states, *that envy is the attendant of glory* [*this* = *that envy is the attendant of glory*].

Est *hoc* commune vitium in magnis liberisque civitatibus, *ut invidia gloriæ comes sit.*

Sometimes the pronoun is understood—not expressed.* Hæc vel summa laus est verbi transferendi, ut sensum ferat id, quod translatum sit. Illa sententia non vera est, ut quemadmodum in se quisque, sic in amicum sit animatus. Vetus est lex illa justæ veræque amicitiæ, ut idem amici semper velint. Extremum illud est, ut te orem et obsecrem, animo ut maximo sis. Fuit hoc in Crasso, ut non tam existimari vellet non didicisse, quam nostrorum hominum prudentiam Græcis anteferre.

3. The infinitive as subject,—the verb *to be*, and a *genitive*, the verb *to be* and *two datives*,† or the verb *to be*, with the prepositions *in*, *ad*, *contra*, etc., as predicate; as,

It is the characteristic of a wise man *to know himself* = *to know himself* is the characteristic of a wise man = *that he should know himself* is the characteristic of a wise man = *knowing himself* is the characteristic of a wise man = *self-knowledge* is the characteristic of a wise man.

Nosse se ipsum est sapientis.

It is an honour to a king *to be loved by the people* = *to be loved by the people* is an honour to a king = *that he should be loved by the people* is an honour to a king = *the love of the people* is an

* This rule, indeed, admits of a wider application, and may be stated more generally thus: that a subject or object may be represented by a demonstrative pronoun in the principal clause, and the equivalent of the demonstrative made by *ut* or *quod*, or placed in apposition.

† Cura is constructed with *ut;* as,

It was his first care *to fortify himself* = *to fortify himself* was his first care = *fortifying himself* was his first care = *that he should fortify himself* was his first care.

Ei primæ curæ fuit *ut sese muniret.*

Est mihi magnæ curæ, ut ita erudiatur Lucullus ut patri respondeat.

honour to a king = *the love of the people* is for an honour to a king.

A populo diligi regi est honori.

It is contrary to truth *to say so* = *to say so* is contrary to truth = *saying so* is contrary to truth.

Ita dicere est contra verum.

Nihil est negotii continere eos quibus præsis, si te ipse contineas. Est hominis ingenui et liberaliter educati velle bene audire a parentibus, a propinquis, a bonis etiam viris. Fortis ægroti est accipere medicinam. Sapientis vero nullo modo, physici præsertim, putare ullum esse cujusquam diem natalem. Clamare contra quam deceat, hominis est impudentis. Sed mandare quemquam literis cogitationes suas, qui eas nec disponere, nec illustrare possit, nec delectatione aliqua allicere lectorem, hominis est intemperanter abutentis et otio et literis. Accusant ii quibus occidi patrem Sex. Roscii bono fuit. Multum posse ad salutem alterius, honori multis; parum potuisse ad exitium, probro nemini fuit. Mihi erat in animo, proficisci in Siciliam Nonis Maiis. Detrahere igitur aliquid alteri, et hominem hominis incommodo suum augere commodum, magis est contra naturam quam mors, quam paupertas, quam dolor, quam cetera quæ possunt corpori accidere, aut rebus externis. Nec contra officium est, majus damnum anteponi minori. In potestate est, abjicere dolorem, quum velis. Cæsari renuntiatur Helvetiis esse in animo per agrum Sequanorum iter in Santonum fines facere. Quam velis, eum obligare in tua manu est. Hoc sentire, prudentiæ est; facere, fortitudinis; sentire vero et facere, perfectæ et cumulatæ virtutis. Bene sentire recteque facere satis est ad bene beateque vivendum.

4. The infinitive as subject,—any of the *impersonal* verbs as predicate; as,

It is his duty *to obey* = *to obey* is his duty = *obeying* is his duty = *obedience* is his duty.

Eum parere oportet.

It is allowed to me *to send soldiers* = *to send soldiers* is allowed to me = *sending soldiers* is allowed to me.
Mittere milites, mihi licet.*

Plura me ad te de hoc scribere pudet. Itaque mihi libet exclamare. Illud parvi refert, vos vectigalia postea recuperare. Licuit esse otioso Themistocli. Licet nemini contra patriam ducere exercitum. Non mihi libet deplorare vitam, quod multi fecerunt. Petebant ut ejus voluntate discedere liceret. Te, annum jam audientem Cratippum, idque Athenis, abundare oportet præceptis institutisque philosophiæ. Sint enim oportet, si miseri sunt. Aut aliquid afferunt quod mihi non displiceat, aut efficiunt ut me non didicisse minus pœniteat. Puderet me dicere † non intelligere, si vos ipsi intelligeretis, qui ista defenditis. Nobis quoque licet in hoc quodammodo gloriari. Nec me pudet, ut istos, fateri nescire quod nesciam. Non pudet philosophum in eo gloriari.

5. The infinitive as subject,—*personal verbs used impersonally* ‡ as predicate; as,

* The impersonal verbs are: libet or lubet, licet,[1] miseret, oportet, piget, pœnitet, pudet, refert, tædet. In the rule, decet, delectat, etc., *oportet* is the only verb really impersonal. Oportet in the sense of duty is always constructed with the infinitive; otherwise, it may be constructed like necesse est.[2] Gelat, pluit, etc., do not admit an infinitive.

† [me] non intelligere. Cicero often omits the pronoun with *dicere* and *fateri*.

‡ Personal verbs used impersonally with an infinitive subject, are such as: apparet, attinet, cadit in aliquem, conducit, constat, convenit,[3] debet,[4] decet, dedecet, delectat, displicet, expedit, fallit, fugit, alicujus habetur, interest,[5] juvat, latet, liquet, maneat, nocet, obest, patet, pertinet, placet,[3] præstat, præterit, prodest, propositum est, quadrat, spectat, stat, vacat, venit in mentem, videtur, visum est (mihi).

[1] Licet may be constructed with the subjunctive *without ut;* as, Fremant omnes licet.

[2] See Infinitive Subject, 2., foot note.

[3] Convenit and placet, as verbs of *resolving* or *ordering*, prefer rather the construction with *ut* and *ne*. Quamobrem placuit ei *ut* ad Ariovistum legatos mitteret. See Verbs of *resolving*.

[4] See Pred. II. *ancillary* verbs.

[5] Interest occurs also with *ut*.

That he should complain does not become him. *It* does not become him *to complain* = *to complain* does not become him = *complaining* does not become him. *Queri* non decet eum.

Interest omnium, recte facere. Non placuit Epicuro medium esse quiddam inter dolorem et voluptatem. Neque enim id est celare quidquid reticeas, sed quum, quod tu scias, id ignorare emolumenti causa velis eos, quorum intersit id scire. Nam in jure cavere, consilio juvare, atque hoc scientiæ genere prodesse, quam plurimis, vehementer et ad opes augendas pertinet, et ad gratiam. Pateat igitur æternum id esse, quod se ipsum moveat. Nobis placet, nec pristinum dicendi studium deponere, et in hac majore et uberiore arte versari. Juvat me, hæc præclara nomina artificum, quæ isti ad cœlum ferunt, Verris æstimatione sic concidisse. Sed hæc tu melius; modo nobis stet illud, unà vivere in studiis nostris. Illud apparebit, verba rebus esse contraria. Neque naturæ attinet repugnare, nec quicquam sequi, quod assequi nequeas. Neque ex omnibus oppidis contrahere copias expedit. Convenit tum in dando munificum esse, tum in exigendo non acerbum. Inter omnes convenit ita esse. Interfectam esse ab Oreste matrem convenit mihi cum adversariis. Conqueri fortunam adversam, non lamentari, decet. Convenit dimicare pro legibus, pro libertate, pro patria. Emori potius quam servire præstat. Fugit me rescribere. Quid tibi in mentem venit ita respondere? Cadit igitur in eundem et misereri et invidere. Et ad tuam fidem et ad rempublicam pertinet, me conservari. Fidei conducit in loco debitum retribuere. Quos nihil attinet nominare. Quid ergo attinet gloriose loqui, nisi constanter loquare. Huic ne perire quidem conceditur. Tempori cedere, sapientis est habitum.

EXCEPTIONS. — 1. When the predicate is any of the

following impersonal verbs, the subject is made by *ut* positive and *ut non* negative, and not by the infinitive:

(*a*) Verbs of *following* (as, conficitur, efficitur, nascitur, *or* ex hoc nascitur, secutum est, sequitur*); as,

It follows *that it is false* = *that it is false* follows.
Sequitur *ut falsum sit.*

(*b*) Verbs of *happening* (as, accidit, contingit, est, evenit, existit, fieri potest, fit, fore, futurum est, incidit, obtingit, occurrit, usu venit); as,

I happened to see him = *it* happened to me *to see him* = *to see him* happened to me = *that I should see him* happened to me.
Mihi evenit *ut eum viderem.*
I happened not to see him = *not to see him* happened to me = *that I should not see him* happened to me.
Mihi evenit *ut eum non viderem.*

(*c*) Verbs of *remaining* (as, reliquum est, relinquitur, restat, superest); as,

That we read remains = *it* remains for us *to read* = *it* remains *that we read.*
Reliquum est *ut legamus.*

(*d*) Abest [longe, tantum, etc.] in eo est, prope est, etc.; as,

The camp was far from being taken = *it* was far from being the case *that the camp was taken.*
Longe abfuit *ut castra caperentur.*
The camp was on the point of being taken = *it* was the case *that the camp was being taken.*
Jam in eo erat *ut castra caperentur.*

Ex. 2. Accedit is constructed with *ut*, and with *quod;* cecidit and addo, or adde, always with *quod;* as,

* *Sequitur* and *efficitur* may, in strict logical reasoning (but only then), be constructed with the accusative and infinitive subject; as, Ex quo efficitur, fortem virum ægritudine nunquam affici.

In addition to this, he had persuaded himself that the nation was very rich = *it* was added to this *that he had persuaded himself that the nation was very rich* = *that he had persuaded himself that the nation was very rich* was added to this = *his persuading himself that the nation was very rich* was added to this.

Ad hoc accedebat *quod sibi persuaserat gentem esse ditissimam.*

Your arrival happened opportunely for me = *it* happened opportunely for me *that you arrived* = *that you arrived* happened opportunely for me = *that you should have arrived* happened opportunely for me.

Cecidit mihi opportune, *quod venistis.*

The *emphatic* form is made with a pronoun (id, hoc, etc.).

What happened opportunely for me was *your arrival* = *your arrival* was *what* happened opportunely for me.

Hoc cecidit mihi opportune, *quod venistis.*

Est, ut plerique philosophi nulla tradant præcepta dicendi. Fieri potest, ut errem. Et id quidem nemini video Græcorum contigisse, ut idem utroque in genere laboraret. Ergo et ii quibus evenit jam, ut morerentur, et ii quibus eventurum est, sunt miseri. Effectumque est ut dando et accipiendo, et permutandis facultatibus et commodis, nulla re egeremus. Fieri autem potest, ut recte qui sentiat, id quod sentit polite eloqui non possit. Restat, ut iis respondeam qui sermonibus ejusmodi nolint personas tam graves illigari. Nec quidquam propius est factum quam ut vivus combureretur. Ad ea cum accedit, ut neque divinum numen horreat, neque præteritas voluptates effluere patiatur, earumque assidua recordatione lætetur, quid est, quod huc possit, quod melius sit, accedere? Quod item in poematibus et picturis usu venit, in aliisque compluribus, ut delectentur imperiti, laudentque ea quæ laudanda non sint. Reliquum est, igitur, ut tibi me in omni re præbeam. Relinquitur, ut summum bonum sit, convenienter congruenterque naturæ vivere. Sequitur, ut de una reliqua parte honestatis dicendum sit. Sed cum ea quæ præterierunt, acri animo et attento intuemur, tunc fit, ut ægritudo sequatur, si illa mala sint. Accidit, ut subito ille interiret. Restat, igitur, ut urbem diruamus. Id autem tantum abest ab officio, ut nihil officio magis possit esse contrarium. Tantum aberat, ut binos scriberent, vix singulos confecerunt. Accedebat huc, quod jam in concilio Æduorum Dumnorix dixerat, sibi a Cæsare regnum civitatis deferri. Accedebat, quod suos ab se liberos abstractos obsidum nomine dolebant. Accedebat, ut, cum sævire ventus cœpisset, et se vento dedissent, et tempestatem ferrent facilius, et in vadis consisterent tutius. Accedit, ut eo facilius animus evadat ex hoc aëre, quem sæpe jam appello. Sed hoc tamen cecidit mihi peropportune, quod, transactis jam meis partibus, ad Antonium audiendum venistis. Addo huc, quod mihi pater misit. Addo huc, quod postridie ille venit.

III. *The Clause of a Sentence Subject.*

1. A clause with *quod;* as,

Your arrival is agreeable to me = *your having arrived* is agreeable to me = *it* is agreeable to me *that you have arrived* = *that you have arrived* is agreeable to me = *that you should have arrived* is agreeable to me.

Quod tu venisti, mihi gratum est.

My belonging to Scotland is against me = *for me to belong to Scotland* is against me = *that I should belong to Scotland* is against me = *that I belong to Scotland* is against me = *it* is against me *that I belong to Scotland.*

Quod Scotus sum, mihi obest.

The masters' conversing on such a subject is something strange = *for the masters to converse on such a subject* is something strange = *that the masters should converse on such a subject* is something strange = *it* is something strange *that the masters should converse on such a subject.*

Quod magistri de ea re colloquuntur est aliquid miri.

Any of these sentences could, according to Subject II. be made with the accusative and infinitive, but with this difference, that the *quod* states an actual fact, while the accusative and infinitive subject states a judgment of the mind or opinion.

Eaque res P. Africano vituperationi fuit, quod ejus auctoritate de sententia deductus Briso putabatur. Dolet mihi, quod tu non stomacharis. Alterum est, quod negatis actionem ullius rei posse in eo esse, qui nullam rem assensu suo comprobet. Illud extremum est, quod recte vivendi ratio meliores efficit. Facile apparet quod me colat. Pungit me rursus quod scribis. Mihi fere satis est, quod vixi. Quintum pœnitet, quod animum tuum offenderit. Me pœnitet quod te offenderim. Quod me amicissime admones, gratum est. Quod me admones, ut me integrum, quoad possim, servem, gratum est. Causa transeundi fuit, quod ab Suevis complures annos exagitati bello premebantur. Causa mittendi fuit, quod iter per Alpes patefieri volebat. Caput est, quod pertinent ad minuendos sumptus civitatum. Illud mihi occurrit, quod inter postulationem uxor a Dolabella discessit. Magnum etiam vinculum, quod iisdem studiis semper usi sumus. Vitium est, quod quidam nimis magnum studium multamque operam in res obscuras atque difficiles conferunt. Multa sunt admirabilia, sed nihil magis quam quod ita stabilis est mundus.

2. A clause with an interrogative and the subjunctive; as,

It is unknown *whether he did so or not* = *whether he did so or not* is unknown.

Utrum nec ne id fecerit ignotum est.

It is uncertain *when he died* = *when he died* is uncertain.

Quo tempore mortuus sit incertum est.

It has not been related *how this happened.*

Quî hoc evenerit non est memoriæ traditum.

It is not so well known *how courageously he conducted himself in war* = *how courageously he conducted himself in war* is not so well known.

Quam fortiter sese in bello gesserit, non tam bene notum est.

It is not doubtful *that they are very influential* = *that they are very influential* is not doubtful = there is no doubt *they are very influential.*

Non dubium est *quin plurimum possint.*

It is doubtful *if the poet was a heathen or a Christian* = *if the poet was a heathen or a Christian* is doubtful.

Utrum ethnicus an Christianus poeta fuerit dubium est.

It is very doubtful *what was the cause of his death* = *what was the cause of his death* is very doubtful.

Quæ mortis ejus causa fuerit valde dubium est.

Sed in omni injustitia permultum interest, utrum perturbatione aliqua animi, quæ plerumque brevis est, et ad tempus, an consulto et cogitato fiat injuria. Neque erat controversia, quid ego intelligerem, sed quid probarem. Perspicuum est enim, quo compositiones unguentorum, quo ciborum conditiones, quo corporum lenocinia processerint. Nos quantum in utroque profecerimus, aliorum sit judicium. Quid rectum sit, apparet; quid expediat, incertum est. Utrum sciant pingere an nesciant, non obscurum est. Prorsus nihil abest quin sim miserrimus. Quarum qualis comparatio fieri soleat et debeat, non est necesse disputare. Ex quo facile apparet, quæ merces Decumani, quæ Prætoria præda esse videatur. Nihil interest utrum hæc fœderati jura constituant, an ea rata esse non possint. Quo id factum nomine appellari oporteat, constat. Illud alterum quam sit difficile, te non fugit. Magnæ est deliberationis, quæ ratio sit ineunda nobis quiescendi. Ambiorix copias suas judicione non conduxerit, quod prœlio dimicandum non existimarit, an tempore exclusus et repentino equitum adventu prohibitus fuerit, cum reliquum exercitum subsequi crederet, dubium est. Venit in contentionem, utrum sit probabilius. Ipsi animi, magni refert, quali in corpore locati sint. Tantum refert, quam magna dicam. Tamdiu autem velle debebis, quoad te, quantum proficias, non pœnitebit. Me ipsum non pœnitet quanta sint. Quid refert, utrum voluerim fieri an gaudeam factum? Nihil enim mea refert, utrum tu nihil unquam ausus sis scribere ad eum; an amici tui tabulas abdiderint. Quid sit porro ipse animus, aut ubi, aut unde, magna dissensio est.

THE PREDICATE.

The Predicate may be,—

1. A verb, or a verb with its case or cases.
2. A verb with the infinitive governed by it.
3. A verb with its complement of opinion.
4. A verb with an adjective or substantive, and the complement in the infinitive, etc.

The Predicate may be amplified or extended in the same way as the Subject. See Subject I.

I. *A Verb, or a Verb with its Case or Cases.*

1. A verb, or a verb with its case:—

James *sleeps* = James *is sleeping* = James *does sleep.*
Jacobus *dormit.*
The mother *grieves* = the mother *is grieving* = the mother *does grieve.*
Mater *dolet.*
The king *seemed good* = the king *did seem good* = the king *was seeming good.*
Rex *videbatur bonus.*
The boy *was reckoned wise.*
Puer *habebatur sapiens.*
We *have believed you.*
Nos *tibi credidimus.*
The father *consulted the son's interest.*
Pater *filio consuluit.*
The father *consulted the son.*
Pater *filium consuluit.**

Luget Senatus, mœret equester ordo, tota civitas confecta senio est, squalent municipia, afflictantur coloniæ. M. Brutus per se homo magnus evaserat. Hæc gemebant boni, sperabant improbi. Memini, enim, memini, nec unquam obliviscar noctis illius. Iste certe cum aliquo dolore flagitiorum suorum recordabitur. Audite, quæso, judices, et aliquando misereminí sociorum. Nec si grando quippiam nocuit, id Jovi fuit animadvertendum. Quis minus unquam pepercit hostium castris, quam hic omnibus corporis sui partibus? Sapiens parebit, et obediet præcepto illi veteri. Qui parti civium consulunt, partem negligunt, rem perniciosissimam in civitatem inducunt. Sed ne ipse quidem te consuluisti. Considerares quibus crederes et quos caveres. Caverat enim ille sibi. Non omnes loci in omnem causam conveniunt. Magna multitudo homi-

* For a very full list of verbs varying their meaning with their construction, see Ruddiman's Larger Grammar.

num convenit ad iudicium. Animus separatus a corpore meminit præteritorum, præsentia cernit, futura providet. Huic loco, per deos immortales, judices, consulite et providete. Nulla vitæ pars vacare officio potest. Hos ille moderatione, non inventione vicit. Odi hominem, et odero; illum ulciscantur mores sui. Neque nos te fruimur, et tu nobis cares. Lysias est functus omni civium munere. Filius plus pollet, potiorque est patre. Circumventos interfecerunt.* Eodem modo constitutum est, ut non liceret sui commodi causa nocere alteri. Id est cujusque proprium quo quisque fruitur atque utitur. Sapiens et præterita grate meminit, et præsentibus potitur. Salus hominum non veritate solum, sed etiam fama nititur. Nihil opus est simulatione et fallaciis. Senes multi se agri cultione oblectarunt. Admiratione afficiuntur ii qui anteire ceteros virtute putantur. Regno carebat Tarquinius, quum regno esset expulsus. Cæsar a lacu Lemano ad montem Juram millia passuum decem novem murum fossamque perducit. Curionis adventum L. Cæsar filius ad Clupeam præstolabatur. In Formiano tibi præstolor. Magnis viris prospere semper eveniunt omnes res.

2. A verb with its cases:—

The master *accused the boy of theft.*
Magister *puerum furti accusavit.*
The boy *compared himself with the master.*
Puer *se magistro comparavit.*
The father *gave a book to the son.*
Pater *librum filio dedit.*
The father *took away the book from the son.*
Pater *librum filio eripuit.*
The father *taught the son everything.*
Pater *filium omnia docuit.*

* When two actions are contemporaneous they may be expressed in Latin in one proposition; as, *He took the city and set it on fire* = *he set on fire the taken city: Urbem captam incendit.*

Ego et librarios tuos culpa libero, neque te accuso. Nunc non modo te hoc crimine non arguo, sed ne illa quidem communi vituperatione reprehendo. Fannius Verrem insimulabat avaritiæ et audaciæ. Condemnabo eodem ego te crimine. Piso sceleris condemnat generum suum. Prorsus eum libero omni suspicione cupiditatis. Is auctoritatem suam quam magni æstimat. Hic salutem populi Romani vitæ suæ præposuit. Et longe Academiæ illi et Lyceo tuum hoc suburbanum antepono. Puer tuus mihi literas abs te reddidit. Tribuit sapientiam eis, qui eam sibi arrogant. Gladiumque hosti in pectus infixerat. Non adimit ei libertatem. Ego me tibi non offerebam. Racilius de privatis me primum sententiam rogavit. Spoliavit enim virtutem suo decore. Filio meo satis amplum patrimonium relinquam in memoria nominis mei. Lælius id parvi ducit. Ego, ex quo tempore tu me diligere cœpisti, quotidie te pluris feci. Viros primos et homines honestissimos summo beneficio in perpetuum tibi tuisque devinxeras. Quid nunc te, asine, literas doceam? Illud ad extremum te oro et hortor. Ægritudo me somno privat. Metropolitæ muros armatis compleverunt. Sibi jam iis rebus in Gallia auctoritatem comparaverat. Se ipsi acutissimis vallis induebant.

Verbs of *teaching*, which admit of two accusatives, may have, instead of the latter accusative, an *infinitive* to complete the predicate; as,

I shall teach you *to be silent.*
Ego docebo te *silere.*

Verbs of *appointing* (as adscisco, capio, constituo, creo, declaro, designo, dico, lego, renuntio), *making* (as efficio, facio, reddo), *naming* (as appello, dico,* inscribo, nomino, saluto, voco), *regarding* (as arbitror, duco, existimo,

* In an example like this, *Mori nemo sapiens miserum dixerit*, the infinitive *mori* is not governed by *dixerit*, but is the secondary subject before *miserum*, *esse* being understood.

habeo, judico, numero, perhibeo, puto), *showing one's self to be* (as exhibeo, præbeo, præsto), complete the predicate in the active voice both in English and Latin with two accusatives; as,

The people *made Numa king.*
Populus *creavit Numam regem.*
Show you yourself a man.
Præbe te virum.

With *duco, existimo, judico, puto*, the infinitive may be expressed, but not with *habeo* in this sense.

Docebo te in his tacere rebus. Ferre laborem consuetudo docet. Avaritia reddit homines cæcos. Deos æternos et beatos habemus. Montem Vesontionis murus circumdatus arcem effecit. Hunc ego unum potissimum delegissem generum. Deinde te senatui, bonisque omnibus, auctorem, principem, ducem præbeas. Imperatores appellati sumus. L. Murenam consulem renuntiavi. Et tamen cum ita vivit, neminem præ se ducit hominem. Alienæ igitur culpæ me reum facies? Voluptatum perceptarum recordatio vitam beatam facit.

II. *A Verb with the Infinitive governed by it.*

As a general rule, verbs that directly govern the infinitive in the English do so in the Latin also.*

Verbs of *hoping, promising* [*engaging, undertaking,* etc.], *refusing, swearing, trusting, threatening, vowing,* which are in English sometimes followed by the infinitive, belong to Predicate III.

The *Ancillary Verbs* (cœpi, debeo, desino, incipio, nequeo, possum, queo, soleo) are used *personally* to govern a *personal* infinitive, but *impersonally* to govern an *impersonal* infinitive; as,

I begin to see.
Incipio videre.

* To obviate any objection to this rule as too general, we give an example of every verb we have met with governing the infinitive.

I begin to repent.
Incipit me pœnitere.
I began to be resisted.
Cœptum est mihi resisti.

Verbs directly governing the infinitive are such as:

1. Verbs of *ability* and *inability* to do;* as,

I *can tell you.*
Ego *possum dicere tibi.*

Nos commovere nequeunt. Non queo tantum, quantum vereor, scribere. Habeo audire quid hic sentiat. Facere non possum, ut nihil ad te dem literarum. Ab eo honeste dissentire non possum. Potest fieri ut fallar. Qui mortem in malis ponit, non potest eam non timere. Hæc fere dicere habui de natura deorum. Id, quod parati sunt facere, mihi nocuerit.

2. Verbs of being *accustomed* to do;† as,

Cæsar *was not in the custom of granting help* = Cæsar *was not accustomed to grant help.*
Cæsar *auxilium dare non solebat.*

Gallinas alere permultas quæstûs causâ solent. Has Græci stellas Hyadas vocitare sueverunt. Est animadversum a venatoribus quo se recipere alces consueverint. Quo in loco ad fluctum aiunt declamare solitum Demosthenem, ut fremitum assuesceret voce vincere. Cum minus idoneis verbis uti consuescerem. Solet Dionysium, quum aliquid furiose fecit, pœnitere.

3. Verbs of *beginning* and *ending*, *delaying* and *persevering* to do;‡ as,

* As, habeo, nequeo, paratus est, possum, queo.

† As, assuesco,[1] consuesco, soleo, suesco (rare).

‡ As, adorior, aggredior,[2] cœpi, cesso, cunctor, desino, desisto, exordior, festino, incipio, ingredior, instituo, insto (rarely), intermitto, maturo, moror, omitto, ordior, pergo, persevero, prætermitto, propero.

[1] *Assuefacio* is constructed with the accusative and infinitive; as, Cæsar ceteras nationes imperio Romano parere assuefecit.

[2] *Aggredior* is also constructed with *ad*.

The master *began to speak.*
Magister *cœpit dicere.*
The master *persevered speaking.*
Magister *perseveravit dicere.*

Quodque sese movet, nunquam moveri desinit. Pompeium hortari et orare non desistimus. Itaque omittamus lugere. Illos libros scribere non cessavi, neque cesso. Si latro rursus in Italiam se recipere cœperit, Bruti erit officium occurrere ei. Hortensius, cum admodum adolescens orsus esset in foro dicere, celeriter ad majores causas adhiberi cœptus est. Homines mortem optare incipiant, vel certe timere desistant. Quod facere nunc ingredimur. Itaque ad eum ire perreximus. Quare, mi Cicero, persevera constanter nos defendere. Sed ductus odio, properavit rem deducere in judicium. Te expecto et oro ut matures venire. Neque ille intermittit affirmare se venturum. Quam ob causam non est cunctandum profiteri, hunc mundum animal esse. Tum incipiat aliis imperare, cum ipse improbissimis dominis, dedecori ac turpitudini, parere desierit. Ne convellere adoriamur ea quæ non possunt commoveri. De quibus dicere aggredior, si pauca prius de instituto, ac de judicio meo dixero. Quæ cum ille dixisset, tum ego rursus quasi ab illo principio sum exorsus dicere. Ei bellum moremur inferre. Deinde, ut migrare tantopere festines. Undique lapides in murum jaci cœpti sunt. Athenis primum monumentis et literis oratio est cœpta mandari. Veteres orationes a plerisque legi sunt desitæ.

4. Verbs of *endeavouring* to do;* as,

The Gauls *attempted to destroy the Romans.*
Galli *Romanos delere conati sunt.*

Eruptionem facere contendit. Frequentes profecto

* As, conor, contendo, molior, nitor; but, except *conor*, verbs of *endeavouring* generally prefer the construction with *ut*. See Pred. IV. 3. (*d*).

talibus conatibus obviam ire nitemur. Perrumpere nituntur. Aliquod munus efficere molitur. Hæc, si verbis explicare conemur, frustra laboremus. Si impetum in me facere conabitur, resistam, et ejus conatus refutabo.

5. Verbs of *inclination* and *disinclination* to do;* as,

James *desires to learn.*
Jacobus *cupit discere.*†
The man *did not hesitate to go.*
Homo *non dubitavit*‡ *ire.*
I *am afraid to do it.*
Ego *id facere vereor.*§

* As, appeto, audeo, aveo, cogito, concupisco, consentio, non curo,[1] cupio, debeo, desidero, dubito, erubesco, exopto, fugio, gestio, gravor, in animo habeo, horreo, hortor,[2] in animum induco, jubeo,[3] malo, meditor, moneo,[2] nolo, odi, paro, pervolo, prægestio, præopto, probo, puto, recuso, reformido, satis habeo, simulo, studeo, suadeo,[2] timeo, vereor, veto,[3] mihi videor, volo.

† Verbs of desire (as cupio, exopto, malo, nolo, volo, studeo) are constructed with the infinitive when there is but one subject; as, *I desire to learn: cupio discere;* but if there be a secondary subject in the sentence, as, *I desire* HIM *to learn* = *I desire that he learn,* they may be constructed with the accusative and infinitive; as, *cupio* EUM *discere;* or in the case of malo, nolo, and volo, with *ut* and the subjunctive, or in short unambiguous sentences, the subjunctive without *ut.* *Exopto* with a *secondary subject* always with *ut.* *Opto* is found with the accusative and infinitive; as, Spero et opto nobis hanc conjurationem voluptati fore; but it is better *always* to construct *opto* with *ut;* as, Senectutem ut adipiscantur omnes optant, eandem accusant adeptam. Optavit ut in currum patris tolleretur.

‡ For the construction of *dubito* as a verb of *doubting,* see Verbs of *doubting.*

§ Of Verbs of fearing, *horreo, paveo* (doubtful—some read *avet* in the example), *reformido, refugio, timeo, vereor,* are in good prose constructed with the infinitive, but *only* in the sense of *not having courage to do.* In Livy and the poets, *metuo* also is constructed with the infinitive. For *fearing* ONE'S SELF [OR ANOTHER] *doing,* see Verbs of *fearing,* Pred. IV. 3. (*f*).

1 *Curo* itself is not constructed with the infinitive,—only *non* curo.

2 Hortor, moneo *aliquem,* suadeo *aliqui,* see Verbs of *advising,* Pred. IV. 3. (*e*).

3 Jubeo and veto *aliquem,* see Verbs of *ordering,* Pred. IV. 3. (*h*).

The general *was thinking of crossing the river* = *had in view to cross the river* = *had in view the crossing of the river.*
Dux *cogitabat flumen transire.*
The general *did not care to cross the river.*
Dux *non curavit flumen transire.*

Ego conservare coloniam populi Romani cupio, tu expugnare studes. Pavet animus apud consilium illud pro reo dicere. Principia causarum propria esse debent. Quis audeat bene comitatum aggredi? Vide ne facinus facias, cum mori suadeas. Cato ipse jam servire quam pugnare mavult. Valde aveo scire quid agas. Antonius Senatum delere gestit. Noli putare me quidquam maluisse quam ut mandatis tuis satisfacerem. Sed is Stoicus esse voluit; orator autem nec studuit unquam, nec fuit. Quos ego non tam ulcisci studeo, quam sanare. Is Sassiam in matrimonium ducere concupivit. Appetit animus aliquid agere semper; neque ulla conditione quietem sempiternam potest pati. Quid dubitamus igitur affirmare, nihil inter hæc interesse. Sed ex hoc genere toto perspici potest levitas orationis eorum qui omnia cupiunt confundere. Refugit animus, eaque reformidat discere. Mithridates Bosporanis finitimis suis bellum inferre simulavit.* Quocirca vereor committere ut non bene provisa et diligenter explorata principia ponantur. Ausus es hoc ex ore tuo, Ennius inquit, me rogare. Curtius consensit cum Hispanis quibusdam, si Pompeius in oppidum venisset, eum comprehendere, ad Cæsaremque deducere. Te rogo ne gravere exædificare id opus quod instituisti. Ego vero, inquit, istis obsequi studeo, neque gravabor breviter, meo more, quid quaque de re sentiam, dicere. Id sacrificium nemo unquam vir adspicere non horruit. Neque sane redire curat. Erubescunt pudici etiam loqui de pudicitia. Pater istum exhæredare in animo habebat. Tu igitur animum induces causam hanc

* See also Pred. III. 1.

defendere? Cum hominem nomino, satis mihi videor dicere. Non satis habet avaritiam suam pecunia explere. Adeone oblitus constantiæ meæ esse videor, ut in animum inducam, cujus nuper ferrum retuderim, flammamque restinxerim, ejusdem nunc causam, vitamque defendere? Cæsar non multos annos regnare meditatus est. Ego autem multis de causis te exopto quamprimum videre. Cogito proficisci. Cogito trans Tiberim hortos aliquos parare. Itaque ea nolui scribere, quæ nec indocti intelligere possent, nec legere curarent. Si volent grati esse, debebunt Pompeium hortari, ut mihi sit amicus. Barbari, confisi loci natura, cum dimicare non recusarent, si forte Romani subire collem conarentur, paulatimque copias distributas dimittere non auderent, ne dispersi perturbarentur, in acie permanserunt. Nunc publice literas Romam mittere parabam. Non dubitat, si ita melius sit, migrare de vita. Pietas officium erga parentes conservare monet. Nam quum solitudo et vita sine amicis insidiarum et metus plena sit, ratio ipsa monet amicitias comparare. E numero primus est ausus Leontinus Gorgias in conventu poscere quæstionem, id est, jubere dicere qua de re quis vellet audire. Maxime probat, coactis navibus, mare transire et Pompeium sequi. Isti, qui ad nos causas deferunt, ita nos plerumque ipsi docent, ut non desideres plenius dici. Turpiter facere cum periculo fugiamus. Servire et contumelias pati, pejus odi malis omnibus aliis. Sed scire ex te pervelim. Prægestit animus videre. De vino aut salsamento putes loqui, quæ evanescunt vetustate. Gallis magno ad pugnam erat impedimento, quod pluribus eorum scutis uno ictu pilorum transfixis et colligatis, cum ferrum se inflexisset, neque evellere, neque, sinstra impedita, satis commode pugnare poterant; multi ut, diu jactato brachio, præoptarent scutum manu emittere, et nudo corpore pugnare. Reipublicæ dignitas, quæ me ad sese rapit, hæc minora relinquere hortatur.

EXCEPTION.—Such phrases as, *I am glad to see you* = *I glad see you; Ego lætus te video:* or = *I am glad that I see you*, see Pred. III. 4., and Pred. IV. 4.

6. Verbs of *knowing*, *forgetting*, and *remembering* to do, or *how* to do;* as,

I *know how to write* = I *know to write.*
Scio scribere.

Varroni memineris excusare tarditatem literarum mearum. Proinde ita parent se in vita, ut vinci nesciant. Scribere oblitus es. Mihi verba desunt, dedidicique loqui. Hæc didiceram tractare. Voluptatem sequi nesciunt. Antonius diem edicti obire neglexit. Epicurei nostri Græce fari nesciunt, nec Græci Latine.

7. Verbs of *resolving* to do;† as,

The earl *resolved to conciliate the king.*
Comes statuit‡ *regem sibi conciliare.*

Hæc deinceps facere constitui. Decreveram cum eo valde familiariter vivere. Is certe statuerat et deliberaverat non adesse. Cum instituissem ad te scribere. Capit consilium de amicorum sententia, non adesse judicio. Sed cum statuissem aliquid hoc tempore ad te scribere, et multa posthac, ab eo ordiri volui maxime, quod et ætati tuæ esset optatissimum et auctoritati meæ. Lepidus ad Forum Voconii castra habet, ibique me expectare constituit. Maxime ea quæ ad usum navium pertinent, providere instituunt.

Also such phrases as *do bibere, ministro bibere;* as, Homerus Ganymedem a diis raptum ait propter formam, ut Jovi bibere ministraret. Gallinis meridie bibere dato.

* As, dedisco, disco, memini, negligo, nescio, obliviscor, scio.

† As, consilium capio, constituo, decerno, deliberavi (mihi deliberatum est), destino, instituo, statuo.

‡ Verbs of resolving are constructed with the infinitive when there is but one subject; as, He resolved to go = *statuit ire;* but, if there is a *secondary* subject, they are constructed with *ut* or *ne*, as, He resolved that *they* should go = *statuit ut irent.* See Pred. IV. 3. (*i*).

TO = IN ORDER TO = FOR THE PURPOSE OF.

When *to*, the sign of the infinitive, means *in order to* or *for the purpose of*, the infinitive cannot be rendered by the Latin infinitive, but must be made in some other way; as,

Cæsar *comes to seek help* = *comes in order to seek help* = *comes with the view of seeking help* = *comes for the sake of seeking help* = *comes for the purpose of seeking help* = *comes for the seeking of help* = *comes for seeking help.*

Cæsar *venit auxilium petiturus;* or,
Cæsar *venit* (sup.) *petitum auxilium;* or,
Cæsar *venit auxilium petendi causâ;* or,
Cæsar *venit auxilii petendi causâ;* or,
Cæsar *venit ad auxilium petendum* (gerundive); or,
Cæsar *venit ut auxilium petat.*

Cæsar *sends men to seek help* = *sends men who should seek help.*

Cæsar *homines mittit qui auxilium petant.*

Of these general forms for expressing purpose, observe:

1. Use the participle in *rus*, and the supine in *um*, only after verbs of motion.

2. Turn the gerund into the gerundive *only* when the active voice of the verb governs the accusative; except in the case of the gerundives of *fruor*, *fungor*, *utor*, which are used as if these verbs governed the accusative.

3. Use the genitive of the *gerund* (*not* the *gerundive*), when its *object* is a neuter adjective or a pronoun (as, cupiditas habendi *falsum*, or cupiditas habendi *eum*, *not* falsi or ejus), except when the adjective denotes a general idea (as, nec modus est ullus investigandi *veri*).

4. Use the *gerundive* (*not* the *gerund*) with a sub-

stantive or adjective for its object with prepositions (as, ad petendAM pacem, *not* ad petendUM pacem).

5. Use *qui* after verbs of motion in the active voice governing the accusative.

Perspicuum est, eos ad imperandum deligi solitos, quorum de justitia magna esset opinio multitudinis. Facillime cognoscuntur adolescentes, qui se ad claros et sapientes viros contulerunt; quos sibi ipsi delegerunt ad imitandum. Quum ad me in Cumanum salutandi causa uterque venisset, pauca primo inter nos de literis erant. Est difficile nobis, qui, antequam ad discendum ingressi sumus, obruimur ambitione. Hîc ego cum ad respondendum surrexi, qua cura, qua sollicitudine animi? Et ad subeundum periculum et ad vitandum, multum fortuna valuit. Multa enim sæpe ad te cohortandi gratia scripsimus. Quotannis singula millia armatorum bellandi causa ex finibus educunt. Neque longius anno remanere uno in loco incolendi causa licet. Atque ea juventutis exercendæ ac desidiæ minuendæ causa fieri prædicant. Dumnorigi custodes ponit, ut, quæ agat, quibuscum loquatur, scire possit. His opibus ac nervis non solum ad minuendam gratiam sed pæne ad perniciem ejus utitur. Cum bellum civitas aut illatum defendit aut infert, magistratus, qui ei bello præsint, ut vitæ necisque habeant potestatem, deliguntur. Idem facit Cæsar, equitatumque omnem præmittit, qui videant, quas in partes hostes iter faciant. Legatos ad Cæsarem mittunt rogatum auxilium. Cæsar copias suas in proximum collem subducit, equitatumque, qui sustineret hostium impetum, misit. Quare omnis oratio suscipitur a nobis, ut retineamus eam definitionem quam Philo voluit evertere. Hi, vitandi æstûs causa, plerumque silvarum ac fluminum petunt propinquitates. Inita æstate, in interiorem Galliam qui legiones deduceret, Q. Pedium legatum misit. Bello Helvetiorum confecto, totius fere Galliæ legati principes civitatum, ad Cæsarem gratulatum convenerunt. Quamobrem placuit ei, ut ad Ariovistum legatos mitteret, qui ab eo hæc postularet. Legati ab Æduis veniebant questum quod Harudes fines eorum popularentur. Nonnulli, pudore adducti, ut timoris suspicionem vitarent, remanebant. Quid ad se venirent? an speculandi causa? Ipse in citeriorem Galliam ad conventus agendos profectus est. Equidem sæpe emori, si fieri posset, vellem, ut ea, quæ dico, mihi liceret invenire. Iphigenia Aulide duci se immolandam jubet, ut hostium sanguis eliciatur suo. Ut exeamus e vita læti et agentes gratias, paremus. Cicero eo tendit, id agit, ad eum exitum properat, ut sit illi Octavius propitius. Cum Pompeio agebatur ut eam rem susciperet. Atque ut omittam has artes elegantes et ingenuas, ne opifices quidem tueri sua artificia possent, nisi vocabulis uterentur nobis incognitis, usitatis sibi. Elaborandum est, ut hoc non in nostris solum artibus, sed etiam in illorum ipsorum consequamur. Commentarios quosdam, inquam, Aristotelicos, quos hic sciebam esse, veni, ut auferrem, quos legerem, dum essem otiosus. C. Canius, eques Romanus, nec infacetus, et satis literatus, cum se Syracusas, otiandi (ut ipse dicere solebat) non negotiandi causa, contulisset, dictitabat, se hortos aliquos velle emere, quo invitare amicos, et ubi se oblectare sine interpellatoribus posset. Hi magno nobis usui ad bellum gerendum erant. Ad cohortandos milites decucurrit. Sed tempus est, inquit, jam hinc abire me, ut moriar; vos, ut vitam agatis. Torquem detraxit hosti, et quidem se texit ne interiret. Quæ prima signa conspexit, ad hæc constitit, ne, in quærendis suis, pugnandi tempus dimitteret. Legatos senatus non ad pacem deprecandam, sed ad bellum denunciandum, miserat. Introducebat Carneades, non quo probaret, sed ut opponeret Stoicis, summum bonum esse, frui iis rebus, quas primas natura conciliavisset. Legatos ad Cæsarem mittunt rogatum auxilium. Admonitum venimus te, non flagitatum. Domi nihil erat, quo famem tolerarent.

III. *A Verb with its Complement of Opinion.*

The complement *of opinion* is in the *accusative* and *infinitive;* except when the infinitive is an *impersonal* verb governing the *dative,* when the complement will be in the *dative* and *infinitive.*

To this construction belongs *every verb* and *every phrase* that completes the predicate with the simple conjunction *that.**

Verbs that complete the predicate with the simple conjunction *that* are such as:

1. Verbs of *declaring* or *denying that something is,* or *that something was,* or *that something is to be;* † as,

> Charles *said he could declare he had never done it* = *said that he could declare that he had never done it.*
> Carolus *dixit se declarare posse, se id nunquam fecisse.*

* *That* may be a *relative*, an *adjective*, a *conjunction* denoting *purpose* or *end*, or a *simple conjunction.* Verbs of *asking, causing, commanding, entreating, exhorting, fearing,* etc., are constructed with the *that* denoting end. See Pred IV. 3.

† As, abnuo, acclamo, addo, adjicio, adjungo, admoneo, affero, affirmo, agnosco, ago cum aliquo, aio, aperio, arguo, assevero, cavillor, clamito, cogo, commemoro, concedo, concionor, conclamo, concludo, confirmo, confiteor, consentio, contendo, convinco, criminor, declaro, defendo, defero, demonstro, denuntio, dico, dictito, dissimulo, divino, do, doceo, edico, efficio, ementior, enuntio, expono, fac, facio certiorem, fama fert, fateor, increpo, indico, inficior, insimulo, interpretor, introduco, jacto, loquor, memoro, mitto (with an ellipsis of some verb of saying), moneo, narro, nego, nitor, nuntio, objicio, ostendo, præcipio, prædĭco, prædīco, præ me fero, præsagio, perhibeo, perscribo, persuadeo, pono, portendo, postulo, probo, prodo or trado memoriæ, pronuntio, propono, proscribo, refero, renuntio, repugno, rescribo, respondeo, scribo, sententiam dico, significo, simulo, statuo, suadeo, subscribo, sumo, testificor, trado, verba facio, vinco, voco in dubium.

Several of these verbs (as admoneo, concedo, contendo, dico, do, edico, efficio, enuntio, fero, mitto, moneo, nitor, persuadeo, postulo, rescribo, suadeo, vinco) may be used in another sense than that of *declaring that a thing is, etc.,*—viz., *declaring to one* TO DO SOMETHING, or *declaring* THAT ONE SHOULD DO SOMETHING, when, of course, the construction will be different. See Pred. IV. 3.

Solon *pretended to be insane* = *pretended that he was insane.*

Solon *se furere simulavit.*

The father *boasted of having done it* = *boasted that he had done it.*

Pater *gloriatus est se id fecisse.*

Messengers *brought intelligence of his being continued in the consulship* = *brought intelligence that he was continued in the consulship.*

Nuncii *attulerunt consulatum ei continuatum esse.*

The boy *confessed having done it* = *confessed that he had done it.*

Puer *confessus est se id fecisse.*

The messengers *inform the king of the laws being obeyed* = *inform the king that the laws are obeyed.*

Nuncii *regem certiorem faciunt legibus pareri.*

Pro his Divitiacus facit verba, Bellovacos omni tempore in fide atque amicitia civitatis Æduæ fuisse. Insimulant eum simulatione insaniæ militiam subterfugere voluisse. Me abs te cupisse laudari, aperte atque ingenue confitebor. Critoni enim nostro non persuasi, me hinc avolaturum, neque quidquam mei relicturum. Sed fac, ut isti volunt, animos non remanere post mortem; video nos, si ita sit, privari spe beatioris vitæ. Allobroges, qui trans Rhodanum vicos possessionesque habebant, fuga se ad Cæsarem recipiunt, et demonstrant, sibi præter agri solum nihil esse reliqui. Biduo post Ariovistus ad Cæsarem legatos mittit, velle se de his rebus, quæ inter eos agi cœptæ, neque perfectæ essent, agere cum eo. Publium Scipionem, Marce fili, eum qui primus Africanus appellatus est, dicere solitum scripsit Cato, qui fuit fere ejus æqualis, nunquam se minus otiosum esse, quam cum ostiosus; nec minus solum, quam cum solus esset. Cui cum exposuisset, patriam se liberare velle, causamque docuisset, a rege opulento vir summus facile impetravit, ut grandi pecunia adjuvaretur. Ad hæc Ariovistus respondit, jus esse belli, ut qui vicissent, iis, quos vicissent, quemadmodum vellent, imperarent. Legatis respondit, diem se ad deliberandum sumpturum. Ambarri Cæsarem certiorem faciunt, sese, depopulatis agris, non facile ab oppidis vim hostium prohibere. Simulas enim quærere te de sapiente; quæris autem fortasse de te. Addunt etiam quidquid valde utile sit, id fieri honestum. Id autem non modo non summum malum, sed ne malum quidem esse, maxima auctoritate philosophi affirmant. Beatos esse deos sumpsisti, concedimus; beatum esse sine virtute neminem posse, id quoque damus, et libenter quidem; virtutem autem sine ratione constare non posse, conveniat id quoque necesse est; adjungis, nec rationem esse, nisi in hominis figura. Quis neget, omnes leves, omnes cupidos, omnes denique improbos, esse servos? Cum eum ne liberum quidem esse, ratio et veritas ipsa convincat. Apollinem ex Hyperboreis Delphos ferunt advenisse. Cujus rei tantæ, tamque difficilis facultatem consecutum esse me non profiteor; secutum esse præ me fero. Principes consilium hoc ceperunt, nomen Tarquiniorum memoriamque regni esse tollendam. Platonem ferunt, ut Pythagoreos cognosceret, in Italiam venisse, et didicisse Pythagorea omnia, primumque de animorum æternitate non solum sensisse idem quod Pythagoram, sed rationem etiam attulisse. Nitamur igitur nihil posse percipi. Ego quia curo, attendoque, id tibi affirmo, te in istis molestiis non diutius futurum. Innumerabilia sunt ex quibus effici cogique possit, nihil esse, quod sensum habeat, quin id intereat. Nemo me vocabit in dubium, me pro concione dixisse.

2. Verbs of *believing*, *determining*, or *thinking that something is*, or *that something was*, or *that something is to be*, etc.;* as,

* As, arbitror, æstimo, censeo, cogito, conjicio, consentio, consilium capio, constituo, credo, decerno, duco, existimo, exploratum

The Romans *believed that certain epigrams were his = believed certain epigrams to be his.*

Romani *crediderunt quædam epigrammata ejus esse.*

The Senate *determined that it is so = determined it to be so.*

Senatus *decrevit id ita esse.*

The boy *thought that he would be equal in renown to Cæsar = thought himself to be about to be equal in renown to Cæsar.*

Puer *existimavit se parem Cæsari gloriâ fore.*

Quid mihi animi in navigando censes fore? Ullum tu decus in quotidianis periculis et laboribus cum hac tranquillitate conferendum putas? Quod quia patriæ non utile putavit, idcirco sibi honestum, et sentire illa et pati, credidit. Quod opinatus sum, me in provinciam exiturum. Suspicabor, vel potius intelligebam, nihil fuisse, quod scriberes. Illos, in quibus eas virtutes esse remur, a natura ipsa diligere cogimur. Namque (dicam enim non reverens assentandi suspicionem) neminem esse oratorem paullo illustriorem arbitror, neque Græcum neque Latinum, quem ætas nostra tulerit, quem non et sæpe et diligenter audierim. Atque ego is, qui sum, quantuscumque sum ad judicandum, omnibus auditis oratoribus, sine ulla dubitatione sic statuo et judico, neminem omnium tot, et tanta, quanta sunt in Crasso, habuisse ornamenta dicendi. Mihi gratias egistis singularibus verbis, et mea virtute atque diligentia, perditorum hominum patefactam esse conjurationem, decrevistis. Ipse mihi assentor fortasse, cum ea esse in me fingo. Tenendum est, igitur, nihil curandum esse post mortem, cum multi inimicos etiam mortuos puniant. Multi de diis prava sentiunt; omnes tamen esse vim et naturam divinam arbitrantur. Ad eas res conficiendas

or pro explorato habeo, fingo, animum induco, judico, opinor, persuasum habeo, præmeditor, puto, ratiocinor, reor, reputo, satis habeo, sentio, somnio, statuo, statutum habeo, suspicor, teneo.

biennium satis esse duxerunt. Itaque existimo, Panætium, cum dixerit, homines solere in hac comparatione dubitare, hoc ipsum sensisse, quod dixerit, solere modo, non etiam oportere. Statuebat enim ignem esse ipsam naturam, quæ quidque gigneret, et mentem atque sensus.

3. Verbs of *despairing*, *hoping*,* *promising*, *swearing*, *threatening*, *trusting*, *vowing that something is*, or *that something was*, or *that something is to be*, etc.;† as,

I *hope to see him* = I *hope that I shall see him.*

Spero me eum visurum esse, or *Spero fore ut eum videam.*

I *hope to be able to see him* = I *hope that I shall be able to see him* [the future infinitive of *posse* is not used].

Spero me eum videre posse, or, as this is ambiguous, *Spero fore ut eum videre possim.*

I *hope I see him.*

Spero me eum videre.

I *despair of seeing him* = I *despair that I shall see him.*

Despero me eum visurum esse.

* An opinion seems to prevail in some quarters that expecto, constructed with *ut*, is used as a verb of *expecting* or *hoping that something will happen.* This is a misconception. Expecto means *I wait*, and, like any other active verb, may have an object; but it never has a complement of opinion either with or without *ut.* An *ut* may occur in the same sentence (as, in Cæsar, *B. C.*, i. 6, Neque expectabant ut de eorum imperio ad populum feratur: Nor did they wait that a reference might be made to the people about their authority. Cicero, 8, *Att.* 4, Expecto tuas literas, ut sciam, quid respondeas consultationi meæ: I wait your letters that I may know what you reply to my advice); but it is the usual *ut* of purpose, which may follow any verb, and which is in no way whatever dependent on the verb *expecto.*

† As, despero, magna in spe sum, spero, in spem adducor, spem affero, in spem inducor, in spem venio, spe ducor, spes me tenet, spes deserit, spes deficit, spem habeo, spes me obtentat; fidem facio, promissum facio, fidem meam obligo, polliceor, præsto, profiteor, promitto, in me recipio, repromitto, restipulor, spondeo; adjuro, juro, cautione, execratione, fœdere, jurejurando devincio, jusjurandum do; minitor, minor, testificor, testor omnes deos; confido, diffido, voveo.

The *soldiers promised to surrender* = *promised that they would surrender.*

Milites *polliciti sunt se in deditionem venturos esse.*

The father *swears to do it* = *swears that he will do it.*

Pater *jurat se facturum esse.*

The father *swears that it is so.*

Pater *jurat ita esse.*

Magnam in spem Cæsar veniebat, pro suis tantis populique Romani in eum beneficiis, cognitis suis postulatis, fore, ut pertinacia desisteret. Spero, quæ tua temperantia est, et hercule, ut me jubet Acastus, confido, te jam, ut volumus, valere. Inter se fidem et jusjurandum dant, et, regno occupato, per tres potentissimos populos totius Galliæ sese potiri posse sperant. Namque et operum magnitudinem et timorem suum sperabat fiduciam barbaris allaturum. Speravit iisdem se copiis cum illo posse confligere, quibuscum ego noluissem dimicare. Spero fore, ut contingat id nobis. Præterea in extremo libro tertio, de hac parte pollicetur se deinceps esse dicturum. Dixit, plus quam pollicitus esset, Cæsarem facere; pollicitum, se in cohortis prætoriæ loco decimam legionem habiturum, nunc ad equum rescribere. Cæsar Gallorum animos verbis confirmavit, pollicitusque est sibi eam rem curæ futuram. Præstabo, si Cæsarem bene novi, eum tuæ dignitatis rationem habiturum. Jurarem per Jovem Deosque Penates me et ardere studio veri reperiendi et ea sentire quæ dicerem. Marcellus, duo templa dedicaturum se Romæ, voverat. Nautæ quidam, cum adversa tempestate in alto jactarentur, voverunt, si eo portu, quem conspiciebant, potiti essent, ei deo, se vitulum immolaturos. Quare quanquam a Cratippo nostro, principe hujus memoriæ philosophorum, hæc te assidue audire atque accipere confido; tamen conducere arbitror, talibus aures tuas vocibus undique circumsonare. Spondeo, in meque recipio, eos esse M. Curii mores. Sed tamen separatim promitto, in meque recipio, fore eum tibi et voluptati et usui. Diffido me posse in hac causa consistere. Perfuga ab eo venit in castra Fabricii, eique est pollicitus, si præmium sibi proposuisset, se, ut clam venisset, sic clam in Pyrrhi castra rediturum et eum veneno necaturum. At ille, ut ingressus est, confestim gladium destrinxit, juravitque se illum statim interfecturum, nisi jusjurandum sibi dedisset, se patrem missum esse facturum. Cum hæc scribebam, censorem jam te esse sperabam. Spero nostram amicitiam non egere testibus. Cæsar in eam spem venerat, se sine pugna rem conficere posse.

4. Verbs expressive of *feeling that something is*, or *that something was*, or *that something is to be*, etc.;* as,

> I *rejoice in your welfare* = *rejoice that you are well* = *rejoice that you should be well.*
>
> *Gaudeo te valere.*
>
> The Macedonians *took it amiss that Eumenes was preferred to them* = *took amiss Eumenes' being preferred to them* = *took it amiss that Eumenes should be preferred to them.*
>
> Macedones *Eumenem sibi anteponi indigne ferebant.*

Si quis ægre ferat, se pauperem esse; idne disputes, paupertatem malum non esse; an, hominem ægre ferre nihil oportere? Gaudeo tibi jucundas meas esse literas. Equidem angor animo, non consilii, non ingenii, non auctoritatis armis egere rempublicam. Is mihi etiam gloriabitur, se omnes magistratus sine repulsa assecutum esse. Hoc a Panætio prætermissum esse miror. Doleo, te in tam leves, ne dicam in tam ineptas sententias, incidisse. Equidem vehementer lætor, eum esse me, in quem, cum cuperes, nullam contumeliam jacere potueris. Virtutes autem noli vereri ne expostulent et

* As, admiror, angor, demiror, doleo, ægre, indigne or moleste fero, gaudeo, glorior, gratulor, indignor, indoleo, invideo, lætor, mæreo, miror, queror, sollicitor, stomachor.

querantur se relictas esse. Eleus Hippias, quum Olympiam venisset, gloriatus est nihil esse ulla in arte rerum omnium, quod ipse nesciret. In quo valde delector, me ante providisse. Minime miramur, te tuis præclaris operibus lætari. Nihil me magis sollicitabat, quam in his molestiis non me, si qua ridenda essent, ridere tecum.

Verbs of *feeling*, instead of the accusative and infinitive, complete the predicate with *quod*,—seldom *quum*,—when it is intended to indicate not so much the feeling as the cause or reason of the feeling; as,

> I am glad *that you are well* = *because you are well.*
> Gaudeo, *quod salvus es.*
> She said she wondered *to find she had married a slave* = *insomuch as she found she had married a slave.*
> Dixit se mirari *quum invenisset se servo nuptam esse.*
> The father congratulated the son *on gaining such a victory* = *because he had gained such a victory.*
> Pater filio gratulatus est *quod tantam victoriam reportasset.*

Sane gaudeo, quod te interpellavi, quandoquidem tam præclarum mihi dedisti judicii tui testimonium. Quod scribis, te a Cæsare quotidie plus diligi, immortaliter gaudeo. Cato mirari se dicebat, quod non rideret aruspex, aruspicem cum vidisset. Delectat hoc ipso, quod inter se omnes partes cum quodam lepore consentiunt. Admiratus sum, quod nihilominus ad me tua manu scripsisses. Non dubito quin mirere, atque etiam stomachere quod tecum de eadem re sæpius agam. Tamen quod abes, gratulor. Gloriari solebat Hortensius quod nunquam bello civili interfuisset. In hoc admodum delector, quod in aliis rebus, aliisque sententiis versaris, atque ille. In qua tibi invideo, quod unis vestimentis tamdiu lautus es. Dolebam quod consortem gloriosi laboris amiseram.

5. Verbs of *knowing* and *not knowing that something is*, or *that something was*, or *that something is to be*, etc.;* as,

I *perceive it is true* = *that it is true* = *it to be true.*
Sentio verum esse.

The king *found there were many troublesome persons in the city* = *found that there were many troublesome persons in the city* = *found many troublesome persons to be in the city.*
Rex *invenit multos homines turbulentos in urbe esse.*

The Ædui *saw his vast machines approach their walls* = *saw that his vast machines were approaching their walls* = *saw his vast machines to be approaching their walls.*
Ædui *viderunt ingentes ejus machinas mœnibus suis appropinquare.*

We *hear he is come* = *that he is come* = *that he has come.*
Audimus† *eum venisse.*

Ex quo intelligi debet, illum mentis agitatione, investigationeque earum rerum, quas cogitando consequebatur, nec otiosum, nec solum unquam fuisse. Animadvertit Cæsar, unos ex omnibus Sequanos nihil earum rerum facere, quas ceteri facerent; sed tristes, capite demisso, terram intueri. Sic ab hominibus doctis accepimus, non solum ex malis eligere minima oportere, sed etiam excerpere ex his ipsis, si quid inesset boni. Paullatim Germanos consuescere Rhenum transire, et in Gal-

* As, accipio, agnosco, animadverto, attendo, audio, cerno, certum or pro certo habeo, cognosco, colligo, compertum habeo, commemini, concipio, comperio, mihi conscius sum, disco, ignoro, intelligo, invenio, memini, nescio, obliviscor, perspicio, recordor, reperio, pro certo scio, scio, sentio, video, etc.

† Observe: Ex Crasso audivi, *cum diceret*, sibi certum esse. Socratem audio *dicentem*, cibi condimentum esse famem, potionis sitim. Catonem vidi in bibliotheca *sedentem*, multis circumfusum Stoicorum libris.

liam magnam eorum multitudinem venire, populo Romano periculosum videbat. Video te alte spectare et velle in cœlum migrare. Conscius sum mihi nihil a me commissum esse, quod boni cujusque offenderet animum. Neque vero tum ignorabat, se ad crudelissimum hostem, et ad exquisita supplicia proficisci; sed jusjurandum conservandum putabat. Græcas literas M. Catonem in senectute didicisse accepimus. Æduos, fratres consanguineosque sæpenumero ab senatu appellatos, in servitute atque in ditione videbat Germanorum teneri, eorumque obsides esse apud Ariovistum ac Sequanos intelligebat. Mihi conscius sum nunquam me cupidum fuisse vitæ. Memini, me ex multis audire, te de glorioso et celeri reditu meo confirmare. Faciam, quod te sæpe animadverti facere. Id ego agnovi meo jussu esse factum. Eversam in perpetuum provinciam nos invenisse scito. Pompeios, celebrem Campaniæ urbem, desedisse terræ motu audivimus. Platonem Tarentum venisse, L. Camillo, Appio Claudio consulibus, reperio. An nesciebam vitæ brevem esse cursum, gloriæ sempiternum?

6. Verbs of *wishing that one's self* or *another do* or *be*, etc.; * as,

> I *wish that you know this = wish that you should know this = wish you to know this.*
> *Volo te hoc scire.*

Qui se ex his minus timidos existimare volebant, non se hostem vereri, sed angustias itineris et magnitudinem silvarum timere dicebant. Id ea maxime ratione fecit, quod noluit eum locum, unde Helvetii discesserant, vacare. Quod, ut te plurimum diligam, facere necesse est, si volo is esse, quem tu me esse voluisti. Nolo viros primarios esse temeritati et mendacio conscios.

* As, cupio, expeto, malo, nolo, postulo (rare), studeo, volo. Malo, nolo, volo, may be constructed also with the subjunctive. See Pred. II. 5. foot note.

Oratorem ne physicorum quidem esse ignarum volo. Malo non intelligi orationem meam quam reprehendi. Cujus principatum in capite, sicut in arce, posuit; et duas partes parere voluit, iram et cupiditatem. Nostram gloriam tua virtute augeri expeto. Nos in hac sententia sumus, ut te cupiamus etiam in libera republica magnum atque honestum esse. Dissensionem nascentem extingui summe studui. Remque ad arma deduci studebat. Quæ me P. Quinctius cupit commemorare. Tantum quisque se in republica posse postulat, quantum habet virium. Judicem me esse, non doctorem volo. Vellem adesse posset Panætius. Sed, nisi quid necesse erit, malo ne roges. Nunc idem (nisi molestum est) quoniam tibi non omnino displicet definire, et id facis quum vis; velim definias, quid sit voluptas. Velim demum ad tuos scribas, ut mihi libri pateant. Quod mecum per literas agis, unam ob causam mallem coram egisses.

Credor, *dicor*, *habeor*, *putor*, *videor*, *fertur*,* are seldom in the *present* and *imperfect* passive used impersonally, but in the *perfect* and *pluperfect* passive the impersonal form is used; *videor* meaning to *seem fit* is impersonal; as,

It is said that James is good = *James is said to be good.*

Jacobus dicitur esse bonus.

It seems that James is good = *James seems to be good.*

Jacobus videtur esse bonus.

It is believed that James is good = *James is believed to be good.*

Jacobus creditur esse bonus.

* So also *Arguitur:* Occidisse patrem Sex. Roscius arguitur. *Auditur:* Bibulus nondum audiebatur esse in Syria. *Nuntiatur:* Pons in Ibero prope effectus nuntiabatur. *Scribitur:* Avis quædam scribitur conchis se complere solere. *Reperitur:* Pythagoras venisse reperitur. *Traditur:* Aristides unus omnium justissimus fuisse traditur.

But,—*It seems good to James.*

Jacobo videtur. See Infinitive Subject, 5.

Quamquam magni ad honorem nostrum interest, quam primum ad urbem me venire, tamen peccasse mihi videor, qui a te decesserim. Sed quia tua voluntas ea videbatur esse ut prorsus, nisi confirmato corpore, nolles navigare, approbavi tuum consilium. Itaque mihi videris Latine docere philosophiam, et ei quasi civitatem dare; quæ quidem adhuc peregrinari Romæ videbatur. Idque princeps Isocrates instituisse fertur. Dicitur etiam Flaminius ad populum valuisse dicendo. Cyclops Ætnam solam tenuisse dicitur. Quo facto statuisse Commius dicebatur, nunquam in conspectum cujusquam Romani venire. Terentii fabellæ propter elegantiam sermonis putabantur a C. Lælio scribi. Themistocles fertur Seriphio cuidam respondisse.

THAT = IN ORDER THAT.

When *that* means *in order that*, it cannot be made by the accusative and infinitive; but it may be made by *ut*, or especially when accompanying a comparative by *quo*, and the negative by *ne;* as,

Read *that you may understand.*

Lege *ut intelligas.*

He reads *that he may not be ignorant.*

Legit *ne ignarus sit.*

The fugitives were forced to throw away the booty *that they might flee the faster.*

Fugitivi coacti sunt prædam abjicere *quo celerius fugerent.*

Eo opere perfecto, præsidia disponit, castella communit, quo facilius, si se invito transire conarentur, prohibere possit. Carinæ aliquanto planiores factæ erant quam nostrarum navium, quo facilius vada ac decessum æstûs excipere possent. In quos eo gravius Cæsar vindicandum statuit, quo diligentius in reliquum tempus a barbaris jus legatorum conservaretur. Geometræ solent non omnia docere, sed postulare, ut quædam sibi concedantur, quo facilius, quæ velint, explicent. Omnes, quæ rem ullam virtutis expertem aut in bonis aut in malis numerant, eas non modo nihil adjuvare arbitror, neque affirmare, quo meliores simus, sed ipsam depravare naturam. Sed ex hoc primum error tollendus est, ne quis sequi existimet, ut duo sint ultima bonorum. Cæsar respondit, consuesse Deos immortales, quo gravius homines ex commutatione rerum doleant, quos pro scelere eorum ulcisci velint, his secundiores interdum res et diuturniorem impunitatem concedere. Quinetiam necesse erit cupere et optare ut quam sæpissime peccet amicus, quo plures det sibi tanquam ansas ad reprehendendum. Ista sequimur, ut sine cura, metuque vivamus, animumque et corpus, quantum efficere possimus, ut molestia liberemus. Justitia sola restat, ut de omni virtute sit dictum. Iidem etiam dolorem sæpe perpetiuntur, ne, si id non faciant, incidant in majorem. Domi vero etiam contumelias servorum ancillarumque pertulit, ut ad id aliquando, quod cupiebat, perveniret. Idem tibi censeo faciendum, ut par sis in utriusque orationis facultate. Sed meos amicos, in quibus est id studium, in Græciam mitto, id est, ad Græcos ire jubeo, ut ea a fontibus potius hauriant, quam rivulos consectentur. Quæ autem nemo adhuc docuerat, nec erat, unde studiosi scire possent; ea, quantum potui (nihil enim magnopere meorum miror) feci, ut essent nota nostris. Nam nos in nostra urbe peregrinantes, errantesque, tamquam hospites, tui libri quasi domum deduxerunt, ut possemus aliquando, qui et ubi essemus, agnoscere. Qui stadium, inquit, currit, eniti et contendere debet, quam maxime possit, ut vincat. Omnia patefacienda, ut ne quid omnino, quod venditor norit, emptor ignoret. Ne noster quidem Gratidianus officio boni viri functus est tum, cum prætor esset, collegiumque prætorum tribuni plebis adhibuissent, ut res nummaria de communi sententia constitueretur. Has civitates L. Sulla, pecunia accepta, ex senatus consulto liberavisset, ut hæ rursus vectigales essent. In omni officio consuetudo exercitatioque capienda, ut boni ratiocinatores esse possimus. Omnis, quæ a ratione suscipitur de aliqua re, institutio debet a definitione proficisci, ut intelligatur, quid sit, de quo disputetur. Non enim te puto meas epistolas delere, ut reponas tuas. Hos Cæsar, ut in miseros ac supplices usus misericordia videretur, diligentissime conservavit. Sub vesperum Cæsar portas claudi jussit ne quam noctu oppidani ab militibus injuriam acciperent.

IV. *A Verb and an Adjective or Substantive, with the complement in the infinitive, the infinitive not being a complement of opinion.*

We find this complemental English infinitive with various signs; as, *at*, *for*, *from*, *in*, *of*, *to*, *with*, *without;* as, The Romans formed a plan *for* taking* the city; He put me to the trouble *of* coming; We had a facility *in* learning languages; Ye kept me *from* coming; etc. Sometimes we meet with this complemental infinitive without any sign; as, He prevented me *doing* it; I will make him *come;* etc.

This complemental English infinitive cannot be made by the Latin infinitive. It may be made by the *supine* in *u*, the *gerund* or *gerundive; ut*, *qui*, *quo*, affirmatively; *ne*, *quin*, *quominus*, negatively; *cur*, *quare*, etc.

Here we may set down these general rules:—

When the complemental infinitive depends upon

1. An *adjective*,

The complemental infinitive may be made in some cases by the *supine* in *u*, in others by the *gerund;* as,

* *Taking* is sometimes regarded as a *participial;* it is really a corruption of the Saxon infinitive in *an* or *en;* and so with *coming*, etc.

This is *easy to understand.*
Hoc est *facile intellectu;* or,
Hoc est *facile ad intelligendum.*

2. A *substantive,**

The complemental infinitive may be made by the *gerund;* as,

James put me to the *trouble of coming.*
Jacobus imposuit mihi *laborem veniendi.*

3. If the complemental infinitive is an *end* or *purpose,*

The infinitive may be made by *ut,* positive, and *ne,* negative, with the *subjunctive;* as,

Cæsar *was the proposer of levying a tax.*
Cæsar *fuit auctor ut vectigal cogeretur.*
The Romans *permitted him to triumph.*
Romani *permiserunt ei ut triumpharet.*
I *exhort you to fear God.*
Hortor te ut Deum timeas.
The Romans *condemned him to be crucified.*
Romani *condemnaverunt eum ut in crucem ageretur.*
The inhabitants *told them not to go away.*
Incolæ *iis dixerunt ne abirent.*
I *kept myself from doing it.*
Me tenui ne id facerem.

4. If the complemental infinitive assigns a *reason,*

The infinitive may be made by *qui, quod, cur,* etc.; as,

The king *was just in punishing him.*
Rex *justus fuit qui eum puniret.*
The citizens *accused me of doing this* = *accused me because* [as they said] *I had done this.*
Cives *accusarunt me quod hoc fecissem.*
You *were the cause of me being dismissed* = *were the cause why I was dismissed.*
Tu *causa fuisti cur dimitterer.*

* For substantives of *doubt* and *fear,* see Verbs of *doubting* and *fearing.* See also foot note, Pred. IV. 2.

5. If the complemental infinitive is a *condition*,

The infinitive must be made by *si* with the *subjunctive.*

Be you content with defending yourself = be content if you defend yourself.

Satis habeas si te defendas.

I *shall give you this book to do it = shall give you this book, if you do it.*

Tibi hunc librum dabo si id feceris.

1. When the complemental infinitive depends upon an *adjective.**

(*a*) The complemental infinitive made by the *supine* in *u.*†

This [*i.e.*, some particular thing] *is easy to say*, or *be said.*

Hoc *est facile dictu.*

[But *it is easy to say = saying is easy*, must be made, according to Subject II., *dicere est facile.*]

This *deserves to be mentioned* = this *is worthy to be mentioned.*

Hoc *est dignum commemoratu.*

Instead of the construction with the *supine* in *u*, we may employ the *gerund* with *ad;* as,

This matter *is easy to understand.*

Hæc res *est facilis ad intelligendum.*

Ex quo facile intellectu est, verbis eos, non re dissidere. Perfacile factu esse, illis probat, conata perficere, propterea quod ipse suæ civitatis imperium obtenturus esset. Quum suo cuique judicio sit utendum, difficile factu est,

* The construction of an *infinitive*, which depends on an *adjective*, is the same in the amplification of the *subject* as in the *predicate.*

† The supines in *u* in use are,—auditu, cognitu, commemoratu, dictu, gustatu, factu, intellectu, inventu, memoratu, perpessu, scitu, tactu, visu. *Fas. nefas*, and *opus* also have this construction, as if they were adjectives.

me id sentire semper, quod tu velis. Quod scire vis, qua quisque in te fide et voluntate sit, difficile dictu est de singulis. Quid est tam jucundum cognitu atque auditu quam sapientibus sententiis gravibusque verbis ornata oratio. Humanus autem animus, nisi cum ipso Deo, si hoc fas est dictu, comparari potest. Nefas dictu est, miseram fuisse talem senectutem. Uva succo terræ et calore solis augescens primo est peracerba gustatu. Erit vel acerbum aditu vel incredibile.

(*b*) The complemental infinitive made by the *gerund* in *di.*

When the adjective denotes an *affection of the mind*,* the predicate is completed by the *gerund* in *di.*†

The boy is *desirous to learn.*
Puer est *cupidus discendi.*

Equidem, inquit, ita sum cupidus te in illa longiore ac perpetua disputatione audiendi, ut, si id mihi minus contingat, vel hoc sim quotidiano tum sermone contentus. Hoc quidem sane luculenter, ut ab homine perito definiendi. Iste restituendi mei, quam retinendi studiosior. Tanquam ad picturam probandam, adhibentur etiam inscii faciendi cum aliqua solertia judicandi. Neque est ex multis res una quæ magis oratorem ab imperito dicendi, ab ignaroque distinguat, quam quod ille rudis incondite fundit, quantum potest; et id quod dicit, spiritu, non arte, determinat. Qua de causa homines bellandi cupidi magno dolore afficiebantur. Dumnorix Æduus insuetus navigandi mare timebat. Zeno perpessus est omnia potius quam conscios delendæ tyranidis indicaret.

(*c*) The complemental infinitive made by the *gerund* with *ad.*

* As, avidus, avarus, conscius, cupidus, ignarus, imperitus, inscius, insuetus, inops, peritus, studiosus.

† The gerund can be used *only* when the complemental infinitive is *active.*

When the adjective denotes *fitness* or *unfitness*,* the predicate may be completed with the *dative of the gerund*, or with the *gerund with ad*; as,

> This water is *useful for drinking*.
> Hæc aqua est *utilis bibendo*; or,
> Hæc aqua est *utilis ad bibendum*.†

Cum te unum ex omnibus ad dicendum maxime natum aptumque cognossem. Eum puto esse, qui verbis ad audiendum jucundis, et sententiis ad probandum accommodatis uti possit in causis forensibus, atque communibus. Menses tres ad dicendum maxime appositos mihi eripuistis. His tantis in rebus, tantisque in periculis, est tuum, M. Cato, qui non mihi, non tibi, sed patriæ natus es, videre quid agatur, retinere adjutorem, defensorem, socium, in republica consulem non cupidum, consulem (quod maxime tempus hoc postulat) fortuna constitutum ad complectendum otium, scientia ad bellum gerendum, animo et usu ad quod velis negotium. Marcellus promptus et non inexercitatus ad dicendum fuit. Alii ad permovendos animos instructi et parati erant. Ad imitandum mihi propositum exemplar illud est. Te hilari animo et prompto ad jocandum esse, valde gaudeo. Ardens et erectus [est] ad libertatem recuperandam. Non convenit, cum ego ad promerendum officium fuerim

* As, accommodatus, acutus, alacer, amplus, appositus, aptus, audax, bonus, celer, comparatus, concinnus, concitatus, copiosus, difficilis, diligens, erectus, exercitatus, expeditus, expositus, facilis, factus, fatalis, figuratus, firmus, fortis, habilis, hilaris, idoneus, imbecillus, imparatus, impiger, ineptus, inexercitatus, infirmus, instructus, intentus, intolerabilis, inutilis, jucundus, lætabilis, mollis, munitus, natus, necessarius, opportunus, ornatus, par, paratus, peritus, perfectus, piger, plenus, præparatus, promptus, propositus, sagax, salutaris, satis, segnis, tardus, tempestivus, uber, utilis, vacuus, vicinus.

Paratus, in Cicero and Cæsar, and *insuetus*, in Livy, are constructed with the infinitive. Is est maxime docilis, qui atten tissime est paratus audire. Mœsta civitas fuit, vinci insueta.

† Cicero rather uses *ad* with the *gerund*.

expeditus, vos ad referendam gratiam esse tardiores. Domitius non satis firmus est ad castra facienda. Mihi semper frequens conspectus vester multo jucundissimus, hic autem locus ad agendum amplissimus, ad dicendum ornatissimus est visus. Rem quæris præclaram juventuti ad discendum, nec mihi difficilem ad docendum. Ac multum proficiet, si se misericordem in potestate, et propensum ad ignoscendum fuisse ostendet. Nunc in uno cive respublica ad resistendum imbecilla est. Ad probandum utraque res infirma nugatoriaque est.

Dignus, *indignus*, and *idoneus*,* and sometimes *aptus*, especially when the predicate of a *personal subject*, complete the predicate with *qui* and the subjunctive; as,

> Robert was *qualified to be a king* = was *qualified who should be a king.*
>
> Robertus fuit *idoneus qui esset rex.*

O virum magnum, dignumque qui in nostra republica natus esset. Tibi fortasse idoneus fuit nemo, quem imitarere. Pompeius idoneus non est qui impetret. Res est idonea de qua quæratur. An qui petebant, indigni erant, qui impetrarent? Homines digni erant quibuscum disseratur. Vibillium Rufum Cæsar idoneum judicaverat, quem cum mandatis ad Pompeium mitteret.

For such forms as, *I am glad to do it* = *I glad do it* = *Ego lætus id facio*, see *Verbs of inclination and disinclination*, Pred. II. 5.

For such forms as, *James is the best to do it* = *James is the best of all who should do it* = *Jacobus maxime idoneus omnium est qui id faciat*, see Pred. V. 3.

Forms with ordinals,—novissimus, postremus, primus, princeps, ultimus,—thus,

> The boy *was the first to do it* = the boy *first did it.*
>
> *Id* puer *primus fecit.*

* *Idoneus* and *indignus* are found also with *ut.*

Qui ex iis novissimus venit, in conspectu multitudinis omnibus cruciatibus affectus necatur. Hæc quum dixisset, primus ex dextro cornu procurrit. Alteram insulæ partem distinendæ manûs causa cum constratis navibus aggreditur, præmiis magnis [ei] propositis, qui primus insulam cepisset. Ita sive casu, sive consilio Deorum immortalium, quæ pars civitatis Helvetiæ insignem calamitatem populo Romano intulerat, ea princeps pœnas persolvit.

When there is a *relative* along with the ordinal, it *follows* the ordinal in the English, but *precedes* the ordinal in the Latin; as,

That was Scipio, the first who was called Africanus
= Scipio *who first* was called Africanus.
Is Scipio erat, *qui primus* Africanus appellatus est.

2. When the complemental infinitive depends upon a *substantive*.*

The complemental infinitive may be made by the

* The *genitive of the gerund* occurs after such substantives as, Adjumentum, administrator, alacritas, amor, animus, arbitrium, argumentum, ardor, ars, artifex, artificium, assiduitas, auctoritas, auctor, aviditas, beneficium, causa, celeritas, cœptus, comes, conatus, conditio, consilium, consuetudo, contentio, copia, cupiditas, cursus, delectatio, descriptio, dies, difficultas, diligentia, disciplina, doctrina, dulcedo, dux, elegantia, elementum, eventus, excogitatio, exemplum, expectatio, experientia, facilitas, facultas, figura, finis, forma, formula, fortuna, fundamentum, genus, gloria, gratia, illecebra, impudentia, impunitas, initium, inscitia, intercapedo, jus, labor, laus, levitas, libertas, libido, licentia, locus, ludus, magister, materia, maturitas, mediocritas, mercatura, modus, mora, mos, natura, necessitas, occasio, occupatio, onus, opera, optio, ornamentum, otium, particeps, partitio, perpetuitas, potestas, princeps, principium, professio, profluentia, progressio, prudentia, ratio, sal, sapientia, satietas, scientia, sedatio, sensus, signum, societas, solertia, sonus, spatium, species, spes, spina, status, studium, stylus, subtilitas, tempus, usus, venia, verecundia, via, vis, virtus, voluntas, voluptas. For Substantives of *apprehension* and *bargaining*, see Infinitive Subject, 1., Exceptions 2. and 3.; of *allowing*, see Pred. IV. 3. (*a*); of *fearing*, see Pred. IV. 3. (*f*); of *hindering* and *doubting*, see Pred. IV. 3. (*g*); of *ordering* and *resolving*, see Pred. IV. 3. (*h*) and (*i*).

genitive of the *gerund* or *gerundive*, or with *ad* and the *gerund* or *gerundive*; as,

We *have cause to doubt* = *cause of doubting.*
Nos *habemus causam dubitandi.**
You *have a right to attack them* = *right of attacking.*
Vobis *est jus eos impugnandi.*
The Romans *formed a plan to take the city* = *plan of taking the city.*
Romani *urbis capiendæ consilium ceperunt.*
The boy *gets time to study* = *time for studying.*
Puer *tempus ad studendum nanciscitur.*†
The son *employed every means to ruin them.*
Filius *usus est omni ratione ad eos perdendos.*

Sometimes the complemental infinitive must be made with the subjunctive; as,

* A substantive cannot govern the infinitive in Latin; but the *gerund* is a *verbal substantive*, and one substantive governs another in the genitive,—hence the construction, *causam dubitandi.*

When, in the amplification of the subject, an infinitive depends upon a substantive, the construction is the same as in the predicate.

† We have the accusative of *purpose* with *ad* after these verbs, especially when, in the case of the transitive verbs, they are followed by an *impersonal substantive*:—Accedo, accommodo, acquiro, addo, adduco, adhibeo, adhortor, adipiscor, adjungo, adjuvo, advoco, affero, aggredior, allecto, allicio, applico [me], ardeo, arripio, attinet, attribuo, colloco, commoveo, comparo, concilio, conduco, confero, congredior, conspiro, constituo, contendo, convenio, converto, creo, decurro, deest, delego, depromo, descendo, desidero, dimitto, discedo, do, duco, elicio, erigo, excio, excito, expono, existo, figuro, firmo, gigno, habeo, hortor, impello, incendo, incito, inclino, incumbo, induco, ingredior, intendo, introvoco, invito, invoco, lacesso, largior, mitto, munio, nitor, obsum, offero, oppono, opus est, paro, patefacio, permaneo, pertineo, polleo, pono, porrigo, postulo, præparo, prodest, proficiscor, proficit, propono [mihi], rapio, redeo, refero, reperio, reviresco, satis est, sollicito, specto, stimulo, sumo, suppedito, suppeto, suscipio, tempus est,[1] trado, transfero, tribuo, usui esse, utor, valeo, voco.

[1] *Tempus est urbis defendendæ* or *ad urbem defendendam* = it is time to defend the city = it is time for defending the city. But, *tempus est defendere urbem* = it is high time to defend the city = *tempestivum est.*

I *have nothing to write.*
Habeo nihil quod scribam.
I *have nothing to accuse you of.*
Habeo nihil cujus te accusem.
The general *permitted them to retain their arms to defend themselves against their neighbours.*
Dux *iis permisit ut arma retinerent quibus se contra finitimos suos defenderent.*
The father *sent a letter to the boy not to go.*
Pater *misit ad puerem literas ne iret.*

So also when an *interrogative* precedes the complemental infinitive; as,

I *know not what to do.*
Nescio quid agam.
I *know not whether to do it or not.*
Nescio utrum necne id faciam.

Literas ad Trebonium mittit ut, quam celerrime posset, legionem xiii. arcesseret. Turmas mittit ad insequendum. Legionem mittit ad colonias civium Romanorum tuendas. Legatos ad eum mittit, qui dicerent sibi esse in animo sine ullo maleficio iter per provinciam facere. Ad Lingones literas nuntiosque misit, ne eos frumento neve alia re juvarent. Tu Cæsari causam belli contra patriam inferendi dedisti. Non committam ut, si defugerim, tibi causam aliquam dem recusandi. Hic mihi gravissimus auctor ad instituendam, fidelissimus socius ad comparandam, fortissimus adjutor ad rem perficiendam fuit. Habeo auctores et magistros religionum colendarum majores nostros. Nullam aliam ob causam me auctorem fuisse Cæsaris interficiendi criminatur, nisi ut in me veterani incitentur. Ille legibus per vim et contra auspicia ferendis auctor; ille in adoptando Clodio augur; ille restituendi mei quam retinendi studiosior. Maximis et miserrimis rebus perturbatus, cum coram te mihi potestas deliberandi non esset, uti tamen tuo consilio volui. Nulli improbo locus est ad rempublicam violandam. Nullum habeo instituendi aut docendi locum. Affert enim et temporis reliqui recuperandi rationem, et præsentis tuendi. De qua re alienum tempus est mihi tecum expostulandi, purgandi autem mei necessarium. Miloni nulla facultas manendi, exeundi non causa solum, sed etiam necessitas fuit. Ne irato testi facultas ad dicendum data videatur. Quæ cum viderem, nullam moram interponendam insequendi M. Antonium putavi. Quî igitur convenit, quæ causa fuerit ad constituendum judicium, eandam moram esse ad judicandum. Quoniam ut medicina valetudinis, navigationis gubernatio, sic vivendi ars est prudentia. Naturâ inest mentibus nostris insatiabilis quædam cupiditas veri videndi; et oræ ipsæ locorum illorum quò pervenerimus, quo faciliorem nobis cognitionem rerum cœlestium, eo majorem cognoscendi cupiditatem dabunt. Fannius ædificandi consilium abjecerat.

This complemental infinitive is often the *manner* or *cause*, and is made in Latin by the *gerund* or *gerundive*, with or without a preposition; as,

The boy wastes his time *playing*.
Puer tempus *ludendo* consumit.

Hominis mens discendo alitur et cogitando. Epicurus nihil de dividendo ac partiendo docet. Virtutes cernuntur in agendo. Injurias ferendo majorem laudem quam ulciscendo mereberis. Non pudendo, sed non faciendo id, quod non decet, impudentiæ nomen effugere debemus. Invidiæ verbum ductum est a nimis intuendo fortunam alterius. Omnis loquendi elegantia augetur legendis oratoribus et poetis. Exercenda est memoria ediscendis ad verbum quam plurimis et Ciceronis scriptis et aliorum. Sepulcris legendis redeo in memoriam mortuorum. In voluptate spernenda et repudianda virtus vel maxime cernitur. Plerisque in rebus gerendis tarditas et procrastinatio odiosa est. Ejus autem vinculum est ratio et oratio, quæ docendo, discendo, communicando, disceptando, judicando, conciliat inter se homines. Omne desiderium literis mittendis accipiendisque leniam. Is fuit mediocris in dicendo. Non in agendo solum, sed in meditando etiam fuit vehemens. Demosthenes perfecit meditando, ut nemo planius eo loqueretur. Fabricius ad Pyrrhum de captivis recuperandis missus est.

Some verbs, especially when the complemental infinitive is *passive*, prefer the participle in *dus*,* agreeing with the substantive; as,

The father *sent a book to be given to him.*
Pater *misit librum ei dandum.*
The general *undertook the besieging of the city* = *undertook the city to be besieged.*
Dux *suscepit urbem obsidendam.*
Cæsar *caused a bridge to be built over the river.*
Cæsar *curavit pontem in flumine faciendum.*

Redemptor, qui columnam illam de Cotta et de Torquato conduxerat faciendam. An vero in Syria diutius est Semiramis illa retinenda? cujus iter in provinciam fuit ejusmodi, ut rex Ariobarzanes consulem vestrum ad cædem faciendam, tamquam aliquem Thracem, conduceret. Alexander ex eo auro buculam curavit faciendam. Eo ad te scripsi, ut eam epistolam mihi curares referendam. Tu fasciculum, qui *Curio* descriptus est, velim cures ad eum perferendum. Quod me cogitare jubes, cogitabo equidem, etsi tibi dederam superiore epistola cogitandum. Utque quæstores eam basim statuamque faciendam et in rostris statuendam locent. Hic majore pecunia quatuor columnas dealbandas, quam ille omnes ædificandas locaverat. Qui

* As, accipere, censere, conducere, curare, dare, locare, mandare, mittere, permittere, proponere, putare, relinquere, suscipere, tradere.

singulis diebus ediscendos fastos populo proposuit. Plerique autem victi et debilitati tradunt se libidinibus constringendos. Tot prædia, tam pulchra, tam fructuosa pater filio suo colenda ac tuenda tradiderat. Quamobrem tradamus nos ei curandos. Tu cadaver P. Clodii nocturnis canibus dilaniandum reliquisti.

The *dative* of the participle in *dus* completes the predicate after certain phrases;* as,

The consul *takes pains to pacify the gods* = *gives endeavour to the gods being pacified.*
Consul *dat operam diis placandiis.*
The tribune *was over the tilling of the land* = *was over the land being tilled.*
Tribunus *præerat agro colendo.*

Ut quisque eis rebus tuendis conservandisque præfuerat. [Tu es] qui præesse agro colendo flagitium putes. Demosthenes curator muris reficiendis fuit. Omnibus hibernis Cæsaris oppugnandis erat dies dictus.

3. When the complemental infinitive is an *end* or *purpose.*†

The complement may be made in the *subjunctive* by *ut* positive and *ne* negative; but, in the case of verbs of *doubting*, by *an* positive, *quin* negative; as,

The Romans *condemned him to be crucified* = *condemned him that he should be crucified.*
Romani *eum condemnaverunt ut in crucem ageretur.*
Cæsar *commanded Catulus to give an account of*

* Dicere diem alicui, capere locum alicui, dare operam[1] alicui, præesse alicui, præficere aliquem alicui, studere alicui, and in the titles of officials; as, decemviri legibus scribendis.

† General Rule.—Whenever the complement of the predicate or the complement of the complement (as in the case of the indirect speech) is in a conjunctional or relative clause, the conjunctional or relative clause is put in the subjunctive.

[1] Also with *ut*.

the money = commanded Catulus that he should give an account of the money.

Cæsar *Catulo imperavit ut pecuniæ rationem redderet.*

The father *commanded the boy not to go away = commanded the boy that he should not go away.*

Pater *puero imperavit ne abiret.*

A friend *kept me from doing it = kept me that I should not do it.*

Amicus *prohibuit quominus id facerem.*

I *doubt him doing it = doubt if he will do it = doubt whether he will do it.*

Dubito an ille id faciat.

I *don't doubt him doing it = don't doubt but that he will do it.*

Non dubito quin ille id faciat.

These are the general forms of this complemental infinitive, but, for the sake of the beginner, we shall endeavour to classify the examples according to the nature of the leading verb.

(*a*) Verbs of *allowing* or *conceding* * *to one* to do.

The complement is made by *ut* positive and *ne* negative; as,

The general *permitted the soldiers to retain their arms = permitted to the soldiers that they should retain their arms.*

Dux *militibus permisit* † *ut arma retinerent.*

* As, assentio, cedo, concedo, do, largior, permitto, potestatem or optionem do or facio, remitto, sino (but sino only when in the imperative, and then generally without *ut*, as: *Sine dicas*), tribuo, veniam do. Sino, with the exception mentioned above, patior, and quiesco, follow the English construction of accusative and infinitive; as,

The master *suffered the boy to wear the mark.*

Magister *sivit puerum gerere notam.*

† Verbs like *permitto*, that govern only the *dative* in the active voice, must, if used in the passive voice, be used *impersonally;* as,

The soldiers are permitted to retain their arms = it is permitted to the soldiers to retain their arms = it is permitted to the soldiers that they should retain their arms:

Militibus permittitur ut arma retineant.

But *patior*, *quiesco*, and *sino* take the accusative and infinitive. See foot note.

Tibi remitto atque concedo ut Cn. Plancium defendas. Si quis deus mihi largiatur, ut ex hac ætate repuerascam, valde recusem. Cæsar postulavit ut, Sequanis permitteret ut, quos illi haberent, voluntate ejus obsides reddere illis liceret. Quod autem suades, ut ab eo petam, ut mihi concedat, ut idem tribuam Pompeio, quod ipsi tribuerim; id me jampridem agere intelliges ex literis Balbi. Assentio tibi ut in Formiano potissimum commorer. Tauris naturâ datum est ut pro vitulis contra leones summa vi impetuque contendant. Primique ex omnibus philosophis a natura tributum esse docuerunt, ut ii qui procreati essent, a procreatoribus amarentur. Dabis hanc veniam, mi frater, ut nostros Græcis anteponam.

Itaque non ob ea solum incommoda, quæ eveniunt improbis, fugiendam improbitatem putamus, sed multo etiam magis, quod cujus in animo versatur, nunquam sinit eum respirare, nunquam acquiescere. Hi Senatum Senatui parere non siverunt. Torquato nostro officia grata esse facile patior, eaque augere non desinam. Consilium meum a te probari facile patior.

(*b*) Verbs of *asking* or *entreating** *one* to do.

The complement is made by *ut* positive, and *ne* negative; as,

> The *general demanded of them to give an account* = *that they should give an account.*
>
> Dux *ab iis postulavit ut rationem redderent.*
>
> The father *asked the son not to do it* = *that he should not do it.*
>
> Pater *filium rogavit ne id faceret.*

* As, appello, contendo, deprecor, exigo, efflagito, exopto, exoro, expeto, exposco, exsecror, flagito, imploro, invito, obsecro, obtestor, opto, oro, peto, posco, postulo, precor, quæso, reposco, requiro, rogo, supplex est.

Two of the tribes *begged him to come to their assistance* = *begged that he would come to their assistance.*

Duæ ex tribubus *ab eo petierunt ut sibi auxilio veniret.*

Per fortunas tuas, Cicero, per liberos, te oro, et obsecro, ne quid gravius de salute et incolumitate tua consulas. Petit atque hortatur ut sine ejus offensione animi vel ipse de eo, causa cognita, statuat, vel civitatem statuere jubeat. Hæc cum pluribus verbis flens a Cæsare peteret, Cæsar ejus dextram prendit; consolatus, rogat finem orandi faciat. Tum Pythius, qui esset, ut argentarius, apud omnes ordines gratiosus, piscatores ad se convocavit, et ab his petivit ut ante suos hortulos postridie piscarentur. Ut geometræ solent non omnia docere, sed postulare, ut quædam sibi concedantur, quo facilius, quæ velint, explicent; sic ego a te postulo, mi Cicero, ut mihi concedas, si potes, nihil, præter id quod honestum sit, propter se esse expetendum. Ut lætetur etiam, non postulo. Primum, inquam, deprecor, ne me, tanquam philosophum, putetis, scholam vobis aliquam explicaturum. Exigerem ex te, cogeremque, ut responderes, nisi vererer, ne Herculem ipsum ea, quæ pro salute gentium summo labore gessisset, voluptatis causa gessisse diceres. Deos immortales precari, venerari, atque implorare debetis, ut urbem defendant. Precorque ab iis ut hodiernum diem, et ad hujus salutem conservandam, et ad rempublicam constituendam, illuxisse patiantur. Quæso ut eum diem memoriæ mandetis. Te quoque magnopere quæso, ut qualem te jam antea populo Romano præbuisti, cum huic idem quæstioni judex præesses, talem te et nobis et populo Romano hoc tempore impertias. Quæso a vobis, judices, ut hæc pauca, quæ restant, ita audiatis, ut partim me dicere pro me ipso putetis, partim pro Sex. Roscio. Nec dubito, quin Cæsar a me contendat ut ad urbem veniam. Passis manibus obtestabantur Romanos, ut sibi parcerent. Incensus Canius cupiditate, contendit a Pythio ut venderet. Immo vero obsecrabit patrem ne id faciat. A me postulat, ne dicendo tempus absumam. Sol Phæthonti filio facturum se esse dixit, quidquid optasset; optavit, ut in currum patris tolleretur. Ut sempiternæ laudi tibi sit iste tribunatus, exopto. Exoro enim, ut mecum cœnet. Ariovistus postulavit ne quem peditem ad colloquium Cæsar adduceret. Eo mulieres imposuerunt, quæ in prœlium proficiscentes, milites passis crinibus flentes implorabant, ne se in servitutem Romanis traderent.

(*c*) Verbs of *acquiring*, *effecting*, or *causing one* to do.*

The complement is made by *ut* positive, and *ne* negative; as,

I *will make him come.*
Efficiam ut veniat.
The sun *causes everything to flourish.*
Sol *efficit ut omnia floreant.*
I *will cause him not to go away.*
Efficiam ne abeat.
The master *carried the day that the boys should read.*
Magister *vicit ut pueri legerent.*

Efficias ne quid mihi fiat injuriæ. Negotium magistratibus est datum, ut curarent, ut sine vi mihi ædificare liceret. Impetravi a Salaminiis ut silerent. Tu tuas inimicitias ut reipublicæ donares, vicisti. Non assequor ut scribam, quod æquo animo legas. Hoc prœlio facto, reliquas copias Helvetiorum ut consequi posset, pontem in Arari faciendum curat. Quid mereas,

* As, adipiscor, assequor, cogo,[1] committo, consequor, curo,[2] efficio, evinco, extorqueo, facio,[3] impetro, mereo, obtineo, perficio, pervinco, teneo, vinco.

[1] *Cogo* frequently follows the English construction of accusative and infinitive, and *assuefacio* always.

[2] *Curo*, when the complement is a passive infinitive, takes the participle in *dus;* as, Cæsar curavit pontem faciendum.

[3] *Facere*, to represent, is constructed with the accusative and the infinitive, or with the present participle; as, Xenophon Socratem *disputantem* facit; Plato facit mundum *ædificari* a Deo.

ut Epicureus esse desinas? Pollicitus sum, curaturum me, Bruti causa, ut ei Salaminii pecuniam solverent. Vos adepti estis ne quem civem timeretis. Rem suscipit et a Sequanis impetrat ut per fines suos Helvetios ire patiantur, obsidesque uti inter sese dent, perficit. Feci igitur atque effeci, ut neuter quemquam omnium pluris quam me faceret. Nos autem teneamus, ut nihil censeamus esse malum, quod sit a natura datum omnibus. Nec, ut omnia, quæ præscripta et quasi imperata sint, defendamus, necessitate ulla cogimur. Sed quoniam coëgisti, ut concederem, qui mortui essent, eos miseros non esse, perfice, si potes, ut ne moriendum quidem esse miserum putem. Ut enim non efficias, quod vis, tamen, mors ut malum non sit, efficies. Cum sibi quisque primum itineris locum peteret et domum pervenire properaret, fecerunt ut consimilis fugæ profectio videretur. Nonne tibi satis prodesse videor, si perficio ut nolint obesse, qui possunt. Extorsisti ut faterer, qui omnino non essent, eos ne miseros quidem esse posse. Quid ergo? hic non noceat, qui quodam quasi veneno perficiat, ut veros heredes moveat, in eorum locum ipse succedat? Non committam ut tibi insanire videar. Socrates respondit, sese meruisse, ut amplissimis honoribus et præmiis decoraretur. Dii immortales faxint ne sit alter.

(*d*) Verbs of *endeavouring* or *exerting one's self* to do.*

The complement is made by *ut* positive, and *ne* negative; as,

The master *did his endeavour to expel the boy.*
Magister *operam dedit ut puerum expelleret.*
The master *did his endeavour not to expel the boy.*
Magister *operam dedit ne puerum expelleret.*

* As, id ago, ago cum aliquo, annitor, connitor, contendo, operam do, elaboro, enitor, experior, incumbo,[1] laboro, id molior, nitor,[2] obnitor, pugno.

[1] *Incumbo* more frequently with *ad* and gerund.

[2] *Conor* almost always follows the English construction with the infinitive, and *nitor* often follows it.

Nos autem id agimus, ut id in sapiente nullum sit omnino. Non minus se id contendere et laborare, ne ea quæ dixissent, enuntiarentur, quam uti ea quæ vellent, impetrarent. Quis reprehendet nostrum otium, qui in eo non modo nosmet ipsos hebescere et languere nolumus, sed, ut plurimis prosimus, enitimur. Laboro ut assentiar Epicuro. Deinde reliquæ legiones per tribunos militum et primarum ordinum centuriones egerunt, uti Cæsari satifacerent. Bene sane facis; sed enitar, ut Latine loquar. Dedi Antiocho operam diligentius ut causam ex eo totam cognoscerem. Cum autem paulum firmitatis accesserit, connituntur ut se erigant; et manibus utuntur. Dabo operam, ne Ventidius elabatur. Quare effice et elabora ut excellas. Equidem illud molior ut mihi Cæsar concedat ut absim.

(*e*) Verbs of *exhorting*, *impelling*, or *persuading one to do*.*

The complement is made by *ut* positive, and *ne* negative; as,

The boy *persuaded me to do it* = *that I should do it.*
Puer *mihi persuasit*† *ut id facerem.*
This *provoked the father to deprive the son of the inheritance.*
Hoc *patrem provocavit ut filium hereditate privaret.*
I *advise you to return home.*
Tibi *auctor sum ut domum redeas.*
The Romans *induced him not to undertake the work.*
Romani *eum adduxerunt ne opus susciperet.*

* As, adduco, adhortor, admoneo, auctor sum, censeo, cohortor, commoneo, commonefacio, confirmo, corrumpo, dehortor, dissuadeo, duco, hortor, impello, incito, induco, insisto, insto, moneo, moveo, permoveo, præmoneo, persuadeo, provoco, sollicito, suadeo, urgeo. Several of these verbs also take *ad*. See Verbs completing predicate with *ad*.

† Remember that verbs that govern *only* the dative in the active must be used impersonally in the passive. See Pred. IV. 3 (*a*) foot note.

Reliquas civitates sollicitant, ut in ea libertate, quam a majoribus acceperant, permanere, quam Romanorum servitutem perferre mallent. Eodem tempore persuadent Rauracis finitimis uti, eodem usi consilio, oppidis suis vicisque exustis, una cum iis proficiscantur. Alii, cuneo facto, ut celeriter perrumpant censent, quoniam tam propinqua sint castra; alii, ut in jugo consistant, atque eundem omnes ferant casum. Dumnorigem ad se vocat; monet ut in reliquum tempus omnes suspiciones vitet; præterita se Divitiaco fratri condonare dicit. His persuaderi, ut diutius morarentur neque suis auxilium ferrent, non poterat. Monet igitur ut caveat, ne prœlium ineat. Impellitque, ut hominum cœtus et celebrationes esse et a se obiri velit. Nec vero minus Lepidus ursit me et suis et Antonii libris, ut legionem trigesimam mitteret sibi. Quamobrem magnopere te hortor, mi Cicero, ut non solum orationes meas, sed hos etiam de philosophia libros, qui jam illos fere æquarunt, studiose legas. Ea difficultas induxit imperitos ut errarent. Adducis me ut tibi assentiar. Quid est aliud igitur, quam adhortari adolescentes, ut turbulenti, ut perniciosi, ut seditiosi cives velint esse? Caninius noster me tuis verbis admonuit, ut scriberem de suis consiliis. Sed auctor non sum, ut te urbi committas. Te hortor ne defatigere, neu diffidas semper in præsentibus malis prohibendis. Admonebat me res, ut hoc quoque loco intermissionem eloquentiæ, ne dicam interitum, deplorarem. Milites non longiore oratione [est] cohortatus, quam uti suæ pristinæ virtutis memoriam retinerent. Impellimur natura, ut prodesse velimus quamplurimis. Sed nunquam sum adductus, ut crederem.

(*f*) Verbs of *fearing* * *one doing.*

The predicate is completed with *ut* or *ne non*, *that not*, and *ne*, *that* or *lest;* as,

* As, extimesco, metuo, pertimesco, subtimeo, subvereor, timeo, vereor.

The son *fears his father coming* = *fears his father will come* = *fears lest his father come* [and prays that he may not come].*

Filius *timet ne pater veniat.*

The son *fears his father not coming* = *fears his father will not come* = *fears lest his father do not come* [and prays that he may come].

Filius *timet ut pater veniat.*

An hoc timebam, ne mecum ageretur, more institutoque majorum ut possem præsens sustinere? Et hic metuit, ne vix sibi constet. Habet enim aliquantum a physicis, ut verear, ne majorem largiar ei qui contra dicturus est libertatem et licentiam. Ac vereor interdum, ne talium personarum, quum amplificare velim, minuam etiam gloriam. Nam, ne ejus supplicio Divitiaci animum offenderet, verebatur. Quo facto, cum alius alii subsidium ferrent, neque temerent ne aversi ab hoste, circumvenirentur, audacius resistere ac fortius pugnare cœperunt. Et tamen veremur, ut hoc, quod a tam multis et quod tot locis perferatur, natura patiatur. Quod vos fœdus non jusseritis, vereor ut satis firmum sit. Itaque non extimesco ne Cn. Plancio custodia meæ salutis apud eos obsit, qui meipsum maxime salvum videre voluerunt. Vereor ut idem interitus sit animorum et corporum. Quoniam tu abfuisti, vereor ut satis diligenter actum sit. Quid metuebat ut oppugnaretur a perdito? an, ne accusaretur a condemnato? Videris

* Verbs of *fearing* may be regarded as verbs of *praying*. This is perhaps the simplest view for the beginner. When one fears that a thing will happen, and yet desires that it may not happen, he naturally prays that it may not happen—*ne;* when one fears that it will not happen and yet desires it to happen, he prays that it may happen—*ut:*

Timeo ne,—I fear he will,
Timeo ut,—I fear he won't.

So in Greek:

δέδοικα μή,—I fear he will.
δέδοικα μὴ οὐ,—(= ne non = ut) I fear he won't.

vereri ut epistolas illas acceperim. Tamen vereor ne consolatio ulla possit vera reperiri. Metuo ne id consilii ceperimus, quod non facile possimus explicare. Timeo ut sustineas. Metuit ut eam ipse posset opibus suis sustinere. Timebam ne evenirent ea quæ acciderunt.

(*g*) Verbs of *hindering* and *doubting one doing.**

Verbs of *hindering* generally imply a negative complement made with *ne;* as,

Anguish of mind *prevents me saying more* = *prevents me from saying more.*

Dolor animi *impedit ne plura dicam.*

A friend *kept me from doing it.*

Amicus *prohibuit quominus id facerem.*

But *impedio* and *prohibeo*† may follow the English construction of accusative and infinitive; as,

What *hinders me approving of these things?* = *hinders me from approving of these things?*

Quid *impedit me hæc probare?*

Instead of *ne*, the complement may be made with *quominus;* as,

The general *prevented the enemy making incursions* = *prevented the enemy from making incursions.*

Dux *prohibuit quominus hostes incursiones facerent.*

* As, abstineo, adversor, antepono, contineo, desidero, deterreo, eripio, per me fit, impedio, inhibeo, intercedo, interdico, intermitto, interpello, interpono moram, moror, obsisto, obsto, officio, perturbo, prohibeo, pugno, reclamo, recuso, repugno, retineo, per me stat, sustineo, tempero, teneo, terreo.

† *Prohibeo*, in Cæsar, always has the accusative and the infinitive, and *prohibeor* the infinitive; as, Hos Cæsar, dispositis in vallo custodiis, recipi prohibebat. Fit in hostes impetus; sed e muro, sagittis tormentisque, fugientes persequi prohibentur. We have, in Cicero, an example of *prohibeo*, as a verb of *praying*, with *ut*,—Dii prohibeant, judices, ut hoc præsidium sectorum existimetur. If *prohibeo* is constructed with *quominus*, it cannot take an accusative after it, though *deterreo* may. We can say, *deterreo aliquem quominus;* but we *cannot* say, *prohibeo aliquem quominus*, —only *prohibeo quominus aliquis.*

Sometimes a verb of hindering completes the predicate with the gerund; as,

Cæsar *kept sane men from writing.*
Cæsar *deterruit sanos homines a scribendo.*

Verbs of hindering, *when they are preceded by a negative* [by a direct negative, such as, haud, nihil, non, nunquam, or by an implied negative, such as, ægre, paulum, haud multum, vix, quis est ?], may complete the predicate by *quin;* as,

The master *scarcely refrains from laughing.*
Magister *vix se continet quin rideat.*

But *impedio, intercedo, interdico,* and *prohibeo,* rarely in this case take *quin,*—almost always *quominus.*

Nec vero, ut noster Lucilius, recusabo, quominus omnes mea legant. Sententiam ne diceret, recusavit. Cimbros intra fines suos ingredi prohibuerunt. Nam libero tempore, quum soluta nobis est eligendi optio, quumque nihil impedit, quominus id, quod maxime placeat, facere possimus, omnis voluptas assumenda est, omnis dolor repellendus. Per eos, ne causam diceret, se eripuit. Miserunt qui dicerent, tantum esse eorum omnium furorem, ut ne Suessiones quidem, fratres consanguineosque suos, qui eodem jure et eisdem legibus utantur, unum imperium unumque magistratum cum ipsis habeant, deterrere potuerint, quin cum his consentirent. Quod quum audissemus, nullam moram interponendam putavimus quin videremus hominem, nobiscum et studiis eisdem et vetustate amicitiæ conjunctum. Si te, inquit, Luculli oratio flexit quæ est habita memoriter, accurate, copiose, taceo, neque te, quominus, si tibi ita videatur, sententiam mutes, deterrendum puto. Nec vero Aristotelem in philosophia deterruit a scribendo amplitudo Platonis. Neque hæc in eam sententiam disputo, ut homines adolescentes a dicendi studio deterream. Itaque non deterret sapientem mors, quominus in omne tempus reipublicæ consulat. Nec mihi, ne faciam, interdictum puto. Neque enim interdictum est a rerum natura, aut a lege aliqua, atque more, ut singulis hominibus ne amplius quam singulas artes nosse liceat. Interpellent me, quominus honoratus sim, dum ne interpellent, quo minus respublica a me administrari possit. Cæsar nunquam interpellavit, quin, quibus vellem, atque etiam quos ipse non diligebat, tamen iis uterer. Quid autem obstat, quominus sit beatus, si non sit bipes? Neque repugnabo, quominus omnia legant. Non cunctandum existimavit quin pugna decertaret. Contineo igitur me ne incognito assentiar. Quintus a ducenda uxore abhorret. Videmus ne, ut pueri, ne verberibus quidem a contemplandis rebus perquirendisque deterreamur? Non recusabat Quinctius, quin ita satisdare juberet. Nihil desideramus, quominus Epirum ipsam possidere videamur. In urbe mundove communi non adversatur jus, quominus suum quidque cujusque sit. Unius legionis hibernis non potuerant contineri, quin bellum pararent conjurationesque facerent. Quid obstat quominus deus sit beatus. Cæsar eisdem de causis, quominus dimicare vellet, morabatur. Per te factum est, quominus pax fieret. Nemo se anteponat, quominus reus fiat. Tu nullam moram interposuisti, quin quam primum maximo gaudio frueremur. Hominem multis verbis deterret, ne auctionetur. Neque sibi homines feros ac barbaros temperaturos existimabat, quin, cum omnem Galliam occupassent, ut ante Cimbri, Teutonique fecissent, in Provinciam exirent atque inde in Italiam contenderent. Colloquendi Cæsari causa visa non est; et eo magis, quod pridie ejus diei Germani retineri non poterant, quin in nostros tela conjicerent. Cæsar cognovit, per Afranium stare, quominus dimicaretur. Cæsar ad T. Sextium legatum mittit, ut si nostros depulsos loco vidisset, quominus liberè hostes insequerentur, terreret.

Verbs of *doubting*,* *preceded by a negative*, complete the predicate with *quin*; as,

I *don't doubt him doing it* = *don't doubt but that he will do it.*

Non dubito quin id faciat.

There *is no doubt of him doing it* = *no doubt but that he will do it.*

Nihil dubii *est quin id faciat.*

But, if there be no negative,

I *doubt him doing it* = I *doubt if he will do it* = I *doubt whether he will do it.*

Dubito an ille id faciat. See Pred. V. 2.

Non quod dubitaretis, quin ab isto nihil jure esset actum,

* As, non dubito, non dubium est, nihil dubii est, nihil dubitationis habeo. Dubito, I hesitate, and non dubito, I don't hesitate, are constructed with the infinitive. See Pred. II. 5. Non dubito and dubium est are sometimes constructed with the accusative and infinitive, like verbs of declaring. *Dubito num*, in a single indirect question, occurs in Pliny,—Dubito num idem tibi suadere, quod mihi, debeam; but in the very same letter he has also written: Dubito an idem nunc tibi quod tunc mihi suadeam. *Ne* in a single indirect question is found in Cicero's letters: Antea dubitabam, venturæne essent; nunc mihi non est dubium quin venturæ non sint; and also in Cæsar, *B. G.* v. 54.

Doubts having been expressed about Dr Melvin's construction of *dubito*, we give the following from our notes:—"*Dubito* governs no case, and therefore the word that comes after it must be put in the ablative with *de;* as, I doubt the matter, *De re dubito;* and, therefore, in the passive it must be used impersonally with what is doubted in the ablative, as above, as, Whose bravery cannot be doubted: *Cujus de virtute dubitari non potest.* It is doubtful if this could have been done before: *Dubium est an hoc antea fieri potuerit.* I doubt the justice of this: *Dubito an hoc justum sit.* The historian expresses a doubt whether Hercules being alone could have killed many thousand persons: *Historicus dicit, se dubitare an Hercules, quum solus esset, multa millia hominum interficere potuisset.* I don't doubt but he would have done it: *Non dubito quin facturus fuisset.* When a relative comes after *dubito*, the accusative and infinitive must be used, because we cannot say *quin qui;* as, They went to the king, who they doubted not would do it: *Ad regem iverunt, quem non dubitabant facturum esse.* He did many things, in regard to which he doubted if they were just: *Multa fecit, quæ an justa essent dubitavit.*"

sed quia, etc. Quid illud? num dubitas, quin specimen naturæ capi debeat ex optima quaque natura? Dionysius non dubitabat quin ei crederemus. Non potest dubitari, quin decretum nullum falsum possit esse. Dubitabis quin hunc vindices? Cum igitur hic locus nihil habet dubitationis, quin homines plurimum hominibus et prosint et obsint, proprium hoc est virtutis, conciliare sibi animos hominum et ad usus suos adjungere. Nisi forte tanta ubertas, et varietas pomorum, earumque jucundus non gustatus solum, sed odoratus etiam et adspectus dubitationem offert, quin hominibus solis ea natura donaverit. Dubiumne est, quin ista omnis improbatio cogendæ pecuniæ causa nata sit? Quis unquam dubitavit quin in republica nostra primas eloquentia tenuerit semper?

(*h*) Verbs of *ordering*, *providing*, *taking care*, or *taking on one's self* to do.*

The complement is made by *ut* positive and *ne* negative; as,

> The son *wrote to his father to introduce him to the king* = *wrote to his father that he should introduce him to the king.*
>
> Filius *ad patrem scripsit ut se ad regem introduceret.*
>
> The inhabitants *told them not to go away* = *told them that they should not go away.*
>
> Incolæ *iis dixerunt ne abirent.*
>
> *Take you care of getting yourself new chains* = *take care lest you get yourself new chains.*
>
> *Cave [ne] nova tibi vincula compares.*

* As, arrogo, assumo, caveo, clamo, conclamo, condemno, consulo, curo, denuncio, dico, edico, eloquor, exclamo, impero,[1] impono, inclamo, instituo, lego, loquor, mando, mitto, negotium do, præcipio, prædīco, præmando, præscribo, pronuntio, prospicio, provideo, reclamo, scribo, sententiam dico, significo, sumo, suscipio,[2] video.

[1] Also, Postremo imperavi egomet mihi assentari omnia, Cic. de Am. 94; but this construction is hardly to be imitated.

[2] Suscipio often takes an accusative and gerundive; as, Suscepit hoc faciendum.

Jubeo and *veto* follow the English construction of accusative and infinitive; as,

The Romans *ordered him to let Egypt alone.*
Romani *jusserunt eum omittere Ægyptum.*
His father forbade him to go.
Pater *vetuit eum ire.* See Pred. II. 5.

Vetat enim dominans ille in nobis Deus injussu hinc nos suo demigrare. Trium mensium molita cibaria sibi quemque domo efferre jubent. Ponere jubebam, de quo quis audire vellet. Cæsar ad Lingones literas nuntiosque misit, ne eos frumento, neve alia re juvarent; qui si juvissent, se eodem loco, quo Helvetios, habiturum. Cave quidquam putes esse verius. Hoc, quæso, cave ne te terreat. Cave facias. Caverat enim ille sibi, ut, si tibi provinciam dedisset, omnium suorum scelerum adjutorem te præberes. Quare Januario ineunte, ut constituisti, cura ut Romæ sis. Cura ut valeas. Interim paucis post diebus fit ab Ubiis certior, Suevos omnes unum in locum copias cogere, atque iis nationibus, quæ sub eorum sint imperio, denunciare, ut auxilia peditatus equitatusque mittant. Ubiis imperat ut pecora deducant, suaque omnia ex agris in oppida conferant. Cæsar suis imperavit ne quod omnino telum in hostes rejicerent. His mandavit ut, quæ diceret Ariovistus, cognoscerent, et ad se referrent. Non enim, credo, id præcipit, ut membra nostra aut staturam figuramve noscamus. Scripsi ad eum, ut mihi Heracleam occurreret. Negotium magistratibus est datum ut curarent, ut sine vi mihi ædificare liceret. Est oratori providendum, non ut illis satisfaciat, quibus necesse est, sed ut illis, quibus liberè liceat judicare. Arcesilaus eum morem revocavit, instituitque ut ii qui se audire vellent, non de se quærerent, sed ipsi dicerent, quid sentirent. Videndum est, igitur, ut ea liberalitate utamur quæ prosit amicis, noceat nemini. Cato ad Pompilium scripsit, ut, si eum pateretur in exercitu remanere, secundo eum obligaret militiæ sacramento. Provide etiam ne uni tibi istam sententiam minime liceat defendere. Vide, igitur, ne etiam si divinationem tibi esse concessero, quod nunquam faciam, neminem tamen divinum reperire possimus. Sed Pompeius suis prædixerat, ut Cæsaris impetum exciperent, neve se loco moverent, aciemque ejus distrahi paterentur. Atque etiam hoc natura præscribit ut homo homini, quicunque sit, ob eam ipsam causam, quod is homo sit, consultum velit. Tantum tibi arrogas, ut exponas disciplinam sapientiæ. Deinde ut concludamus atque ita peroremus, natura ipsa præscribit. Atque etiam omnes, qui rempublicam gubernabunt, consulere debebunt, ut earum rerum copia sit, quæ sunt necessariæ. Suscipio ut me putem præstare debere.

(*i*) Verbs of *resolving*, *decreeing*, or *determining that* one do.*

The complement is made by *ut* positive and *ne* negative; as,

> The general *resolved that the soldiers should march.*
> Dux *statuit ut milites proficiscerentur.*
> The senate *decreed that no one go away.*
> Senatus *decrevit ne quis abiret.*

Pompeius contendit ut decem tribuni plebis ferrent ut absentis ratio haberetur. Natura fert ut extrema ex altera parte graviter, ex altera autem acute sonent. Natura fert ut eis faveamus qui eadem pericula, quibus nos perfuncti sumus, ingrediantur. Conscripserunt communiter edictum cum pœna, atque judicio, constitueruntque, ut omnes simul in rostra post meridiem escenderent. Habeo enim regulam, ut talia visa vera judicem, qualia

* As, animum induco, comparo, condemno, consilium capio, constituo, decerno, depaciscor, excipio, facio decretum, fero, instituo, judicium do, paciscor, sancio, scisco, statuo, vota facio. Verbs of resolving complete the predicate with the infinitive when there is no secondary subject, as, He resolved to go: *Statuit ire.* See Pred. II. 7.

falsa esse non possint. Ea re permissa, diem concilio constituerunt, et jurejurando, ne quis enuntiaret, nisi quibus communi consilio mandatum esset, inter se sanxerunt. Sententiis dictis, constituunt, ut, qui valetudine aut ætate inutiles sint bello, oppido excedant. Lex ipsa naturæ decernit profecto, ut ab homine inerti atque inutili, ad sapientem, bonum, fortemque virum, transferantur res ad vivendum necessariæ. Sanxerunt ne quis emeret mancipium nisi in demortui locum. Athenienses, cum Persarum impetum nullo modo possent sustinere, statuerentque, ut, urbe relicta, conjugibus et liberis Trœzene depositis, naves conscenderent, libertatem Græciæ classe defenderent, Cyrsilum quendam, suadentem, ut in urbe manerent, Xerxemque reciperent, lapidibus obruerunt. Prætores, ut considerate fieret, comparaverunt. Tibi decernit, ut regem deducas. Hic decernit ut miser sit. Quod ne liceret fieri ad alterius injuriam, lege sanxerunt. Decurionum decretum statim fit ut decemprimi proficiscantur ad Sullam.

4. When the predicate or complement contains a *reason.*

All *words* and *phrases* denoting a *cause* or *reason* * complete the predicate with *qui*, *quippe qui*, *utpote qui*, *quod*, *ex eo quod*, *quia*, *quare*, *quamobrem*, *cur*, *etc.*

(*a*) Qui, quippe qui, quia, quod, utpote qui; as,

The citizens *accused me of doing this* = *that I had done this* = *because* [as they said] *I had done this.*

Cives *me accusarunt* † *quod hoc fecissem.*

* See Causal Particles.

† Verbs of accusing, blaming, praising, surprise (as, accuso, criminor, incuso, laudi or vitio alicui do, excuso, gratias alicui ago, invehor, objicio, objurgo, reprehendo, subscribo, invideo, vitupero, laudo, admiror, miror, etc.), complete the predicate with *quod* and the indicative, when the speaker or writer is giving *his own* reason; but with *quod* and the subjunctive when he is giving the *alleged* reason, or the reason *of another.*

I *find fault with you for speaking = because you speak.*

Reprehendo te quod dicis, or *Reprehendo te in eo quod dicis.*

I *am surprised at you saying so = because you say so.*

Miror quod tu ita dicis.

I *praise him for saying so = because he says so.*

Laudo eum quod ita dicit.

I *thank you for noting my observations.*

Tibi gratias ago quod mea dicta observas.

This *arises from your neglecting my admonitions.*

Hoc *oritur inde quod meas admonitiones neglexisti.*

James *seems to have been the elder from his being always mentioned first.*

Jacobus *major natu videtur fuisse ex eo quod ejus nomen semper prius commemoratur.*

You *are a fool to say so = inasmuch as you say so.*

Tu *es stultus qui ita dicas.*

Livy *must have been very diligent, to have written this history = inasmuch as he has written this history.*

Livius *diligentissimus fuerit necesse est, qui hanc historiam scripserit.*

The king *was just in punishing him.*

Rex *justus fuit qui eum puniret.*

The king *said we were unjust in obstructing him in his right.*

Rex *dixit nos esse iniquos qui in suo jure se interpellaremus.*

Neptune *was entitled to the honour as having given what was more useful = from having given what was more useful.*

Neptuni honor jure erat, quippe qui id quod utilius erat dedisset.

Is filium, Macedonum legatis accusantibus, quod

pecunias prætorem in provincia cepisse arguerent, causam apud se dicere jussit. Quo in libro in hoc maxime admirabor Platonem, quod mihi in oratoribus irridendis ipse esse orator summus videbatur. Princeps decima legio per tribunos militum ei gratias egit quod de se optimum judicium fecisset. De animo ergo bene facis, quod non dubitas. Criminabatur quod Titum filium ab hominibus relegasset. Vehementer eos incusavit, quod aut quam in partem aut quo consilio ducerentur, sibi quærendum aut cogitandum putaret. Æschines in Demosthenem invehitur, quod is septimo die post filiæ mortem hostias immolasset. Quod eo magis miror, quia scriptum a discipulo ejus Posidonio est. Graviter eos accusat, quod cum frumentum neque emi, neque ex agris sumi posset, tam necessario tempore, tam propinquis hostibus, ab iis non sublevetur; præsertim cum magna ex parte eorum precibus adductus bellum susceperit; multo etiam gravius, quod sit destitutus, queritur. Fecisti mihi pergratum quod Serapionis librum ad me misisti. Bene facis, inquit, quod me adjuvas. Non tibi objicio quod hominem omni argento spoliasti. Laudat Africanum Panætius quod fuerit abstinens. Urbs, quæ, quod in ea Fortunæ fanum fuit, Tyche nominata est. Aristoteles, veteres philosophos accusans, qui existimavissent, philosophiam suis ingeniis esse perfectam, ait, eos aut stultissimos aut gloriosissimos fuisse. Quis autem vel eum jure reprehenderit, qui in ea voluptate velit esse, quam nihil molestiæ consequatur, vel illum qui dolorem eum fugiat quo voluptas nulla pariatur? Reperiebat Nervios increpitare atque incusare reliquos Belgas, qui se populo Romano dedidissent. Excusavit [eum] Vespa Terentius, quod eum brachium fregisse diceret. Vitio mihi dant, quod mortem hominis necessarii graviter fero. Aristoteles nos reprehendit, qui has pecuniarum effusiones non admiremur, quæ fiunt ad multitudinem deleniendam. Mihi es visus esse inconstans, qui eundem et læderes et laudares. Frater ejus, utpote qui peregre depugnarit, familiam ducit. Epicurus istam voluptatem interdum nimis etiam novit, quippe qui testificetur.

(*b*) Cur, quamobrem, quare, quod; as,

He saw no reason *for departing from his practice* = *why he should depart from his practice.*

Vidit nullam causam *cur a consuetudine decederet.*

There is no reason *for his doing it* = *no reason why he should do it.*

Non est *cur id faciat.*

This *need not appear surprising* = there is no reason *why this should appear surprising.*

Non est *quod hoc mirum videatur.*

You were the cause *of my dismissal* = *of my being dismissed* = *why I was dismissed.*

Tu causa fuisti *cur dimitterer.*

Non justa [erat] causa cur Laomedonti tanta fieret injuria. Satis esse causæ arbitrabatur quare in eum aut ipse animadverteret, aut civitatem animadvertere juberet. Secundum ea multæ res eum hortabantur quare sibi eam rem cogitandam et suscipiendam putaret. Quid est, cur dubitemus dicere, et sapientiam propter voluptatem expetendam et insipientiam propter molestias esse fugiendam? Nec tamen mihi sane quidquam occurrit cur non Pythagoræ sit et Platonis vera sententia. Neque est quidquam, cur incredibilis his animorum videatur æternitas. Affers omnia argumenta cur dii sint. Quid est causæ cur repudietur? Iste multa signa dederat quamobrem ei responsurus non videretur. Multa mihi veniebant in mentem quamobrem ita fore putarem. Quære rationem cur ita videatur. Credo equidem, et cur credam afferre possum. Nego fuisse causam, cur postularet. Multa ab Cæsare in eam sententiam dicta sunt, quare negotio desistere non posset.

5. When the complement contains a *condition, exception*, or *limitation*.*

The limitation or exception is put in the *subjunctive;* as,

> The boy *would have died, but for me.*
> Puer *mortuus esset, nisi ego fuissem.*
> I *never go out without seeing him.*
> *Nunquam exeo quin eum videam.*
> I *will tell him, if I see him.*
> *Ei dicam, si eum videam.*
> You *would have conquered him by forgiving the son for the sake of the father = would have conquered him if you had forgiven the son to the father.*
> *Eum vicisses, si filium patri condonavisses.*
> I *will give you the book to go.*
> *Librum tibi dabo si iveris.*

An vero vir fortis, nisi stomachari cœperit, non potest fortis esse? Audax id negotium est, dicerem impudens, nisi hoc institutum postea translatum ad philosophos nostros esset. Possumusne scire, hoc quale sit, nisi contulerimus inter nos, quam finem bonorum dixerimus, quid finis, quid etiam sit ipsum bonum? Auctoritas tanta plane me movebat, nisi tu opposuisses non minorem tuam. Cæsar nunquam ad suorum quemquam

* But, except, for, unless, without, etc., nisi, nisi si, quin, si, ut non, etc.

Without cannot be made by *nisi*, or *quin*, or *ut non*, *unless a negative precedes.* He never went away without reading = he never went away unless he had read: *Nunquam abiit nisi legisset.* Or = he never went away that he did not read = he never went away but he read: *Nunquam abiit quin legeret.* He went away without reading = he went away and he read not = he went away nor did he read: *Abiit neque legit.* He went away without reading the book = he went away, the book not having been read: *Abiit libro non lecto.* Or = he went away, nor did he read the book: *Abiit, neque librum legit.* He went away without being asked = not having been asked: *Abiit non rogatus.*

literas misit, quin Attico mitteret quid ageret. Dolorem justissimum, si non potero frangere, occultabo. Lutatius, eques Romanus, sponsionem fecerat, ni vir bonus esset. Memoria minuitur, nisi eam exerceas. Sæpe homines ægri, quum æstu febrique jactantur, si aquam gelidam biberint, primo relevari videntur. Non possunt una in civitate multi rem atque fortunas amittere, ut non plures secum in eandem calamitatem trahant. Quis unquam templum illud adspexit, quin avaritiæ tuæ testis esset? Literas ad te nunquam habui, cui darem, quin dederim. In castello nemo fuit omnium militum quin vulneraretur. Non dubitari debet quin fuerint ante Homerum poëtæ. Nullum patior esse diem, quin aut in foro dicam, aut mediter extra forum.

V. *When there are Intensives in the Predicate, or when the Complement of the Predicate is an Interrogative, Relative, etc.*

1. When there are *intensives** in the predicate.

The complement is made by *ut* and *qui*, positive, and *ut non*, or *qui non*, or *ut nihil*, *ut nunquam*, etc., negative; as,

You *are too powerful to be hindered.*
Tu *potentior es quam ut prohibearis.*
The man *is too great for you to hurt him.*
Homo *major est quam cui tu nocere possis.*
The boys *were foolish enough to lend it to him.*
Pueri *fuerunt tam stulti ut ei id commodarent.*
The father *was so glad that he asked him.*
Pater *tantopere gavisus est ut eum rogaret.*
The state *was so far from complying with the conditions that it violated them.*
Civitas *conditionibus adeo non paruit ut eas violaret.*
The master *was so angry that he did not speak.*
Magister *adeo iratus fuit ut non loqueretur.*

* As, adeo, is, ita, sic, talis, tam, tantus, tot, usque eo, etc.

Horum adventu tanta rerum commutatio facta est, ut nostri, etiam qui vulneribus confecti procubuissent, scutis innixi, prœlium redintegrarent. Idque natura loci sic muniebatur, ut magnam ad ducendum bellum daret facultatem. Tantus subito timor omnem exercitum occupavit, ut non mediocriter omnium mentes animosque perturbaret. Tantumque valuit error ut corpora cremata quum scirent, tamen ea fieri apud infernos fingerent, quæ sine corporibus nec fieri possent, nec intelligi. Quæ est anus tam delira, quæ timeat ista, quæ vos videlicet, si physica non didicissetis, timeretis? Tot autem rationes attulit, ut velle [persuadere] ceteris, sibi certe persuasisse videatur. Adeone me delirare censes, ut ista esse credam? Quis enim tam excors, quem ista moveant? Zeno igitur nullo modo is erat, qui, ut Theophrastus, nervos virtutis incideret. Nemo est tam senex, qui se annum non putet posse vivere. In quo tantopere apud nostros justitia culta est, ut ii, qui civitates, aut nationes devictas bello in fidem recepissent, earum patroni essent more majorum. Deinde postulas ut, si mundus ita sit par alteri mundo, ut inter eos ne minimum quidem intersit, concedatur tibi, ut in hoc quoque nostro mundo aliquid alicui sic sit par, ut nihil differat, nihil intersit. Usque eo morosi sumus, ut nobis non satisfaciat ipse Demosthenes. Tales enim nos esse putamus, ut jure laudemur. Hoc vero ejusmodi esse statuo, ut sine talium virorum et amicorum benevolentia, neque in adversa neque in secunda fortuna, quisquam vivere possit. Neque enim tu is es, qui, qui sis, nescias. Id autem tantum abest ab officio, ut nihil magis possit esse contrarium. Inferiorem se esse patitur duntaxat usque eo, ne inimicorum crudelitati dedatur. Est ergo ulla res tanti, aut commodum ullum tam expetendum, ut viri boni et splendorem et nomen amittas? Verum usque eo permanat ad animum, ut summus furor atque amentia consequatur. Nihil adeo arduum sibi existimabant, quod non virtute consequi possent.

2. When an *interrogative* with its verb completes the predicate.*

The verb of the interrogative is put in the *subjunctive*; as,

* This is called the *interrogative put indefinitely*. Dubito, haud scio, incertus sum, nescio, are constructed with *an* in a single indirect question. See Verbs of *doubting*.

No useful general rule can be given for translating *dubito, haud scio, incertus sum*, and *nescio an*. In every case, the *intention* of the writer or speaker must be learned by an examination of the context. It is no doubt quite true that, in rendering sentences with *nescio an*, etc., into English, we may often, but certainly not by any means always, assert *seemingly the opposite* of the proposition following *an*; as,

Haud scio an ulla[1] vita beatior esse possit.

I don't know that there can be *any* happier life = I rather think that there can be *no* happier life.

But we accept this as the translation only on the *supposition* that the *original direct* question, Ulla vita beatior esse potest? is a *rhetorical affirmative* question.[2] *Suppose*, however (and *independent of the context*, either supposition is equally probable), that the original direct question, Ulla vita beatior esse potest? is *not* a rhetorical question, but a question seeking information, we have then the *doubtful* or *confession of ignorance* case; and

Haud scio an ulla vita beatior esse possit

cannot be translated

I rather think that there can be *no* happier life,

but the translation now must be,

I don't know if [= whether] there is *any* happier life;

haud scio being now not the polite assertion of what is implied in the original question, but the confession of ignorance of what the question asks,—*I don't know*.

The practice of the Latins is to give the original question, changing, if necessary, its *mood* (but not changing in the least its *import*), on prefixing dubito, haud scio, incertus sum, or

[1] Observe ulla, and not nulla, as given by Arnold.

[2] Rhetorical *affirmative* questions have always a *negative* meaning, and rhetorical *negative* questions an *affirmative* meaning. Or thus: the *rhetorical* question, Ulla vita beatior esse potest? = the statement, Nulla vita beatior esse potest; and the *haud scio an*, so far from contradicting this statement, politely (or sometimes ironically) asserts, *Indeed*, there can be no happier life. So also the *rhetorical* question, Nulla vita beatior esse potest? = the statement, Non nulla vita beatior esse potest; and this statement, implied in the original question, we must bring out in translating.

I *know not what* to do* = *know not what I should do.*
Nescio quid agendum sit.
I *know not whether to do it or not* = *know not whether I should do it or not.*
Nescio utrum necne id facere debeam.
These words *showed who he was.*
Hæc verba *demonstrarunt quis esset.*
The man *asked me what I was doing.*
Homo *me rogavit quid facerem.*
The master *is inquiring how you know that.*
Magister *quærit unde id scias.*
The event *showed how vain this opinion was.*
Eventus *ostendit quam vana hæc opinio fuerit.*

nescio an. We must therefore, before rendering into English or into Latin, determine these points:—

1. Is the *original direct* question a rhetorical question, or a question properly so called?

2. What is the *drift* of the original question?

3. What is the *force* of haud scio, nescio an, etc.? *i.e.* are they a polite assertion of what is implied in the original question, = *I rather think*? or are they a confession of ignorance of its contents, = *I don't know*?

We give a few examples, with the context:—

Solonis quidem sapientis elogium est, quo se negat velle suam mortem dolore amicorum et lamentis vacare. Vult, credo, se esse carum suis. Sed haud scio, an melius Ennius: nemo me lacrymis decoret, neque funera fletu faxit.

Quod cum omnibus est faciendum, qui vitam honestam ingredi cogitant, tum haud scio, an nemini potius quam tibi.

Non quaero, quis fuerit [summus orator] sed quid sit illud, quo nihil possit esse præstantius: quod in perpetuitate dicendi non sæpe, atque haud scio an unquam,[1] in aliqua autem parte eluceat aliquando, idem apud alios densius, apud alios fortasse rarius.

Sapientem et bonum virum fingimus, qui celaturus Rhodios non sit, si id turpe judicet; sed dubitet, an turpe non sit.

Quinti fratris domus inflammata est jussu Clodii, inspectante urbe, conjectis ignibus, magna querela et gemitu, non dicam bonorum, qui nescio an ulli sint, sed plane hominum omnium.

Atque haud scio, an satis sit eum, qui lacessierit, injuriæ suæ pœnitere, ut et ipse ne quid tale posthac, et ceteri sint ad injuriam tardiores.

* *What* is sometimes not the interrogative but the compound relative = *that which;* as, He is saying what he thinks: *Dicit quod sentit.*

[1] Not nunquam, as given by Arnold.

Neque quo signa ferantur, neque quam in partem quisque conveniat, provident. Simul commonefacit, quæ ipso præsente in concilio Gallorum de Dumnorige sint dicta, et ostendit quæ separatim quisque de eo apud se dixerit. Dumnorigem ad se vocat; quæ in eo reprehendat, ostendit; quæ ipse intelligat, quæ civitas queratur, proponit. Qualis esset natura montis et qualis in circuitu ascensus, qui cognoscerent, misit. Neque quo se reciperent, neque quemadmodum oppida defenderent, habebant. Neque erat unquam controversia, quid ego intelligerem, sed quid probarem. Habebam, quo confugerem, ubi conquiescerem, cujus in sermone et suavitate omnes curas doloresque deponerem. Causæ nihil erat quin secus judicaret ipse de se Quintius. Utrum autem sit melius, Dii immortales sciunt. Ecqui ergo intelligis, quantum mali de humana conditione dejeceris? Videsne, ut in proverbio sit ovorum inter se similitudo? Præcurrunt equites, et quanto sit res in periculo, cognoscunt. Cum ab his quæreret, quæ civitates, quantæque in armis essent, et quid in bello possent, sic reperiebat. Ego autem satis mirari non queo unde hoc sit tam insolens domesticarum rerum fastidium. Nos quantum in utroque profecerimus, aliorum sit judicium. Utro me minus deceat uti, non intelligo. Hæc negotia quomodo se habeant, ne epistola quidem narrare audeo tibi. Verebar quorsum id casurum esset. Quem haud scio an recte dixerim principem philosophorum. Haud scio an melius fuerit. Nescio an melius patientiam possim dicere. Haud scio an minus hoc vobis sim probaturus. Gracchus, si diutius vixisset, eloquentia nescio an habuisset parem neminem. An dubium vobis fuit utrum vis aliqua videretur, necne? De quo alterum potest habere dubitationem, adhibendumne fuerit hoc genus, quod in divisione Panætii tertium est, an plane omittendum. Non dubito quid nobis agendum putes. Restat, judices, ut hoc dubitemus, uter potius Sex.

Roscium occiderit, is ad quem morte ejus divitiæ venerint, an is ad quem mendicitas? Fiat necne fiat, id quæritur. Dii utrum sint necne sint, quæritur. Sed dubitet turpe sit an non sit. Quæro num id injuste an improbe fecerit. Rogavit, essentne fusi hostes? Quid enim interest, expetas an eligas? Deliberant utrum id sequantur, quod honestum esse videant, an se scientes scelere contaminent. Ille, igitur, vidit, non modo quot fuissent adhuc philosophorum de summo bono, sed quot omnino esse possent sententiæ. Dubitatis an coitio facta sit? Sed ea res haud scio an plus mihi profuerit, quam si mihi tum essent omnes congratulati. Sed haud scio, an recte ea virtus frugalitas appellari possit. Hanc si nostri transirent, hostes expectabant.* Expectabam si quid de eo consilio ad me scriberes. Prima luce productis omnibus copiis, quid hostes consilii caperent expectabat. Helvetii nonnunquam interdiu, sæpius noctu, si perrumpere possent, conati, operis munitione et militum concursu et telis repulsi, hoc conatu destiterunt. Si cogitata præclare eloqui possent, nonnulli studio et usu elaboraverunt. Quid est causæ quin, si longe aliter possedit quam prætor edixit, iste ex edicto non possederit. Haud scio, an satis sit, eum, qui lacessierit, injuriæ suæ pœnitere. Videmusne, ut pueri aliquid scire se gaudeant? ut aliis narrare gestiant? Cæsar docebat, ut omni tempore totius Galliæ principatum Ædui tenuissent. Illud dubium est, ad id quod summum bonum dicitis, ecquænam fieri possit accessio. Moriendum certe est, et id incertum, an eo ipso die. Qualis sit animus, ipse animus nescit. Non quantum quisque possit, sed quanti quisque sit, ponderandum est. Non est, cur eorum, qui se studio eloquentiæ dediderunt, spes infringatur, aut languescat industria. Difficile dictu est, quænam causa sit.

* *Si* = if = whether, with expecto, and verbs of attempting (conor, experior, tento, etc.). Sometimes the verb of attempting is understood, not expressed.

3. When a *relative* with its verb completes the predicate.

The verb of the relative is put in the *subjunctive*; as,

There are some *who believe.*
Sunt *qui credant.*
There is no one *who knows.*
Nemo est *qui sciat.*
There is no one *who does not know.*
Nemo est *qui non sciat* = there is no one *but knows* = nemo est *quin sciat.*
Who is there *who does not discern?*
Quis est *qui non cernat?* = who is there *but discerns?* = quis est *quin cernat?*
Socrates was wont to execrate him, *who was the first to disjoin nature from utility.*
Socrates execrari eum solebat, *qui primus utilitatem a natura sejunxisset.*
The king spared no one, *who hurt a citizen.*
Rex nemini pepercit, *qui civem læsisset.*

Sunt autem qui dicant, fœdus quoddam esse sapientum, ut ne minus quidem amicos quam se ipsos diligant. Quis animo æquo videt eum quem impure ac flagitiose putet vivere? aut quis est qui majorum, aut Africanorum, aut ejus, quem tu in ore semper habes, proavi mei, ceterorumque virorum fortium atque omni virtute præstantium, facta, dicta, consilia cognoscens, nulla animo afficiatur voluptate? Et quod, omnibus fructibus amissis, domi nihil erat, quo famem tolerarent, Allobrogibus imperavit, ut iis frumenti copiam facerent. Quis enim tam excors, quem ista moveant? Nihil est enim apud istos, quod non atomorum turba conficiat. Sapientia enim est una, quæ mœstitiam pellat ex animo, quæ nos exhorrescere metu non sinat. Neque enim tempus est ullum, quo non plus habeat voluptatum quam dolorum. Hic vero nulla munitio est, quæ perterritos recipiat. Fere nemo est, quin acutius atque acrius vitia in dicente quam recta videat. Sunt enim multi, qui omnino Græcas non ament literas. Nihil est enim, quod de suo genere in aliud genus transferri possit. Nulla est celeritas, quæ possit cum animi celeritate contendere. Dolores autem, si qui incurrant, nunquam vim tantam habent, ut non plus habeat sapiens, quod gaudeat, quam quod angatur. Quamobrem, ne sit æs alienum, quod reipublicæ noceat, providendum est. Nam qui e divisione tripartita duas partes absolverit, huic necesse est restare tertiam. Exempli causa, ponatur aliquid quod pateat latius. Est in animis tenerum quiddam, quod ægritudine quasi tempestate quatiatur. Bene præcipiunt, qui vetant, quidquam agere, quod dubites, æquum sit, an iniquum. Epicurus unum genus posuit earum cupiditatum, quæ essent et naturales et necessariæ. Justitia non modo nunquam nocet cuiquam, sed contra semper alit aliquid tum vi sua atque natura, quod tranquillet animos. Sin autem voluptatem putat adjungendam eam, quæ sit in motu, quid tendit? Nec ullum habet ictum, quo pellat animum status hic non dolendi. Deinde illa exponunt duo, quæ quasi contineant omnem hanc quæstionem. Supplantare eum, quicum certet, aut manu depellere, nullo modo debet. Capitalis Eteocles, vel potius Euripides, qui id unum, quod omnium sceleratissimum fuerit, exceperit. Quid ergo est, quod percipi possit, si ne sensus quidem vera nuntiant? Nihil video quod timeam, nisi quod omnia sunt incerta. Erat autem nihil novi, quod aut scriberem aut ex te quærerem. Nunquam est enim, quin aliquid memoriæ tradere velimus, et tum maxime, cum aliquo majore negotio detinemur. Duo tum excellebant oratores, qui me imitandi cupiditate incitarent, Cotta et Hortensius. Pompeius unus inventus est, quem socii in urbes suas cum exercitu venisse gaudeant. Nactus sum, qui Xenophontis similem esse se cuperet.

4. When the predicate is completed by a *particle of comparison.**

The verb of the particle of comparison is put in the subjunctive; as,

The Roman fights *as if he contended for his life.*
Romanus pugnat *quasi de vita contendat.* [*Contendat*, because the contending is of the same time with the fighting.]
The Roman fought *as if he had contended for his life.*
Romanus pugnavit *quasi de vita contenderet.*
He speaks *as if he were a king* [and is a king still].
Loquitur *quasi rex sit.*
He speaks *as if he had been a king* [but is not now a king].
Loquitur *quasi rex fuerit.*
He spoke *as if he were a king* [and was a king still].
Locutus est *quasi rex esset.*
He spoke *as if he had been a king* [but was not now a king].
Locutus est *quasi rex fuisset.*

Declarant quædam esse vera; deinde ibidem, inter falsa visa et vera nihil interesse; ut primum sumpseras tamquam interesset. Hunc igitur ipsum annulum, si habeat sapiens, nihilo plus sibi licere putet peccare, quam si non haberet. Atque hoc loco philosophi quidam, minime mali illi quidem, sed non satis acuti, fictam et commenticiam fabulam dicunt prolatam a Platone; quasi vero ille, aut factum id esse, aut fieri potuisse defendat. Neminem reperies, qui, tanquam si arma militis inspicienda sint, ita probet armatum. Qui, tanquam si offusa reipublicæ sempiterna nox esset, ita ruebant. Similes enim sunt dii, si ea nobis objiciunt,

* As, ac si, juxta ac si, pro eo ac si, non secus ac si, similiter ac si, perinde quasi, quasi, sicut, tanquam si, velut si, etc.

quorum neque scientiam, neque explanationem habeamus, tanquam si Pœni aut Hispani in senatu nostro sine interprete loquerentur. Quasi tua res aut honos agatur, ita labores. Non poteram, credo, ante hiemem (sic enim scribis), quasi vero ad cognoscendum ego ad illos, non illi ad me venire debuerint. Tu autem, qui id quæris, similiter facis, ac si me roges, cur te duobus contuear oculis, et non altero tantum, cum idem uno assequi possim. Quem tracta, non secus ac si ego essem imperator. Qui me omnibus officiis, juxta ac si meus frater esset, sustentavit. Pro eo ac si concessum sit, concludere oportebit argumentationem. Quod nunquam factum est, perinde quasi factum sit, confirmare. Qui aliis nocent, ut in alios liberales sint, in eadem sunt injuria, ut si in rem suam aliena convertant. Metelli sperat sibi quisque fortunam, perinde quasi certi quidquam sit in rebus humanis. Quasi domi nummos haberet, ita constituit Scapulis daturum. Qui modum igitur vitio quærit, similiter facit, ut si posse putet eum, qui se e Leucata præcipitaverit, sustinere se, quum velit. Consulem languentem reliquit, atque ipse privatus, ut si consul esset, qui rempublicam salvam esse vellet, se sequi jussit.

NARRATION.

Narration is either *direct* or *indirect.*

1. *Direct Narration.*

Narration is *direct* when the *very words* or *thoughts* of the writer or speaker are given in his own person ; as,

Quod si facerem, quasi te erudiens, jure reprehenderer. Sed ab eo plurimum absum ; neque ut ea cognoscas, quæ tibi notissima sunt, ad te mitto, sed quia facillime in nomine tuo acquiesco, et quia te habeo æquis-

simum eorum studiorum, quæ mihi communia tecum sunt, existimatorem, et judicem. Attendes igitur, ut soles, diligenter, eamque controversiam dijudicabis, quæ mihi fuit cum avunculo tuo divino, ac singulari viro.

Here Cicero is stating his own thoughts in his own proper person, and the narration is direct; but if Cicero had reported his views in the *third* person, the narration would not be direct. Thus: *Cicero says, that if he should have done this, as if he were teaching him* (*Brutus*) *he would have been justly blamed; that he was very far from that,* etc. = indirect narration.

Indirect narration may occur in a direct narrative, and *vice versa;* as,

In Cumano nuper quum mecum Atticus noster esset, nuntiatum est nobis a M. Varrone, *venisse eum Roma pridie, et, nisi de via fessus esset, continuo ad nos venturum fuisse.*

In reporting speeches directly, the reporter's remark (said he, said she, etc., *inquit* or *ait*) is introduced parenthetically, and does not affect the construction; as,

On this Marius said: *I accept of the consulship in order that I may conquer the Cimbri, as I have done the Teutones; but as for the triumph, I should like it deferred till I complete my victory. As long as there are any barbarians, who may prove troublesome to the Romans, the pomp of a triumph would be disagreeable to me, and I beg that you would, in the meantime, allow me to finish my undertaking.*

Tum Marius, *Consulatum,* inquit, *accipio ut Cimbros vincam, quemadmodum Teutones vici; quod autem ad triumphum attinet, eum deferri velim quoad victoriam perfecero. Quamdiu ulli sunt barbari, qui Romanis molesti esse possint, pompa triumphi mihi ingrata foret; et peto ut interim me inceptum absolvere patiamini.* —MELVIN.

Only *inquit* and *ait* can be used for *said he, she*, etc., in direct narration, except in such a sentence as this, where *dicere* must be used: But, he proceeded to say, you were doing it. Sed, perrexit *dicere*, id faciebas.

Quo proficiscimur, inquit, milites? Omnis noster equitatus, omnis nobilitas interiit; principes civitatis, Eporedorix et Virdumarus, insimulati proditionis ab Romanis, indicta causa, interfecti sunt. Hæc ab iis cognoscite, qui ex ipsa cæde fugerunt; nam ego, fratribus atque omnibus meis propinquis interfectis, dolore prohibeor, quæ gesta sunt, pronunciare.

Quasi vero, inquit ille, consilii sit res, ac non necesse sit nobis, Gergoviam contendere, et cum Arvernis nosmet conjungere. An dubitamus, quin, nefario facinore admisso, Romani jam ad nos interficiendos concurrant? Proinde, si quid est in nobis animi, persequamur eorum mortem, qui indignissime interierunt; atque hos latrones interficiamus.

Nolite hos vestro auxilio exspoliare, qui vestræ salutis causa suum periculum neglexerint, nec stultitia, ac temeritate vestra, aut imbecilitate animi, omnem Galliam prosternere, et perpetuæ servituti addicere. An, quod ad diem non venerunt, de eorum fide constantiaque dubitatis? Quid ergo? Romanos in illis ulterioribus munitionibus animine causa quotidie exerceri putatis? Si illorum nunciis confirmari non potestis, omni aditu præsepto, iis utimini testibus, appropinquare eorum adventum; cujus rei timore exterriti, diem noctemque in opere versantur. Quid ergo mei consilii est? Facere, quod nostri majores, nequaquam pari bello Cimbrorum Teutonumque, fecerunt; qui, in oppida compulsi, ac simili inopia subacti, eorum corporibus, qui ætate inutiles ad bellum videbantur, vitam toleraverunt, neque se hostibus tradiderunt.

Tum ille: Tu, autem, quum ipse tantum librorum habeas, quos hic tandem requiris?

Commentarios quosdam, inquam, Aristotelios, quos hic sciebam esse, veni ut auferrem, quos legerem, dum essem otiosus; quod quidem nobis (ut scio) non sæpe contingit.

Quam vellem, inquit, te ad Stoicos inclinavisses! Erat enim, si cujusquam, certe tuum, nihil præter virtutem in bonis ducere.

Vide, ne magis, inquam, tuum fuerit, quum re idem tibi, quod mihi videretur, non nova te rebus nomina imponere. Ratio enim nostra consentit, pugnat oratio.

Quæ adhuc, Cato, a te dicta sunt, eadem, inquam, dicere posses, si sequerere Pyrrhonem aut Aristonem. Nec enim ignoras, similiter his istud honestum, non summum modo, sed etiam (ut tu vis) solum bonum videri. Quod si ita est, sequitur id ipsum, quod te velle video, omnes semper beatos esse sapientes.

Non ignoranti, inquit, tibi, quid sim dicturus, sed aliquid, ut ego suspicor, ex mea brevi responsione arripere cupienti, non respondebo ad singula; explicabo potius, quoniam otiosi sumus, nisi alienum putas, totam Zenonis Stoicorum sententiam.

Minime, id quidem, inquam, alienum; multumque ad ea, quæ quærimus, explicatio tua ista profecerit.

Experiamur, igitur, inquit, etsi habet hæc Stoicorum ratio difficilius quiddam et obscurius. Nam quum in Græco sermone hæc ipsa quondam rerum nomina novarum non videbantur, quæ nunc consuetudo diuturna trivit; quid censes in Latino fore?

Quid mihi, inquit, aut vita aut civitate opus est, quam beneficio Cæsaris habere videbor? Cujus rei opinio tolli non poterit, cum in Italiam, ex qua profectus sum, reductus existimabor.

Nam mores et instituta vitæ resque domesticas ac familiares nos profecto et melius tuemur et cautius; rem vero publicam nostri majores certe melioribus temperaverunt et institutis et legibus. Quid loquar de re militari? in qua quum virtute nostri multum valuerunt, tum plus etiam disciplina.

Quod quum audissemus, nullam moram interponendam putavimus, quin videremus hominem, nobiscum et studiis eisdem, et vetustate amicitiæ conjunctum. Itaque confestim ad eum ire perreximus; paullumque quum ejus villa abessemus, ipsum ad nos venientem vidimus; atque illum complexi, ut mos amicorum est, satis, eum longo intervallo ad suam villam reduximus.

2. *Indirect Narration.*

Narration is *indirect* when only the *substance* of what the speaker has said is given, and *in the third person* (for there can be *only* third persons in the indirect), either in the historical present or in the past tense.

1. Historical present; as,

Sabellius says *that he may be called the last of the ancient poets, and the first of the modern, and that among those who imitate Virgil there is no one more like the model.*

Sabellius dicit *eum poëtarum veterum ultimum, recentiorum autem primum dici posse; atque inter eos qui Virgilium imitentur exemplari neminem esse similiorem.* —MELVIN.

2. Past tense; as,

Arundel and his friends contended *that a public honour by whomsoever bestowed, ought to stand good every where;* but the ancient nobles maintained *that no person could receive such an honour but from his own sovereign; that this was the case in other countries; and that Atticus, for example, had refused being enrolled a citizen of Athens, lest he should lose his privileges as a citizen of Rome.*

Arundellius et amici ejus contenderunt, *honorem publicum, a quocunque tributum, ubique ratum esse debere;*

sed veteres nobiles affirmarunt *neminem posse talem honorem, nisi a rege suo accipere; rem ita in aliis terris se habere; et verbi causâ Atticum in civitatem Atheniensium adscisci recusasse, ne sua civis Romani jura amitteret.*—Melvin.

The indirect speech, it will be observed, is the *complement* of a predicate. Hence,

Rule I.—If the indirect speech be a *complement of opinion* [Pred. III.] the leading verbs of the indirect speech will be all in the *infinitive*, and the qualifying clauses* will be all in the *subjunctive;* as,

His Cæsar ita *respondit* [Pred. III. 1.]; Eo sibi minus dubitationis *dari*, quod eas res, quas legati Helvetii *commemorassent*, memoria *teneret;* atque eo gravius *ferre*, quo minus merito populi Romani *accidissent;* qui si alicujus injuriæ sibi *conscius fuisset*, non *fuisse* difficile cavere.

The direct speech here would be: The less doubt is occasioned to me, because I remember those things which the Helvetian ambassadors related; and I take it the more amiss the less it happened through the desert of the Roman people. If they had been conscious to themselves of any injury, it would not have been difficult for them to be on their guard.

Cæsar *cognovit* [Pred. III. 5.] et montem a suis *teneri* et Helvetios castra *movisse*, et Considium, timore perterritum, quod non *vidisset*, pro viso sibi *renuntiasse.*

Cæsar *pollicitus est* [Pred. III. 3.], sibi eam rem curæ *futuram* [esse]; [dixit] magnam se *habere* spem, et beneficio suo et auctoritate adductum, Ariovistum finem injuriis *facturum.*

Obsides *daturos*, quæque *imperâsset*, sese *facturos*, *polliciti sunt.*

* Gen. Rule, Pred. IV. 3, foot note.

Rule II.—If the indirect speech be a *complement of Pred. IV. 3. or 4. or of Pred. V. 2.* the leading verbs of the indirect speech will be, according to the rules for the formation of those complements, generally in the *subjunctive*, and the qualifying clauses also in the *subjunctive;* as,

Cæsar vehementer eos *incusavit* [Pred. IV. 4. (*a*)] primum, quod aut quam in partem, aut quo consilio ducerentur, sibi quærendum aut cogitandum *putarent.*

Cæsar *hortatus est* [Pred. IV. 3. (*e*)] ne ea, quæ accidissent, graviter *ferrent;* neve his rebus *terrerentur;* multisque secundis prœliis unum adversum, et id mediocre, *opponerent.*

Multa ab Cæsare in eam sententiam dicta sunt, *quare* [Pred. V. 2.] negotio desistere non *posset.*

Docet, latum ab x. tribunis plebis, ut sui ratio absentis haberetur, ipso consule Pompeio; qui si improbasset, *cur* ferri passus *esset?* sin probasset, *cur* se uti populi beneficio *prohibuisset?*

Rule III.—In an indirect speech there may be complements of Pred. III., Pred. IV. 3. and 4., and Pred. V. 2., the leading verb being given only at the beginning of the speech, and the change of leading verb being indicated only by the change of construction; as,

Divitiacus *obsecrare* [Pred. IV. 3. (*b*)], cœpit, ne quid gravius in fratrem *statueret;* [Pred. III. 1.] *scire* se illa esse vera; nec quemquam ex eo plus quam se doloris *capere.*

Ariovistus legatos mittit [Pred. III. 1.], *velle* se de his rebus, quæ inter eos agi cœptæ neque perfectæ essent, agere cum eo; [Pred. IV. 3. (*h*)] uti aut iterum colloquio diem *constitueret;* aut si id minus vellet, ex suis legatis aliquem ad se *mitteret.*

Cæsar *docebat quam* [Pred. V. 2.], veteres *quamque* justæ causæ necessitudinis cum Æduis *intercederent;*

quæ senatûs-consulta, *qualia* quamque honorifica in eos facta essent; ut omni tempore totius Galliæ principatum Ædui *tenuissent*, prius etiam quam nostram amicitiam appetissent; [Pred. III. 1.] populi Romani hanc *esse* consuetudinem, ut socios atque amicos non modo sui nihil deperdere, sed gratia, dignitate, honore, auctiores velit esse; quod vero ad amicitiam populi Romani attulissent, id iis eripi, *quis* [Pred. V. 2.] pati *possit*?

RULE IV.—An explanatory clause or sentence by the reporter, not forming part of the direct speech, is in the *indicative;* as,

Nuntiatum est ei, Ariovistum cum suis omnibus copiis ad occupandum Vesontionem, *quod est oppidum maximum Sequanorum*, contendere. [Here, *quod est oppidum maximum Sequanorum* is no part of the message sent, but is supplied by Cæsar himself for the information of the reader; and because it is no part of the message, it is in the *indicative.*]

Imperatives of the direct, when they become indirect, evidently depend on, or are the complement of, a verb of Pred. IV. 3. (*b*) or (*e*), understood generally, not expressed, and are, of course, in the *subjunctive;* as,

Direct.—*Here is the book: read it. Hîc est liber: hunc lege.*

Indirect.—*He said that the book was there, and he commanded him to read it. Dixit librum ibi esse; legeret. Imperavit ei ut* is here understood, but need not be expressed, because it is indicated by the change of construction.

Exclamatory and *interrogative* sentences of the direct, becoming indirect, being *interrogatives put indefinitely* [Pred. V. 2.], are also in the subjunctive, a verb of Pred. III. or IV. 3. being understood; as,

Direct.—*Here is the book: who wrote it? how won-*

derful it is! Hic est liber: quis hunc scripsit? quam mirus est!

Indirect.—*He said that the book was there; and he asked who wrote it; how wonderful it was! Dixit librum ibi esse; quis hunc scripsisset; quam mirus esset!** *Rogavit*, etc. is here understood.

* It is generally admitted that questions of the second person, becoming indirect, are in the subjunctive; but some have laid down the rule that questions of the *first* and *third* persons are in the indirect in the infinitive. It certainly does not seem very much in accordance with the analogy of the language that an indirect question, whatever its person, should be in the infinitive, the standing rule of the language being, that all indirect questions are in the subjunctive. If a *statement of opinion* can be put in the form of a question, that statement we should expect to be in the infinitive; but we should be slow to believe that *every* question of the first and third persons is constructed like a *complement of opinion*. We are not aware that any examples from Cicero are advanced in favour of this rule for the first and third persons, and it receives but little countenance from the examples in Cæsar. In Cæsar we have only two undoubted examples of questions of the third person in the infinitive, *B. G.*, v. 28, and *B. C.*, i. 9; and one doubtful example of the first person, *B. G.*, i. 14. But it is to be observed respecting the undoubted examples, that they are all *rhetorical* questions,[1] which neither expect nor admit of an answer, but are only a more forcible way of *affirming an opinion*. In this case, the construction is *ad sensum*, not *ad formam*. Thus, in *B. G.*, v. 28, we read: Quid esse levius aut turpius, quam auctore hoste de summis rebus capere? but this, though more forcible in the form of a question, is evidently otherwise equal to the statement of opinion: Nihil esse levius aut turpius quam auctore hoste de summis rebus capere consilium. All the examples from Livy are of the same rhetorical character. Consult, on the other hand, *B. G.*, i. 40, 43; ii. 30; v. 29; vii. 37; *B. C.*, i. 72; iii. 19.

A full examination of the subject will show that the rule for the construction of *rhetorical questions*, or, as they are sometimes called, *questions of appeal*, in indirect speech, is: Rhetorical questions may be put in the *infinitive*, but they may also be put in the *subjunctive*. The rule for *questions* in indirect speech,—*questions*, properly so called, that seek information and look for an answer,—is: Questions in indirect speech are always in the subjunctive.

[1] *Rhetorical questions, i.e., assertions*, expressed in the form of questions, to which one cannot refuse his assent.—Ramshorn.

Translate, first indirectly, then directly:

Divico ita cum Cæsare agit: Si pacem populus Romanus cum Helvetiis faceret, in eam partem ituros, atque ibi futuros Helvetios, ubi eos Cæsar constituisset, atque esse voluisset; sin bello persequi perseveraret, reminisceretur et veteris incommodi populi Romani et pristinæ virtutis Helvetiorum.

Ariovistus respondit; Æduis se injuria bellum illaturum non esse, si in eo manerent, quod convenisset stipendiumque quotannis penderent; si id non fecissent, longe iis fraternum nomen populi Romani abfuturum.

Cæsari Divico respondit, ita Helvetios a majoribus suis institutos esse, uti obsides accipere, non dare consuerint; ejus rei populum Romanum testem esse.

Ubi de ejus adventu Helvetii certiores facti sunt, legatos ad eum mittunt, nobilissimos civitatis, qui dicerent, sibi esse in animo, sine ullo maleficio iter per Provinciam facere, propterea quod aliud iter haberent nullum; rogare, ut ejus voluntate id sibi facere liceat. Legatis respondit, diem se ad deliberandum sumpturum; si quid vellent, a. d. Idus Apr. reverterentur.

Miserunt qui dicerent, se suaque omnia in fidem atque potestatem populi Romani permittere; paratosque esse et obsides dare, et imperata facere, et oppidis recipere, et frumento ceterisque rebus juvare. . . . Germanosque, qui cis Rhenum incolunt, sese cum his conjunxisse; tantumque esse eorum omnium furorem, ut ne Suessiones quidem, fratres consanguineosque suos, deterrere potuerint, quin cum his consentirent.

Cæsar respondit, hæc omnia et se tulisse patienter, et esse laturum; neque nunc id agere, ut ab illis abductum exercitum teneat ipse (quod tamen sibi difficile non sit) sed ne illi habeant, quo contra se uti possint; proinde, ut esset dictum, provinciis excederent, exercitumque dimitterent; si id sit factum, nociturum se nemini; hanc unam atque extremam pacis esse conditionem.

Quos cum apud se in castris Ariovistus conspexisset, exercitu suo præsente, conclamavit, Quid ad se venirent? an speculandi causâ?

Ariovistus respondit se prius in Galliam venisse, quam populum Romanum; nunquam ante hoc tempus exercitum populi Romani Galliæ provinciæ fines egressum; quid sibi vellet? cur in suas possessiones veniret? provinciam suam hanc esse Galliam, sicut illam nostram.

[Respondit], Ariovistum, se consule, cupidissime populi Romani amicitiam appetisse; cur hunc tam temere quisquam ab officio discessurum judicaret? sibi quidem persuaderi, cognitis suis postulatis, atque æquitate conditionum perspecta, eum neque suam neque populi Romani gratiam repudiaturum; quod si, furore atque amentia impulsus, bellum intulisset, quid tandem vererentur? aut cur de sua virtute aut de ipsius diligentia desperarent?

Interim Cæsari nunciatur, Sulmonenses, quod oppidum a Corfinio vii. millium intervallo abest, cupere ea facere quæ vellet, sed a Q. Lucretio senatore et Attio Peligno prohiberi, qui id oppidum vii. cohortium præsidio tenebant.

Ubii magnopere orabant, ut sibi auxilium ferret, quod graviter ab Suevis premerentur, vel, si id facere occupationibus reipublicæ prohiberetur, exercitum modo Rhenum transportaret; id sibi ad auxilium spemque reliqui temporis satis futurum; tantum esse nomen apud eos, atque opinionem ejus exercitus, uti opinione et amicitia populi Romani tuti esse possint.

Comprehendunt utrumque et orant, ne sua dissensione et pertinacia rem in summum periculum deducant; facilem esse rem, seu maneant, seu proficiscantur, si modo unum omnes sentiant ac probent; contra in dissensione nullam se salutem perspicere.

Ariovistus postulavit, ne quem peditem ad colloquium Cæsar adduceret; vereri se, ne per insidias ab eo circumveniretur; uterque cum equitatu veniret; alia ratione se non esse venturum.

Cæsar in eam spem venerat, se, sine pugna et sine vulnere suorum, rem conficere posse: quod re frumentaria adversarios interclusisset. Cur etiam secundo prœlio aliquos ex suis amitteret? cur vulnerari pateretur optime de se meritos milites? cur denique fortunam periclitaretur? præsertim cum non minus esset imperatoris consilio superare, quam gladio.

Ariovistus respondit, neminem secum sine sua pernicie contendisse; cum vellet, congrederetur.

Ita cum Cæsare agit, quod improviso unum pagum adortus esset, quum ii, qui flumen transissent, suis auxilium ferre non possent, ne ob eam rem, aut suæ magnopere virtuti tribueret, aut ipsos despiceret; se ita a patribus majoribusque suis didicisse, ut magis virtute quam dolo contenderent, aut insidiis niterentur; quare ne committerent, ut is locus, ubi constitissent, ex calamitate populi Romani et internecione exercitûs nomen caperet, ac memoriam proderet.

Cum iis præmium communicat, hortaturque, ut se liberos, et imperio natos, meminerint: unam esse Æduorum civitatem, quæ certissimam Galliæ victoriam distineat.

QUESTIONS.

Questions are *direct* or *indirect*. Sometimes instead of *direct* or *indirect*, they are called *independent* and *dependent*.

Direct questions differ nothing in construction from a direct proposition save in the sign of the question.

Direct questions are *single* or *double*, i.e. *alternative*.

1. *Single Direct Questions.*

A *single* direct question may be expressed

(*a*) By a pronoun or adverb;* as,

What did he say?

Quid dixit?

The question in this class has reference to a single *point*, and not to the whole proposition.

Quando hoc bellum populus Romanus suscepit? Quando igitur est turpe: quando est pœna peccati? Quid expectas quam mox ego eos dicam ordine esse Senatores? Quamdiu nos etiam furor iste tuus eludet? In integro res nobis erit; quanquam quicum loquor? Deum nisi sempiternum quî possumus intelligere? Quid? testes quid aiunt? Quid ni iste neget? Quis erat tu? Quorsum tandem aut cur ista quæris? Quot, quantas, quam incredibiles calamitates hausit? Quousque ludemur? Quo igitur spectat hæc oratio? Sed isti, qui Clodii leges timuerunt, quemadmodum ceteras observaverunt? Quanti autem hæc philosophia æstimanda est? Qualis oratoris et quanti hominis in dicendo putas esse, scribere historiam? Id autem quantulum est? Ubi sunt, qui Antonium Græce negant scire? Unde appares? Uter igitur facilius hoc faceret? Ecqui ergo intelligis, quantum mali de humana conditione dejeceris? Quam? Ecquæ poterit in agnoscendo esse distinctio? Quid jaces? aut quid mœres? aut cur succumbis, cedisque fortunæ? Quin prodis? Quin tu aspicias ad te venientem patrem Paulum?

(*b*) By the tone of the voice; as,

Did he say *that?* [Surprise if he said it, and doubt whether he could have said it.]

Id dixit?

* As, cur, qualis, quam, quamdiu, quamobrem, quemadmodum, quando, quanti, quare, quî, quid, quin, quis, quo, quod, quorsum, quot, quantus, ubi, unde.

Did he *not* say *that?* [Surprise that he did not say that, and doubt whether he could have said anything else.]
Id non dixit?

Tho question is indicated by the tone of the voice, without any interrogative particle, when it is meant to express *surprise* or *doubt.* Whether the answer should be positive or negative, depends very much on the context. Generally, when there is no negative or word equivalent to a negative in the question, a negative answer is expected.

Quid? si te rogavero aliquid, non respondebis? Anaxagoras nivem nigram dixit esse; ferres me, si ego idem dicerem? Nihil igitur cernis? nihil audis? nihil tibi est perspicuum? Mihi, ne ut dubitem quidem, relinquatur? Dicitis etiam, esse e regione nobis, e contraria parte terræ, qui adversis vestigiis stent contra nostra vestigia, quos Antipodas vocatis? Putas solem esse tantulum? Illi unquam dicerent, sapientes solos reges? solos divites? solos formosos? insipientes omnes, peregrinos, exsules, servos, furiosos? Non igitur patria præstat omnibus officiis? immo vero. Et tu oblivisci jubes, quod contra naturam est? Non elogia monumentorum id significant, velut hoc ad portam? Non statuebas, tibi non solum de te, sed etiam de illorum factis rationem esse reddendam? Non igitur existimas cadere in sapientem ægritudinem? Non vobis videor cum aliquo declamatore disputare?

(*c*) By *ne* at the end of a word; as,

Was it a *sword* [or some other instrument] he was killed with?
Gladione interfectus est?
Was it *Rome* [or some other place] he went to?
Romamne ivit?

Was it to *you* he gave the book [or to some other body]?
Tibine librum dedit?
Was it a *book* he gave to you [or something else]?
Librumne tibi dedit?
Did he *give* you the book [or lend it, etc.]?
Deditne tibi librum?

Ne for the most part merely seeks information; and the *ne* is put at the end of the word about which information is sought.

Potestne igitur quisquam dicere, inter eum, qui doleat, et inter eum, qui in voluptate sit, nihil interesse? aut, ita qui sentiat, non apertissime insaniat? Tune, quum tantis laudibus philosophiam extuleris, Hortensiumque nostrum dissentientem commoveris, eam philosophiam sequere, quæ confundit vera cum falsis, spoliat nos judicio, privat approbatione, omnibus orbat sensibus? Videorne tibi non, ut Saturninus, nominare modo illustres homines, sed etiam imitari nunquam, nisi clarum, nisi nobilem? Videsne navem illam? stare nobis videtur; at iis qui in navi sunt, moveri hæc villa. Jamne vides, bellua? jamne sentis? Dasne hoc nobis, deorum immortalium numine naturam omnem regi? Quid? mundum præter hunc unquamne vidisti? Quid tot tantosque viros ob rempublicam interfectos cogitasse arbitramur? iisdemne ut finibus nomen suum, quibus vita terminaretur?

(*d*) By *num* at the beginning of the question; as,

It is not through our fault, is it? [No.]
Num nostra culpa est? [Non.]
There was no investigation proposed about the death of Africanus, was there? [Certainly none.]
Num ulla quæstio de Africani morte lata est? [Certe nulla.]

Num generally expects a negative answer.

Num eloquentia Platonem superare possumus? Quid ergo istud ad nos? num nostra culpa est? Num censes Ennium, quum in hortis cum Ser. Galba, vicino suo, ambulavisset, dixisse, visus sum mihi cum Galba ambulare? Num illud attendimus in hoc omni genere, quam inconstanter loquamur? Num censes etiam eosdem fuisse? Num ergo is excæcat nos, aut orbat sensibus, si parum magnam vim censet in his esse ad ea, quæ sub eos subjecta sunt, judicanda? Quid igitur nobis faciendum est? num argumentis utendum in re ejusmodi? Quærendum est, credo, Heus iste num æs alienum habuerit, num auctionem fecerit? Memini, inquit ille, sed num ista societas talis est, ut nihil suum cujusque sit? Num te emere coegit, qui ne hortatus quidem est? Num iratum timemus Jovem? Num igitur fortem virum, num magno animo, num patientem, num gravem, num humana contemnentem potes te dicere? aut Philoctetam illum?

(*e*) By *nonne;* as,

What! is not a dog like a wolf?

Quid! canis *nonne* lupo similis?

Nonne generally expects an affirmative answer.

Quid! qui vivimus, quum moriendum sit, nonne miseri sumus? Quid! si te rogavero aliquid, nonne respondebis? Nonne etiam bis exclamavit se videre, quum omnino non videret? non perinde movebatur falsis, ut veris moveretur? Quid? quum ipse Antiochus dissentit quibusdam in rebus ab his, quos amat, Stoicis, nonne indicat, non posse illa probanda esse sapienti? Quid! quæ dicuntur quidem et acuta mihi videntur in utramque partem, et paria; nonne caveam, ne scelus faciam? Quid! nostros Gracchos, Ti. Gracchi, summi viri, filios, Africani nepotes, nonne agrariæ contentiones perdiderunt? Nonne id agendum nobis fuit ut materiem subtraheremus furori tuo?

Nonne hoc vestra voce vulgatum est, si quid cum periculo experiri velis, in Caria id potissimum esse faciendum? Nonne ita est?

II. *Double Direct or Disjunctive Questions.*

The first question may be made by *utrum*, or the enclitic *ne*, and the remaining questions, however many there may be of them, by *an;* or the first question, especially if it is short and unambiguous, may be made by the tone of the voice alone, and the remaining questions by *an;** as,

Did he say it *or* write it? = *whether* did he say it, *or* write it?
Utrum id dixit *an* scripsit? or,
Id*ne* dixit *an* scripsit? or,
Id dixit *an* scripsit?

If there are only two questions, the one excludes the other; and however many suppositions there may be, the one that is true excludes all the rest; as,

Is he going *or* staying? [He cannot both go *and* stay,—only the one or the other is possible.]
Abit *an* manet?
Do I go to Rome, or remain here, or shall I flee to Arpinum?
Romam*ne* venio, *an* hic maneo, *an* Arpinum fugiam?

In cases where more than one answer is in the nature of things possible, only one of the events is conceived as having actually happened; as,

Did he say it *or* write it?
Id dixit *an* scripsit?

* Sometimes we find *anne*. *An* also is very common in seemingly single direct questions in Cicero, but there is always a previous *utrum* to be supplied from the context.

A person might both say and write a thing, but it is conceived here that he has done only the one or the other, and it is asked *which* he has done.

Or not is, in direct disjunctive questions, generally made by *an non.* There are a few examples of *necne* even in direct questions; but *an non* is more frequent in direct, and *nec ne* in indirect questions; as,

Did he say it or not?
Utrum id dixit *an non?*

Hæc vera an falsa sunt? Utrum ea vestra an nostra culpa est? Quid fiet artibus? quibus? iisne, quæ ipsæ fatentur conjectura se plus uti, quam scientia; an his, quæ tantum id, quod videtur, sequuntur, nec habent istam artem vestram, qua vera et falsa dijudicent? Utrum igitur nos impudentes, qui labi nolumus; an illi arrogantes qui sibi persuaserint, scire se solos omnia? Si est, tresne partes habeat, ut Platoni placuit, rationis, iræ, cupiditatis; an simplex unusque sit? Si unus et simplex, utrum sit ignis, an anima, an sanguis? an, ut Xenocrates, mens nullo corpore? Utrum igitur utilius vel Fabricio, qui talis in hac urbe, qualis Aristides Athenis fuit, vel senatui nostro, qui nunquam utilitatem a dignitate sejunxit, armis cum hoste certare, an venenis? Senatus an populus, an judices, an frequentes, an pauci, an singuli? Utrum existimatis minus operis esse, facere hoc, an illud? Utrum aliquid gravius in quempiam dici potest, an certius quid objici potest? Ea, quæ dixi, ad corpusne refers? an est aliquid quod te sua sponte delectet? Utrum igitur tandem perspicuis dubia aperiuntur, an dubiis perspicua tolluntur? Utrum asseveratur in hoc, an tentatur? Utrum aliquem exhortari oportuit, qui ista prohiberet, an non? In geometriane, quid sit verum vel falsum, dialecticus judicabit, an in literis aut in musicis? Utrum nescis quam alte ascenderis, an pro nihilo id putas?

III. *Indirect Questions.*

RULE I.—*Ne*, *nonne*, *num*, etc., in indirect questions, lose their distinctive meanings, and are simply signs of questions.

RULE II.—The indirect question, being the complement of a predicate, is always in the subjunctive.

For examples, see Pred. V. 2., and Indirect Narration.

For indirect rhetorical questions, see Indirect Narration.

NOTES ON THE CONSTRUCTION OF SOME PARTICLES.

TEMPORAL, ETC., PARTICLES.

Temporal particles are used in two ways: they either *mark time simply*, or, besides time, they express also the idea of *end*, *design*, *occasion*, *cause*, *condition*, *succession*, etc. This twofold usage determines their twofold construction. When they do nothing else than mark time, they are constructed with the *indicative;* when, along with time, the writer intends them to express any other idea, they are constructed with the *subjunctive.*

I. *Marking only Time.*

1. Antequam, postquam, priusquam; as,

Romulus, *after* he had *founded* the city, called the people together.

Romulus, *postquam* urbem *condidit*, populum convocavit.

Before he *did* this, he went out.

Antequam hoc *fecit*, exiit.

The general arrived in Italy, *before* the enemy *had observed* him.

Dux in Italiam pervenit, *priusquam* hostes eum *animadverterunt.*

Antequam and *priusquam* are constructed with the *perfect.*

When *postquam* notes time, it is generally constructed with the *perfect* of the indicative; though, in instances denoting repeated time = as often as, or continued states, it is found with the *imperfect.* When a definite portion of time is mentioned, *postquam* is constructed with the *pluperfect;* as,

> On the *eleventh day after I had departed* from you, I scribbled this.
>
> *Undecimo die postquam* a te *decesseram*, hoc exaravi.

Itaque postquam adamavi hanc quasi senilem declamationem, studiose equidem utor nostris poetis. Ego autem non commemini, antequam sum natus, me [esse] miserum. Postquam id animum advertit, copias suas Cæsar in proximum collem subducit. Eo postquam Cæsar pervenit, obsides, arma, servos, qui ad eos perfugissent, poposcit. Numa magnus vir habendus est, cum eam sapientiam constituendæ civitatis duobus prope seculis ante cognovit, quam eam Græci natam esse senserunt. Seculis multis ante gymnasia inventa sunt, quam in iis philosophi garrire cœperunt. Postero die quam illa erant acta, Catulus venit. Tabellarii venerunt post diem xlvi. quam a nobis discesserant. Quod ego, simul ac te aspexi, priusquam loqui cœpisti, sensi. Neque in hac re solum fuit ejusmodi, sed antequam ego in Siciliam veni, in maximis rebus ac plurimis. Cui fui semper amicus, antequam ille reipublicæ est factus inimicus. Sed priusquam illa conor attingere, proponam breviter hoc. Erat comœdus nuper, qui posteaquam e scena sibilis explodebatur, sicut in aram, confugit in Roscii domum. P. Africanus, posteaquam bis consul et censor fuerat, L. Cottam in judicium vocabat. Labienus, postquam neque aggeres neque fossæ vim hostium sustinere poterant, Cæsarem per nuntios facit certiorem, quid faciendum existimet. Sed, postquam non modo hordeum, sed etiam fructus ex arboribus deficiebant, Pompeius hoc existimavit.

2. Dum, donec,* quoad; as,

While men teach they learn.

Homines *dum docent* discunt.

Milo was in the senate-house that day *till* the senate was *dismissed.*

Milo in curia fuit eo die, *quoad* senatus *dimissus* est.

Hæc dum Romæ geruntur, Quintius interea contra jus, detruditur. Videte majorum diligentiam, qui nihil dum ejusmodi suspicabantur, veruntamen, ea quæ parvis in rebus accidere poterant, providebant. Fuit hæc gens fortis, dum Lycurgi leges vigebant. Dum hæc in Venetis geruntur, Sabinus pervenit. Quanquam, quoad fuit in urbe, ejus consiliis obstiti. Juris consulti jus civile eatenus exercuerunt, quoad populo præstare voluerunt. Ille navi, quoad potuit, est opitulatus. Primum ei te commodes, quoad fides tua dignitasque patietur. Operam des, quoad tibi æquum et rectum videbitur. Omnia cogitando, quoad facere potui, sum prosecutus.

3. Quum or cum; as,

We all, *when* we *are well,* give good advice to the sick.

Omnes, *quum valemus,* recta consilia ægrotis damus.

The matter, *when* I *was writing* these, had been brought to the greatest extremity.

Res, *quum* hæc *scribebam,*† erat in summum adducta discrimen.

* *Dum* prefers the pres. ind. to the perfect. *Donec* is very seldom used by Cicero.

† If an action is *only* referred to time, so that *quum* signifies *at the time when,* the indicative is employed; though, in speaking of *past* time, the imperfect conjunctive is likewise admissible. —Madvig. Perhaps, according to present ideas on the subject, the best rule for the young student to follow is: Prefer the imperfect and pluperfect subjunctive even to express time.

When may often be elegantly expressed by means of a parti-

When this battle *was fought*, Cæsar was absent.
Quum hoc prœlium *factum est*, Cæsar aberat.
Scarcely had they entered, *when* the king *got* intelligence of the affair.
Vix ingressi erant, *quum* rex certior de re *factus est*.

Deinde quo modo suscipere aliquam rem aut agere fidenter audebit, quum certi nihil erit quod sequatur? Sic ad malam domesticam disciplinam vitamque umbratilem et delicatam quum accesserunt etiam poëtæ, nervos omnis virtutis elidunt. Sed videamus Herculem ipsum, qui tum dolore frangebatur, quum immortalitatem ipsa morte quærebat. Quis igitur Epicurum sequitur dolor, quum hoc ipsum dicit, summum malum esse dolorem? Quare satis mihi dedisti, quum respondisti, majus tibi videri malum dedecus, quam dolorem. Definis tu mihi, non tollis dolorem, quum dicis asperum, contra naturam. Quum varices secabantur C. Mario, dolebat, cum æstu magno ducebat agmen, laborabat. Quum vero sontes ferro depugnabant, auribus fortasse multæ, oculis quidem nulla poterat esse fortior contra dolorem et mortem disciplina. Faciunt idem, quum exercentur, athletæ; pugiles vero, etiam quum feriunt adversarium in jactandis cæstibus, ingemiscunt. Fulgentes gladios hostium videbant Decii, quum in aciem eorum irruebant. Qui, quum magnam speciem doctrinæ sapientiæque præ se tulerunt, audiuntur. Num manus affecta recte est, quum in tumore est. Haec renovabam, quum licebat, legendo. Quin etiam Græcis licebit utare, quum voles, si te Latina forte deficient. Physici raro admodum, quum hærent aliquo

ciple; as, *When* an evil *is beginning*, it is easily crushed: Malum *nascens* facile opprimitur. *When* the king *was walking* in his garden, a stranger met him: Regi in horto *ambulanti* advena occurrit. *When* I *returned* home I found him: Domum *reversus* eum inveni. *When* the king *died*, there was a full meeting of the senate: Rege *mortuo*, frequens senatus fuit. *When* the consul *said* these things, he departed: His consul *dictis* abiit.

loco, exclamant, quasi mente incitati. Nam, quum vim, quæ esset in sensibus, explicabamus, simul illud aperiebatur, comprehendi multa et percipi sensibus. Hi, quum ovum inspexerant, quæ id gallina peperisset, dicere solebant. Qualis vis id fuerit aut furentium aut somniantium tum, quum commovebantur. Quum aliquid hujusmodi inciderat, sic ludere Carneades solebat. Cum Collatino collegæ Brutus imperium abrogabat, poterat videri facere id injuste. Vix annus intercesserat ab hoc sermone, cum iste accusavit Norbanum. Una nox intercesserat, cum iste illum sic diligebat, ut diceres, inter eos omnia esse communia. Curius, cum Appius de plebe consulem non accipiebat, patres auctores fieri coëgit. Bene facitis, cum venitis. Unum quidem erat tempus, cum Flacco portas tota Asia claudebat, Cappadocem autem illum recipiebat. Fuit quoddam tempus, cum in agris passim homines bestiarum more vagabantur. Jam anni quadringenti sunt, cum hoc accidit. Cum diutius in negotio curaque fueram, ad Carpinatium revertebar. Unus et alter dies intercesserat, cum res parum certa videbatur. Quid? apud Euripidem Hercules, quum ut Eurysthei filios, ita suos configebat sagittis; quum uxorem interimebat, quum conabatur etiam patrem; non perinde movebatur falsis, ut veris moveretur?

4. Simul ac (atque, before a vowel), ubi, ubi primum, ut primum, quum primum, statim ut, ut, prefer the perf. to the plp. ind., and may be translated, *no sooner .... than*, *the moment that*, *immediately when*, *as soon as*, *the instant that*, etc.; as,

> *No sooner had* he *been elected*, than he was obliged to take the field.
>
> *Simul atque electus est*, in aciem prodire coactus est.
>
> *As soon as* he *was informed*, he removed his camp.
>
> *Ubi primum* certior *factus est*, castra movit.

Quod ubi Cæsar resciit, quorum per fines ierant, his,

ut conquirerent et reducerent, imperavit. Simul atque natum animal est, gaudet voluptate, et eam appetit, ut bonum. Omne enim animal simul ut ortum est, et seipsum, et omnes partes suas diligit. Non, simul ac se ipse commovit, atque ad se revocavit, sentit, quid intersit inter perspicua et inania? Quod ubi auditum est, conclamant omnes, occasionem negotii bene gerendi amittendam non esse. At ille, ut ingressus est, confestim gladium destrinxit. Is, ut me salutavit, statim Romam profectus est. Ut primum Oppianicus cœpit suspicari, statim se ad Staleni familiaritatem applicavit. Male se res habet, quæ, statim ut dici cœpta est, non melior fieri videtur. Literas scripsi statim ut tuas legeram. Serpentes quædam, simul ac primum niti possunt, aquam persequuntur. Simul ut experrecti sumus, visa nocturna contemnimus.

II. *Noting Relationship of Cause, Occasion, Succession, Condition, etc.*

1. Antequam and priusquam;* as,

There must be fire *before* there *is* smoke.
Ignis sit necesse est *priusquam sit* fumus.
We must be diligent *before* we *learn*.
Nos esse diligentes necesse est, *priusquam discamus*.

In each of these examples the temporal particle and its verb may be regarded not so much as a mark of time as the *limitation* or the *complement* of the *predicate;* and in conformity with the genius of the language the complement will be in the subjunctive. See General Rule, Pred. IV. 3. foot note.

Neque prius finem sequendi fecerunt, quam muro oppidi appropinquarent. Itaque priusquam quicquam

* *Postquam* is hardly ever used for any purpose but to mark time, and of course is constructed with the indicative, except in indirect speech, when it is with the subjunctive.

concederetur, Divitiacum ad se vocari jubet. Omnes hostes terga verterunt, neque prius fugere destiterunt, quam flumen Rhenum pervenirent. Postridie ejus diei, Cæsar, priusquam se hostes ex terrore ac fuga reciperent, in fines Suessionum exercitum duxit. His rebus adducti, non prius Viridovicem reliquosque duces ex concilio dimittunt, quam ab his sit concessum, arma uti capiant. Hoc tibi ante explicandum est, quam illuc proficiscare, quo te dicis intendere. In omnibus autem negotiis, priusquam aggrediare, adhibenda est præparatio diligens. Ac priusquam aggrediar ad causam, quiddam de communi conditione breviter commemorandum videtur. Nihil habebam novi, quod ante accidisset quam dedissem ad te liberto tuo literas. Utinam, dii immortales, P. Clodius viveret, antequam hoc spectaculum viderem. Posteaquam mihi nihil de adventu tuo scriberetur, verebar, ne id ita caderet, quod etiam nunc vereor, ne antequam tu in provinciam venisses, ego de provincia decederem. His de rebus multa disputata sunt quondam in Hortensii villa, quum eo Catulus et Lucullus nosque ipsi postridie venissemus, quam apud Catulum fuissemus.

2. Dum, donec quoad; as,

Wait *till he come.*

Expecta *dum* ille *veniat.*

I was unwilling to be a leader in the civil war *so long as* they *were treating* about peace.

Ego me ducem in civili bello, *quoad* de pace *ageretur*, nolui esse.

Ad properationem meam quiddam interest, non te expectare donec ad locum venias. Virtus vetat spectare fortunam, dum præstetur fides. Expectas fortasse dum dicas. Quoad perventum sit eo, quo sumpta navis est, non domini est navis, sed navigantium. Si mea pericula neglexi, dum timorem a patria propulsarem.

3. Quum or cum; as,

Quintius, *having been* prætor the year before, was sent into Asia = Quintius, *inasmuch* as he *had been* prætor the year before, was sent into Asia = Quintius, *since* he *had been* prætor the year before, was sent into Asia. = Quintius, *in consequence* of his having been prætor the year before, was sent into Asia.

Quintius, *quum* prætor anno superiore *fuisset*, in Asiam missus est.

Loving the good, he will avoid the evil = *Since* he *loves* the good, he will avoid the evil.

Quum bonum *amet*, malum vitabit.

When the king *had intimated* his intention of passing into Italy, many dissuaded him = *Inasmuch* as the king *had intimated* his intention of passing into Italy, many dissuaded him.

Quum rex *significasset* se in animo habere in Italiam transire, multi eum dehortati sunt.

Quum in this sense may generally be best Englished by the present or perfect participle.

Quum is sometimes used instead of *quod* after verbs of *feeling*, and then it is constructed, like *quod*, with the indicative.

Zenonem, quum Athenis essem, audiebam frequenter. Epaminondas, quum vicisset Lacedæmonios apud Mantineam atque ipse gravi vulnere exanimari se videret, quæsivit, salvusne esset clypeus. Quæ, quum dixisset, sic rursus exorsus est. Sæpe soles audire Roscium, quum ita dicat, se adhuc reperire discipulum, quem quidem probaret, potuisse neminem. Contendi cum P. Clodio, quum ego publicam causam, ille suam defenderet. In Cumano nuper quum mecum Atticus noster esset, nuntiatum est nobis a M. Varrone, venisse eum Roma pridie vesperi. Quod quum audissemus, nullam moram interponendam putavimus. Paullumque quum ejus villa abessemus, ipsum ad nos venientem vidimus. Quæro, quid sit, cur, quum multa scribas, genus hoc prætermittas, præsertim quum et ipse in eo excellas. Nam quum philosophiam viderem diligentissime Græcis literis explicatam, existimavi nos Græca potius quam nostra lecturos. Sed Zeno quum Arcesilaum anteiret ætate, valdeque subtiliter dissereret et peracute moveretur, corrigere conatus est disciplinam.

4. Simul ac, etc., generally indicate only time.

ILLATIVE.

Nam, namque, enim, etenim, form distinct propositions, and the construction is not affected by the particle; only *enim* can never stand first in the proposition; it must be at least in the second, and it may be in the third place in the sentence; as,

That canton was called Tigurinus: *for* the whole Helvetian state is divided into four cantons.

Is pagus appellabatur Tigurinus: *nam* omnis civitas Helvetia in quatuor pagos divisa est.

Justice will come, and indeed quickly; *for* time flies.

Veniet justitia, et quidem celeriter; volat *enim* ætas.

Quid refert? Adsunt enim qui hæc non probent. Acerrime autem deliciæ meæ, Dicæarchus, contra hanc immortalitatem disseruit; is enim tres libros scripsit, in quibus vult efficere, animos esse mortales. Laudo id quidem, etsi nihil nimis oportet confidere; movemur enim sæpe aliquo acute concluso; labamus, mutamusque sententiam clarioribus etiam in rebus; in his enim est aliqua obscuritas. Jus et omne honestum sua sponte est expetendum; etenim omnes viri boni ipsam æquitatem et jus ipsum amant. Vellem fortasse; quis enim id potest, aut unquam poterit imitari? Amici non solum se colent inter se ac diligent, sed etiam verebuntur; nam maximum ornamentum amicitiæ tollit, qui ex ea tollit verecundiam. Dici vix potest, quanta sit [ejus rei] vis in utramque partem; namque et incitat languentes, et languefacit excitatos, et tum remittit animos, tum contrahit. Perturbatis nostris novitate pugnæ, tempore opportunissimo Cæsar auxilium tulit; namque ejus adventu hostes constiterunt, nostri se ex timore receperunt.

CAUSAL.

Quia, quippe, quando, quandoquidem, quod, quoniam, are constructed with the indicative; as,

I say so, *because* I *think* so.

Ita dico *quod* ita *sentio.*

But the *false* reason, *i.e.*, the reason which is denied to be the true reason, is always in the *subjunctive*, whether it be introduced by quia, quo, quod, quin, or quippe; as,

I read these books, *not that I feel disposed*, but because I am forced.

Hos libros lego, *non quod velim*, sed quia cogor.

The *alleged* reason also is put in the subjunctive; as,

Aristides was expelled from his country *because* he *was* too just.

Aristides ob eam causam patriâ expulsus est, *quod* præter modum justus *esset.*

[*Erat* here would designate the reason as the writer's, whereas it is the reason alleged by Aristides' countrymen].

Quod = *quoad* is also used with the *subjunctive*, as it then rather limits the predicate than assigns a reason; as,

This, *as far as I know*, is true.

Hoc, *quod sciam*, verum est.

A culpa quando tantum absumus, ut etiam optime senserimus, et quando præstitimus, quod debuimus, moderate, quod evenit, feramus. Leve nomen habet utraque res; quippe leve enim est totum hoc risum movere. Jam fateor, inquit, in Gabinium me nefarium fuisse; quippe vides. Urbs, quæ, quod in ea Fortunæ fanum fuit, Tyche nominata est. Bene facis, inquit, quod me adjuvas. Sane gaudeo, quod te interpellavi. Non tibi objicio, quod hominem omni argento spoliasti. Urbs, quæ quia postrema ædificata est, Neapolis nominatur. Sed quia natura mutari non potest, idcirco veræ amicitiæ sempiternæ sunt. Tamen ei moriendum fuit, quoniam homo nata erat. Et quoniam tu ita vis, nimium me gratum esse concedam. In eoque summum bonum poni necesse est, quandoquidem id tale esse debet, ut rerum expetendarum sit extremum. Tu te posse dicito, quandoquidem potes. Quoniam nacti te, inquit, sumus aliquando otiosum, certe audiam, quid sit. Non me aliquid juvare potes; quippe res est in manibus; tu autem abes longe gentium. Ut ab urbe discessi, nullum adhuc intermisi diem, quin aliquid ad te literarum darem, non quod haberem magnopere quod scriberem, sed ut loquerer tecum absens. Pugiles in jactandis cæstibus ingemiscunt, non quod doleant animove succumbant, sed quia profundenda voce omne corpus intenditur venitque plaga vehementior. Magnæ pecuniæ coactæ sunt, non quod jugerum numerum vere profiteri esset difficile, sed, etc. Hoc mihi Latinis literis illustrandum putavi, non quia philosophia Græcis et literis et doctoribus percipi non posset, sed meum judicium semper fuit.

Qui, quippe qui, utpote qui, ut qui, quum, are joined to the *subjunctive*. Examples of quippe qui and utpote qui are found with the indicative, but they are hardly to be imitated; for examples of qui, quippe qui, utpote qui, see Pred. IV. 4.; for examples of quum, see Temporal Particles, quum.

CONCESSIVE.

Etsi, etiamsi, quanquam tametsi, are usually joined to the *indicative*, and quamvis, quum, ut to the *subjunctive;* but etsi, etiamsi, quanquam, tametsi, are joined to the subjunctive when they introduce a *conditional* rather than a concessive clause.

Cæsar, *although* he had as yet *received* no intelligence of their designs, yet had a general suspicion of what happened.

Cæsar, *etsi* nondum eorum consilia cognoverat, tamen fere id, quod accidit, suspicabatur.

Pompey *might have wished*, on account of their friendship, *to recall* Clodius from the shades, yet he would not, on account of the republic, have done it.

Pompeius, *etiamsi* propter amicitiam *vellet* Clodium ab inferis evocare, tamen propter rempublicam non fecisset.

Optimi homines faciunt, quod rectum, quod honestum est, etsi nullum consecuturum emolumentum vident. Etsi duce natura congregabantur homines, tamen spe custodiæ rerum suarum urbium præsidia quærebant. Homo, quod crebro videt, non miratur, etiamsi, cur fiat, nescit. Quæ tametsi Cæsar intelligebat, tamen, quam mitissime potest,* legatos appellat. Quamquam omnis virtus nos ad se allicit, facitque, ut eos diligamus, in quibus ipsa inesse videatur, tamen justitia et liberalitas id maxime efficit. Quamquam in utroque vestrum summum esse ingenium studiumque perspexi, tamen hæc in te, Sulpici, divina sunt. Huc accedit quod, quamvis ille felix sit, sicut est, tamen in tanta felicitate nemo potest esse in magna familia. Quamvis suasor non fueris profectionis meæ, approbator certe fuisti. Quanquam in amicitia alii dicant æque caram esse sapienti rationem amici, ac suam; alii autem sibi cuique cariorem suam, tamen hi quoque posteriores fatentur, alienum esse ab justitia, detrahere quid de aliquo, quod sibi assumat. Ut quæras omnia, quomodo Græci ineptum appellent, non reperies. Ut rationem Plato nullam afferret (vide quid homini tribuam), ipsa auctoritate me frangeret. Equidem, etiamsi oppetenda mors esset, domi atque in patria mallem quam in externis atque alienis locis. Sunt, qui, quod sentiunt, etsi optimum sit, tamen invidiæ metu non audent dicere. Quod turpe est, id quamvis occultetur, tamen honestum fieri nullo modo potest. Quum omnibus virtutibus me affectum esse cupiam, tamen nihil est quod malim, quam me et gratum esse et videri. Toto prœlio, quum ab hora septima ad vesperum pugnatum sit, aversum hostem videre nemo potuit.

CONDITIONAL.

Si, sin, sive...sive, nisi, ni, are used in two ways:

1. They introduce a statement that is either true or *assumed* as true (not that it is necessarily true), and then they are joined to the *indicative;* as,

If God *is* omnipotent, he is also good.

Si Deus omnipotens *est*, etiam est bonus. [If we were to make it omnipotens *sit*, it would imply that we regard it as doubtful whether God is omnipotent.]

If the heart, or the blood, or the brain, is the soul, certainly, since it is body, it will die with the rest of the body = *Grant* [for the sake of argument] that the heart, or the blood, or the brain, is the soul = *be it* [as you say] that the heart, or the blood, or the brain, is the soul, certainly, since it is body, it will die with the rest of the body.

Si cor, aut sanguis, aut cerebrum, *est* animus, certe, quoniam est corpus, interibit cum reliquo corpore.

Whether he be wise *or* foolish, he is my son = *Be it* that he is wise, *or be it* that he is foolish, he is my son.

Sive bonus *sive* stultus *est*, meus est filius.

I see nothing to fear, *unless* that all things *are* uncertain.

Nihil video quod timeam, *nisi* quod omnia *sunt* incerta.

Si nihil interest, nulla regula est. Si tempus est ullum jure hominis occidendi, quæ multa sunt, certe illud est non modo justum, sed etiam necessarium, cum vis illata defenditur. Si quid generis istiusmodi me delectat, pictura delectat. Quod si Græci faciunt, quanto id magis nobis concedendum est. En miserum hominem! si dolor summum malum est, dici aliter non potest. Si nudus es, da jugulum; sin tectus Vulcaniis armis, resiste. Quare, si, ut initio concessisti, turpitudo pejus est, quam dolor; nihil est plane dolor. Et, si verum quærimus, in omnibus officiis persequendis, animi est adhibenda contentio. Nunc idem, nisi molestum est, quoniam tibi non omnino displicet definire, et id facis quum vis, velim definias quid sit voluptas. Nunquam a Philone discessit, nisi posteaquam ipse cœpit, qui se audirent, habere. Nisi ego insanio, stulte omnia agi judico. Frangite eos, si potestis, ne molesti sint; erunt enim, nisi cavetis. In animi cognitione dubitare non possumus, nisi plane in physicis plumbei sumus, quin nihil sit animis admixtum. Si nihil aliud fecerunt nisi rem detulerunt, nonne satis fuit his gratias agi? Nam illo loco libenter uti soleo, sive quid mecum ipse cogito, sive aliquid scribo aut lego. Cretum leges, quas sive Jupiter sive Minos sanxit, laboribus erudiunt juventutem. Veniet tempus mortis, et quidem celeriter; et sive retractabis sive properabis. Ita sive dissipantur, procul a terris id evenit; sive permanent, et conservant habitum suum, hoc etiam magis necesse est ferantur ad cœlum. Si vales, bene est; valeo. Si dubium tibi est, posse te illius regno potiri, non est conandum.

2. They introduce a statement which is regarded either as not true or as doubtful, and then they are joined to the *subjunctive;* as,

> *If* you *were* in my position [which you are not] you would think otherwise.
>
> *Si* hic *sis*, aliter sentias.
>
> *If* the master *has* money [but I don't know whether he has or not], he will give you.
>
> *Si* magister pecuniam *habeat*,* tibi dabit.

Often *nisi, si, si non*, are the complement of the predicate, and, of course, in the subjunctive. This is the case whenever it is implied that something *does not*, or *would not* happen, unless *another thing happen previously;* as,

> You cannot learn *unless* you *study* = *without studying.*
>
> Non potes discere, *nisi studeas.*
>
> Cæsar would not have joined battle *unless* he *had* seen the enemy near.
>
> Cæsar prœlium non commisisset, *nisi* hostes prope *vidisset.*
>
> He would have died *had* it not *been* for Conon.
>
> Mortuus esset, *si* Conon non *fuisset.*

Non hercule, inquit, si ego Seriphius essem, nobilis; nec tu si Atheniensis esses, clarus unquam fuisses. Quod si quis deus diceret, nunquam putarem me in Academia, tanquam philosophum, disputaturum. Sim impudens, si plus postulem, quam homini a rerum natura tribui potest. Thucydidis orationes ego laudare soleo;

* The present or perfect of the subjunctive is used when the supposition is regarded as probable; the imperfect or pluperfect, when it is regarded as improbable. *Sive*, unless in indirect speech, is very seldom found with the subjunctive.

imitari neque possim, si velim, nec velim fortasse si possim. Cur et Camillus doleret, si hæc post trecentos et quinquaginta fere annos eventura putaret? Id si acciderit, simus armati. Sapientia, quæ ars vivendi putanda est, non expeteretur, si nihil efficeret. Non possem vivere, nisi in literis viverem. Pompeius munitiones Cæsaris prohibere non poterat, nisi prœlio decertare vellet. Memoria minuitur nisi exerceas. Quæ nunquam quinque nuntiis animus cognosceret, nisi ad eum omnia referrentur. Quod si ante accidisset, tum eventum omnino amisisset. An vir fortis, nisi stomachari cœperit, non potest fortis esse? Etenim nec justitiæ nec amicitiæ esse omnino poterunt, nisi ipsæ per se expetantur. Helvetii, seu quod timore perterritos Romanos discedere a se existimarent, sive eo quod re frumentaria intercludi posse confiderent, commutato consilio, atque itinere converso, nostros a novissimo agmine insequi ac lacessere cœperunt.

CONSECUTIVE.

Ut, ut non, quin, *as consecutives*, or stating the *consequence* of the leading verb, are joined to the *subjunctive*; as,

Cato was *so* glad *that* [as a consequence] he *asked* him to live with him.

Cato *tantopere* gavisus est *ut* eum *rogaret* ut apud se viveret.

Cæsar was *so* incensed at this *that* [as a consequence] *he showed them* no mercy.

Hoc Cæsar *adeo* incensus fuit, *ut* nulla in eos misericordia *uteretur*. See Pred. V. 1.

I do not refrain from laughing = I do not refrain myself *that* [as a consequence] *I do not laugh.**

Non me contineo,† *quin rideam.*

* Rule: whenever, in the same affirmation or interrogation, we have two negatives, real or implied, *the one in the predicate* and *the other in the complement*, the complement may be made by *quin*.

† For examples of verbs of *hindering* and *doubting*, see Pred. IV. 3. (*g*.).

Prorsus nihil abest, quin sim miserrimus. Abesse non potest, quin ejusdem hominis sit. Neque abest suspicio, ut Helvetii arbitrantur, quin ipse sibi mortem consciverit. Quis ignorat quin tria Græcorum genera sint? Quis musicis penitus se dedidit quin comprehenderit. Quid est causæ, quin decemviri coloniam in Janiculum possint deducere? Quis est, quin cernat, quanta vis sit in sensibus? Nullus locus est, quo in loco Populi Romani nomen sit, quin eodem perscriptum hoc indicium pervenerit. Dies fere nullus est quin hic Satrius domum meam ventitet. Facere non possum quin ad te mittam. Non necesse est expectare quin [quid] mox fiat. Nemo est quin malit. Nullum intermisi diem quin aliquid ad te literarum darem. Hortensius nullum patiebatur diem, quin aut in foro diceret aut meditaretur extra forum. Nunquam venit in contentionem de accusando, qui quæstor fuisset, quin repudiaretur. Quis unquam templum illud aspexit, quin avaritiæ tuæ testis esset? Deesse mihi nolui quin te admonerem. Facere non possum, ut non scribam. Nego ullam gemmam aut margaritam fuisse, quin quæsierit, inspexerit, abstulerit. Causæ nihil dico, quin ita sit. De musicis rebus non poterit quin dicat, hoc opere suscepto, recusare. Ego nihil prætermisi, quantum facere potui, quin Pompeium a Cæsaris conjunctione avocarem. Non possumus, quin alii a nobis dissentiant, recusare. Dignitatis autem tuæ nemo est, quin existimet habitam esse rationem ab senatu. Non enim possum quin exclamem, ut ait ille in Trinummo. Omnium voces audientur, exspectari diutius non oportere, quin ad castra iretur. At controversia non erat, quin verum dicerent. Non cunctandum existimavit, quin pugna decertaret. Nemo fere studuisse ei scientiæ vehementius videtur, quin quod voluerit consecutus sit. Parum abfuit quin occideretur. Adest fere nemo, quin acutius atque acrius vitia in dicente quam recta videat. Cæsarem non fefellit quin ab iis cohortibus, quæ contra equitatum in quarta acie collocatæ essent, initium victoriæ oriretur. Cæsar oppido potitur, perpaucis ex hostium numero desideratis quin cuncti vivi caperentur.

FINAL.

Ut, ne, quo, quominus, as final conjunctions, are joined to the *subjunctive.*

For examples of ut and ne, see Pred. IV. 3, etc.

Bargains, laws, treaties, etc., are made by *ut* positive, *ne* negative.

Quo is generally used when the complement is a *comparative.* See Pred. III. *that* = *in order that.*

Quo minus or *quominus* is used for the complement after verbs and phrases, implying *hindrance* or *want.*

Nihil desideramus, quo minus Epirum ipsam possidere videamur. Qui quidem in triumviratu judicavit contra P. Africani avunculi sui testimonium, vocationem augures, quo minus judiciis operam darent, non habere. Quæ religio C. Mario non fuerat, quo minus C. Glauciam prætorem occideret. Nihil de me tulistis, quo minus essem in civium numero. Illud non perficis, quo minus tua causa velim. Nemo est qui nesciat, quo minus discessio fieret, per adversarios tuos esse factum. Tanquam nihil denegatum sit ei, quo minus quam paratissimus esset. Nullis terminis circumscribit jus suum quo minus ei liceat vagari quo velit. Nemini civi ulla, quo minus adesset, satis justa excusatio est visa. Quid autem dici poterit, si turpitudinem non ipsam per se fugiendam esse statuerimus quo minus homines, tenebras et solitudinem nacti, nullo dedecore se abstineant.

COMPARISON—QUAM, AC, ETC.

Quam, strictly speaking, does not couple like moods and cases, and when it seems to couple like moods and cases, the like moods and cases depend on something else than quam.

Quam is the sign of comparison, either between two propositions, or between different parts of the same proposition.

When it is the sign of comparison between two propositions, *quam* is constructed with the *indicative.*

When it is the sign of comparison between parts of the same proposition, *quam*, being then the complement of the predicate, is joined to the subjunctive.

Ac and atque (*ac* before a consonant, *atque* before a vowel) are also used as signs of comparison, but only between propositions denoting similarity or dissimilarity; and are put after such words as par, pariter, aliter, æque, idem, contrarium, etc.

1. When two propositions are compared; as,

He conferred on no one more benefits *than* on me = he conferred on no one more benefits *than* he conferred benefits on me.

Nemini plura beneficia tribuit *quam* mihi.

Here, *he conferred on no one more benefits* is one proposition, and *he conferred benefits on me* is another proposition, and the relation between them is shown to be one of comparison, by the presence of the particle *than, quam;* but words common to both propositions, like *conferred* and *benefits*, are not repeated.

The Æqui were fiercer *than* the Volsci = the Æqui were fiercer *than* the Volsci were fierce.

Æqui ferociores fuerunt *quam* Volsci.

He said that the Æqui were fiercer *than* the Volsci = he said that the Æqui were fiercer *than* he said that the Volsci were.

Dixit Æquos ferociores esse *quam* Volscos.

You think me better *than* I feel myself to be = you think me to be better *than* I feel myself to be.

Me meliorem existimatis *quam* ego me esse sentio.

I will read rather *than* write [*i.e.*, the subject will either read or write, but prefers reading] = I will read rather *than* I will write.

Legam potius *quam* scribam.

He sings rather *than* reads = he sings rather *than* he reads [*i.e.*, he sings—he does not read].

Canit potius *quam* legit.

He said that he would rather tell a story *than* sing = he said that he would rather tell a story *than* he said that he would sing.

Dixit se fabulam narraturum esse potius *quam* canturum esse.

When the governing word is not common to both propositions, it must be supplied after the *quam* in Latin, even though it is not expressed in English; as,

You have slain a braver man *than* yourself.

If we make this *virum fortiorem interfecisti quam te ipsum*, the English of this would be, *you have slain a man braver than you have slain yourself;* but the *meaning* of the sentence is, *you have slain a man braver than you yourself are*, and therefore it must be made:

Virum fortiorem interfecisti *quam* ipse *es*.

You can build a better house *than* that of Romulus.

Domum meliorem ædificare potestis quam Romuli domus *est*.

We have an orator as eloquent as Cicero.

Habemus oratorem tam eloquentem *quam* Cicero *fuit*.

Quod me magno animi motu perturbatum putas, sum equidem; sed non tam magno quam tibi fortasse videor. Nobis, ut quidam putant, nihil est timendum magis, quam ille consul. Non mehercule quidquam libentius facio, quam scribo ad te. Quorum neutrum tam facile, quam tu arbitraris, conceditur. Eloquentia pluris est, quam juris civilis scientia. Considerate agere pluris est, quam cogitare prudenter. Ager nunc multo pluris est quam tunc fuit. Quos prudentes possumus dicere, divinos nullo modo possumus, non plus quam Milesium Thalem. Hoc non plus quam in duas partes posse distribui puto. Si amplius sestertio nummo petisti, quam tibi debitum est, causam perdidisti. Præstitimus enim patriæ non minus certe, quam debuimus. Hic majorem pecuniam prætori pollicetur, quam quantum tu dedisti. Iis plus frumenti imperabatur quam quantum exaraverant. Multa præclara in eo viro cognovi, sed nihil admirabilius, quam quomodo ille mortem filii tulit. Nulla re una magis commendatur orator, quam splendore verborum. Major et melior actionum, quam sonorum concentus est. Qui sæpius cum hoste conflixit, quam quisquam cum inimico concertavit. Citius veterem conjunctionem diremissem, quam novam conciliassem. Sophistæ concinnas magis sententias exquirunt quam probabiles. Illud vereor, ne majorem vim ad deterrendum habeat quam ad cohortandum. Rempublicam condere meo discessu, quam omnium interitu occidere malui. Num, igitur, quæ tempestas impendeat, vates melius conjiciet, quam gubernator? Malo Tyronis verecundiam in culpa esse quam liberalitatem Curii. Magis adeo id facilitate, quam ulla alia culpa mea contigit. Reperiam multos non tam curiosos, nec tam molestos, quam vos estis. Sperabam, honoris potius L. Flacci me adjutorem futurum quam miseriarum deprecatorem.

Contrarium decernis, ac paulo ante decreveras. Omnia aliter ac vos in monumentis habetis, pronunciavit. Nam et lætamur amicorum lætitia æque ac nostra, et pariter dolemus. Iste aliter atque ut edixerat, decreverat. Nunc contrarium est atque antea fuit. Sed ratio ordoque agminis aliter se habebat, ac Belgæ ad Nervios detulerant.

2. Between different parts of the same proposition; as,

He has more skill *than* do that [*than do that* = complement of predicate] = he has more skill *than that he should do that.*

Majorem scientiam habet, *quam ut id faciat.*

He will do anything rather *than* sing = he will do anything rather *than that he should sing* [*i.e.*, he won't sing].

Potius faciet quid *quam canat.*

He sings rather *than* read = he sings rather *than that he should read* [*i.e.*, he sings that he may *not* read].

Canit potius *quam legat.*

He will rather go away than do this.

Potius abibit *quam hoc faciat.*

He said that he would die rather than flee.

Dixit se potius moriturum esse *quam fugeret.*

Observe that the one member of the comparison excludes the other member [= *in order that not*], and that the *excluded* or *negative* member is in the *subjunctive.*

Hoc majus est quam ut profiteri scribere audeamus. Majore mihi ingenio videtur esse Isocrates, quam ut cum orationibus Lysiæ comparetur. Stirpibus natura nihil tribuit amplius, quam ut eas alendo atque augendo tueretur. Zeno proponatur Eleates, qui perpessus est omnia potius, quam conscios delendæ tyrannidis indicaret. Nihil ægrius factum est multo labore meo, quam ut manus ab illo abstinerentur. Nihil est in dicendo majus, quam ut faveat oratori auditor. Sed hoc majus est quoddam, quam ab aliis postulandum sit. Hoc inferius est quam ut patre tuo dignum videatur. See also Pred. V. 1.

VOCABULARY.

ABBREVIATIONS, ETC.

a.	Active.
abl. . . .	Ablative.
adj. . . .	Adjective; or adjectives are indicated by their terminations, as bon*us*, a, um.
adv. . . .	Adverb.
c.	Common gender.
comp. . .	Comparative.
conj. . .	Conjunction.
dat. . . .	Dative.
def. . . .	Defective.
dep. . . .	Deponent.
f.	Feminine.
gen. . . .	Genitive.
imp. . . .	Impersonal.
ind. . . .	Indeclinable.
interj. . .	Interjection.
inter. . .	Interrogative.
irr. . . .	Irregular.
m.	Masculine.
n.	Neuter.
obs. . . .	Obsolete,
p.	Passive.
pl.	Plural.
prep. . .	Preposition.
pron. . .	Pronoun.
s. or *sub.*	Substantive; or substantives are indicated by their termination, as hom*o*, inis.
sing. . .	Singular.
sup. . . .	Superlative.

The inflected part of a word is printed in *Italics*.

Verbs are known by the infinitive; and, when regular, only the present and infinitive are given, as Am*o*, āre.

The general rule for the quantity of Latin words is: A vowel before another vowel is short; a diphthong is long; a vowel before two consonants is long, *j*, *x*, and *z* having the same effect as two consonants.

VOCABULARY.

A

A, ab, abs, *prep.* from, by.
Ab*do*, dĭdi, dĭtum, dĕre, *a.* to hide, to conceal.
Abdū*co*, xi, ctum, cĕre, *a.* to lead away.
Ăb*eo*, ii, ĭtum, ĭre, *n. irr.* to go away.
Abhorr*eo*, ui, —, ēre, *a.* and *n.* to dread; to abhor; to be remote; to differ.
Abj*icio*, ēci, ectum, icĕre, *a.* to throw away; to reject; to despise.
Abrŏg*o*, āre, *a.* to repeal, to annul.
Absen*s*, ns, ns, ntis, absent.
Absol*vo*, vi, ūtum, vĕre, *a.* to finish; to absolve, to acquit.
Abstĭnen*s*, ns, ns, ntis, abstinent, not covetous.
Abstĭ*neo*, inui, —, inēre, *a. et n.* to keep from, to abstain.
Abstră*ho*, xi, ctum, hĕre, *a.* to take from by force; to divert from.
Ab*sum*, fui, esse, *n. irr.* to be absent, to be wanting.
Absūm*o*, psi, ptum, ĕre, *a.* to take away; to consume; to spend.
Ăbund*o*, āre, *n.* to overflow; to abound.
Ăb*ūtor*, ūsus, ūti, *a.* to consume; to make full use of; to abuse.
Ac, *conj.* and; than; as.
Ăcădēmĭ*a*, æ, *f.* the gymnasium or academy, where Plato taught; one of Cicero's villas.
Acast*us*, i, one of Cicero's slaves.
Ac*cēdo*, cessi, cessum, cedĕre, *n.* to go to, to approach; to apply one's self to; accedit, *imp.* it is added.

Accessi*o*, ōnis, *f.* an approaching; an addition.
Accĭd*o*, i, —, ĕre, *n.* to fall to; to happen; accidit, *imp.* it happens.
Accĭ*pio*, ēpi, eptum, ipĕre, *a.* to take; to receive; to accept; to learn; to hear.
Accommŏdāt*us*, a, um, accommodated, adapted, suitable.
Accommŏd*o*, āre, *a.* to adapt one thing to another; to accommodate; to gratify; to lend.
Accūrātè, *adv.* accurately, carefully.
Accūs*o*, āre, *a.* to accuse; to blame.
Ăcer *vel* ācris, ācris, ācre, sharp; quick; eager; passionate.
Ăcerb*us*, a, um, unripe, bitter; harsh, cruel.
Ăci*es*, ēi, *f.* the edge, or point of a weapon; the eye, or sight; battle array; an army in battle array.
Acqui*esco*, ēvi, ētum, escĕre, *n.* to repose, or rest; to be pleased, or satisfied with.
Acr*ĭter*, *adv.*, *comp.* rius, *sup.* acerrĭme, sharply; keenly; bravely; fiercely, vehemently.
Acti*o*, ōnis, *f.* an action.
Acūte, *adv.* sharply, acutely.
Ăcūt*us*, a, um, sharp; shrill; acute, ingenious.
Ad, *prep.* to, at, before.
Ădăm*o*, āre, *a.* to love greatly.
Addīc*o*, xi, ctum, ĕre, *a.* to adjudge; to make over; to assign.
Add*o*, ĭdi, ĭtum, ĕre, *a.* to add, to put to; to occasion.
Addū*co*, xi, ctum, cĕre, *a.* to lead; to bring to; to induce.

Ădeo, *adv.* so, so much, so far.
Ădeo, ii, ĭtum, īre, *n. irr.* to go to.
Ădhĭbeo, ui, ĭtum, ēre, *a.* to use; to apply; to employ.
Ădhortor, ātus, āri, *dep.* to exhort.
Ădhuc, *adv.* as yet, hitherto, still.
Ădĭmo, ēmi, emptum, imĕre, *a.* to take to one's self; to take away.
Ădĭpiscor, eptus, ipisci, *dep.* to get, obtain, accept.
Ădĭtus, ûs, *m.* an approach; access, liberty of approach; a passage.
Adjungo, xi, ctum, gĕre, *a.* to add, to join to, to unite; to acquire.
Adjūtor, ōris, *m.* an assistant.
Adjŭvo, ūvi, ūtum, uvāre, *a.* to assist; to favour.
Admĭnistro, āre, *a.* to take care of; to manage; to perform.
Admīrābĭlis, is, e, wonderful; worthy of admiration.
Admīrātio, ōnis, *f.* wonder, admiration.
Admīror, ātus, āri, *dep.* to wonder greatly; to admire.
Admisceo, scui, stum *et* xtum, scēre, *a.* to mix with.
Admitto, īsi, issum, ittĕre, *a.* to admit; to commit.
Admŏdum, *adv.* very.
Admŏneo, ēre, *a.* to admonish; to put in mind.
Ădŏlescens, tis, *c.* a young man or woman, from fifteen to thirty.
Ădŏlescentŭlus, i, *m.* a very young man.
Ădopto, āre, *a.* to accept; to adopt.
Ădŏrior, tus, īri, *dep.* to attack; to apply one's self to.
Adspicio. *See* Aspicio.
Adsum, fui, esse, *n. irr.* to be present; to assist.
Advĕnio, ēni, entum, enīre, *n.* to come to; to arrive.
Adventus, ûs, *m.* a coming, an arrival.
Adversārius, a, um, opposite to; *sub.* an opponent, an adversary.
Adversor, ātus, āri, *dep.* to oppose.
Adversus, a, um, opposite; adverse.
Adversus *et* adversum, *prep.* against, opposite.
Adverto, ti, sum, tĕre, *a.* to turn towards, observe.
Advŏcātus, i. *m.* a helper, an advocate.
Ædĭfĭco, āre, *a.* to build.
Ædui, ōrum *m.* a people of Gaul on the Arar.
Æduus, a, um, belonging to the Ædui.
Æger, ra, rum, sick; distressed.
Ægre, ægrius, ægerrime, *adv.* with difficulty; hardly; with dislike.
Ægrĭtūdo, ĭnis, *f.* sickness, sorrow.
Ægrōtus, a, um, sick, disordered.
Æquālis, is, e, equal; contemporary.
Æque, *adv.* equally.
Æquĭtas, ātis, *f.* evenness of mind; justice, equity.
Æquo, āre, *a.* to make level; to make equal; to compare; *n.* to equal.
Æquus, a, um, level; equal, just; advantageous; fit.
Aër, aëris, *m.* the air
Æs, æris, *n.* brass; money.
Æschĭnes, is, an Athenian orator.
Æstas, ātis, *f.* summer.
Æstĭmātio, ōnis, *f.* a valuing; a valuation; esteem.
Æstĭmo, āre, *a.* to estimate, to value, to esteem.
Æstus, ûs, *m.* the tide; restlessness; force.
Ætas, ātis, *f.* age; time; a season.
Æternĭtas, ātis, *f.* eternity.
Æternus, a, um, eternal.
Ætna, æ, *f.* a volcanic mountain in Sicily.
Affectus, ûs, *m.* an affection, disposition.
Affĕro, attŭli, allātum, afferre, *a. irr.* to carry to; to report; to occasion; to allege; to offer.
Affĭcio, ēci, ectum, icĕre, *a.* to affect, to move; to bestow, to furnish.
Affirmo, āre, *a.* to affirm, to declare.
Afflicto, are, *a.* to injure; to distress, to vex.
Afflictus, a, um, distressed; despised.
Afrĭcānus, a, um, African; a surname of the two Scipios.

Ager, ri, *m.* a field; land; a district.
Agg*er*, ĕris, *m.* a heap, rubbish; mound, rampart.
Aggrĕd*ior*, ssus, di, *dep.* to go to; to accost or address; to attempt; to attack, or assault.
Ăgĭtāti*o*, ōnis, *f.* motion, agitation, exercise.
Agm*en*, ĭnis, *n.* an army on march; a multitude.
Agn*osco*, ōvi, ĭtum, oscĕre, *a.* to know, discern; to recognise, acknowledge; to approve.
Ăgo, ēgi, actum, agĕre, *a.* to drive; to act, to do; to treat; to transact; — gratias, to give thanks; — cum aliquo, to treat with, to converse.
Agrāri*us*, a, um, relating to land, rural.
Aio, *def.* I say.
Ălăcer *or* ălăcris, ălăcris, ălăcre, cheerful; active; impatient.
Alc*es*, is, *f.* (probably) the elk.
Alcidām*us*, i, a rhetorician.
Alĕo, ōnis, (*for* aleator) *m.* a gamester.
Alexand*er*, ri, name of several persons; Alexander, king of Macedon.
Ăliēn*us*, a, um, belonging to another; foreign; disadvantageous; averse.
Ălĭquando, *adv.* at some time; sometime or other.
Ălĭquanto, alĭquantum, *adv.* somewhat, a little.
Ălĭ*quis*, qua, quod *vel* quid, some one; any.
Ălĭquo, *adv.* to some place.
Ălĭter, *adv.* otherwise.
Ăli*us*, a, ud, *gen.* alĭus, other, another; different.
Allĭ*cio*, ēxi, ectum, icere, *a.* to allure, to attract.
Allobrŏg*es*, um, a people of Dauphiné in Gaul.
Ăl*o*, ui, ĭtum *or* altum, ĕre, *a.* to maintain, to support; to nourish, to foster.
Alp*es*, ium, *f.* the Alps.
Alte, *adv.* highly; deeply.
Alter, a, um, *gen.* ĭus, another (of two); cne of two; the other, the second.
Alt*us*, a, um, high; deep.
Ambarr*i*, ōrum, a branch of the Ædui on the Arar.
Ambiori*x*, gis, a king of the Eburones, in Gaul.
Ambĭti*o*, ōnis, *f.* a going round; canvassing for any public employment; ambition.
Ambŭl*o*, are, *n.* to walk; to go.
Āmenti*a*, æ, *f.* madness; stupidity.
Āmĭce, *adv.* in a friendly manner; *sup.* amicissime.
Āmĭcĭti*a*, æ, *f.* friendship.
Āmĭc*us*, a, um, friendly; courteous.
Āmĭc*us*, i. *m.* a friend.
Āmi*tto*, ĭsi, issum, ittĕre, *a.* to send away; to let go; to lose.
Ām*o*, āre, *a.* to love, to take delight in.
Amplĭfĭc*o*, āre, *a.* to make wide; to dilate upon.
Amplĭtūd*o*, ĭnis, *f.* largeness; honour.
Amplius, *adv. comp. of* amplè, more, moreover.
Ampl*us*, a, um, large, ample; great, noble.
An, *adv.* et *conj.* whether, or.
Ănāxăgŏr*as*, æ, an Athenian philosopher.
Ancill*a*, æ, *f.* a maid-servant.
An*go*, xi, —, gĕre *a.* to vex.
Angusti*a*, æ, *f.* narrowness; difficulty; indigence.
Ănĭm*a*, æ, *f.* air, breath; the soul; life.
Ănĭmadver*to*, ti, sum, tĕre, *a.* to turn the mind to, to consider, attend to; to punish.
Ănĭma*l*, lis, *n.* an animal.
Ănĭman*s*, tis, *f. m.* et *n.* a living creature.
Ănĭmāt*us*, a, um, disposed; courageous.
Ănĭm*us*, i. *m.* the mind; will; disposition; courage.
Annon, *or* an non, *adv.* whether or not.
Annŭl*us*, i, *m.* a ring.
Ann*us*, i, *m.* a year.
Ans*a*, æ, *f.* a handle; an opportunity.

Ante, *prep.* before.
Ante *et* Antea, *adv.* before, formerly.
Antĕcēdo, ssi, ssum, dĕre, *a.* et *n.* to go before; to excel.
Anteeo, ii, ĭtum, īre, *a. irr.* to go before; to excel; to prevent.
Antĕfĕro, tŭli, lātum, ferre, *a. irr.* to carry before; to prefer.
Antĕpōno, ŏsui, ŏsĭtum, ōnĕre, *a.* to place, or set before; to prefer.
Antĕquam, *conj.* before that.
Antiŏchus, i, a king of Syria; a philosopher.
Antĭpŏdes, um, *m.* the Antipodes.
Antīquĭtas, ātis, *f.* antiquity.
Antīquus, a, um, old, ancient.
Antŏnīnus, i, a Roman family name; Marcus Aurelius, Emperor, famous for his virtues.
Antonius, a, um, a Roman family name; Marcus, the friend of Julius Cæsar and avenger of his death.
Ănus, ûs, *f.* an old woman.
Ăpĕrio, ui, tum, īre, *a.* to open; uncover, disclose; declare.
Ăperte, apertius, apertissime, *adv.* openly; plainly.
Ăpertus, a, um, open; clear; candid.
Ăpollo, ĭnis, son of Jupiter and Latona, god of the fine arts, of music, poetry, etc.
Appāreo, ēre, *n.* to appear, to be visible; to be evident.
Appello, āre, *a.* to call, or name; to address, or speak to.
Appello, pŭli, pulsum, pellĕre, *a.* to drive; to turn to; to land.
Appĕto, īvi, ĭtum, ĕre, *a.* to desire greatly; to endeavour; to draw near to.
Appius, i, a Roman prænomen; Claudius, the decemvir, notorious in the case of Virginia.
Applĭco, āvi, ātum, *or* ui, ĭtum, āre, *a.* to lay one thing to another; to attach, or join; to apply.
Appŏsĭtus, a, um, fit, suitable.
Apprŏbātio, ōnis, *f.* approbation.
Apprŏbātor, ōris, *m.* an approver.
Apprŏbo, āre, *a.* to approve.
Apprŏpinquo, āre, *a.* to approach, to draw near.
Aprīlis, is, e, April.
Aptus, a, um, fit, suitable.
Ăpud, *prep.* at, nigh, with.
Ăqua, æ, *f.* water.
Ăquītānia, æ, a part of Gaul.
Āra, æ, *f.* an altar.
Ărar *et* Ărăris, is, *m.* the Saône.
Arbitror, ātus, āri, *dep.* to decide a dispute; to judge, to think.
Arbor *et* arbos, ŏris, *f.* a tree.
Arcesso, īvi, ītum, ĕre, *a.* to send for; to call; to accuse.
Arcesilāus, i, *or* Arcĕsĭlas, æ, a philosopher, the founder of the middle academy.
Ardens, ns, ns, ntis, burning; ardent.
Ardeo, si, sum, dēre, *n.* to burn; to be inflamed with.
Arduus, a, um, steep; difficult.
Argentārius, i, *m.* a banker.
Argentum, i, *n.* silver, money.
Argūmentātio, ōnis, *f.* argument; proof.
Argūmentum, i, *n.* an argument; a proof.
Arguo, ŭi, ūtum, uĕre, *a.* to show; to prove; to accuse; to convict.
Ariŏbarzānes, is, king of Cappadocia.
Ariovistus, i, king of the Germans.
Ăristīdes, is, an Athenian, celebrated for his justice.
Aristo, ōnis, the sceptic philosopher of Chios.
Ăristŏtĕles, is, the famous Grecian philosopher.
Ăristŏtĕlicus, a, um, Aristotelian.
Arma, ōrum, *n.* arms or armour.
Armĕnius, a, um, belonging to Armenia.
Armo, āre, *a.* to arm; to equip; to furnish.
Arpineius, i, a Roman knight.
Arpīnum, i, the birthplace of Cicero.
Arrĭpio, ipui, eptum, ipĕre, *a.* to snatch by violence, to seize; to learn quickly; to engage in eagerly.
Arrŏgans, ns, ns, ntis, arrogant.
Arrŏgantia, æ, *f.* arrogance.

Arrŏgo, āre, *a.* to arrogate.
Ars, tis, *f.* art, skill, ability; a trade.
Artĭfex, ex, ex, ĭcis, artificial; artful; *sub.* an artificer.
Artĭfĭcium, i, *n.* exercise of any art; skill; stratagem,
Aruspex, ĭcis, *m.* a priest; a predictor of events.
Arverni, ōrum, a people of Aquitania.
Arx, cis, *f.* a fortress; a citadel.
Ascendo, di, sum, dĕre, *a.* to go up, to mount, ascend.
Ascensus, ûs, *m.* an ascendency; an ascent.
Ăsia, æ, Asia.
Ăsĭnus, i, *m.* an ass; a stupid person.
Aspectus, ûs, *m.* a seeing; the sight; aspect.
Asper, a, um, rough; cruel.
Aspicio, exi, ectum, icĕre, *a.* to look at, to see, to behold.
Assensus, ûs, *m.* an assent.
Assentio, si, sum, tīre, *n.*, *or* Assentior, sus, tīri, *dep.* to assent; to approve.
Assentor, ātus, āri, *dep.* to flatter; approve.
Assĕquor, cūtus, qui, *dep.* to reach; come up to; to attain; to understand.
Assĕvēro, āre, *a.* to assert earnestly.
Assidue, *adv.* perpetually, assiduously.
Assĭduus, a um, constant, continual; diligent, assiduous.
Assuēfăcio, ēci, actum, acĕre, *a.* to render accustomed.
Assuesco, ēvi, ētum, esĕre, *n.* to become accustomed.
Assūmo, psi, ptum, ĕre, *a.* to take; to take to one's self, assume, acquire, arrogate.
At, *conj.* but.
Athlēta, æ, *m.* a wrestler.
Athēnæ, ārum, the capital of Attica.
Athenienses, ium, Athenians.
Atŏmus, i, *f.* an atom.
Atque, *conj.* and.
Attendo, di, tum, dĕre, *a.* to attend, to apply.
Attente, *adv.* attentively.
Attentus, a, um, attentive.
Atticus, i, Titus Pomponius, a Roman knight, called Atticus on account of his long residence in Athens.
Attĭneo, ui, —, ēre, to reach; to concern; attinet, *imp.* it belongs to, it is necessary.
Attingo, ĭgi, actum, ingĕre, *a.* to touch gently; to study; to bestow some attention upon; to take in hand.
Attius, a, um, a Roman family name.
Auctio, ōnis, *f.* an auction.
Auctiōnor, ātus, āri, *dep.* to sell by auction.
Auctor, ōris, *c.* an author, founder; an adviser, proposer; an inventor.
Auctōrĭtas, ātis, *f.* authority, influence.
Auctus, a, um, grown; increased.
Audācia, æ, *f.* boldness, confidence, temerity.
Audax, ax, ax, ācis, bold, daring.
Audeo, ausus, audēre, *n. p.* to dare, to attempt.
Audio, īre, *a.* to hear, to listen; to assent, to obey.
Audītor, ōris, *m.* a hearer, a disciple.
Aufĕro, abstŭli, ablātum, auferre, *a. irr.* to take away, to carry off.
Augeo, xi, ctum, gēre, *a.* to increase; to furnish.
Augesco, —, —, ĕre, to become greater.
Augur, ŭris, *c.* an augur.
Auris, is, *f.* the ear.
Aurum, i, *n.* gold, money.
Auspĭcium, i, *n.* an augury, a sign.
Aut, *conj.* or, either.
Autem. *conj.* but, however.
Aulis, ĭdis, *f.* a town of Bœotia.
Auxĭlium, i, *n.* aid, help; *pl.* auxiliaries.
Ăvārĭtia, æ, *f.* avarice, covetousness.
Ăvārus, a, um, covetous, greedy of money, avaricious.
Aveo, —, —, ēre, to desire.
Ăvernus, i, a lake in Campania.

Āversus, a, um, turned from; averse, adverse.
Āverto, ti, sum, tĕre, a. to turn away from; to cause to retire; to turn off; to detain, keep off; to carry off.
Āvŏco, āre, a. to call away; to divert from.
Āvŏlo, āre, n. to fly away; to flee; to haste.
Ăvuncŭlus, i, m. a maternal uncle.

B

Balbus, i, surname of several Romans.
Barbărus, a, um, foreign; barbarous; s. a barbarian.
Băsis, is, f. a base, a pedestal.
Beāte, adv. happily.
Beātus, a, um, blessed, happy.
Belgæ, ārum, the bravest people of ancient Gaul.
Bello, āre, n. to wage war, to fight.
Bellŏvăci, ōrum, the bravest people among the Belgæ.
Bellua, æ, f. a large wild beast.
Bellum, i, n. war.
Bĕnĕ, melius, optime, adv. well, better, best.
Bĕnĕfĭcium, i, n. a deed of kindness, a benefit, a favour.
Bĕnĕvŏlentia, æ, f. benevolence, kindness.
Bĕnigne, adv. kindly.
Bestia, æ, f. a beast.
Bĭbo, i, ĭtum, ĕre, a. tŏ drink.
Bĭduum, i, n. a space of two days.
Biennium, i, n. a space of two years.
Bīni, æ, a, two by two; *with words that have no singular, or the singular in a different sense*, two.
Bĭpes, pes, pes, ĕdis, two-footed; biped.
Bĭs, adv. twice.
Bŏnus, a, um, good, virtuous.
Bospŏranus, a, um, Thracian.
Brăchium, i, n. the arm from the wrist to the elbow.
Brĕvis, is, e, short, brief.
Brĕvĭter, adv. shortly, briefly
Briso, ōnis, M. Antius, a Roman tribune.
Brūtus, i, a surname of the Junian family; Marcus, the murderer of Cæsar.
Būcŭla, æ, f. a heifer.

C

C. = Caius.
Cădāver, ĕris, n. a dead body.
Cădo, cecĭdi, cāsum, cadĕre, n. to fall; to happen; to incur.
Cæcus, a, um, blind, dark; hidden.
Cædes, is, f. slaughter, murder.
Cædo, cecīdi, cæsum, cædĕre, a. to beat or strike; to kill.
Cæsar, ăris, the surname of a branch of the Julian family.
Cæstus, ûs, m.; *in the pl.* boxing-gloves.
Călămĭtas, ātis, f. calamity, misfortune.
Călor, ōris, m. warmth; heat.
Camillus, i, a surname of the Furian family.
Campania, æ, a district of Italy.
Caninius, i, an intimate friend of Cicero.
Cănis, is, c. a dog, a bitch.
Canius, i, C. a Roman knight.
Cantus, ûs, m. a singing; song; melody.
Căpio, cēpi, captum, capĕre, a. to take, to receive; to contain; to seize; to understand.
Căpĭtālis, is, e, relating to the head; capital; mortal; hurtful; wicked.
Cappadox, ŏcis, an inhabitant of Cappadocia.
Captīvus, a, um, captive; s. m. a captive.
Căput, ĭtis, n. the head; the life; the chief part; source.
Căreo, ui, ĭtum, ēre, n. to be without, to want.
Căria, æ, a country of Asia Minor.
Cărīna, æ, f. the keel of a ship.
Carmen, ĭnis, n. a verse, a poem.
Carneădes, is, a philosopher, the founder of the new academy.
Carnūtes, um, a people of Celtic Gaul.

Carpinatius, i, publicanus in Sicilia.
Carrus, i, m. and carrum, i, n. a car.
Cārus, a, um, dear or loved; expensive.
Cassiānus, a, um, of Cassius.
Cassius, i, a Roman surname.
Castellum, i, n. a little fort, a castle.
Castrum, i, n. a fort; pl. a camp.
Casus, ûs, m. a fall; a chance or misfortune.
Cătĭlīna, æ, surname of the Sergian family; a Roman patrician and conspirator.
Căto, ōnis, a surname of the Porcian family.
Cătŭlus, i, a surname of the Lutatian family.
Causa, æ, f. a suit at law; a cause; reason; defence.
Cautus, a, um, legally secured; safe; cautious.
Căveo, cāvi, cautum, cavēre, a. to beware; to guard against; n. to take care; to provide for; to give security.
Căvo, āre, a. to hollow.
Cēdo, cessi, cessum, cedĕre, n. to give place, to depart; to yield.
Cĕlĕber, or ris, ris, re, frequented; numerous; renowned.
Cĕlĕbrātio, ōnis, f. an assembly; a festival.
Cĕler, or ĕris, ĕris, ĕre, swift, quick.
Cĕlĕrĭtas, ātis, f. swiftness, quickness.
Cĕlĕrĭter, adv. quickly, speedily; comp. celerius; sup. celerrime.
Cēlo, āre, a. to conceal, to hide.
Censeo, ui, um, ēre, a. to think, to judge; to deliver one's opinion; to decree; to estimate the fortunes of the people, in order to tax them.
Censor, ōris, m. a censor.
Centŭrio, ōnis, m. a centurion.
Cerno, —, —, cernĕre, a. to separate; to see, discern.
Certāmen, ĭnis, n. a contest, a battle.
Certè et certo, adv. certainly, at least.
Certo, āre, n. to contend.
Certus, a, um, sure; trusty.
Cesso, āre, n. to be at leisure; to cease.
Cētĕra, um (nom. sing. mas. wanting), the other, the rest.
Cĭbāria, ōrum, n. victuals, rations.
Cĭbus, i, m. meat, food.
Cĭcĕro, ōnis, a surname of the Tullian family; the Roman orator.
Cimbri, ōrum, a people of Jutland.
Circa et circum, prep. about, around.
Circuitus, ûs, m. a going round; the circuit or compass of a thing.
Circumdo, ĕdi, ătum, ăre, a. to put round, to surround.
Circumscrībo, psi, ptum, bĕre, a. to write round, describe; to circumscribe; to surround.
Circumsŏno, ui, ĭtum, āre, n. to resound on all sides.
Circumsto, stĕti, —, stāre, a. to stand round, to surround.
Circumvĕnio, ēni, entum, enīre, a. to come round, to surround; to circumvent.
Cis, prep. on this side.
Cĭtĕrior, us, comp. (from citer, obsolete) sup. citimus, nearer, sup. nearest.
Cĭto, adv. quickly, soon.
Cīvīlis, is, e, of or pertaining to a citizen; civic; civil; courteous.
Cīvis, is, c. a citizen; a fellow-citizen.
Cīvĭtas, ātis, f. an assemblage of citizens; city or state; citizenship.
Clam, adv. secretly; prep. without the knowledge of.
Clāmo, āre, n. and a. to complain; to cry out.
Clārus, a, um, clear, bright; famous.
Classis, is, f. a fleet.
Claudo, si, sum, dĕre, a. to close; to shut in.
Clōdius, i, a Roman family name.
Clŭpea, æ, f. a town of Africa.
Clўpeus, i, m. a round shield, buckler.
Cn. = Cneius.

Cœlestis, is, e, heavenly.
Cœlum, i, n.; pl. cœli, ōrum, m. heaven; the sky, the air.
Cœno, āre, n. to sup; to be at supper.
Cœpi, sse, et cœptus sum, def. to begin; to undertake.
Cœtus, ûs, m. a company, an assembly.
Cŏgĭtātio, ōnis, f. thought, reflection.
Cŏgĭtāto, adv. with consideration; designedly.
Cŏgĭto, āre, a. to think; to devise; to intend.
Cognĭtio, ōnis, f. an inquiry; knowing; knowledge.
Cognosco, ōvi, ĭtum, oscĕre, a. to find out; to know.
Cōgo, coēgi, coactum, cōgĕre, a. to drive together, to assemble; to compel; to conclude.
Cŏhĭbeo, ui, ĭtum, ēre, a. to restrain.
Cŏhors, tis, f. a cohort; a division of the Roman army.
Cŏhortor, ātus, āri, dep. to exhort.
Coĭtio, ōnis, f. a coming together, meeting.
Collatinus, a, um, belonging to Collatia.
Collēga, æ, m. a colleague.
Collēgium, i, n. a number of colleagues, a college, a society; a guild.
Collĭgo, āre, a. to tie together; to comprehend.
Collĭgo, ēgi, ectum, igĕre, a. to gather together, to collect; to conclude.
Collis, is, m. a hill.
Collŏco, āre, a. to place, lay.
Collŏquium, i, n. a conversation; a conference.
Collŏquor, cūtus or quutus, qui, dep. to speak with one, to speak together, to have a conference.
Cŏlo, ŏlui, ultum, ŏlĕre, a. to bestow pains on; to cultivate; to inhabit; to esteem; to worship.
Cŏlōnia, æ, f. a colony, colonists.
Cŏlumna, æ, f. a column.
Combūro, ssi, ustum, rĕre, a. to burn; to consume.
Cŏmĭtor, ātus, āri, dep. to accompany, to attend.
Commĕmĭni, isse, def. to remember.
Commĕmŏro, āre, a. to mention, to remind.
Commendo, āre, a. to entrust; to recommend; to commend.
Commentĭcius, a, um, invented; fictitious.
Commentārius, i, m., et commentarium, i, n. a journal; a commentary.
Commeo, āre, n. to come, or go; to move.
Committo, īsi, issum, ittĕre, a. to join; to begin; to entrust; to cause; to be the occasion, to act so that; to undertake; to do.
Commius, i, king of the Atrebătes, a Gallic nation.
Commŏde, adv. fitly, conveniently.
Commŏdo, āre, a. to adopt; to lend.
Commŏdum, i, n. advantage, convenience.
Commŏdus, a, um, convenient, advantageous, agreeable.
Commŏnĕfăcio, ēci, ăctum, ăcĕre, a. to remind.
Commŏror, āri, dep. to tarry.
Commŏveo, ōvi, ōtum, ovēre, a. to move together; to excite.
Commūnĭco, āre, a. to make common; to impart; to participate.
Commūnio, īre, a. to fortify.
Commūnis, is, e, common.
Commūnĭter, adv. in common; commonly.
Commūtātio, ōnis, f. a change.
Commūto, āre, a. to change; to exchange.
Cōmœdus, i, m. a comic actor.
Compărātio, ōnis, f. a preparing; an acquiring; a comparing.
Compăro, āre, a. to procure; to compare; to ordain.
Compello, āre, a. to address; to accuse.
Compello, ŭli, ulsum, ellĕre, a. to drive together; to compel.
Complector, xus, cti, dep. to embrace; to comprehend; to esteem.
Compleo, ēvi, ētum, ēre, a. to fill up; to finish.

Complūres, es, a, several; many.
Compŏsĭtio, ōnis, *f.* an agreement; an arrangement.
Comprĕhendo, di, sum, dĕre, *a.* to lay hold of; to perceive; to comprehend; to embrace.
Comprŏbo, āre, *a.* to prove; to approve.
Cōnātum, i, *n.* an attempt, endeavour.
Cōnātus, ûs, *m.* an endeavour, attempt.
Concēdo, ssi, ssum, dĕre, *n.* to yield, to give place; *a.* to grant, allow.
Concentus, ûs, *m.* a concert; harmony.
Concerto, āre, *n.* to dispute.
Concīdo, di, sum, dĕre, *a.* to cut to pieces; to slay.
Concĭdo, i, —, ĕre, *n.* to fall down; to fail; to cease.
Concĭlio, āre, *a.* to unite; to conciliate; to procure.
Concĭlium, i, *n.* a council, assembly.
Concinnus, a um, concise, neat, elegant.
Concio, ōnis, *f.* an assembly of people; an oration.
Conclāmo, āre, *n.* et *a* to cry out.
Conclūdo, si, sum, dĕre, *a.* to shut up; to contain; to conclude.
Concŭpisco, īvi, ītum, iscĕre, *a.* to desire earnestly; to aspire to.
Concurro, curri *or* cŭcurri, cursum, currĕre, *n.* to run together; to engage in battle; to join; to agree.
Concursus, ûs, *m.* a running; a meeting, hostile or otherwise.
Condemno, āre, *a.* to condemn.
Condĭtio, ōnis, *f.* the condition of anything; an offer, proposal.
Condo, ĭdi, ĭtum, ĕre, *a.* to lay up; to found, to build; to hide; to compose; to make.
Condōno, āre, *a.* to give; to forgive; to remit.
Condūco, xi, ctum, cĕre, *a.* to bring together; to lead; to hire; to contract; *n.* to be serviceable.
Condūcit, ebat, it is of use, serviceable.
Confĕro, contŭli, collātum, conferre, *a. irr.* to bring together; to betake (one's self); to compare; to attribute; to occasion; to bestow; to agree.
Confestim, *adv.* immediately, forthwith.
Confĭcio, ēci, ectum, ĭcĕre, *a.* to finish, to make; to waste; to kill. Conficitur, it follows.
Confīdo, sus, dĕre, *n. pass.* to trust, confide; to be assured.
Confīgo, xi, xum, gĕre, *a.* to fasten together; to pierce.
Confirmātus, a, um, strong, certain, resolute.
Confirmo, āre, *a.* to strengthen, confirm; to affirm, or declare solemnly.
Confĭteor, essus, itēri, *dep.* to confess.
Conflīgo, xi, ctum, gĕre, *n.* to contend, fight; to strive.
Confluo, xi, xum, ĕre, *n.* to flow together.
Confŭgio, ūgi, ŭgĭtum, ŭgĕre, *n.* to flee for refuge.
Confundo, ūdi, ūsum, undĕre, to pour out; to mingle; to unite.
Congrātŭlor, ātus, āri, *dep.* to wish joy; to congratulate.
Congrĕdior, ssus, di, *dep.* to gc together; to accost; to engage in battle; to dispute.
Congrĕgo, āre, *a.* to assemble together; to combine.
Congruenter, *adv.* agreeably, fitly.
Conjectūra, æ, *f.* a conjecture; a conjecturing.
Conjĭcio, ēci, ectum, icĕre, *a.* to throw together; to aim; to conjecture.
Conjunctio, ōnis, *f.* a uniting; an agreement.
Conjunctus, a, um, united; related; agreeable.
Conjungo, xi, ctum, gĕre, *a.* to join together; to unite; to associate; to procure.
Conjūrātio, ōnis, *f.* a conspiracy, a combination.
Conjux, ŭgis, *c.* a husband or wife.
Connītor, nīsus *et* nixus, nīti, *dep.* to try to the utmost; to strive to.

Cōnor, ātus, āri, *dep.* to endeavour, try, attempt.

Conquĕror, estus, eri, *dep.* to complain; grieve.

Conquiesco, ēvi, ētum, escĕre, *n.* to rest; to take repose; to find repose.

Conquīro, sīvi, sītum, rĕre, *a.* to search for diligently; to collect; to acquire.

Consanguīneus, a, um, related by blood, akin.

Conscendo, di, sum, dĕre, *a.* to climb, to mount; to embark.

Conscientia, æ, *f.* consciousness; conscience.

Conscisco, īvi, ītum, iscĕre, *a.* to execute, commit; to resolve upon.

Conscius, a, um, privy to; conscious.

Conscrībo, psi, ptum, bĕre, *a.* to write; to enrol.

Consector, ātus, āri, *dep.* to follow after diligently; to overtake; to obtain.

Consensio, ōnis, *f.* agreement, consent.

Consensus, ûs, *m.* a consent; an agreement.

Consentāneus, a, um, agreeable; agreeable to reason.

Consentio, si, sum, tīre, *n.* to agree; to consent; to combine.

Consĕquor, quūtus *or* cūtus, qui, *dep.* to follow, to pursue; to get.

Conservo, āre, *a.* to keep; to preserve; to observe.

Consīdĕrāte, *adv.* considerately, cautiously.

Consīdĕro, āre, *a.* to consider; to observe.

Consīdius, i, one of Cæsar's lieutenants.

Consīlium, i, *n.* advice; a purpose.

Consīmīlis, is, e, like.

Consisto, tĭti, tĭtum, istĕre, *n.* to stand firmly; to consist in; to depend upon.

Consōlātio, ōnis, *f.* consoling, consolation.

Consōlor, ātus, āri, *dep.* to comfort, to console.

Consors, tis, *c.* sharing; a partner.

Conspectus, ûs, *m.* sight, view.

Conspĭcio, exi, ectum, ĭcĕre, *a.* to see; to consider.

Conspĭcor, ātus, āri, *dep.* to discover; to perceive.

Constanter, *adv.* uniformly; constantly.

Constantia, æ, *f.* constancy, firmness.

Consterno, strāvi, strātum, sternĕre, to cover; constrata navis, a decked ship.

Constĭtuo, ui, ūtum, uĕre, *a.* to place together; to establish; to appoint; to determine.

Consto, ĭti, ĭtum *or* ātum, āre, *n.* to stand together; to halt; to consist; to be; to be consistent; to last; to cost; to be evident.

Constringo, nxi, ctum, ngĕre, to bind together; to restrain.

Consuesco, ēvi, ētum, escĕre, *n.* to be accustomed.

Consuētūdo, ĭnis, *f.* custom; acquaintance.

Consul, ŭlis, *m.* a consul.

Consŭlo, ui, tum, ĕre, *a.* to consult; *n.* to consult for.

Consulto, *adv.* designedly; on purpose.

Consultum, i, *n.* a resolution.

Consūmo, psi, ptum, ĕre, *a.* to consume, to spend.

Contāmĭno, āre, *a.* to touch together; to contaminate.

Contĕgo, xi, ctum, gĕre, *a.* to cover all over; to hide,

Contemno, psi, ptum, nĕre, *a.* to despise, contemn.

Contemplor, ātus, āri, *dep.* to gaze upon; to contemplate.

Contendo, di, tum, dĕre, *a.* to stretch, strain; to affirm confidently; to entreat; *n.* to hasten; to contend; to ask.

Contentio, ōnis, an earnest endeavour; a contest.

Contentus, a, um, content.

Contĭneo, inui, entum, inēre, *a.* to hold together; to contain; to restrain.

Contingo, ĭgi, actum, ingĕre, *a.* to touch; contingit, *imp.* it happens.

Contĭnuo, *adv.* forthwith; instantly.
Contra, *prep.* against; opposite to.
Contrăho, xi, ctum, hĕre, *a.* to draw together; to contract.
Contrārius, a, um, contrary.
Contrōversia, æ, *f.* a quarrel; controversy.
Contueor, ĭtus, ēri, *dep.* to behold steadily; to survey.
Contŭmēlia, æ, *f.* an affront, injury.
Convello, elli, ulsum, ellĕre, *a.* to tear away; to destroy; to refute.
Convĕnienter, *adv.* conveniently.
Convĕnio, ēni, entum, enīre, *n.* to come together; to agree; convĕnit, *imp.* it is agreed; it is meet.
Conventus, ûs, *m.* a meeting; an agreement.
Converto, ti, sum, tĕre, *a.* to turn; to apply; to convert.
Convinco, ci, ctum, ncĕre, *a.* to prove clearly; to convict; to refute.
Convŏco, āre, *a.* to call together, to summon.
Cōpia, æ, *f.* plenty; ability; supply; *pl.* forces.
Cōpiōse, *adv.* copiously; diffusely.
Cōram, *prep.* before, in presence of; *adv.* openly.
Corfīnium, i, the capital of the Peligni.
Cornu, *n. sing. indecl., pl.* cornua, um, a horn; a trumpet; the wing of an army.
Corpus, ŏris, *n.* a body; a society.
Corrĭgo, exi, ectum, igĕre, *a.* to correct.
Corrumpo, ūpi, uptum, umpĕre, *a.* to spoil; to corrupt.
Cotta, æ, a Roman orator.
Crassus, i, surname of the Licinian family; a Roman famed for his riches.
Crastĭnus, a um, of to-morrow.
Crătippus, i, a philosopher of Mitylene.
Crēbro, *adv.* frequently.
Crēdo, ĭdi, ĭtum, ĕre, *a. et n.* to believe; to trust.
Crēdŭlĭtas, ātis, *f.* credulity.
Crĕmo, āre, *a.* to burn.
Creo, āre, *a.* to create; to beget.
Cres, tis, *m.* a Cretan.
Crēta, æ, *or* Crēte, es, *f.* an island south of Greece.
Crīmen, ĭnis, *n.* a crime; an accusation.
Crīmĭnor, ātus, āri, *dep.* to accuse.
Crīnis, is, *m.* hair.
Crito, ōnis, a friend of Socrates.
Crœsus, i, the last king of Lydia, esteemed the richest of men.
Crŭciātus, ûs, *m.* torment; torture.
Crūdēlis, is, e, cruel, inhuman.
Crūdēlĭtas, ātis, *f.* cruelty; barbarities.
Crus, crūris, *n.* the leg.
Culpa, æ, *f.* a fault.
Culpo, āre, *a.* to blame.
Cultio, ōnis, *f.* a cultivating.
Cŭm, *prep.* with, together with.
Cum *or* quum, *adv.* and *conj.* when, seeing that, since, while, whereas, although.
Cūmānus, a, um, belonging to Cumæ.
Cŭmŭlātus, a, um, loaded with; the highest degree of perfection.
Cunctor, ātus, āri, *dep.* to loiter; to delay; to hesitate.
Cunctus, a, um, all, whole.
Cŭneus, i, *m*, a wedge; a body of soldiers in the form of a wedge.
Cŭpĭde, *adv. com.* ius, *sup.* ĭssime, eagerly, fondly.
Cŭpĭdĭtas, ātis, *f.* desire; covetousness.
Cŭpĭdus, a, um, desirous; covetous.
Cŭpio, īvi, ītum, ĕre, *a.* to desire; to covet.
Cūr, *adv.* why? wherefore? because.
Cūra, æ, *f.* care.
Cūrātio, ōnis, *f.* a taking care of anything; a guardianship; a cure.
Cūrātor, ōris, *m.* an overseer.
Cūria, æ, *f.* the senate-house.
Curio, ōnis, a Roman family name.
Cūriōsus, a, um, careful; curious.
Cūrius, i, a Roman family name.
Cūro, āre, *a.* to take care of; to care about; to cause; to cure.
Curro, cŭcurri, cursum, currĕre, *n.* to run.

Currus, ûs, m. a car.
Cursus, ûs, m. a running; a race; a voyage.
Curtius, i, a Roman family name.
Custōdia, æ, f. a keeping; a charge; custody.
Custos, ōdis, c. a guardian or guard; a watch.
Cyclōpes, um, giants living in Sicily.
Cyrsilus, i, name of an Athenian.

D

Damnum, i, n. loss, damage.
Darīus, i, king of Persia.
Dē, prep. of, concerning.
Dealbo, āre, a. to whitewash.
Dēbeo, ēre, a. to owe; to be obliged; debet, imp. it ought.
Dēbĭlĭto, āre, a. to weaken; to discourage.
Dēbĭtum, i, n. a debt.
Dēcēdo, ssi, ssum, dĕre, n. to depart; to forego.
Dĕcem, adj. indecl. ten.
Dĕcemprīmi, ōrum, m. the ten chief men.
Dĕcemvir, i, m. a decemvir.
Dēcerno, crēvi, crētum, cernĕre, a. to think; to decree; n. to fight.
Dēcerto, āre, n. to contend vehemently; to fight.
Dēcessus, ûs, m. a departure; death.
Dĕcet, uit, ēre, imp. it becomes.
Dĕcĭmus, a, um, the tenth.
Dĕcius, i, a Roman family name.
Declāmātio, ōnis, f. a declaiming.
Declāmātor, ōris, m. a declaimer.
Dēclāmo, āre, n. to cry aloud; to declaim; to inveigh.
Declāro, āre, a. to make evident; to declare.
Dĕcŏro, āre, a. to adorn; to praise.
Decrētum, i, n. a decree.
Dĕcŭmānus, a, um, relating to the tenth; [porta] the principal gate of a Roman camp.
Dĕcŭrio, ōnis, a senator in any town out of Rome; decuriones, the senators, senate.
Dēcurro, curri et cŭcurri, cursum, currĕre, n. to run down; to have recourse to; a. to run through.
Dĕcus, ŏris, n. an ornament; an honour.
Dēdĕcet, imp. it is unbecoming.
Dēdĕcus, ŏris, n. what is unbecoming; disgrace.
Dēdĭco, āre, a. to dedicate.
Dēdisco, didĭci, discĕre, a. to unlearn; to forget.
Dēdo, dĭdi, dĭtum, dĕre, a. to surrender, to submit.
Dēdūco, xi, ctum, cĕre, a. to bring down; to lead.
Dēfătīgo, āre, a. to fatigue.
Dēfendo, di, sum, dĕre, a. to avert; to defend; to maintain.
Dēfensor, ōris, m. an averter; a defender.
Dēfĕro, tŭli, lātum, ferre, a. irr. to bring or carry; to give; to report; to inform against; to defer.
Dēfĭcio, ēci, ectum, ĭcĕre, a. et n. to fail; to be discouraged; to revolt.
Dēfīnio, īre, a. to limit; to prescribe; to define; to end.
Dēfīnītio, ōnis, f. a limiting; a prescribing, a defining.
Dēfŭgio, fūgi, fŭgĭtum, fŭgĕre, a. to flee; to avoid.
Dĕhortor, ātus, āri, dep. to discourage, to dissuade.
Dĕinceps, adv. successively; henceforth.
Dĕinde, adv. then, after that.
Dējĭcio, ēci, ectum, ĭcĕre, a. to throw down; to degrade; to remove.
Dēlectātio, ōnis, f. a delighting; pleasure.
Dēlecto, āre, a. to allure; to delight; delectat, imp. it delights.
Dēleo, ēvi, ētum, ēre, a. to blot out; to destroy utterly.
Dēlībĕrātio, ōnis, f. a deliberating.
Dēlībĕro, āre, a. to deliberate; to consult.
Dēlĭcātus, a, um, that serves for pleasure; luxurious; over-nice.
Dēlĭciæ, ārum, f. delight; a darling; sport.

Dēlĭgo, ēgi, ectum, igĕre, *a.* to choose, to pick out.
Dēlīnio *or* dēlēnio, īre, *a.* to soothe; to charm.
Dēlīro, āre, *n.* to be crazy.
Dēlīrus, a, um, crazed.
Delphi, ōrum, chief town of Phocis, famous for its oracle.
Dēmētrius, i, a philosopher.
Dēmigro, āre, *n.* to remove.
Dēmitto, īsi, issum, ittĕre, *a.* to send down; to cause to go.
Dēmocrĭtus, i, the philosopher of Abdēra.
Dēmōlior, ītus, īri, *dep.* to demolish.
Dēmonstro, āre, *a.* to point out; to name; to prove; to represent.
Dēmortuus, a, um, dead.
Dēmosthĕnes, is, the Athenian orator.
Dēmum, *adv.* at length, at last.
Dēnĕgo, āre, *a.* to deny; to refuse.
Dēnĭque, *adv.* at last, finally.
Densus, a, um, dense, thick, concise.
Dēnuncio, āre, *a.* to announce; to denounce.
Dēpĕcūlor, ātus, āri, *dep.* to rob.
Dēpello, ŭli, ulsum, ellĕre, *a.* to drive away.
Dēperdo, dĭdi, dĭtum, dĕre, *a.* to lose.
Dēplōro, āre, *n.* to weep; *a.* to bewail.
Dēpōno, ŏsui, ŏsĭtum, ōnĕre, *a.* to lay down; to lay aside.
Dēpŏpŭlor, ātus, āri, *dep.* to lay waste; to pillage.
Dēprāvo, āre, *a.* to pervert; to make worse.
Dēprĕcātor, ōris, *m.* an intercessor.
Dēprĕcor, ātus, āri, *dep.* to pray earnestly for; to deprecate.
Dēpugno, āre, *n.* to fight eagerly; to contend.
Dērĭpio, ipui, eptum, ipĕre, *a.* to tear away; to diminish.
Dērŏgo, āre, *a.* to repeal; to take away.
Descrībo, psi, ptum, bĕre, *a.* to write over; to describe, designate; to distribute.
Dēsĕro, ui, tum, ĕre, *a.* to leave, forsake.
Dēsĭdĕrium, i, *n.* regret for a thing lost; longing.
Dēsīdĕro, āre, *a.* to desire or regret a thing lost; to long for; to need; to miss.
Dēsĭdia, æ, *f.* idleness.
Dēsīdo, sēdi, —, sīdĕre, *n.* to sink down.
Dēsĭno, īvi *or* ii, ĭtum, inĕre, *n.* to leave off; *a.* to omit.
Dēsisto, stĭti, stĭtum, istĕre, *n.* to desist from; to cease.
Despēro, āre, *a. et n.* to despair.
Despĭcio, exi, ectum, icĕre, *a.* to look down upon, to despise.
Destĭno, āre, *a.* to fasten; to appoint; to determine.
Destĭtuo, ui, ūtum, uĕre, *a.* to forsake; to give up; to leave off.
Destringo, inxi, ctum, ingĕre, *a.* to draw, to unsheathe.
Dēsum, fui, esse, *n. irr.* to be wanting; to be absent; to fail in one's part.
Dētermĭno, āre, *a.* to finish; to bound.
Dēterreo, ēre, *a.* to frighten from; to deter.
Dētĭneo, inui, entum, inēre, *a.* to keep back.
Detrăho, xi, ctum, hĕre, *a.* to draw down; to take from; to detract.
Detrūdo, si, sum, dĕre, *a.* to thrust down; to dispossess; to compel.
Deus, i, *m.* God; a deity; *pl. nom. et voc.* dii, *dat. et abl.* diis.
Dēvincio, xi, ctum, cīre, *a.* to bind; to oblige; to entangle.
Dēvinco, īci, ictum, incĕre, *a.* to vanquish completely.
Dexter, ĕra, ĕrum *or* ra, rum, right, on the right hand; lucky.
Dextra, æ, *f. sc.* manus, the right hand.
Diălectĭcus, a, um, dialectical; *s.* a dialectician.
Dĭcæarchus, i, a pupil of Aristotle.
Dīco, xi, ctum, cĕre, *a.* to say; to plead; to name; to appoint.
Dictĭto, āre, *a.* to say frequently; to give out.
Dictum, i, *n.* a saying; a proverb.
Dies, ēi, *m. or f.*, *pl. m.* a day; time.

Di*ffĕro*, stŭli, lātum, fferre, *a. irr.* to scatter; to differ; to delay.
Diffĭcĭle, *adv.* hardly, with difficulty.
Diffĭcĭl*is*, is, e, difficult; morose.
Diffĭcult*as*, ātis, *f.* difficulty.
Diffī*do*, sus, dĕre, *n. p.* to distrust; to despair of.
Dignĭt*as*, ātis, *f.* dignity.
Dign*us*, a, um, worthy, deserving of.
Dījūdĭc*o*, āre, *a.* to judge; to determine.
Dīlănio, āre, *a.* to tear in pieces.
Dīlĭge*ns*, ns, ns, ntis, fond, diligent, careful.
Dīlĭgenter, *adv.* diligently, carefully; *comp.* diligentius; *sup.* diligentissime.
Dīlĭgenti*a*, æ, *f.* diligence; attention.
Dīl*igo*, exi, ectum, igĕre, *a.* to love, to esteem highly.
Dīmĭc*o*, āvi, ātum, āre, *n.* to fight, to contend.
Dīmi*tto*, si, ssum, ttĕre, *a.* to send away; to dismiss; to give up; to give way; to omit.
Diŏnȳsĭ*us*, i, a philosopher; also the tyrant of Syracuse.
Dīr*ĭmo*, ēmi, emptum, imĕre, *a.* to separate; to break off; to decide.
Dīr*uo*, ui, ŭtum, uĕre, *a.* to pull down; to destroy.
Di*s*, tis, rich.
Discē*do*, ssi, ssum, dĕre, *n.* to go away, depart.
Discept*o*, āre, *a.* to decide; to debate.
Dis*cerno*, crēvi, crētum, cernĕre, *a.* to separate; to discern; to determine.
Discessi*o*, ōnis, *f.* a separation; a voting.
Discess*us*, ûs, *m.* a separation; a departure.
Discĭplīn*a*, æ, *f.* instruction; discipline; method.
Discĭpŭl*us*, i, *m.* a scholar.
Disco, dĭdĭci, —, discĕre, *a.* to learn.
Discrīm*en*, ĭnis, *n.* a difference; a contest.
Disper*go*, si, sum, gĕre, *a.* to disperse, scatter.
Displĭc*eo*, ēre, *n.* to displease.
Disp*ōno*, ŏsui, ŏsĭtum, ōnĕre, *a.* to arrange; to appoint; to distribute.
Dispŭtāti*o*, ōnis, *f.* a disputation.
Dispŭtāt*or*, ōris, *m.* a disputant.
Dispŭt*o*, āre, *a.* to reason; to dispute.
Dissensi*o*, ōnis, *f.* difference, disagreement; dissension.
Dissen*tio*, si, sum, tīre, *n.* to differ in opinion, to dissent.
Dissĕr*o*, ui, tum, ĕre, *n.* to set asunder; to discuss.
Diss*ĭdeo*, ēdi, —, idēre, *n.* to be at variance; to differ.
Dissĭpāt*us*, a, um, scattered.
Dissĭp*o*, āre, *a.* to put asunder, scatter; to destroy; to rout; to publish.
Dissol*vo*, vi, ūtum, vĕre, *a.* to dissolve; to destroy; to pay; to rid.
Distincti*o*, ōnis, *f.* a distinction; an ornament.
Dist*ĭneo*, inui, entum, inēre, *a.* to keep back; to keep asunder; to divide.
Distin*guo*, xi, ctum, guĕre, *a.* to distinguish; to adorn.
Distră*ho*, xi, ctum, hĕre, *a.* to draw asunder; to separate, to divide.
Distrĭbu*o*, ui, ūtum, ĕre, *a.* to distribute.
Distr*ingo*, nxi, ctum, ngĕre, *a.* to pull asunder; to strip.
Dĭti*o*, ōnis, *f.* dominion; authority.
Diu, *adv.*, *comp.* diutius, *sup.* diutissĭme, long, a long time.
Diūturn*us*, a, um, long, lasting.
Dīv*ello*, elli, ulsum, ellĕre, *a.* to tear asunder; to separate; to break off.
Dīvers*us*, a, um, *a.* turned aside; different.
Dīv*es*, ĭtis, rich.
Divic*o*, ōnis, a chief of the Ædui.
Dīv*ĭdo*, īsi, īsum, ĭdĕre, *a.* to divide, distribute.
Dīvīnāti*o*, ōnis, *f.* foretelling future events, divination.
Dīvīn*us*, a, um, divine, heavenly.
Dīvīsi*o*, ōnis, *f.* a division.

Divitiăcus, i, an Æduan.
Dīvĭtiae, ārum, *f.* riches.
Do, dĕdi, dătum, dăre, *a.* to give; to grant.
Dŏceo, ui, tum, ēre, *a.* to teach.
Dŏcĭlis, is, e, apt to learn, docile.
Doctor, ōris, *m.* a teacher, an instructor.
Doctrīna, æ, *f.* learning, doctrine.
Doctus, a, um, learned; skilful.
Dolabella, æ, surname of a family of the Cornelia gens; Cicero's son-in-law.
Dŏleo, ui, ĭtum, ēre, *n.* to be in pain; *a.* to grieve.
Dŏlor, ōris, *m.* grief; pain.
Dŏlus, i, *m.* deceit; stratagem.
Dŏmestĭcus, a, um, domestic.
Dŏmĭnātrix, icis, *f.* a female ruler.
Dŏmĭnor, ātus, āri, *dep.* to be lord; to domineer.
Dŏmĭnus, i, *m.* a master; a lord.
Dŏmĭtius, i, a Roman consul.
Dŏmus, ûs, and i, *f.* a house; home.
Dōnĕc, *adv.* until.
Dōno, āre, *a.* to give freely; to present.
Dŭbĭtātio, ōnis, *f.* doubt.
Dŭbĭto, āre, *n.* to doubt; to hesitate.
Dŭbius, a, um, doubtful, uncertain.
Dūco, xi, ctum, cĕre, *a.* to lead; to draw; to think.
Dulcis, is, e, sweet.
Dum, *adv.* while, whilst; until.
Dumnŏrix, ĭgis, a chief among the Ædui.
Dumtaxat *or* duntaxat, *adv.* only; at least.
Duo, æ, o, two.
Duŏdĕcim, *pl. indec.* twelve.
Dux, dŭcis, *c.* a leader; a general.

E

Ē *or* ex, *prep.* of, out of, from.
Eātĕnus, *adv.* so far.
Ēbutius *or* Æbutius, a, um, a Roman family name; a tribune, author of the lex Ebutia.
Ecqui, *adv.* = num, whether?
Ecquis, quæ *or* qua, quod *or* quid, whether any?
Ecquisnam, quænam, quodnam *or* quidnam, whether any?
Ēdīco, xi, ctum, cĕre, *a.* to make known; to order; to appoint.
Ēdīctum, i, *n.* an edict, a proclamation.
Ēdisco, edĭdĭci, —, ediscĕre, *a.* to learn by heart.
Ēdūco, xi, ctum, cĕre, *a.* to lead forth; to draw out; to bring up.
Edŭco, āre, *a.* to bring up; to nurture.
Effĕro, extŭli, elātum, efferre, *a.* to carry out; to extol; to endure.
Effĭcio, ēci, ectum, icĕre, *a.* to finish; to cause; to effect; bring about; to prove.
Efflāgĭto, āre, *a.* to demand earnestly.
Effluo, xi, xum, ĕre, *n.* to flow out; to fail or pass away quickly.
Effŭgio, ūgi, ĭtum, ugĕre, *a.* to flee from; to elude.
Effūsio, ōnis, *f.* a pouring forth.
Ēgeo, ui, —, ēre, *n.* to want; to be needy.
Ĕgo, mei, *m. or f. pron.* I.
Ĕgŏmet, meimet, *pron.* I myself.
Egrĕdior, ssus, di, *dep.* to go out.
Ejusmŏdi, of that sort.
Ēlābor, psus, bi, *dep.* to slip away; to escape.
Ēlăbōro, āre, *a.* to bestow pains on; *n.* to endeavour.
Ēleātes, æ, belonging to Elea.
Ēlĕgans, ns, ns, ntis, elegant; handsome.
Ēlĕgantia, æ, *f.* elegance; politeness.
Ēlēus, a, um, belonging to Elis.
Ēlĭcio, ui, ĭtum, ĕre, *a.* to draw out; to allure.
Ēlīdo, si, sum, dĕre, *a.* to strike out; to dash to pieces; to weaken.
Ēlĭgo, ēgi, ectum, igĕre, *a.* to choose.
Ēlŏgium, i, *n.* any short writing, an inscription; a clause in a will.
Ēlŏquentia, æ, *f.* eloquence.
Ēlŏquor, cutus, qui, *dep.* to speak out; to say.
Ēluceo, xi, —, cēre, *n.* to shine forth; to be conspicuous.

Ēlūdo, si, sum, dĕre, *n.* to play; *a.* to parry; to mock.
Ēmitto, īsi, issum, ittĕre, *a.* to send out; to throw away; to let go; to die.
Ĕmo, ēmi, emptum, emĕre, *a.* to take; to buy.
Ēmŏlŭmentum, i, *n.* profit; advantage.
Ēmŏrior, tuus, i, *dep.* to die.
Emptor, ōris, *m.* a buyer.
Ēn, *interj.* lo, behold.
Ĕnim, *conj.* for, indeed.
Ēnitor, nisus, niti, *dep.* to endeavour; to strive.
Ennius, i, a Roman poet.
Ēnŭmĕro, āre, *a.* to reckon up; to recount.
Ēnuncio *or* ēnuntio, āre, *a.* to declare; to spread abroad.
Eo, īvi, ītum, īre, *n. irreg.* to go.
Eo, *adv.* thither, to that extent; so far; for that reason; there; *with a comp.*, by so much.
Ĕpaminondas, æ, a Theban, famous as a general.
Ĕpīcūrus, i, a Greek philosopher.
Epīrus, i, the kingdom of Pyrrhus, in Greece.
Ĕpistŏla, æ, *f.* a letter, an epistle.
Ĕpŏrēdŏrix, īgis, an Æduan chief.
Ĕques, ītis, *m.* a horseman; a knight.
Ĕquus, i, *m.* a horse.
Ĕquester *or* ris, ris, re, pertaining to horse, or cavalry; equestrian.
Ĕquīdem, *adv.* indeed.
Ĕquītātus, ûs, *m.* cavalry; the equestrian rank.
Ērectus, a, um, erect; encouraged; elevated.
Erga, *prep.* towards.
Ergŏ, *conj.* therefore, then; ergō, *adv.* for the sake of.
Ērīgo, exi, ectum, igĕre, *a.* to raise up; to build; to encourage.
Ērīpio, ipui, eptum, ipĕre, *a.* to take away by force; to rescue; to induce, extort by entreaties.
Erro, āre, *n.* to wander; to mistake.
Error, ōris, *m.* a wandering; a mistake; error.
Ērŭbesco, bui, —, bescĕre, *n.* to blush; to be ashamed.
Ērŭdio, īre, *a.* to teach, instruct.
Ērŭdītus, a, um, learned; skilful.
Ēruptio, ōnis, *f.* a bursting forth; an assault.
Escendo, di, sum, dĕre, *n.* to ascend.
Et, *conj.* and; et...et, both...and.
Ĕtĕnim, *conj.* for; because that; truly.
Ĕteocles, is, son of Œdipus.
Ĕtiam, *conj.* also; even.
Ĕtiamsi, *conj.* even if; although.
Etsi, *conj.* although.
Eurīpīdes, is, an Athenian tragic poet.
Eurystheus, ĕi *et* ĕos, king of Mycene.
Ēvādo, si, sum, dĕre, *n.* to go out; to escape; to become.
Ēvānesco, ui, itum, escĕre, *n.* to vanish; to become vapid.
Ēvello, elli, ulsum, ellĕre, *a.* to tear out; to remove.
Ēvĕnio, ēni, entum, enīre, *n.* to come out; to happen; evenit, *imp.* it happens.
Ēventum, i, *n.* an event.
Ēverto, ti, sum, tĕre, *a.* to overturn; to destroy.
Ēvŏco, āre, *a.* to call out; to invite.
Ex, *prep.* of, out of, from.
Exædĭfĭco, āre, *a.* to build; to finish.
Exăgĭto, āre, *a.* to drive out; to harass; to agitate; to excite.
Exănĭmo, āre, *a.* to exhaust; to astonish; to frighten to death.
Exăro, āre, *a.* to plough; to write hastily.
Excæco, āre, *a.* to make blind.
Excēdo, ssi, ssum, dĕre, *n.* to go out; to depart; to exceed.
Excello, ui, —, ĕre, *n.* to excel; to be eminent.
Excerpo, si, tum, ĕre, *a.* to pick out; to separate.
Excĭpio, ēpi, eptum, ipĕre, *a.* to take; to receive; to entertain; to except; to attack by surprise; to follow.
Excĭto, āre, *a.* to stir up; to excite.
Exclāmo, āre, *n.* to cry out, to say with a loud voice.

Exclūdo, si, sum, dĕre, *a.* to shut out; to reject.
Excors, s, s, dis, without understanding; foolish.
Excūsātio, ōnis, *f.* an excuse; a defence.
Excūso, āre, *a.* to excuse; to allege as an excuse.
Exemplar, āris, *n.* a copy; an example.
Exemplum, i, *n.* an example; a copy.
Exeo, ii, ĭtum, īre, *n. irr.* to go out; to be divulged; to die; to end.
Exerceo, ēre, *a.* to exercise; to follow an occupation.
Exercĭtātio, ōnis, *f.* exercise, practice, custom.
Exercĭtus, ûs, *m.* an army.
Exhærēdo, āre, *a.* to disinherit.
Exhorresco, ui, —, escĕre, *n.* to shudder; to be frightened.
Exhortor, ātus, āri, to exhort.
Exĭgo, ēgi, actum, igĕre, *a.* to drive out; to pass over; to demand; to examine.
Existĭmātor, ōris, *m.* one who gives his opinion, a valuator.
Existĭmo, āre, *a.* to think; to determine; to esteem.
Exĭtium, i, *n.* an end; destruction.
Exĭtus, ûs, *m.* a going out; an end; an event; death.
Exopto, āre, *a.* to wish for.
Exordior, sus, dīri, *dep.* to begin.
Exōro, āre, *a.* to entreat; to obtain by entreaty.
Expecto, āre, *a.* to look or wait for.
Expĕdit, *imp.* it is expedient.
Expĕdītus, a, um, disengaged; free; ready; light.
Expello, ŭli, ulsum, ellĕre, *a.* to drive out, to expel.
Expergiscor, rectus, gisci, *dep.* to awaken.
Expĕrior, tus, īri, *dep.* to try; to prove; to experience.
Expers, s, s, tis, having no part in; free from.
Expĕto, ivi, ītum, ĕre, to desire greatly; to covet.
Explānātio, onis, *f.* an explanation.
Expleo, ēvi, ētum, ēre, *a.* to fill up; to complete.
Explĭcātio, ōnis, *f.* an unfolding; an explication; a paying.
Explĭco, ui, ĭtum, āre, *a.* to unfold; āvi, ātum, tc explain.
Explōdo, si, sum, dĕre, *a.* to hiss off; to drive out; to reject.
Explōrātor, ōris, *m.* an examiner; a spy.
Explōro, āre, *a.* to search out; to examine diligently; to explore.
Expōno, ŏsui, ŏsĭtum, ōnĕre, *a.* to put out; to expose; to explain; to mention.
Exportātio, ōnis, *f.* an exportation.
Expostŭlo, āre, *a.* to demand; to complain.
Expugno, āre, *a.* to take by storm; to vanquish.
Exquīro, sīvi, sītum, rĕre, *a.* to inquire; to investigate; to demand; to seek out.
Exquīsītus, a, um, select; exquisite; far-fetched.
Exscindo, ĭdi, issum, indĕre, *a.* to cut off; to destroy.
Exspŏlio, āre, *a.* to rob; to spoil.
Externus, a, um, outward, foreign, alien.
Exterreo, ui, ĭtum, ēre, *a.* to frighten, terrify.
Extĭmesco, ui, —, escĕre, *n.* to be greatly afraid of.
Extinguo, xi, ctum, guĕre, *a.* to extinguish; to suppress; to kill.
Extorqueo, si, tum, quēre, *a.* to force away; to extort.
Extra, *prep.* without; beyond.
Extrēmus *or* extĭmus, a, um, outermost; last; extremum, extremity.
Exul *or* exsul, ŭlis, *c.* an exile.
Exūro, ussi, ustum, urĕre, *a.* to consume by burning; to consume.

F

Fābella, æ, *f.* a brief narrative; a play.
Fabrĭcius, i, a Roman family name.
Fābŭla, æ, *f.* a narration; a story.

Făcĭlè, *adv.*, *comp.* facilius, *sup.* facillime, easily, readily.
Făcĭl*is*, is, e, easy, gentle.
Făcĭlĭt*as*, ātis, *f.* facility; courteousness.
Făcĭn*us*, ŏris, *n.* a deed; wickedness.
Făcio, fēci, factum, facĕre, *a.* to do; to make; to cause.
Factiōs*us*, a, um, factious, seditious.
Fact*um*, i, *n.* a deed or action.
Făcult*as*, ātis, *f.* ability; power; occasion; a faculty of the mind.
Fallāci*a*, æ, *f.* an artifice.
Fallo, fĕfelli, falsum, fallĕre, *a.* to deceive; to disappoint.
Fals*us*, a, um, false; mistaken.
Fām*a*, æ, *f.* report, fame.
Făm*es*, is, *f.* hunger; famine.
Fămĭli*a*, æ, *f.* the slaves of one master; a family.
Fămĭliār*is*, is, e, of the same family; familiar.
Fămĭliārĭt*as*, ātis, *f.* intimacy, familiarity.
Fămĭliārĭter, *adv.* familiarly, intimately.
Fanni*us*, i, a Roman family name.
Fān*um*, i, *n.* a temple.
Fas, *n.* *indec.* right; possibility.
Fascĭcŭl*us*, i, *m.* a parcel.
Fastīdi*um*, i, haughtiness; loathing.
Fast*us*, a, um, *used only with* dies, a court day.
Fast*us*, ûs, *m.* haughtiness.
Făt*eor*, ssus, tēri, *dep.* to confess, to acknowledge.
Fāt*um*, i, *n.* fate; an accident.
Făveo, fāvi, fautum, favēre, *n.* to favour.
Febr*is*, is, *f.* a fever.
Fēlīcĭt*as*, ātis, *f.* happiness, felicity.
Fēl*ix*, ix, ix, īcis, happy; fortunate.
Fĕr*a*, æ, *f.* a wild beast.
Fĕrè, *adv.* almost; generally.
Fĕr*io*, —, —, ire, *a.* to strike; to kill.
Fĕro, tŭli, lātum, ferre, *a. irr.* to bear; to carry; to endure; to tell; to vote; to praise; to make.
Ferr*um*, i, *n.* iron; a sword.
Fĕr*us*, a, um, wild; cruel.
Festīn*o*, āre, *n.* to hasten.
Fest*us*, a, um, festive; solemn.
Fict*us*, a, um, feigned, false, fictitious.
Fīdēl*is*, is, e, faithful; trusty.
Fidenter, *adv.* confidently.
Fĭd*es*, ĕi, *f.* faith; credit; a promise.
Fīdūci*a*, æ, *f.* trust; confidence.
Fĭgūr*a*, æ, *f.* a figure, an image.
Fīli*a*, æ, *f.* a daughter.
Fīli*us*, i, *m.* a son.
Fi*ngo*, nxi, ctum, ngĕre, *a.* to form; to fashion; to feign.
Fīn*is*, is, *m.* or *f.* the end; *plur.* *m.* territory.
Fīnĭtĭm*us*, a, um, bordering upon; neighbouring.
Fīo, factus, fĭĕri, to be made; to become; to happen.
Firmĭt*as*, ātis, *f.* firmness; strength.
Firm*us*, a, um, firm; strong.
Flacc*us*, i, a Roman family name.
Flāgĭtiōse, *adv.* basely.
Flāgĭti*um*, i, *n.* a flagrant crime; infamy.
Flāgĭt*o*, āre, *a.* to ask with importunity; to demand; to accuse.
Flāmĭni*us*, ii, a Roman family name.
Flamm*a*, æ, *f.* a flame.
Fle*cto*, xi, xum, ctĕre, *a.* to bend; to turn; to persuade.
Fleo, flēvi, flētum, flēre, *n.* to weep.
Flēt*us*, ûs, *m.* a weeping.
Fluct*us*, ûs, *m.* a wave; a commotion.
Flūm*en*, ĭnis, *n.* a river.
Flu*o*, xi, xum, ĕre, *n.* to flow.
Fœdĕrāt*us*, a, um, confederate.
Fœd*us*, ĕris, *n.* a treaty.
Fon*s*, tis, *m.* a fountain.
For [not used], fatus, fāri, *dep.* to say.
Fŏrem, fŏre, *def.* I might, or should be.
Fŏrens*is*, is, e, pertaining to the forum, forensic.
Form*a*, æ, *f.* a form; beauty.
Formiān*us*, a, um, belonging to Formiæ; Formiān*um*, i, Cicero's villa, where he was assassinated.

Formōs*us*, a, um, beautiful in form, handsome.
Fortasse, *adv.* perhaps.
Fortè, *adv.* by chance; perhaps.
Fort*is*, is, e, brave.
Fortĭter, *adv.* bravely.
Fortĭtūd*o*, ĭnis, *f.* bravery; fortitude.
Fortuĭto, *adv.* by chance, accidentally.
Fortuĭt*us*, a, um, accidental.
Fortūn*a*, æ, *f.* fortune.
Fŏr*um*, i, *n.* a market-place; a public court; an assize.
Foss*a*, æ, *f.* a ditch.
Fr*ango*, ēgi, actum, angĕre, *a.* to break; to subdue.
Frāt*er*, ris, *m.* a brother.
Frātern*us*, a, um, fraternal.
Frātrĭcīd*a*, æ, *m.* or *f.* a murderer of a brother; a fratricide.
Fra*us*, dis, *f.* fraud, deceit.
Fremit*us*, ûs, *m.* any kind of noise, murmuring, roaring, etc.
Frĕque*ns*, ns, ns, ntis, crowded; frequent.
Frĕquenter, *adv.* frequently.
Frĕquenti*a*, æ, *f.* a frequency; a great company.
Frēt*us*, a, um, trusting to.
Fructuōs*us*, a, um, fruitful.
Fruct*us*, ûs, *m.* fruit.
Frūgālĭt*as*, ātis, *f.* frugality; moderation.
Frūmentāri*us*, a, um, belonging to corn.
Frūment*um*, i, *n.* corn.
Fru*or*, ĭtus *or* ctus, i, *dep.* to enjoy.
Frustra, *adv.* in vain.
Frux [not used], frugis, *f.* corn.
Fŭg*a*, æ, *f.* a fleeing; flight.
Fŭgio, fūgi, fŭgĭtum, fugĕre, *a.* and *n.* to flee; to escape.
Ful*geo*, si, —, gēre, *n.* to shine, to be bright.
Fundāment*um*, i, *n.* a foundation.
Fundo, fūdi, fūsum, fundĕre, *a.* to pour out; to rout.
Fun*gor*, ctus, gi, *dep.* to discharge a duty.
Fūn*us*, ĕris, *n.* a corpse; funeral.
Fŭriōse, *adv.* furiously.
Fŭriōs*us*, a, um, furious.
Furi*us*, i, a Roman consul.
Fŭr*o*, —, —, ĕre, to rage.
Fŭr*or*, ōris, *m.* fury, rage, passion.
Fŭtūr*us*, a, um, future.

G

Găbīni*us*, i, a Roman family name.
Galb*a*, æ, surname of the Sulpician family.
Galli*a*, æ, *f.* Gaul.
Gallīn*a*, æ, *f.* a hen.
Gall*us*, i, *m.* a Gaul.
Gănȳmēd*es*, is, a son of Tros.
Garrio, īre, *a.* to prattle.
Gaudeo, gavīsus, gaudēre, *n. p.* to be glad.
Gaudi*um*, i, *n.* gladness.
Gĕlĭd*us*, a, um, cold as ice.
Gemm*a*, æ, *f.* a gem.
Gĕmĭt*us*, ûs, *m.* a sighing, a groan.
Gĕm*o*, ui, itum, ĕre, *n.* to sigh.
Gĕn*er*, ĕri, *m.* a son-in-law.
Gĕnĕrōs*us*, a, um, of noble birth; generous; brave.
Gĕnēv*a*, æ, *f.* a town of the Allobroges.
Gen*s*, tis, *f.* a nation; a clan.
Gĕn*us*, ĕris, *n.* a race; descent; a kind.
Geōmetr*a*, æ, *m.* geometrician.
Geōmetrī*a*, æ, *f.* geometry.
Gergŏvi*a*, æ, a town of Aquitania.
Germān*us*, a, um, belonging to Germany.
Gĕr*o*, ssi, stum, rĕre, *a.* to carry; to wear; to conduct; to do.
Gest*io*, īre, *n.* to exult; to rejoice at.
Gigno, genui, genĭtum, gignĕre, *a.* to beget; to cause.
Glădi*us*, i, *m.* a sword.
Glauci*a*, æ, a surname of the Servilian family.
Glōri*a*, æ, *f.* glory; renown.
Glōri*or*, ātus, āri, *dep.* to glory; to boast.
Glōriōsè, *adv.* vain-gloriously; boastfully.
Glōriōs*us*, a, um, boastful; renowned.
Gorgi*as*, æ, a rhetorician of Sicily.
Gracch*us*, i, a Roman family name.
Græcè, *adv.* in Greek.

Græcia, æ, *f*. Greece.
Græcus, a, um, belonging to Greece; Greek.
Grandis, is, e, large; grand.
Grando, ĭnis, *f*. hail.
Grāte, *adv*. with pleasure; gratefully.
Grātia, æ, *f*. favour; *pl*. thanks.
Gratĭdiānus, a, um, belonging to the Gratidian family.
Grātĭfĭcor, ātus, āri, *dep*. to gratify; to oblige.
Grātiōsus, a, um, agreeable; in favour, beloved; showing favour, obliging.
Grātus, a, um, grateful; pleasant.
Grātŭlor, ātus, āri, *dep*. to congratulate; to rejoice.
Grăvis, is, e, heavy; grievous; dignified.
Grăvĭtas, ātis, *f*. heaviness; gravity; dignity; authority.
Grăvĭter, *adv*., *comp*. gravius, heavily; grievously.
Gravor, ātus, āri, *dep*. to hesitate; to make difficulties about.
Gŭbernātio, ōnis, *f*. the act of steering; guiding.
Gŭbernātor, ōris, *m*. a pilot; a governor.
Gŭberno, āre, *a*. to govern.
Gustātus, ûs, *m*. a tasting; flavour.
Gusto, āre, *a*. to taste; to understand.
Gymnăsium, i, *n*. a place of exercise; a school.

H

Hăbeo, ēre, *a*. to have; to suppose; to reckon; to esteem.
Hăbĭlis, is, e, fit, able.
Hăbĭtus, ûs, *m*. a habit; a manner.
Hæreo, hæsi, hæsum, hærēre, *n*. to adhere, be fixed; to hesitate.
Hæres *or* hēres, ēdis, *c*. an heir or heiress.
Harūdes, um, a people of Germany.
Haud, *adv*. not.
Haurio, hausi, haustum, haurīre, *a*. to draw; to swallow; to get.
Hĕbesco, —, —, ĕre, *n*. to grow blunt, dull.
Helvētii, ōrum, Helvetians.
Helvētius, a, um, Helvetian.
Hērăclēus, a, um, belonging to Hercules; Herăclēa [urbs] æ, name of several cities in honour of Hercules.
Hercŭle, by Hercules.
Hercŭles, is, *m*. Hercules.
Hesternus, a, um, of yesterday.
Heus, *interj*. ho!
Hībernus, a, um, relating to winter, wintry; hiberna [castra], winter quarters.
Hīc, hæc, hoc, *pron*. this.
Hīc *vel* hĭc, *adv*. here; hereupon.
Hiems, ĕmis, *f*. winter; a tempest.
Hĭlăris, is, e *or* us, a, um, cheerful, gay.
Hinc, *adv*. hence, from this place; henceforth.
Hippias, æ, the name of a sophist.
Hispānus, a, um, belonging to Spain.
Histŏria, æ, *f*. history.
Histŏrĭcus, i, *m*. a historian.
Hŏdie, *adv*. to-day.
Hŏdiernus, a, um, of to-day.
Hŏmērus, i, the Greek epic poet.
Hŏmo, ĭnis, *m*. a human being, man or woman.
Hŏnestas, ātis, *f*. honesty; dignity.
Hŏneste, *adv*. honourably; honestly.
Hŏnestus, a, um, honourable; honest.
Hŏnor *or* os, ōris, *m*. honour.
Hŏnōrĭfĭcus, a, um, conferring honour; honourable.
Hŏnōro, āre, *a*. to honour.
Hōra, æ, *f*. an hour.
Hordeum, i, barley.
Horreo, ui, —, ēre, *n*. to be terrified; to be astonished; *a*. to be afraid of.
Hortātor, ōris, *m*. an encourager.
Hortensius, i, a Roman family name.
Hortor, ātus, āri, *dep*. to encourage; to advise.
Hortŭlus, i, *m*. a little garden, or country seat.
Hortus, i, *m*. a garden.
Hospes, ĭtis, *c*. a host; a guest.
Hostia, æ, *f*. a victim.

Hostis, is, *c.* an enemy.
Hūc, *adv.* hither.
Hūmānus, a, um, human; humane.
Hŭmĭlis, is, e, low; humble; mean.
Hŭmo, āre, *a.* to bury, inter.
Hyădes, dum, five stars in the head of the Bull.
Hȳperbŏrei, ōrum, a people on the confines of Scythia.

I

Ĭbi, *adv.* there, then.
Ĭbīdem, *adv.* in the same place.
Ictus, ûs, *m.* a blow; incitement.
Ĭdcirco, *adv.* therefore.
Ĭdem, eădem, ĭdem, *pron.* the same.
Ĭdeo, *conj.* therefore.
Ĭdōneus, a, um, fit; deserving.
Īdus, uum, *f.* the Ides; the 15th of March, May, July, and October; the 13th of the other months.
Ĭgĭtur, *conj.* therefore, then.
Ignārus, a, um, ignorant; inexperienced.
Ignāvia, æ, *f.* inactivity; idleness.
Ignis, is, *m.* fire.
Ignōro, āre, *a.* to be ignorant of; to pretend not to know.
Ignosco, ōvi, ōtum, oscĕre, *a. et n.* to pardon.
Ille, a, ud, *pron.* that; he, she, it.
Illĭgo, āre, *a.* to bind; to entangle; to engage.
Illuc, *adv.* thither.
Illūcesco, xi, —, cescĕre, *n.* to become light; to dawn; to appear; illucescit, *imp.* it is growing light.
Illustris, is, e, bright; evident; illustrious.
Illustro, āre, *a.* to make evident; to illustrate; to render famous.
Imbēcillĭtas, ātis, *f.* weakness.
Imbēcillus, a, um, *or is*, is, e, weak.
Imĭtor, ātus, āri, *dep.* to imitate.
Immĭneo, ui, —, ēre, *n.* to overhang; to threaten.
Immĭnuo, ui, ūtum, uĕre, *a.* to lessen; to impair.
Immo *or* imo, *adv.* yes, yea.
Immŏlo, āre, *a.* to offer, to immolate.
Immortālis, is, e, immortal.
Immortālĭtas, ātis, *f.* immortality.
Immortālĭter, *adv.* immortally; infinitely.
Impĕdīmentum, i, *n.* an encumbrance; an impediment; *pl.* the baggage of an army.
Impĕdio, īre, *a.* to entangle; to hinder.
Impello, ŭli, ulsum, ellĕre, *a.* to drive; to impel; to persuade.
Impendeo, di, sum, dēre, *n.* to hang over; to impend.
Impĕrātor, ōris, *m.* a commander; an emperor.
Impĕrītus, a, um, unskilful, ignorant.
Impĕrium, i, *n.* military command; empire.
Impĕro, āre, *n. et a.* to command; to order; to furnish.
Impertio, īre, *a.* to impart; to bestow; — se, to show.
Impetro, āre, *a.* to obtain; to accomplish.
Impĕtus, ûs, *m.* an attack; vehemence.
Implōro, āre, *a.* to implore.
Impōno, ŏsui, ŏsĭtum, ōnĕre, *a.* to place; to put upon; to impose.
Imprīmis *or* in primis, *adv.* in the first place, chiefly.
Imprŏbātio, ōnis, *f.* disapprobation.
Imprŏbe, *adv.* impiously.
Imprŏbĭtas, ātis, *f.* impiety; imprudence.
Imprŏbo, āre, *a.* to disapprove.
Imprŏbus, a, um, wicked.
Imprōvīso, *adv.* unexpectedly.
Impŭdens, ns, ns, ntis, impudent.
Impŭdentia, æ, *f.* impudence.
Impunĭtas, ātis, *f.* impunity.
Impūre, *adv.* impurely; basely.
In, *prep.; when it governs the abl. it signifies* in, among, over; *when the accus.* into, towards, upon, against, etc.
Ĭnānis, is, e, empty; vain.
Incendo, di, sum, dĕre, *a.* to set on fire, to burn; to inflame, incite; to incense.
Incertus, a, um, uncertain; doubtful.

Incĭdo, ĭdi, āsum, idĕre, *n.* to fall into; to meet; to happen.
Incīdo, di, sum, dĕre, *a.* to cut; to engrave.
Incĭpio, ēpi, eptum, ipĕre, *a.* to begin; to attempt.
Incĭto, āre, *a.* to set in motion; to excite; to incense.
Inclīno, āre, *a.* to incline; to dispose towards.
Incognĭtus, a, um, unknown.
Incŏla, æ, *c.* an inhabitant.
Incŏlo, olui, ultum, olĕre, *n.* et *a.* to dwell; to inhabit.
Incŏlŭmĭtas, ātis, *f.* safety.
Incommŏdum, i, *n.* inconvenience.
Incondĭte, *adv.* confusedly.
Inconstans, ns, ns, ntis, inconstant.
Inconstanter, *adv.* inconstantly.
Incrēdĭbĭlis, is, e, incredible.
Incrĕpĭto, āre, *a.* to chide; to blame.
Incurro, curri *or* cŭcurri, cursum, currĕre, *n.* to run against; to attack; to occur; meet with.
Incūso, āre, *a.* to accuse.
Inde, *adv.* thence; ever since.
Indĭcium, i, *n.* a proof; an information.
Indĭco, āre, *a.* to show; to indicate; to give evidence in a court of justice.
Indīco, xi, ctum, cĕre, *a.* to declare; to denounce.
Indignè, *adv.*, *sup.* indignissime, unworthily.
Indignus, a, um, unworthy.
Indĭgus, a, um, needy.
Indoctus, a, um, untaught; ignorant.
Indūco, xi, ctum, cĕre, *a.* to bring in; to introduce; to determine on; to persuade; to think.
Indulgĕo, si, tum, gēre, *a.* to indulge.
Induo, ui, ūtum, ĕre, *a.* to put on; to clothe; to surround.
Industria, æ, *f.* industry.
Ineo, ii, ĭtum, īre, *a. irr.* to go into; to enter upon; to begin.
Ĭneptus, a, um, silly; absurd.
Ĭnermis, is, e *or* us, a, um, unarmed, defenceless.
Ĭners, rs, rs, rtis, inert; unskilled.
Ĭnexercĭtātus, a, um, unexercised; unskilful.
Infăcētus, a, um, unpolished; rude.
Infāmia, æ, *f.* infamy.
Infernus, a, um, lower.
Infĕro, intŭli, illātum, inferre, *a. irr.* to bring into; to attack; to make; to occasion.
Infĕrus, a, um, below, low; *comp.* ior, lower, inferior; *sup.* infimus *or* imus, lowest.
Infĭdus, a, um, unfaithful.
Infīgo, xi, xum, gĕre, *a.* to fix; to infix.
Infīnītus, a, um, infinite; vast.
Infirmus, a, um, infirm; fickle.
Inflammo, āre, *a.* to set on fire; to inflame.
Inflecto, xi, xum, ctĕre, *a.* to bend; to move; to change.
Infringo, ēgi, actum, ingĕre, *a.* to break; to weaken.
Ingĕmisco, ui, —, iscĕre, *n.* to sigh.
Ingĕnium, i, *n.* natural disposition; genius.
Ingĕnue, *adv.* ingeniously.
Ingenuus, a, um, native; ingenuous.
Ingrĕdior, ssus, di, *dep.* to go into; to enter upon; to begin.
Ĭnĭmĭcĭtia, æ, *f.* enmity, hostility.
Ĭnĭmīcus, a, um, unfriendly; hostile.
Ĭnĭmīcus, i, *m.* an enemy.
Ĭnīquus, a, um, unequal; hostile.
Ĭnĭtium, i, *n.* a beginning.
Injūria, æ, *f.* injury; injustice.
Injussu, *m.* (used only in *abl. sing.*) without order.
Injustè, *adv.* unjustly, wrongfully.
Injustĭtia, æ, *f.* injustice.
Injustus, a, um, unjust.
Innītor, sus *or* xus, ti, *dep.* to lean upon; to depend upon.
Innŭmĕrābĭlis, is, e, innumerable.
Ĭnŏpia, æ, *f.* want; indigence.
Inprimis, see Imprimis.
Inquam, is, it, *def.* I say.
Insānia, æ, *f.* insanity.
Insānio, ire, *n.* to be insane; to be foolish.
Insātiābĭlis, is, e, insatiable.
Inscius, a, um, ignorant; unskilful.

Insĕ*quor*, quūtus *or* cūtus, qui, *dep.* to pursue; to persecute.
Insĭdi*ae*, ārum, *f.* an ambush; treachery.
Insignè *et* insignĭter, *adv.* remarkably, excellently.
Insign*is*, is, e, remarkable.
Insimŭl*o*, āre, to feign; to accuse.
Insĭpi*ens*, ns, ns, ntis, foolish.
Insĭpienti*a*, æ, want of wisdom, folly, stupidity.
Insŏle*ns*, ns, ns, ntis, unusual; unaccustomed to; insolent.
Insŏlenti*a*, æ, *f.* want of being accustomed; novelty; insolence.
Inspect*o*, āre, *a.* to look at, behold.
Insp*ĭcio*, exi, ectum, icĕre, *a.* to look into; to view; to understand.
Instĭt*uo*, ui, ūtum, uĕre, *a.* to institute; to erect; to resolve; to educate; to begin.
Instĭtūti*o*, ōnis, *f.* disposition; instruction.
Instĭtūt*um*, i, *n.* a custom, a law.
Instr*uo*, uxi, uctum, uĕre, *a.* to prepare; to draw up in order of battle; to equip; to build.
Instruct*us*, a, um, equipped; instructed.
Insuēt*us*, a, um, unaccustomed; inexperienced.
Insŭl*a*, æ, *f.* an island.
In*sum*, fui, esse, *n. irr.* to be in.
Intĕg*er*, ra, rum, entire; whole; fresh; mihi integrum est, it is in my power.
Intel*lĭgo*, exi, ectum, igĕre, *a.* to understand; to know.
Intempĕranter, *adv.* intemperately.
Inten*do*, di, tum *et* sum, dĕre, *a.* to stretch; to direct.
Inter, *prep.* between, among.
Intercē*do*, ssi, ssum, dĕre, *n.* to go between; to prevent; to come to pass; to be between.
Interclū*do*, si, sum, dĕre, *a.* to hinder; to deprive; to shut in.
Interdīc*o*, xi, ctum, cĕre, *a.* to forbid; to prohibit.
Interdiu, *adv.* in the day time.
Interdum, *adv.* sometimes.
Intĕrea, *adv.* in the meantime.
Intĕr*eo*, ii, ĭtum, īre, *n. irr.* to perish.
Intĕrest, *imp.* it concerns.
Inter*fĭcio*, fēci, fectum, ficĕre, *a.* to kill; to destroy.
Intĕrim, *adv.* in the meantime.
Inter*ĭmo*, ēmi, emptum, imĕre, *a.* to take away; to kill.
Intĕri*or*, or, us, inner, interior.
Intĕrĭt*us*, ūs, *m.* destruction; ruin.
Intermissi*o*, ōnis, *f.* an intermission; a respite.
Interm*itto*, īsi, issum, ittĕre, *a.* to intermit; to omit.
Internĕci*o*, ōnis, *f.* destruction; carnage.
Interpellāt*or*, ōris, *m.* an interrupter.
Interpell*o*, āre, *a.* to interrupt; to disturb.
Interp*ōno*, ŏsui, ŏsĭtum, ōnĕre, *a.* to put in; to interpose.
Interpr*es*, ĕtis, *c.* a mediator; an interpreter.
Inter*sum*, fui, esse, *n. irr.* to be present; to engage in; to be different; to concern.
Intervall*um*, i, *n.* an interval.
Intra, *prep.* within.
Intrōdūc*o*, xi, ctum, cĕre, *a.* to bring into; introduce.
Intu*eor*, ĭtus, ēri, *dep.* to look at; to consider.
Inūsĭtāt*us*, a, um, unusual.
Inūtĭl*is*, is, e, useless.
Inv*ĕho*, exi, ectum, ehĕre, *a.* to import; to inveigh against.
Inv*ĕnio*, ēni, entum, enīre, *a.* to find; to invent.
Inventi*o*, ōnis, *f.* invention.
Invent*or*, ōris, *m.* an inventor.
Investĭgāti*o*, ōnis, *f.* an investigating.
Inv*ĭdeo*, īdi, īsum, idēre, *a. et n.* to envy; to hate.
Invĭdi*a*, æ, *f.* envy; hatred.
Invīt*o*, āre, *a.* to invite.
Invīt*us*, a, um, unwilling.
Invŏc*o*, āre, *a.* to call upon; to implore.
Iphĭgĕnī*a*, æ, a daughter of Agamemnon.
Ips*e*, a, um, *pron.* himself, herself, itself.

Īra, æ, *f.* anger; displeasure.
Īrātus, a, um, angry.
Īrōnīa, æ, *f.* irony.
Irrīdeo, īsi, isum, idēre, *a.* to laugh at.
Irrŭo, ŭi, —, ĕre, *n.* to rush in.
Ĭs, ea, ĭd, *pron.* he, she, it, *or* that; such.
Isocrătes, is, an Athenian orator.
Iste, a, ud, *pron.* that; he, she, it.
Istiusmŏdi, of that kind; such.
Ĭtă, *adv.* so; thus; yes.
Ĭtălia, æ, Italy.
Ĭtăque, *conj.* and so; therefore.
Ĭtem, *adv.* also, likewise, again.
Ĭter, itĭnĕris, *n.* a journey, a way.
Ĭtĕrum, *adv.* again, the second time.

J

Jăceo, ēre, *n.* to lie; to be fallen.
Jăcio, jēci, jactum, jacĕre, *a.* to throw; to declare.
Jacto, āre, *a.* to throw; to toss; to boast.
Jam, *adv.* now, presently.
Jamprīdem, *adv.* long since; already.
Jānĭcŭlum, i, one of the hills of Rome.
Jānuārius, a, um, relating to Janus; January.
Jŏcor, ātus, āri, *dep.* to joke.
Jŭbeo, jussi, jussum, jubēre, *a.* to order.
Jŭcunde, *adv.* agreeably; with pleasure.
Jŭcundus, a, um, pleasant; agreeable.
Jūdex, ĭcis, *c.* a judge.
Jūdĭcium, i, *n.* judgment.
Jūdĭco, āre, *a.* to judge.
Jūgĕrum, *gen.* jugeri and jugeris, *n. in the sing. generally of the second decl., in the pl. of the third,* a portion of land, 240 ft. long, 120 ft. broad, an acre.
Jŭgŭlum, i, n. the throat.
Jugum, i, *n.* a yoke; the ridge of a mountain.
Jungo, xi, ctum, gĕre, *a.* to join.
Junius, i, quidam ex Hispania.
Jūpĭter, Jŏvis, son of Saturn and Ops.
Jūra, æ, a mountain of Gaul.
Jūre, *adv.* by right; rightly.
Jūro, āre, *a.* to swear.
Jūs, jūris, *n.* right, law.
Jusjūrandum, jurisjurandi, *n.* an oath.
Jussum, i, *n.* an order, a command; a mandate.
Jussus, ûs, *m.* a command, *used only in the abl.*
Justĭtia, æ, *f.* justice.
Justus, a, um, just, lawful.
Jŭvat, *imp.* it delights.
Jŭventus, ūtis, *f.* youth.
Jŭvo, jūvi, jūtum, juvāre, *a.* to help.
Juxta, *prep.* near to; juxta ac, atque et, cum *or* quum, just as if.

K

Kălendæ *or* Călendæ, ārum, *f.* the kalends, the first day of the month.

L

L. = Lucius.
Lăbĕfăcio, ēci, actum, acĕre, *a.* to cause to totter; to overthrow.
Lăbiēnus, i, one of Cæsar's officers in Gaul.
Labo, avi, —, āre, *n.* to totter; to waver; to sink.
Lābor, lapsus, labi, *dep.* to slide; to fall.
Lăbor *or* os, ōris, *m.* labour; distress.
Lăbōriōsus, a, um, laborious, toiling; painstaking.
Lăbōro, āre, *n.* to labour; to be in distress.
Lăcĕdæmŏnius, a, um, belonging to Lacedæmon.
Lăcesso, īvi, ītum, ĕre, *a.* to provoke; to harass; to challenge; to fall upon.
Lacrĭma *vel* lacrўma, æ, *f.* a tear.
Lăcus, ûs, *m.* a lake.

Lædo, si, sum, dĕre, *a.* to hurt; to offend.
Lælius, i, a Roman family name.
Lætĭtia, æ, *f.* gladness; mirth.
Lætor, ātus, āri, *dep.* to rejoice.
Lætus, a, um, glad.
Lāmentŏr, ātus, āri, *dep.* to weep; to lament.
Lāmentum, i, *n.* wailing.
Languĕfăcio, ēci, actum, ăcĕre, *a.* to make languid; to tranquillize.
Langueo, gui, —, ēre, *n.* to be faint; to be languid.
Languesco, gui, guescĕre, *n.* to become languid.
Lănio, āre, *a.* to lacerate.
Lăŏmĕdon, ontis, son of Ilus, father of Priam.
Lăpis, ĭdis, *m.* a stone.
Largior, ītus, īri, *dep.* to give liberally; to grant.
Lătīnè, *adv.* in Latin.
Lătīnus, a, um, Latin.
Latobrĭgi, ōrum, neighbours of the Helvetii in Gaul.
Lătro, ōnis, *m.* a robber.
Lătus, a, um, broad; extensive.
Lătus, ĕris, *n.* a side.
Laudābĭlis, is, e, praiseworthy.
Laudātio, ōnis, *f.* praise.
Laudo, āre, *a.* to praise.
Laus, dis, *f.* praise; renown.
Lautus, a, um, elegant; great; dainty; luxurious.
Lector, ōris, *m.* a reader.
Lēgātio, ōnis, *f.* an embassy.
Lēgātus, i, *m.* an ambassador; a lieutenant.
Lĕgio, ōnis, *f.* a legion.
Lĕgo, lēgi, lectum, lĕgĕre, *a.* to gather; to select; to read.
Lĕmānus, i, the lake of Geneva.
Lēnio, īre, *a.* to mitigate; to appease.
Lēnĭter, *adv.* gently.
Lēnōcĭnium, i, *n.* enticement.
Lentŭlus, i, a Roman family name.
Leo, ōnis, *m.* a lion.
Leontīni, ōrum, a town of Sicily. Leontīnus, a, um, belonging to Leontini.
Lĕpĭdus, i, a surname of the Æmilian family; the colleague of Octavianus and Antony in the second triumvirate.
Lĕpor *or* lĕpos, ōris, *m.* pleasantness; humour.
Lĕpus, ŏris, *m.* a hare.
Leucāta, æ, a promontory in Leucadia.
Lĕvis, is, e, light; inconstant.
Lĕvĭtas, ātis, *f.* lightness; levity; fickleness.
Lex, ēgis, *f.* a law.
Lĭbenter *vel* lŭbenter, *adv.* willingly.
Lĭber, ĕra, ĕrum, free; frank.
Lĭber, ri, *m.* a book.
Lĭber, ĕri, *m.* a son.
Lĭbĕrālis, is, e, liberal.
Lĭbĕrālĭtas, ātis, *f.* liberality.
Lĭbĕrālĭter, *adv.* liberally.
Lĭbĕrè, *adv.* freely; candidly.
Lĭbĕri, ōrum, *m.* children.
Lĭbĕro, āre, *a.* to free.
Lĭbertas, ātis, *f.* liberty.
Lĭbertus, i, *m.* a freedman.
Lĭbet *vel* lŭbet, uit, ĭtum est, *imp.* it pleases.
Lĭbīdo, ĭnis, *f.* desire; lust.
Lĭbrārius, i, *m.* a clerk; a copier of books.
Lĭcentia, æ, *f.* licentiousness.
Lĭcet, *conj.* although.
Lĭcet, uit *vel* ĭtum est, ēre, *imp.* it is lawful.
Lĭcĭnius, i, a Roman family name.
Lingŏnes, um, a people of Belgic Gaul.
Lingua, æ, *f.* a tongue; a language.
Lĭtĕra, æ, *f.* a letter of the alphabet; *pl.* an epistle; writing.
Lĭtĕrātus, a, um, learned.
Lŏco, āre, *a.* to place; to hire; to contract.
Lŏcŭples, ētis, rich.
Lŏcus, i, *m.* a place; *pl.* loci *vel* loca, ōrum; loca, places; loci, topics of discourse.
Longè, *adv.* far; far off; *comp.* longius, farther.
Longuinquĭtas, ātis, *f.* distance.
Longus, a, um, long; lasting.
Lŏquor, quutus *vel* cūtus, qui, *dep.* to speak.
Lūcĭlius, i, a Roman family name.
Lucrētius, i, a Roman family name.

Lŭcrum, i, *n.* gain.
Luctor, ātus, āri, *dep.* to wrestle; to contend.
Lūcŭlenter, *adv.* excellently.
Lūcullus, i, a surname of the Licinian family.
Lūdo, si, sum, dĕre, *a. et n.* to play at; to mock.
Lūgeo, xi, —, gēre, *a.* to mourn.
Lutātius, i, a Roman family name.
Lux, lucis, *f.* light.
Lўcēum, i, a celebrated gymnasium near Athens, where Aristotle taught.
Lўcurgus, i, the famous lawgiver of Sparta.
Lўsias, æ, an orator of Athens.

M

M. = Marcus.
Măcĕdo, ŏnis, Macedonian.
Măgis, *adv.* more.
Măgister, ri, *m.* a master.
Măgistrātus, ûs, *m.* a magistrate.
Magnĭfĭcus, a, um, magnificent.
Magnĭtūdo, ĭnis, *f.* greatness.
Magnŏperè, *adv.* greatly, very much.
Magnus, a, um, great.
Măgus, i, *m.* a wise man.
Mājestas, ātis, *f.* majesty; authority.
Mājor, or, us, greater.
Mājōres, um, *m.* ancestors.
Mājus, *or* Māius, a, um, belonging to May; May.
Mălĕ, *adv.* badly; wickedly.
Mălĕfĭcium, i, *n.* an evil deed; mischief, injury.
Mălĕfĭcus, a, um, mischievous.
Mălĭtia, æ, *f.* wickedness; craft.
Mālo, ui, le, *n. irr.* to be more willing.
Mălus, a, um, bad, wicked.
Mălum, i, *n.* an evil; misfortune.
Mancĭpium, i, *n.* property by purchase; a slave.
Mancus, a, um, maimed.
Mandātum, i, *n.* a command; a commission.
Mando, āre, *a.* to give in charge; to commit; to command.
Măneo, si, sum, ēre, *n.* to remain; to wait.
Mānīlius, i, a Roman family name.
Mantinēa, æ, a town of Arcadia.
Mănus, ûs, *f.* a hand; a band of men; in manu esse, to be in one's power.
Marcellus, i, a surname of the Claudian family.
Marcus, i, a Roman prænomen.
Măre, is, *n.* the sea.
Margărīta, æ, *f.* a pearl.
Mărius, i, a Roman family name.
Matăra, æ, *f.* a javelin.
Māter, ris, *f.* a mother.
Mātĕries, ēi, *f.* materials.
Matrĭmōnium, i, *n.* marriage.
Mātūrè, *adv.* soon.
Mātūro, āre, *a.* to ripen; to hasten.
Maxĭmè, *adv.* very much.
Maxĭmus, a, um, very great.
Mĕdeor, —, ēri, *dep.* to heal; to aid.
Mĕdĭcīna, æ, *f.* medicine.
Mĕdiŏcris, is, e, moderate; common.
Mĕdiŏcrĭter, *adv.* ordinarily; easily.
Mĕdĭtor, ātus, āri, *dep.* to think, to meditate.
Mĕdius, a, um, middle.
Mehercule, by Hercules.
Mĕlior, or, us, better.
Mĕlius, *adv.* better.
Membrum, i, *n.* a member.
Mĕmĭni, isse, *def.* to remember.
Mĕmŏria, æ, *f.* memory.
Mĕmŏrĭter, *adv.* by heart.
Mendācium, i, *n.* a lie.
Mendīcĭtas, ātis, *f.* mendicity.
Mēnius, a, um, a Roman family name.
Mens, tis, *f.* the mind.
Mensis, is, *m.* a month.
Mentio, ōnis, *f.* mention.
Merces, ēdis, *f.* hire; rent.
Mĕreo, ui, ĭtum, ēre, *a.* or Mĕreor, ĭtus, ēri, *dep.* to deserve; to gain; quid mereas ut, what would you take for.
Mĕrīdies, ēi, *m.* mid-day.
Mĕrĭto, *adv.* deservedly.
Mĕrĭtum, i, *n.* desert; a reward.
Mĕrĭtus, a, um, deserved, legitimate; deserving.

Met, a syllable added to pronouns.
Mĕtellus, i, a surname of the Cæcilian family.
Mētrŏpŏlītæ, the inhabitants of Metropolis, in Thessaly.
Mĕtuo, i, *rarely* ūtum, ĕre, *a. et n.* to fear.
Mĕtus, ûs, *m.* fear.
Meus, a, um, *pos. pron.* my.
Mīgro, āre, *n.* to migrate.
Mīles, ĭtis, *c.* a soldier.
Mīlēsius, a, um, belonging to Miletus.
Mīlĭtāris, is, e, military; warlike.
Mīlĭtia, æ, *f.* military service; any office.
Mille, *ind. adj. or s.* a thousand; *plur.* millia, um, *n.* thousands.
Mĭlo, ōnis, a surname of the Annian family.
Mĭnĭmè, *adv.* very little; not at all.
Mĭnĭmus, a, um, the smallest, the least, very little.
Mĭnistro, āre, *a.* to serve; to furnish.
Mĭnor, or, us, less.
Mĭnor, ātus, āri, *dep.* to threaten.
Mīnos, ōis, a king of Crete, celebrated for his justice.
Mĭnuo, ui, ūtum, uĕre, *a.* to lessen; to impair.
Mĭnus, *adv.* less.
Mīrābĭlis, is, e, wonderful; strange.
Mīror, ātus, āri, *dep.* to wonder; to admire.
Mĭser, ĕra, ĕrum, wretched.
Mĭsĕreor, ĭtus *or* tus, ēri, *dep.* to pity.
Mĭsĕresco, —, —, ĕre, *a.* to pity.
Mĭsĕret, misertum *or* miseritum, est, ēre, *imp.* it pities.
Mĭsĕria, æ, *f.* misery; trouble.
Mĭsĕrĭcordia, æ, *f.* pity.
Mĭsĕricors, cors, cors, cordis, merciful.
Mĭsĕror, ātus, āri, *dep.* to lament; to pity.
Missus, ûs, *m.* a sending.
Mīte, *adv.*; *sup.* mitissime, gently.
Mitis, is, e, mellow; gentle.
Mithrĭdātes, is, a king of Pontus.
Mithrĭdātĭcus, a, um, belonging to Mithridates.
Mitto, si, ssum, ttĕre, *a.* to send; to throw.
Mŏdĕrātè, *adv.* moderately.
Mŏdĕrātio, ōnis, *f.* moderation.
Mŏdĭcè, *adv.* with proper measure; moderately.
Mŏdŏ, *adv.* only, lately, just now.
Mŏdus, i, *m.* a measure; a manner.
Mœreo, ui, —, ēre, *n. et a.* to mourn.
Mœror, ōris, *m.* grief.
Mœstĭtia, æ, *f.* sadness.
Mŏlestia, æ, *f.* trouble.
Mŏlestus, a, um, troublesome.
Mōlior, ītus, īri, *dep.* to attempt; to contrive.
Mollio, īre, *a.* to soften.
Mŏlo, ui, ĭtum, ĕre, *a.* to grind.
Mŏneo, ēre, *a.* to put in mind; to advise; to admonish.
Mons, tis, *m.* a mountain.
Mŏnŭmentum, i, *n.* a memorial, a monument.
Mŏra, æ, *f.* delay; hindrance.
Morbus, i, *m.* a disease.
Mŏrior, tuus, i, *dep.* to die.
Mŏror, ātus, āri, *dep.* to delay; to hinder.
Mōrōsus, a, um, peevish.
Mors, tis, *f.* death.
Mortalis, is, e, mortal.
Mortuus, a, um, dead.
Mos, ōris, *m.* a custom.
Mōtus, ûs, *m.* motion; a commotion.
Mŏveo, mōvi, mōtum, movēre, *a.* to move; to remove; to excite; to persuade.
Mox, *adv.* presently.
Mulcto, *or* multo, āre, *a.* to punish, to fine.
Mŭlier, ĕris, *f.* a woman.
Multo *or* um, *adv.* by much; much.
Multĭtūdo, ĭnis, *f.* a multitude.
Multus, a, um, much, many.
Munatius, i, a Roman family name.
Mundus, i, *m.* the world.
Mūnĭcĭpium, i, *n.* a town, the citizens of which enjoyed the rights of Roman citizens.
Mūnĭfĭcus, a, um, liberal.
Mūnio, īre, *a.* to fortify.
Mūnītio, ōnis, *f.* a fortifying; a fortification.
Mūnus, ĕris, *n.* a gift; an office.

Mūræna, æ, *f.* a lamprey.
Mūræna, æ, a surname of the Licinian family.
Mūrus, i, *m.* a wall.
Mūsĭcus, i, *m.* a musician.
Mūsĭcus, a, um, musical.
Mūtātio, ōnis, *f.* a change; an exchange.
Mūto, āre, *a.* to change; to exchange.

N

Nam, *conj.* for.
Namque, *conj.* for.
Nanciscor, nactus, nancisci, *dep.* to obtain; to find.
Narro, āre, *a.* to tell; to relate.
Nascor, nātus, nasci, *dep.* to be born; to arise.
Nātālis, is, e, natal; native.
Nātio, ōnis, *f.* a nation.
Nātūra, æ, *f.* nature; disposition.
Nātūrālis, is, e, natural.
Nātus, a, um, born; fit.
Nauta, æ, *m.* a sailor.
Nāvĭgātio, ōnis. *f.* a sailing; navigation.
Nāvĭgo, āre, *a. et n.* to sail.
Nāvis, is, a ship.
Neāpŏlis, is, *f.* a town in Campania.
Nē, *adv.* not; *conj.* lest, that not; *nĕ* at the end of a word, asks a question.
Nĕc, *conj.* neither, nor.
Nĕcessārio, *adv.* of necessity.
Nĕcessārius, a, um, necessary; closely related, relation, friend.
Nĕcesse, *adj. n. ind.* necessary.
Nĕcessĭtas, ātis, *f.* necessity.
Nĕcessĭtūdo, ĭnis, *f.* necessity; intimacy.
Necne, *conj.* or not.
Nĕco, āvi *or* ui, ātum, āre, *a.* to kill.
Nĕfārius, a, um, wicked.
Nĕfas, *s. n. indec.* an unlawful action; *adj.* unlawful, wicked.
Neglĭgo, exi, ectum, ĭgĕre, *a.* to neglect; to slight.
Nĕgo, āre, *a.* to deny; to refuse.
Nĕgōtior, ātus, āri, *dep* to trade.
Nĕgōtium, i, *n.* business; trouble.
Nēmo, ĭnis, *c.* nobody [*gen. and abl.* scarcely used: use instead nullius and nullo.]
Nĕpos, ōtis, *m.* a grandson; a prodigal.
Nēquāquam, *adv.* by no means.
Nĕque, *conj.* neither, nor.
Nĕqueo, ii, ĭtum, ĭre, *n.* to be unable.
Nĕquis, qua, quod *or* quid, lest any one.
Nervii, ōrum, a people in Belgic Gaul.
Nervus, i, *m.* a sinew; a nerve strength.
Nescio, ĭre, *a.* not to know.
Neu, see Neve.
Neuter, ra, rum, neither of the two.
Nēve *or* neu, *conj.* neither, nor.
Nex, nĕcis, *f.* death.
Ni, *conj.* unless.
Nĭger, ra, rum, black.
Nĭhil, *contr.* nĭl, *n. ind.* nothing.
Nĭhĭlōmĭnus, *adv.* nevertheless.
Nĭhĭlum, i, *n.* nothing.
Nĭmis, *adv.* too much.
Nĭmium, *adv.* too much.
Nĭmius, a, um, too much.
Nĭsi, *conj.* unless; if not; except.
Nĭtor, nīsus *or* nixus, niti, *dep.* to exert one's self, to strive; to depend upon; to insist on.
Nix, nĭvis, *f.* snow.
Nōbĭlis, is, e, well known; noble.
Nōbĭlĭtas, ātis, *f.* nobility; fame.
Nŏceo, ēre, *n.* to hurt.
Noctu, *abl.* by night.
Nocturnus, a, um, nightly, nocturnal.
Nōlo, ui, le, *n. irr.* to be unwilling.
Nōmen, ĭnis, *n.* a name; renown.
Nŏmĭno, āre, *a.* to name; to call.
Non, *adv.* not.
Nōnæ, ārum, *f.* the nones, the fifth day of the month; but
In March, July, October, May,
The Nones are on the seventh day.
Nondum, *adv.* not yet.
Nonne, is it not?
Nonnihil, *n. ind.* something.
Nonnullus, a, um, some.
Nonnunquam, *adv.* sometimes.
Nōnus, a, um, ninth.

Norbānus, i, a Roman family name; C. opposed Sylla.
Nosco, nōvi, nōtum, noscĕre, *a.* to know; to learn.
Noster, ra, rum, *pron.* our, ours.
Nŏto, āre, *a.* to observe; to note; to censure.
Nōtus, a, um, acquainted with; remarkable.
Nŏvem, *adj. pl. indec.* nine.
Nŏvĭtas, ātis, *f.* newness; novelty.
Nŏvus, a, um, new; unusual.
Nox, ctis, *f.* night.
Nūbo, psi *or* pta sum, ptum, bĕre, *n.* to veil; to marry; *said properly of a woman only, of a man by way of jest.*
Nūdo, āre, *a.* to make naked; to uncover.
Nūdus, a, um, naked.
Nūgātōrius, a, um, trifling; useless.
Nullus, a, um, no, none.
Num, *adv.* whether? whether or no?
Nūma, æ, the second king of Rome.
Nūmen, ĭnis, *n.* a deity; divine power or will.
Nŭmĕro, āre, *a.* to number; to pay.
Nŭmĕrus, i, *m.* a number; value.
Nummārius, a, um, belonging to money; venal.
Nummus, i, *m.* a piece of money; money.
Nunc, *adv.* now, at this time.
Nuncio *or* nuntio, āre, *a.* to bring news; to announce or report; to tell.
Nuncius *or* nuntius, a, um, announcing; *s.* intelligence; a messenger.
Nunquam, *adv.* never.
Nūper, *adv.* lately.
Nusquam, *adv.* nowhere, in no place; in no way.

O

Ŏb, *prep.* for, on account of.
Obdūco, xi, ctum, cĕre, *a.* to lead against; to cover.
Ŏbēdio, īre, *n.* to obey.
Ŏbeo, ii, ĭtum, īre, *n.* and *a. irr.* to go to; to frequent; to travel over; to discharge; to die.
Objĭcio, ēci, ectum, ĭcĕre, *a.* to throw to; to expose; to object; to oppose.
Oblecto, āre, *a.* to delight.
Oblĭgo, āre, *a.* to tie round; to bind; to oblige.
Oblīviscor, ītus, ivisci, *dep.* to forget.
Obnītor, sus *or* xus, ti, *dep.* to strive against.
Obruo, ui, ŭtum, uĕre, *a.* to cover; to overwhelm; to destroy.
Obscūrĭtas, ātis, *f.* obscurity.
Obscūrus, a, um, dark, obscure.
Obsĕcro, āre, *a.* to beseech; to entreat.
Obsĕquor, quūtus *or* cūtus, qui, *dep.* to comply with; to oblige.
Observo, āre, *a.* to observe; to respect.
Obses, ĭdis, *c.* a hostage.
Obsisto, stiti, *seldom* stĭtum, istĕre, *n.* to oppose.
Obsto, ĭti, ātum *et* ĭtum, āre, *n.* to stand in the way; to obstruct.
Obsum, fui, esse, *n. irr.* to hurt; to hinder.
Obtento, āre, *a.* to support.
Obtestor, ātus, āri, *dep.* to beseech.
Obtĭneo, inui, entum, ĭnēre, *a.* to hold; to effect.
Obtingit, ĭgit, ingĕre, *imp.* it happens; it falls by lot.
Obviam, *adv.* in the way.
Occāsio, ōnis, *f.* an occasion; an opportunity.
Occĭdo, ĭdi, āsum, idĕre, *n.* to fall down; to die.
Occīdo, di, sum, dĕre, *a.* to kill.
Occŭlto, āre, *a.* to hide; to keep secret.
Occŭpātio, ōnis, a taking possession; an occupation, business.
Occŭpo, āre, *a.* to take hold of; to occupy.
Occurro, curri *or* cŭcurri, cursum, currĕre, *n.* to meet; to oppose; to come into; to occur.
Octavianus, i, *and* Octavius, i, Roman family names.
Octōgēsĭmus, a, um, eightieth.

Octōginta, *pl. adj. ind.* eighty.
Ŏcŭlus, i, *m.* the eye.
Ŏdi, ōdi, sse, *def.* to hate.
Ŏdiōsus, a, um, hateful.
Ŏdium, i, *n.* hatred.
Ŏdōrātus, ûs, *m.* a smelling.
Offendo, di, sum, dĕre, *a.* to strike against; to hurt; to offend.
Offensio, ōnis, *f.* a striking against; a hurt; an offence.
Offĕro, obtŭli, oblātum, offerre, *a. irr.* to offer; to expose; to meet.
Offĭcium, i, *n.* a duty; an office.
Offundo, ūdi, ūsum, undĕre, *a.* to pour upon; to spread.
Ŏlympia, æ, a town of Elis.
Ŏlympius, a, um, belonging to Olympia.
Ŏmitto, īsi, issum, ittĕre, *a.* to lay aside; to neglect; to omit.
Omnīno, *adv.* altogether, wholly.
Omnis, is, e, every, all.
Ŏpĕra, æ, *f.* work, endeavour; means.
Ŏpĭfex, ĭcis, *c.* an artificer; a workman.
Ŏpīnio, ōnis, *f.* an opinion; a belief.
Ŏpīnor, ātus, āri, *dep.* to think, to imagine.
Ŏpis, *gen.* of ops, *f. obs.* help; *pl.* power, resources.
Ŏpĭtŭlor, ātus, āri, *dep.* to help.
Ŏportet, uit, ēre, *imp.* it behoves.
Oppĕrior, tus, īri, *dep.* to wait for; to expect.
Oppĕto, ii, ītum, ĕre, *a.* to encounter.
Oppianicus, i, the cognomen of Statius Albius.
Oppĭdānus, a, um, of a town; *s. m.* a townsman.
Oppĭdum, i, *n.* a walled town.
Oppōno, ŏsui, ŏsĭtum, ōnĕre, *a.* to place against; to oppose.
Opportūnus, a, um, commodious; seasonable.
Oppugno, āre, *a.* to fight against; to assail.
Optābĭlis, is, e, desirable.
Optātus, a, um, desired.
Optĭmè, *adv.* very well.
Optĭmus, a, um, very good; best.
Optio, ōnis, *f.* option.
Opto, āre, *a.* to desire.
Ŏpŭlens, ns, ns, ntis, wealthy; abundant.
Ŏpŭlentus, a, um, rich.
Ŏpus, ĕris, *n.* a work; labour.
Ŏpus, *adj. ind.* needful; *s. n.* need.
Ōra, æ, *f.* a coast; a region.
Ōrātio, ōnis, *f.* an oration.
Ōrātor, ōris, *m.* an orator.
Orbis, is, *m.* a circle; the world.
Orbo, āre, *a.* to deprive of.
Ordior, orsus, ordīri, *dep.* to begin.
Ordo, ĭnis, *m.* order; condition; rank.
Ŏrestes, æ *et* is, son of Agamemnon and Clytemnestra.
Orgetorix, īgis, a chief of the Helvetii.
Ŏrior, tus, īri, *dep.* to arise; to be born; to proceed.
Ornāmentum, i, *n.* an ornament; dignity.
Ornātus, a, um, adorned; furnished.
Ornātus, ûs, *m.* an ornament; dress.
Orno, āre, *a.* to adorn; to equip.
Ōro, āre, *a.* to plead; to entreat.
Ōs, ōris, *n.* the mouth; the countenance.
Ŏs, ossis, *n.* a bone.
Ostendo, di, sum *or* tum, dĕre, *a.* to show; to set forth.
Ōtior, āri, *dep.* to be at leisure.
Ōtiōsus, a, um, at leisure, at rest.
Ōtium, i, *n.* leisure; peace.
Ōvum, i, an egg.

P

P. = Publius.
Pæne *or* pene, *adv.* nearly.
Pāgus, i, *m.* a village.
Pălam, *adv.* openly, plainly.
Pānætius, i, a Stoic of Rhodes.
Pando, pandi, pansum, *rather* passum, pandĕre, *a.* to spread.
Pānis, is, *m.* bread.
Pār, pār, pār, păris, equal; meet.
Pār, păris, *n.* a pair.
Părātus, a, um, prepared; fit.
Parco, pĕperci, *seldom* parsi, par-

sum, *seldom* parcĭtum, parcĕre, *n.* to spare; to pardon.
Părens, tis, *c.* a parent.
Pāreo, ēre, *n.* to obey; to appear.
Părio, pĕpĕri, partum *or* parĭtum, părĕre, *a.* to bring forth; to get.
Părĭter, *adv.* equally.
Păro, āre, *a.* to prepare; to procure.
Parrĭcīdium, i, *n.* parricide; an atrocious crime.
Pars, tis, *f.* a part; a party.
Partĭceps, eps, eps, ĭpis, sharing.
Partim, *adv.* partly.
Partior, ītus, īri, *dep.; or* partio, īre, *a.* to distribute; to share.
Părum, *adv.* a little; too little.
Parvus, a, um, little.
Passim, *adv.* here and there; promiscuously.
Passus, ûs, *m.* a pace.
Pătĕfăcio, fēci, factum, făcĕre, *a.* to lay open; to discover.
Păteo, ui, —, ēre, *n.* to be open, accessible; to be manifest; to extend.
Păter, ris, *m.* a father.
Pătienter, *adv.* patiently.
Pătientia, æ, *f.* patience.
Pătior, passus, păti, *dep.* to suffer, to allow, to endure.
Pătria, æ, *f.* one's native country.
Pătrĭmōnium, i, *n.* an inheritance or patrimony.
Pătrōnus, i, *m.* a patron.
Pauci, æ, a, few.
Paulo, *or* paullo *et* paulum, *adv.* a little, somewhat.
Paulus, i, *m.* a surname of the Æmilian family.
Paulŭlum, *adv.* a little, very little.
Paulātim *or* paullātim, *adv.* by degrees.
Pauper, ĕris, poor, needy.
Paupertas, ātis, *f.* poverty.
Păveo, pāvi, —, pāvēre, *n.* to be afraid.
Păvor, ōris, *m.* fear.
Pax, cis, *f.* peace.
Peccātum, i, *n.* a fault; a sin.
Pecco, āre, *n.* to offend; to sin.
Pectus, ŏris, *n.* the breast.
Pĕcūnia, æ, *f.* money.
Pĕcūniōsus, a, um, rich, wealthy.

Pĕcus, ŏris, *n.* sheep; cattle.
Pĕcus, ŭdis, *f.* a sheep.
Pĕdes, ĭtis, *m.* a foot-soldier; *pl.* infantry.
Pĕdĭtātus, ûs, *m.* infantry.
Pedius, i, a Roman family name.
Pĕjor, or, us, worse.
Pĕlignus, a, um, belonging to the Peligni.
Pĕlignus, i, Accius or Attius.
Pello, pĕpŭli, pulsum, pellĕre, *a.* to drive away; to defeat; to banish.
Pĕnātes, ium, *m.* household gods.
Pendo, pĕpendi, pensum, pendĕre, *a.* to weigh; to pay; to suffer (punishment); to judge.
Pēnè, *adv.* almost.
Pĕnes, *prep.* in the power of.
Pĕnĕtro, āre, *n.* to penetrate; to enter.
Pĕnĭtus, *adv.* deeply, completely.
Pĕnus, ûs, *c.* victuals.
Pĕr, *prep.* by; through.
Pĕrăcerbus, a, um, very harsh.
Pĕrăcūte, *adv.* very sharply.
Percĭpio, ēpi, eptum, ĭpĕre, *a.* to take entirely; to receive; to perceive; to understand.
Perdĭtus, a, um, hopeless; abandoned.
Perdo, ĭdi, ĭtum, ĕre, *a.* to lose; to ruin.
Perdūco, xi, ctum, cĕre, *a.* to lead through; to conduct; to persuade.
Pĕrĕgre, *adv.* abroad.
Pĕrĕgrīnor, ātus, āri, *dep.* to be a foreigner; to sojourn.
Pĕrĕgrīnus, a, um, foreign; inexperienced.
Pĕreo, ii, ĭtum, īre, *n. irr.* to perish; to be ruined.
Perfăcĭlis, is, e, very easy.
Perfectus, a, um, perfect.
Perfĕro, tŭli, lātum, ferre, *a. irr.* to carry; to carry through; to endure.
Perfĭcio, ēci, ectum, ĭcĕre, *a.* to perform; to bring to an end; to bring about.
Perfŭga, æ, *m.* a deserter.
Perfŭgio, ūgi, ŭgĭtum, ŭgĕre, *n.* to go over (as a deserter).

Perfungor, ctus, gi, *dep.* to discharge a duty; to undergo.
Pergo, perrexi, perrectum, pergĕre, *n.* to go; *a.* to proceed, go on with a thing.
Pergrātus, a, um, very pleasant; very agreeable.
Pĕrīclĭtor, ātus, āri, *dep.* to make trial; to try; to be in danger.
Pĕrīcŭlōsus, a, um, dangerous; venturesome.
Pĕrīcŭlum, i, *n.* danger.
Pĕrinde, *adv.* just as; equally.
Pĕrītus, a, um, skilful.
Permăneo, si, sum, ēre, *n.* to stay through; to remain.
Permāno, āre, *n.* to flow through; to reach.
Permitto, īsi, issum, ittĕre, *a.* to give up; *n.* to permit.
Permŏveo, ōvi, ōtum, ŏvēre, *a.* to move greatly; to disquiet; to persuade.
Permultum, *adv.* very much.
Permultus, a, um, very much; *pl.* very many.
Permūto, āre, *a.* to alter; to exchange.
Pernīcies, ēi, *f.* destruction; death.
Pernīciōsus, a, um, pernicious, destructive; fatal.
Pĕropportūne, *adv.* very opportunely.
Pĕrōro, āre, *a.* to plead; to conclude an oration, finish speaking.
Perpauci, æ, a, very few.
Perpĕtior, essus, ĕti, *dep.* to suffer; to allow.
Perpĕtuītas, ātis, *f.* perpetuity.
Perpĕtuo, *adv.* perpetually.
Perpĕtuus, a um, perpetual; entire.
Perquīro, sīvi, sītum, rĕre, *a.* to search diligently; to examine.
Perrumpo, rūpi, ruptum, rumpĕre, *n.* to break through; *a.* to rush through; to destroy; to overcome.
Persæ, ārum, Persians.
Perscrībo, psi, ptum, bĕre, *a.* to write fully; to inform by writing; to send in writing.
Persĕquor, quūtus *or* cūtus, qui, *dep.* to pursue; to seek to obtain; to accomplish.
Persĕvēro, āre, *n.* to persevere; *a.* to persevere in a thing.
Persolvo, solvi, sŏlūtum, solvĕre, *a.* to solve; to pay; —pœnas, to suffer.
Persōna, æ, *f.* a mask; a person.
Perspĭcio, exi, ectum, icĕre, *a.* to perceive; to understand; to see.
Perspĭcuus, a, um, clear; manifest.
Persuādeo, si, sum, dēre, *n.* to persuade.
Pertaedet, sum est, dēre, *imp.* it very much wearies.
Perterrĭtus, a, um, terrified.
Pertimesco, ui, —, escĕre, to fear greatly.
Pertinācia, æ, *f.* obstinacy; perseverance.
Pertĭneo, inui, —, ĭnēre, *n.* to reach to; to pertain to.
Perturbātio, ōnis, *f.* disorder; perturbation.
Perturbo, āre, *a.* to disturb greatly; to confound.
Pervĕnio, ēni, entum, enīre, *n.* to come to; to arrive at.
Perverto, ti, sum, tĕre, *a.* to turn upside down; to overthrow; to corrupt.
Pervŏlo, āre, *a.* to fly through; to pass quickly.
Pervŏlo, vŏlui, velle, *n. irr.* to desire very much.
Pēs, ĕdis, *m.* a foot.
Pĕto, īvi, ītum, ĕre, *a.* to seek; to go to; to aim at.
Phaëthon, ontis, a son of Apollo; a slave of Atticus.
Phĭlippus, i, king of Macedon; name of several individuals.
Phĭlo, ōnis, a philosopher.
Philoctēta, æ, *or* Philoctetes, tæ, a son of Pœas; companion of Hercules.
Phĭlŏsŏphia, æ, *f.* philosophy.
Phĭlŏsŏphus, i, *m.* a philosopher.
Philus, i, a surname of the Furian family.
Phȳsĭcus, a, um, natural; physicus, i, a naturalist; physica, ōrum, physics.
Pictūra, æ, *f.* a picture.
Piĕtas, ātis, *f.* piety; natural affection.

Pĭget, uit *or* ĭtum est, ēre, *imp.* it grieves.
Pīlum, i, *n.* a dart.
Pīlus, i, *m.* a company of Triarii; prīmus pīlus, *or* prīmĭpīlus, *s.* the first centurion of the Triarii.
Pingo, pinxi, pictum, pingĕre, *a.* to paint; to embroider.
Pinguesco, —, —, ĕre, *n.* to grow fat.
Piscātor, ōris, *m.* a fisherman.
Piscor, ātus, āri, *dep.* to fish.
Pīso, ōnis, a surname of the Calpurnian family.
Pius, a, um, pious; dutiful.
Plăceo, ēre, *a.* to please; *imp.* placet, it pleases.
Plāco, āre, *a.* to appease.
Plāga, æ, *f.* a wound; a stripe.
Plăga, æ, *f.* a region.
Plancius, i, a Roman family name.
Plānè, *adv.* plainly; certainly; entirely.
Plānus, a, um, plain; level; clear.
Plăto, ōnis, the celebrated Athenian philosopher.
Plebs, ēbis, *f.* the common people.
Plēnus, a, um, full; plentiful.
Plērique, æque, ăque, the most.
Plērumque, *adv.* for the most part.
Plumbeus, a, um, leaden; dull.
Plurĭmum, *adv.* most of all.
Plūrĭmus, a, um, most; very much; very great.
Plus, pluris, *used in sing. neut. in nom. gen. acc.*, more; higher; *pl.* plures, a, more, several.
Plusquam, *adv.* more than.
Poēma, ătis, *n.* a poem.
Pœna, ae, *f.* punishment; a penalty.
Pœni, ōrum, Carthaginians.
Pœnĭtet, uit, —, ēre, *imp.* it repenteth.
Poēta, æ, *m.* a poet.
Pŏlīte, *adv.* neatly.
Polleo, —, —, ēre, *n.* to be able.
Pollĭceor, ĭtus, ēri, *dep.* to promise.
Pompēii, ōrum, a town of Campania.
Pompēĭus, i, a Roman family name.
Pompĭlius, i, a family name.
Pōmus, i, *f.* a fruit-tree; fruit.
Pondĕro, āre, *a.* to weigh; to ponder.
Pōno, ŏsui, ŏsĭtum, ōnĕre, *a.* to put; to place; to lay down; to reckon; to depend.
Pons, tis, *m.* a bridge.
Pŏpŭlor, ātus, āri, *dep.* to lay waste; to ravage.
Pŏpŭlus, i, *m.* the people, a nation.
Porro, *adv.* hereafter; again; on the other hand.
Porta, æ, *f.* a gate; a passage.
Portius, a, um, a Roman family name.
Portus, ûs, *m.* a harbour.
Posco, pŏposci, —, poscĕre, *a.* to ask; to entreat.
Pŏsīdōnius, i, a Stoic philosopher of Rhodes.
Possessio, ōnis, *f.* a possession.
Possĭdeo, ēdi, essum, ĭdēre, *a.* to possess.
Possum, pŏtui, posse, *n. irr.* to be able.
Post, *prep.* after; since.
Posteā, *adv.* afterwards.
Posteăquam, *adv.* after that; after.
Postĕrus, a, um, following.
Posthac, *adv.* hereafter.
Postpōno, ŏsui, ŏsĭtum, ōnĕre, *a.* to place behind; to postpone; to esteem less.
Postquam, *adv.* after that; since.
Postrēmo, *adv.* lastly.
Postrēmus, a, um, the last.
Postrīdiè, *adv.* the day after.
Postŭlātio, ōnis, *f.* a demanding.
Postŭlātum, i, *n.* a demand; a request.
Postŭlo, āre, *a.* to desire; to demand as a right; to accuse.
Pŏtens, ns, ntis, powerful; mighty.
Pŏtestas, ātis, *f.* power; authority.
Pŏtior, ītus, īri, *dep.* to be master of; to obtain.
Pŏtior, or, us, better.
Pŏtis, *adv.* capable; potius, rather; potissime, most of all.
Pŏtissĭmum, *adv.* chiefly; especially.
Pŏtius, *adv.* rather.
Pōto, āre, *a.* to drink.
Præ, *prep.* before; in comparison of.
Præbeo, ēre, *a.* to afford; to show.
Præcēdo, ssi, ssum, dĕre, *a.* to go before; to excel.

Præceptum, i, *n.* a precept; a command.
Præcĭpio, ēpi, eptum, ĭpĕre, *a.* to take beforehand; to instruct; to command; to foresee.
Præcĭpĭto, āre, *a.* to throw headlong; to hasten.
Præcĭpuè, *adv.* chiefly.
Præclārè, *adv.* very clearly; very well.
Præclārus, a, um, very clear; illustrious.
Præcurro, curri *or* cŭcurri, cursum, currĕre, *a. et n.* to run before; to surpass.
Præda, æ, *f.* prey; a prize.
Prædĭco, āre, *a.* to proclaim; to extol.
Prædīco, xi, ctum, cĕre, *a.* to foretell; to admonish.
Prædium, i, *n.* a farm.
Præfĕro, tŭli, lātum, ferre, *a. irr.* to carry before; to prefer.
Prægestio, īre, *n.* to be very desirous.
Prælium, i, *n.* a battle.
Præmitto, mīsi, missum, mittĕre, *a.* to send before.
Præmium, i, *n.* a reward.
Præopto, āre, *a.* to wish rather.
Præpărātio, ōnis, *f.* a preparing.
Præpōno, ŏsui, ŏsĭtum, ōnĕre, *a.* to put before; to set over; to prefer.
Præscrībo, psi, ptum, bĕre, *a.* to write before; to prescribe.
Præsens, ns, ns, ntis, present; favourable.
Præsēpio, psi, ptum, pīre, *a.* to guard; to barricade.
Præsertim, *adv.* especially; chiefly.
Præsĭdium, i, *n.* a guard; a garrison.
Præstans, ns, ns, ntis, excellent.
Præsto, tĭti, tĭtum *or* tātum, tāre, *n.* to stand before; to excel; *a.* to undertake; to perform; to show; to preserve; *imp.* it is better.
Præstōlor, ātus, āri, *dep.* to wait for.
Præsum, fui, esse, *n. irr.* to be over; to command.
Præter, *prep.* besides; except.
Prætĕreā, *adv.* besides; moreover.
Prætĕreo, ii, ĭtum, īre, *a. irr.* to go by; to omit; to surpass.
Prætĕrĭtus, a, um, past.
Prætermitto, īsi, issum, ittĕre, *a.* to let pass by; to omit; to neglect.
Præterquam, *adv.* besides.
Prætor, ōris, *m.* a prætor; a magistrate, next in power to the consuls.
Prætōrius, a, um, prætorian.
Prāvus, a, um, crooked; wicked.
Prĕcis, *f. gen. of* prex, *obs.* a prayer.
Prĕcor, ātus, āri, *dep.* to pray.
Prĕhendo *or* prendo, di, sum, dĕre, *a.* to lay hold of; to seize; to accost.
Prĕmo, ssi, ssum, mĕre, *a.* to press; to oppress; to urge.
Prĕtium, i, *n.* worth, value, price; money.
Prīdem, *adv.* long ago; formerly.
Prīdiè, *adv.* the day before.
Prīmārius, a, um, primary; excellent; of the first rank.
Prīmo, *adv.* firstly; at first.
Prīmum, *adv.* first, firstly; at first; for the first time; quum, ubi, *or* ut primum, as soon as.
Prīmus, a, um, first; best.
Princeps, ĭpis, *c.* the first; the chief; prince or princess; an author.
Princĭpātus, ûs, *m.* the first place; sovereignty.
Princĭpium, i, *n.* a beginning.
Prior, or, us, former; superior.
Pristĭnus, a, um, ancient.
Prius, *adv.* sooner; before.
Priusquam, *adv.* before that.
Prīvātus, a, um, private; peculiar.
Prīvo, āre, *a.* to deprive of.
Prŏ, *prep.* for, in, before; suitable to; in comparison with; on account of; instead of; in favour of.
Proăvus, i, *m.* a grandfather; an ancestor.
Prŏbābĭlis, is, e, probable; plausible.
Prŏbābĭlĭter, *adv.* probably.
Prŏbātor, ōris, *m.* an approver.
Prŏbe, *adv.* virtuously.
Prŏbo, āre, *a.* to prove; to approve.

Prŏbrum, i, *n.* a disgrace.
Prŏbus, a, um, honest.
Prŏcēdo, ssi, ssum, dĕre, *n.* to go forth; to advance; to prosper.
Prŏcrastĭnātio, ōnis, *f.* a delaying.
Prŏcreātor, ōris, *m.* a creator; a father.
Prŏcreo, āre, *a.* to beget; to cause.
Prŏcul, *adv.* at a distance; afar.
Prŏcumbo, cŭbui, cŭbĭtum, cumbĕre, *n.* to fall down, to sink.
Prŏcurro, cŭcurri *et* curri, cursum, currĕre, *n.* to run forth.
Prŏdĭtio, ōnis, *f.* a discovery; treachery.
Prōdo, ĭdi, ĭtum, ĕre, *a.* to make known; to betray; to disclose; to desert.
Prōdūco, xi, ctum, cĕre, *a.* to lead forth; to produce; to draw out.
Prœlium, i, *n.* a battle; a contest.
Prŏfectio, ōnis, *f.* a departure; a journey.
Prŏfecto, *adv.* truly.
Prōfĕro, tŭli, lātum, ferre, *a. irr.* to bring forth; to advance; to publish.
Prōfĭcio, ēci, ectum, ĭcĕre, *n.* to make progress; to be serviceable.
Prŏfĭciscor, ectus, icisci, *dep.* to set out; to advance; to go.
Prŏfĭteor, essus, ĭtēri, *dep.* to profess; to promise.
Prŏfŭgio, ūgi, ŭgĭtum, ŭgĕre, *n.* to flee; to escape.
Prŏfundo, ūdi, ūsum, undĕre, *a.* to pour forth; to squander.
Prōgrĕdior, essus, ĕdi, *dep.* to go forward; to proceed.
Prŏhĭbeo, ui, ĭtum, ēre, *a.* to forbid; to prohibit.
Proinde, *adv.* therefore; *with* ac, atque, quasi, tanquam, *or* ut, as if.
Prōmĕreo, —, —, ēre, *a.* to deserve; to deserve well.
Prōmitto, ĭsi, issum, ittĕre, *a.* to throw forward; to promise.
Prōmo, psi *or* si, ptum *or* tum, ĕre, *a.* to take out; to give forth.
Promptu (*only in the abl.*), in readiness.
Promptus, a, um, ready.
Pronuncio, āre, *a.* to pronounce; to declare; to nominate.
Prŏpè, *adv.* near at hand; almost; *comp.* propius, nearer.
Prōpello, pŭli, pulsum, pellĕre, *a.* to drive before one's self; drive out; to propel.
Prōpensus, a, um, inclined; approaching nearer.
Prŏpĕrātio, ōnis, *f.* a hastening.
Prŏpĕro, āre, *n.* to hasten.
Prŏpinquĭtas, ātis, *f.* nearness; relationship.
Prŏpinquus, a, um, neighbouring; nearly related; allied.
Prŏpior, or, us, nearer.
Prŏpĭtius, a, um, kind, favourable.
Prōpōno, ŏsui, ŏsĭtum, ōnĕre, *a.* to set up to view; to promise; to propose; to declare.
Prōpŏsĭtum, i, *n.* purpose.
Prŏprius, a, um, peculiar; proper.
Propter, *prep.* for, on account of.
Proptĕrea, *adv.* therefore.
Prōpulso, āre, *a.* to drive back.
Prōrŏgo, āre, *a.* to ask to prolong; to prolong.
Prorsus, *adv.* straightway; entirely; exactly.
Prōsĕquor, quūtus *or* cūtus, qui, *dep.* to follow after; to accompany; to pursue; to honour.
Prosper *et* prospĕrus, ĕra, ĕrum, prosperous, fortunate.
Prospĕre, *adv.* prosperously.
Prosterno, trāvi, trātum, ternĕre, *a.* to lay prostrate; to discomfit.
Prōsum, fui, desse, *n. irr.* to do good; to avail.
Prōvĕho, exi, ectum, ĕhĕre, *a.* to carry forward; to advance.
Prōverbium, i, *n.* a proverb.
Prōvĭdentia, æ, *f.* providence.
Prōvĭdeo, ĭdi, ĭsum, idēre, *a.* to foresee; to provide; to take care of.
Prōvincia, æ, *f.* a province; a country acquired by conquest; any office.
Proxĭmus, a, um, nearest; the next in succession; last.
Prūdens, ns, ns, ntis, foreseeing; prudent; skilful.
Prūdenter, *adv.* prudently.

Prūdentia, æ, *f.* foresight; prudence; skill.
Pūbesco, bui, —, bescĕre, *n.* to come to man's estate; to grow up.
Pūblĭcè, *adv.* publicly.
Pūblĭcus, a, um, public.
Publius, i, a Roman prænomen.
Pŭdet, uit *et* ĭtum est, ēre, *imp.* to be ashamed.
Pŭdīcĭtia, æ, *f.* bashfulness; virtuousness.
Pŭdīcus, a, um, shamefaced; virtuous.
Pŭdor, ōris, *m.* shame.
Puer, ĕri, *m.* a boy.
Puerīlis, is, e, puerile.
Pŭgil, ĭlis, *m.* a pugilist.
Pugna, æ, *f.* a fight.
Pugno, āre, *n.* to fight; to resist.
Pulcher, ra, rum, fair, beautiful.
Pulchrè, *adv.* beautifully.
Pungo, pŭpŭgi, punctum, pungĕre, *a.* to prick; to trouble.
Pūnio, īre, *a.* to punish.
Purgo, āre, *a.* to make pure; to justify.
Pŭto, āre, *a.* to think; to value.
Pyrrho, ōnis, the sceptic philosopher of Elis.
Pyrrhus, i, a king of Epirus.
Pȳthăgŏrēus, a, um, belonging to Pythagoras.
Pȳthăgŏras, æ, a celebrated philosopher.
Pythius, i, a banker at Syracuse.

Q

Q. = Quintus.
Quâ, *adv.* which way; where; how.
Quădrāginta, *pl. adj. indec.* forty.
Quădringēni, æ, a, four hundred each.
Quădringenti, æ, a, four hundred.
Quæro, sīvi, sītum, rĕre, *a.* to ask; to inquire.
Quæso, *def.* I pray.
Quæstio, ōnis, *f.* a seeking; an investigation; a question.
Quæstor, ōris, *m.* a quæstor, a Roman magistrate; the paymaster of a legion.
Quæstus, ûs, *m.* gain; a trade.
Quālis, is, e, of what kind.
Quam, *adv.* or *con.*, how, as; *after* tam, as; *after comparatives*, than; *with superlatives*, the highest possible degree, *as*, quam plurimi, as many as possible.
Quamdiu, *adv.* how long; so long as.
Quamobrem, *adv.* why; wherefore.
Quamplūres, a, *or* quam plūres, a, very many.
Quamplūrĭmus, a, um, very many, very much.
Quamprīmum, *adv.* as soon as possible.
Quamvis, *adv.* although; how much soever.
Quando, *adv.* when.
Quandoquĭdem, *adv.* since.
Quanquam *or* quamquam, *conj.* though.
Quantŭlus, a, um, how little; as little as.
Quantum, *adv.* as much as; as far as.
Quantus, a, um, how great; how much.
Quantuscunque, ăcunque, umcunque, how great soever; how much soever.
Quārē, *adv.* wherefore; why.
Quartus, a, um, fourth.
Quăsi, *conj.* as if.
Quătio, quassi, quassum, quatĕre, *a.* to shake violently; disquiet.
Quătuor, *adj. ind.* four.
Que, *insep. conj.* and; both.
Quĕmadmŏdum, *adv.* how, in what manner.
Queo, īvi, ĭtum, īre, *n. irr.* to be able.
Quĕrēla, æ, *f.* a complaint; a lamenting.
Quĕrĭmōnia, æ, *f.* a complaint.
Quĕror, estus, ĕri, *dep.* to complain.
Quī, quæ, quod, *rel. pron.* who, which, *or* that.
Quī, *adv.* how; by which.
Quia, *conj.* because.
Quīcunque, quæcunque, quodcunque, *pron.* whosoever, whatsoever.

Quĭdam, quædam, quoddam *or* quiddam, *pron.* some; a certain person or thing.
Quĭdem, *adv.* indeed, truly; ne — quidem, not even.
Qui*es*, ētis, *f.* rest; quiet.
Qui*esco*, ēvi, ētum, escĕre, *n.* to be quiet; to rest.
Quiēt*us*, a, um, quiet, peaceable.
Quīlĭbet, quælĭbet, quodlĭbet *or* quidlĭbet, *pron.* any one, any.
Quin, *con.* et *adv.* that not; but; but that; why not?
Quinetiam, *adv.* besides; yea, even.
Quincti*us*, i, *or* Quinti*us*, i, a Roman family name.
Quinquāginta, *adj. ind.* fifty.
Quinque, *adj. ind.* five.
Quint*us*, a, um, the fifth; a Roman prænomen.
Quippe, *conj.* for, because, since; as being.
Quis, quæ, quod *or* quid, *inter. pron.* who, which, what?
Quisnam, quænam, quodnam *or* quidnam, *pron.* who, which, what?
Quispiam, quæpiam, quodpiam *et* quidpiam *or* quippiam, *pron.* any one.
Quisquam, quæquam, quodquam *or* quidquam *or* quicquam, *pron.* any one.
Quisque, quæque, quodque *or* quidque, *pron.* each, every one.
Quisquis, —, quidquid *or* quicquid, *pron.* whosoever, whatsoever.
Quīvis, quævis, quodvis *or* quidvis, *pron.* whosoever, whatsoever.
Quō, *adv.* whither; that, to the end that.
Quoad, *adv.* as long as; until.
Quōcirca, *adv.* hence.
Quōcunque, *adv.* whithersoever.
Quod, *conj.* because; that.
Quōdammŏdo, *adv.* or quōdam modo, in a certain measure, in a manner.
Quōmĭnus, *adv.* that...not, but... that; by which the less.
Quōmŏdo, *adv.* how.
Quondam, *adv.* formerly.
Quŏniam, *conj.* because; seeing that; since.
Quŏque, *conj.* also; even.
Quorsum *or* quorsus, *adv.* whitherwards; whither.
Quot, *adj. ind.* how many.
Quŏtannis, *adv.* yearly.
Quŏtĭdiān*us*, a, um, daily.
Quŏtĭdie, *adv.* daily.
Quousque, *adv.* how long.
Quum *or* cum, *adv.* and *conj.* when; seeing; since; although; quum ...tum, both...and.

R

Racili*us*, i, a Roman family name.
Răp*io*, ui, tum, ĕre, *a.* to seize by force.
Rāro, *adv.* rarely; seldom.
Rār*us*, a, um, not thick, thin, rare, unfrequent.
Răti*o*, ōnis, *f.* reason; a cause; a manner; an account.
Rătiōcĭnāt*or*, ōris, *m.* a reckoner.
Răt*us*, a, um, ratified; fixed.
Raurăc*i*, ōrum, a people of Gaul.
Rĕcē*do*, ssi, ssum, dĕre, *n.* to retire; to retract.
Rĕcĭ*pio*, ēpi, eptum, ĭpĕre, *a.* to take again; to recover; to receive; to retreat; to take upon one's self.
Rĕcordāti*o*, ōnis, *f.* a remembering.
Rĕcord*or*, ātus, āri, *dep.* to remember.
Recte, *adv.* rightly; well.
Rect*us*, a, um, straight; upright.
Rĕcŭb*o*, ui, ĭtum, āre, *n.* to lie down.
Rĕcŭpĕr*o*, āre, *a.* to regain, to recover.
Rĕcūs*o*, āre, *a.* to refuse.
Reddo, ĭdi, ĭtum, ĕre, *a.* to give back; to make; to deliver.
Rĕdempt*or*, ōris, *m.* a buyer; a contractor.
Rĕd*eo*, ii, ĭtum, īre, *n. irr.* to go back; to return.
Rĕdintĕgr*o*, āre, *a.* to restore; to renew.
Rĕdĭt*us*, ûs, *m.* a return.
Rĕdūc*o*, xi, ctum, cĕre, *a.* to lead back; to restore; to draw back.

Rĕfĕro, tŭli, lātum, ferre, *a. irr.* to bring back, to restore; to bring back word; to refer to; to apply; to deliver.
Rēfert, *imp.* it concerns.
Rĕfĭcio, ēci, ectum, ĭcĕre, *a.* to restore; to repair; to recruit.
Rĕformīdo, āre, *a.* to dread.
Rĕfringo, ēgi, actum, ingĕre, *a.* to break open; to weaken; to subdue.
Rĕfŭgio, ūgi, ŭgĭtum, ŭgĕre, *n.* to flee away; to flee for refuge; *a.* to shun.
Rĕfūto, āre, *a.* to repress; to refute.
Rĕgio, ōnis, *f.* a line; a district; e regione, in a straight line, over against.
Regno, āre, *n.* to reign.
Regnum, i, *n.* a kingdom.
Rĕgo, rexi, rectum, rĕgĕre, *a.* to direct; to regulate; to rule; to correct.
Rēgŭla, æ, *f.* a rule.
Rējĭcio, ēci, ectum, ĭcĕre, *a.* to throw back; to keep back; to reject; to refer.
Rĕlēgo, āre, *a.* to send away; to banish.
Rĕlĕvo, āre, *a.* to lighten; to refresh.
Rĕlĭgio, ōnis, *f.* religion; a religious scruple.
Rĕlinquo, ĭqui, ictum, inquĕre, *a.* to leave; to relinquish.
Rĕlĭquiæ, ārum, *f.* the remains of anything; the rest.
Rĕlĭquus, a, um, remaining; the rest.
Rĕmăneo, si, sum, ēre, *n.* to remain behind; to continue.
Rĕmĕdium, i, *n.* a remedy.
Rĕmĭniscor, —, ci, to remember.
Rĕmitto, ĭsi, issum, ittĕre, *a.* to send back; to slacken; to remit; to grant.
Rĕmŏveo, ōvi, ōtum, ŏvēre, *a.* to remove.
Rĕnŏvo, āre, *a.* to renew; to refresh.
Rĕnuncio, or rĕnuntio, āre, *a.* to bring back word; to report; to disclaim; to appoint.
Reor, rătus, rēri, *dep.* to think.
Rĕpello, ŭli, ulsum, ellĕre, *a.* to repel; to reject.
Rĕpentè, *adv.* suddenly.
Rĕpentīnus, a um, sudden; unexpected.
Rĕpĕrio, i, tum, īre, *a.* to find; to discover.
Rĕpĕto, īvi, ītum, ĕre, *a.* to seek back; to return to; to repeat.
Rĕpōno, ŏsui, ŏsĭtum, ōnĕre, *a.* to lay back; to lay aside; to replace; to place.
Rĕprĕhendo, di, sum, dĕre, *a.* to catch again; to seize; to blame.
Rĕprĭmo, essi, essum, ĭmĕre, *a.* to repress.
Rĕpŭdio, āre, *a.* to reject; to remove.
Rĕpuĕrasco, —, —, ĕre, *n.* to grow young again; to play the child.
Rĕpugno, āre, *n.* to fight against; to oppose.
Rĕpulsa, æ, *f.* a repulse.
Rĕquīro, sīvi, sītum, rĕre, *a.* to inquire; to require; to search for.
Res, ei, *f.* a thing; an affair.
Rescisco, īvi, ītum, iscĕre, *a.* to learn again; to learn.
Rescrībo, psi, ptum, bĕre, *a.* to write back; to answer; to transfer.
Rĕsisto, tĭti, tĭtum, istĕre, *n.* to stand still; to resist; to prevent.
Respĭcio, exi, ectum, ĭcĕre, *a.* to look back; to consider; to care for.
Respīro, āre, *a.* to respire; to revive; to recover breath; to cease, abate.
Respondeo, di, sum, dēre, *a.* to reply; to correspond to.
Responsio, ōnis, *f.* a reply.
Respūblĭca, reipublĭcæ, *f.* a republic; a state.
Restinguo, xi, ctum, guĕre, *a.* to extinguish; to quench; to destroy.
Restĭtuo, ui, ūtum, uĕre, *a.* to restore; to reinstate.
Resto, stĭti, —, stāre, *n.* to remain; restat, *imp.* it remains.
Rĕtardo, āre, *a.* to delay.

Rěticeo, ui, —, ēre, *n.* to be silent; *a.* to keep secret.
Rětineo, inui, entum, ĭnēre, *a.* to hold back; to retain.
Rětracto, āre, *a.* to handle again; to reconsider; to refuse.
Rětrĭbuo, ui, ūtum, uěre, *a.* to give back; to return.
Rětundo, tŭdi, tūsum *et* tunsum, tunděre, *a.* to hold back; to blunt.
Reus, i, *m.* the accused, a defendant.
Rěvěreor, ĭtus, ēri, *dep.* to fear.
Rěvertor, sus, ti, *dep.* and reverto, ti, sum, těre, *n.* to turn back; to return; to come.
Rěvŏco, āre, *a.* to recall; to restore; to return.
Rex, ēgis, *m.* a king.
Rhēnus, i, *m.* the Rhine.
Rhētor, ŏris, *m.* a rhetorician; an orator.
Rhodănus, i, *m.* the Rhone.
Rhŏdius, a, um, belonging to Rhodos.
Rīdeo, īsi, īsum, ĭdēre, *a.* to laugh at; *n.* to laugh.
Rīsus, ûs, *m.* laughing.
Rītus, ûs, *m.* a rite; a fashion.
Rīvŭlus, i, a brook.
Rŏgo, āre, *a.* to ask; to request.
Rōma, æ, Rome.
Romānus, a um, belonging to Rome.
Roscius, i, a Roman family name.
Rostrum, i, *n.* the beak; *pl.* the orator's pulpit.
Rŏta, æ, *f.* a wheel.
Rŭdis, is, e, rude; inexperienced.
Rūmor, ōris, *m.* a rumour.
Ruo, i, ĭtum, ěre, *n.* to fall down; to rush on; *a.* to throw down; to ruin.
Rursus, *et* um, *adv.* again.

S

S. *or* Sex. = Sextus.
Săbīnus, a, um, belonging to the Sabines.
Săcrāmentum, i, *n.* the military oath.
Săcrĭfĭcium, i, *n.* a sacrifice.
Sæpè, *adv.* often; *comp.* sæpius, *sup.* sæpissime.
Sæpěnŭměro, *adv.* ofttimes.
Sævio, ii *or* ivi, ītum, īre, *n.* to rage.
Săgitta, æ, *f.* an arrow.
Sălămīnius, a, um, belonging to Salamis.
Salsāmentum, i, *n.* fish pickle.
Salto, āre, *n.* to dance.
Sălus, ūtis, *f.* safety; health.
Sălūtāris, is, e, healthful; profitable.
Sălūto, āre, *a.* to salute; to greet.
Salvus, a, um, safe; sound.
Sancio, xi, ctum *or* cīvi, cītum, cīre, *a.* to make sacred; to ratify; to enact.
Sanctè, *adv.* religiously.
Sane, *adv.* truly; then.
Sanguis, ĭnis, *m.* blood; kindred.
Sānĭtas, ātis, *f.* soundness; health; sanity.
Sāno, āre, *a.* to heal; to restore.
Santŏnes, um, a people of Aquitania.
Sānus, a, um, sound.
Săpiens, ns, ns, ntis, wise.
Săpienter, *adv.* wisely; *comp.* sapientius.
Săpientia, æ, *f.* wisdom; knowledge.
Săpio, ivi *or* ui, —, ěre, *n.* to taste of; to be wise.
Sassius, a, um, a Roman family name.
Sătis, *adv.* enough.
Sătisdo, dědi, dătum, dăre, *n.* to give enough; to give security.
Sătisfăcio, ēci, actum, ăcěre, *n.* to satisfy.
Satrius, i, a man's name.
Sāturnīnus, a, um, a Roman family name.
Scapula, æ, a Roman surname.
Scělěrātus, a, um, wicked.
Scělus, ěris, *n.* wickedness.
Scēna, æ, *f.* a scene, a stage.
Schŏla, æ, *f.* leisure; a school; a sect.
Scientia, æ, *f.* knowledge; science.
Scio, īre, *a.* to know.
Scīpio, ōnis, surname of the Cornelian family.

Scrībo, psi, ptum, bĕre, *a.* to write.
Scriptum, i, *n.* a writing.
Scūtum, i, *n.* a shield.
Sēcius, *adv.* otherwise.
Sĕco, cui, ctum, cāre, *a.* to cut; to divide.
Sĕcŭlum, i, *n.* an age.
Sĕcundum, *prep.* according to.
Sĕcundus, a, um, second; favourable.
Sĕcūrus, a, um, free from anxiety.
Sĕcus, *adv.* less; otherwise.
Sĕd, *conj.* but.
Sĕdeo, ēdi, essum, edēre, *n.* to sit.
Sēdĭtiōsus, a, um, seditious.
Sējungo, xi, ctum, gĕre, *a.* to disjoin.
Sĕmel, *adv.* once, once for all.
Sĕmĭrămis, is *et* ĭdis, queen of Assyria.
Semper, *adv.* always.
Sempĭternus, a, um, everlasting.
Sĕnātus, ûs, *m.* a senate.
Sĕnatûs-consultum, i, *n.* a decree of the senate.
Sĕnectus, ūtis, *f.* old age.
Sĕnex, is, old; *comp.* senior; *wants the superlative.*
Sĕnīlis, is, e, senile.
Sĕnium, i, *n.* old age; sorrow.
Sensus, ûs, *m.* sense; feeling; judgment.
Sententia, æ, *f.* opinion; resolution.
Sentio, si, sum, tīre, *a.* to perceive; to think.
Sēpărātim, *adv.* separately.
Sēpăro, āre, *a.* to separate; to divide.
Septem, *pl. adj. ind.* seven.
Septĭmus, a, um, seventh.
Sĕpulcrum, i, *n.* a sepulchre, a tomb.
Sĕquăni, ōrum, a people of Gaul.
Sĕquor, quūtus, *or* cūtus, qui, *dep.* to follow; to pursue; sequitur, *imp.* it follows.
Ser. = Servius.
Sĕrapio, ōnis, surname of several persons.
Serĭphius, i, belonging to the island of Seriphus.
Sermo, ōnis, *m.* talk; speech.
Serpens, tis, *c.* a serpent.
Sertōrius, i, a Roman family name.
Servio, īre, *n.* to serve; to gratify; to conform to.
Servĭtus, ūtis, *f.* slavery; bondage.
Servo, āre, *a.* to keep; to observe; to preserve.
Servus, i, *m.* a slave; a servant.
Sestertius, i, *m.* a sesterce, worth about one penny three farthings.
Seu, *conj.* whether.
Sextius, i, a Roman family name.
Sextus, i, a Stoic philosopher.
Sī, *conj.* if.
Sībĭlus, i, *m.* a hissing.
Sīc, *adv.* so, thus.
Sicilia, æ, Sicily.
Sīcut, *adv.* as; such as.
Signĭfĭco, āre, *a.* to give notice; to signify.
Signum, i, *n.* a sign; a standard.
Sĭleo, ui, —, ēre, *n.* to be silent.
Silva, æ, *f.* a wood.
Sĭmĭlis, is, e, like.
Sĭmĭlĭter, *adv.* similarly.
Sĭmĭlĭtūdo, ĭnis, *f.* likeness.
Simplex, ex, ex, ĭcis, simple; candid.
Sĭmul, *adv.* together; at the same time; simul ut, as soon as.
Sĭmŭlātio, ōnis, *f.* pretence; dissembling.
Sĭmŭlo, āre, *a.* to make like; to pretend.
Sīn, *conj.* but if.
Sĭne, *prep.* without.
Singŭlāris, is, e, single; singular.
Singuli, æ, a, single; one by one.
Sĭnister, ra, rum, belonging to the left hand; unlucky.
Sĭno, sīvi, sĭtum, sinĕre, *a.* to permit.
Sisto, —, —, sistĕre, *n.* to stand; to appear; to be fixed.
Sīve, *conj.* whether, or.
Sōbrius, a, um, sober.
Sŏciĕtas, ātis, *f.* partnership; society.
Sŏcius, i, *m.* a partner; a companion.
Sŏcrătes, is, the celebrated Athenian philosopher, the founder of the ancient Academy.
Sōl, is, *m.* the sun; Apollo.
Sŏleo, ĭtus, ēre, *n. p.* to be accustomed.

Sōlertia, æ, *f.* cleverness; craft.
Sōlĭtūdo, ĭnis, *f.* solitude; a wilderness.
Sollĭcĭto, āre, *a.* to stir; to trouble; to tempt; to allure.
Sollĭcĭtūdo, ĭnis, *f.* solicitude.
Sŏlon, ōnis, the Athenian lawgiver, and one of the seven sages of Greece.
Sōlum, *adv.* only, merely.
Sŏlum, i, *n.* the lowest part of anything; the ground or soil.
Sōlus, a, um, alone; only.
Sŏlūtus, a, um, free.
Solvo, vi, ūtum, vĕre, *a.* to loose; to pay.
Somnio, āre, *a. et n.* to dream.
Somnus, i, *m.* sleep.
Sŏno, ui, ĭtum, āre, *n.* to sound; *a.* to mean.
Sons, tis, guilty.
Sŏnus, i, *m.* a sound.
Sŏphista, æ, *m.* a sophist.
Sotiātes, um, a people of Aquitania.
Spĕcies, ēi, *f.* an appearance; a pretext; a kind.
Spĕcĭmen, ĭnis, *n.* an example; a proof.
Spectācŭlum, i, *n.* a spectacle.
Specto, āre, *a. et n.* to behold; to view with attention; to consider; to have in view; to look to; to belong to.
Spĕcŭlātor, ōris, *m.* an observer; a scout.
Spĕcŭlor, ātus, āri, *dep.* to watch; to pry into.
Sperno, sprēvi, sprētum, spernĕre, *a.* to despise.
Spēro, āre, *a.* to hope.
Spes, ei, *f.* hope.
Spīrĭtus, ûs, *m.* breath, spirit.
Splendor, ōris, *m.* brightness; beauty; respectability.
Spŏlio, āre, *a.* to deprive of; to plunder.
Spondeo, spŏpondi, sponsum, spondēre, *a.* to promise.
Sponsio, ōnis, *f.* a promise; a security.
Spontis, *gen.* (rarely) and *abl.* sponte, of one's own accord.
Squāleo, ui, —, ēre, *n.* to be stiff; to be filthy; to be in mourning.
Stăbĭlis, is, e, stable; lasting.
Stădium, i, *n.* a race-course.
Stalenus, i, a Roman senator.
Statim, *adv.* immediately.
Stătua, æ, *f.* a statue.
Stătuo, ui, ūtum, uĕre, *a.* to set; to appoint; to resolve.
Stătūra, æ, *f.* stature.
Stătus, ûs, *m.* a standing; a condition.
Stella, æ, *f.* a star.
Stīpendium, i, *n.* the pay of soldiers; tribute.
Stirps, is, *c.* the root of a tree; *f.* a family; lineage.
Sto, stĕti, stătum, stāre, *n.* to stand; to continue; *impers.* per te stat, it is owing to you.
Stoicus, a, um, belonging to the Stoics; *s.* a Stoic.
Stŏmăchor, ātus, āri, *dep.* to be indignant.
Stŭdeo, ui, —, ēre, *n.* to study; to desire; to endeavour.
Stŭdiōsè, *adv.* carefully; studiously.
Stŭdiōsus, a, um, careful; fond; studious.
Stŭdium, i, *n.* study; eager pursuit.
Stultè, *adv.* foolishly.
Stultĭtia, æ, *f.* folly; stupidity.
Stultus, a, um, foolish.
Stŭpor, ōris, *m.* stupor; stupidity.
Suādeo, si, sum, dēre, *n.* to advise; to persuade.
Suāsor, ōris, *m.* an adviser.
Suāvĭtas, ātis, *f.* sweetness; pleasantness.
Sŭb, *prep.* under; at; near.
Subdūco, xi, ctum, cĕre, *a.* to withdraw secretly; to free from.
Sŭbeo, ii, ĭtum, īre, *a. irr.* to go under; to undergo.
Subĭgo, ēgi, actum, ĭgĕre, *a.* to subdue; to constrain.
Sŭbĭto, *adv.* suddenly.
Sŭbĭtus, a, um, sudden; unexpected.
Subjĭcio, ēci, ectum, ĭcĕre, *a.* to put under; to subject.
Sublĕvo, āre, *a.* to lighten; to raise up; to support.

Subsĕquor, cūtus, qui, *dep.* to follow immediately; to attend.
Subsĭdium, i, *n.* aid; a body of reserve.
Subterfŭgio, ūgi, ŭgitum, ŭgĕre, *a.* to escape.
Subtīlis, is, e, exquisite; accurate; acute; simple.
Subtīlĭter, *adv.* accurately; fully; with simplicity.
Subtrăho, xi, ctum, hĕre, *a.* to withdraw.
Sŭburbānus, a, um, suburban.
Succēdo, ssi, ssum, dĕre, *n.* to go under; to advance; to succeed.
Succenseo, ui, —, ēre, *n.* to be angry at.
Succumbo, ŭbui, ŭbĭtum, umbĕre, *n.* to sink under; to yield.
Succurro, ri, sum, rĕre, *n.* to hasten to; to come to one's aid; to occur to one's mind.
Succus, i, *m.* juice; moisture.
Suesco, suēvi, suētum, suescĕre, *n.* to be accustomed.
Suessiōnes, um, a people of Belgic Gaul.
Suevi, ōrum, a people of Germany.
Suffōco, āre, *a.* to strangle, choke.
Suffrāgium, i, *n.* a vote.
Sŭi, *pron. gen.* of himself, herself, itself.
Sulla, *see* Sylla.
Sulmonensis, is, e, belonging to Sulmo, a town of the Peligni, and the birthplace of Ovid.
Sulpĭcius, i, a Roman family name.
Sum, fui, esse, *n. irr.* to be.
Summe, *adv.* in the greatest degree.
Summus, a, um, highest; greatest.
Sūmo, psi, ptum, ĕre, *a.* to take; to assume.
Sumptus, ûs, *m.* expense.
Sŭper, *prep.* above; upon; about.
Sŭperbia, æ, *f.* pride.
Sŭperbus, a, um, proud, disdainful.
Sŭpĕrior, or, us, higher.
Sŭpĕro, āre, *a.* to go over; to overcome; to surpass; *n.* to be above.
Sŭperstes, ĭtis, present, remaining.
Sŭpĕrus, a, um, above, high; *comp.* superior; *sup.* supremus *or* summus.
Supplanto, āre, *a.* to supplant.
Supplex, ex, ex, ĭcis, suppliant.
Supplĭcium, i, *n.* a kneeling down; punishment.
Sŭprā, *prep.* above; beyond.
Surgo, rexi, rectum, gĕre, *n.* to rise.
Suscĭpio, ēpi, eptum, ĭpĕre, *a.* to take up; to take; to receive; to undertake.
Suspĭcio, exi, ectum, ĭcĕre, *n.* to look up; *a.* to look up at, to admire.
Suspīcio, ōnis, *f.* suspicion.
Suspĭcor, ātus, āri, *dep.* to suspect; to imagine.
Sustento, āre, *a.* to sustain; to preserve; to endure; to defer.
Sustĭneo, inui, entum, ĭnēre, *a.* to bear; to sustain; to withstand.
Suus, a, um, *poss. pron.* his own, her own, its own, their own.
Sylla *or* **Sulla**, æ, a surname of the Cornelian family.
Sȳrăcūsæ, ārum, Syracuse.
Sȳria, æ, a country of Asia.

T

T. = Titus.
Tăbellārius, i, *m.* a letter carrier.
Tăbŭla, æ, *f.* a board; a table.
Tăceo, ēre, *n.* to be silent.
Tædet, uit *et* ĭtum est, ēre, *imp.* it wearies.
Tālis, is, e, such, like.
Tam, *adv.* so, so much.
Tamdiu, *adv.* so long.
Tămen, *conj.* however, nevertheless.
Tămetsi, *conj.* although.
Tandem, *adv.* at length; at last.
Tanquam, *adv.* as if.
Tanto, *adv.* by so much.
Tantŏpĕre, *adv.* so greatly, so much.
Tantŭlus, a, um, so little.
Tantum, *adv.* so much, only.
Tantus, a, um, so great, so much.
Tardĭtas, ātis, *f.* slowness.

Tardus, a, um, slow; heavy; stupid.
Tărentum, i, a town of Calabria.
Tarquĭnius, a, um, belonging to Tarquinii.
Tarquĭnius, i, the name of two Roman kings.
Taurus, i, *m.* a bull.
Tĕgo, texi, tectum, tegĕre, *a.* to cover; to conceal; to protect.
Tellus, ūris, *f.* the earth.
Tēlum, i, *n.* a dart, an arrow.
Tĕmĕrārius, a, um, rash, violent.
Tĕmĕre, *adv.* rashly.
Tĕmĕrĭtas, ātis, *f.* rashness.
Tempĕrantia, æ, *f.* temperance.
Tempĕro, āre, *n.* to be moderate; to abstain, restrain; *a.* to moderate; to mitigate, regulate.
Tempestas, ātis, *f.* time; a season of the year; weather; a storm.
Templum, i, *n.* a temple.
Tempus, ŏris, *n.* time; opportunity; circumstances.
Tendo, tetendi, tensum *or* tentum, tendĕre, *a.* to stretch out; to give; *n.* to go; to intend; to aim at.
Tĕnĕbræ, ārum, *f.* darkness.
Tĕneo, ui, tum, ēre, *a.* to hold; to possess; to refrain.
Tĕner, ĕra, ĕrum, tender.
Tento, āre, to try; to attempt.
Tĕnuis, is, e, slender; weak; trifling.
Tĕrentius, i, a writer of comedies.
Tergum, i, *n.* the back.
Termĭno, are, *a.* to enclose; to regulate; to end.
Termĭnus, i, *m.* a boundary; a limit; an end.
Tĕro, trīvi, trītum, terĕre, *a.* to rub; to use often; to make common; to spend.
Terra, æ, *f.* the earth.
Terreo, ui, ĭtum, ēre, *a.* to frighten.
Terror, ōris, *m.* terror.
Tertius, a, um, third.
Testāmentum, i, *n.* a testament.
Testĭfĭcor, ātus, āri, *dep.* to call to witness; to bear witness; to show.
Testĭmōnium, i, *n.* an evidence; testimony.
Testis, is, *c.* a witness.
Testor, ātus, āri, to bear witness; to declare; to call to witness.
Teutŏnes, um, *and* Teutoni, ōrum, a people of Germany.
Thăles, *or* Thaletis, is, a Greek philosopher.
Thēbæ, ārum, Thebes, the capital of Bœotia.
Thĕmistŏcles, is, an Athenian, the rival of Aristides.
Theŏphrastus, i, a Greek philosopher.
Thrax, ācis, Thracian.
Thūcydĭdes, is, a celebrated Greek historian.
Ti. = Tiberius.
Tĭbĕris, is, *m.* the Tiber.
Tigrānes, is, a king of Armenia.
Tĭmeo, ui, —, ēre, *a. et n.* to fear.
Timĭdus, a, um, fearful.
Tĭmor, ōris, *m.* fear.
Tĭtus, i, a Roman prænomen.
Tŏlĕro, āre, *a.* to endure; to sustain.
Tollo, sustŭli, sublātum, tollĕre, *a.* to raise; to extol; to remove.
Torquātus, i, a surname of the Manlian family.
Torqueo, torsi, tortum, torquēre, *a.* to turn; to twist awry; to torture; to afflict.
Torquis or **es**, is, *c.* a necklace.
Tŏt, *adj. pl. ind.* so many, as many.
Tōtus, a, um, whole.
Tracto, āre, *a.* to handle; to treat.
Trādo, ĭdi, ĭtum, ĕre, *a.* to give up; to hand down, relate.
Trādūco, xi, ctum, cĕre, *a.* to bring over; to lead past; to spend; to traduce.
Trăgula, æ, *f.* a missile weapon.
Trăho, xi, ctum, hĕre, *a.* to draw; to attract; to prolong.
Tranquillĭtas, ātis, *f.* tranquillity.
Tranquillo, āre, *a.* to make calm; to tranquillize.
Trans, *prep.* beyond; over.
Transduco, *see* Tradūco.
Transeo, ii, ĭtum, īre, *n. irr.* to go over; *a.* to pass over; to exceed.
Transfĕro, tŭli, lātum, ferre, *a. irr.* to carry over; to transfer;

to translate; to accommodate; to direct.
Transfīgo, xi, xum, gĕre, *a.* to pierce through; to transfix.
Transĭgo, ēgi, actum, ĭgĕre, *a.* to drive through; to stab; to pass time; to finish; to transact.
Transporto, āre, *a.* to carry over; to transport; to banish.
Trĕbōnius, i, a Roman family name.
Trĕcenti, æ, a, three hundred.
Trĕpĭdo, āre, *n.* to be in a bustle; to tremble.
Trēs, tres, tria, three.
Trĭbūnātus, ûs, *m.* the office of tribune.
Trĭbūnus, i, *m.* a tribune.
Trĭbuo, ui, ūtum, uĕre, *a.* to give; to allot; to ascribe.
Trīgēsĭmus, a, um, the thirtieth.
Trinummus, i, the name of one of Plautus' comedies.
Trĭpartītus, a, um, divided into three parts.
Trĭplex, ex, ex, ĭcis, threefold; triple.
Tristis, is, e, sorrowful; morose; cruel.
Triumvir, ĭri, *m.* one of three men united in office; a triumvir.
Triumvĭrātus, ûs, *m.* the office of a triumvir.
Trœzen, ēnis, a town of Argolis.
Trōja, æ, Troy.
Tū, tui, *m. or f. pron.* thou.
Tŭba, æ, *f.* a trumpet.
Tueor, tuĭtus *or* tūtus, tuēri, *dep.* to see; to defend; to keep.
Tullius, a, um, a Roman family name.
Tum, *adv.* then; *conj.* tum ... tum, *or* quum ... tum, both ... and.
Tŭmor, ōris, *m.* a tumour; a commotion.
Tumultus, ûs, *m.* a tumult.
Tunc, *adv.* then.
Turba, æ, *f.* a crowd; a tumult.
Turbŭlentus, a, um, disturbed; turbulent.
Turma, æ, *f.* a troop; a crowd.
Turpis, is, e, ugly; base.
Turpĭter, *adv.* basely.
Turpĭtūdo, ĭnis, *f.* ugliness; baseness.
Turris, is, *f.* a tower; a besieging tower.
Tūto, *adv.* safely; *comp.* tutius.
Tūtus, a, um, safe.
Tuus, a, um, *pron.* thy *or* thine.
Tyche, es, a part of Syracuse.
Tўrannis, ĭdis, *f.* tyranny; despotism.
Tўro, us, the wife of Cretheus.

U

Ūber, er, er, ĕris, rich; fertile.
Ūbertas, ātis, *f.* fruitfulness; abundance.
Ŭbī, *adv.* where; when.
Ubii, ōrum, a people on the Rhine.
Ulciscor, tus, cisci, *dep.* to avenge; to punish.
Ullus, a, um, *gen.* ullīus, any; any one.
Ultĕrior, or, us, farther.
Ultimus, a, um, the first; the utmost.
Umbrātĭlis, is, e, fond of the shade; retired.
Unā, *adv.* together.
Undè, *adv.* whence.
Undĭque, *adv.* on every side.
Unguentum, i, *n.* a perfume.
Unĭversus, a um, the whole; universal.
Unquam, *adv.* ever.
Ūnus, a, um, one; alone.
Urbs, is, *f.* a city.
Urgeo, ursi, —, urgēre, *a.* to press; to oppress; to incite.
Ūro, ussi, ustum, urĕre, *a.* to burn.
Usĭtātus, a, um, usual.
Usquam, *adv.* anywhere.
Usque, *adv.* constantly; as far as; even unto.
Usus, ûs, *m.* use; utility; occasion; intimacy.
Ŭt *or* uti, *conj.* and *adv.* that, as, how, when, although, as soon as.
Ŭter, ra, rum, whether of two.
Ŭterque, ŭtrăque, ŭtrumque, utriusque, both, the one and the other; each.
Ūtĭlis, is, e, useful; profitable.
Ūtĭlĭtas, ātis, *f.* utility; profit.
Ŭtĭnam, conj. O that! I wish that!

Ūtor, ūsus, ūti, *dep.* to use; to enjoy.
Utpŏte, *adv.* as; seeing; inasmuch as.
Utrum, *adv.* whether.
Ūva, æ, *f.* a grape.
Uxor, ōris, *f.* a wife.

V

Văco, āre, *n.* to be at leisure; to be free from; to be void, empty.
Vădum, i, *n.* a ford.
Văgor, ātus, āri, *dep.* to wander about; to waver.
Valdè, *adv.* very much; exceedingly.
Văleo, ēre, *n.* to be in health; to be able; to prevail.
Vălētūdo, ĭnis, *f.* health.
Vallum, i, *n.* a rampart.
Vānus, a, um, vain; empty.
Văriĕtas, ātis, *f.* variety; fickleness.
Vărius, a, um, various; changeable.
Varix, ĭcis, *c.* a swollen vein in the leg.
Varro, ōnis, a surname of the Terentian family; Terentius, the contemporary of Cicero.
Vasto, āre, *a.* to lay waste.
Vātes, is, *c.* a prophet; a poet.
Vĕ, *an enclitic conj.* or; either.
Vectīgal, ālis, *n.* a toll; revenue.
Vectīgālis, is, e, what is paid as a tax; bound to pay to taxes; tributary; producing revenue.
Vĕhĕmens, ns, ns, ntis, vehement; strong.
Vĕhĕmenter, *adv.* vehemently.
Vĕl, *conj.* or, either; even.
Vĕlut, *adv.* as; as if.
Vēnātor, ōris, *m.* a hunter; one who inquires into.
Vendĭtor, ōris, *m.* a seller.
Vendo, ĭdi, ĭtum, ĕre, *a.* to sell.
Vĕnēnātus, a, um, poisoned; poisonous.
Vĕnēnum, i. *n.* poison.
Vēneo, ii, —, īre, *n.* to be sold.
Vĕnĕror, ātus, āri, *dep.* to venerate; to worship.
Vĕnĕtus, a, um, belonging to Venetia.
Vĕnia, æ, *f.* leave; pardon.
Venio, ēni, entum, enīre, *n.* to come; venit, *imp.* it happens.
Vēnor, ātus, āri, *dep.* to hunt.
Ventĭdius, i, a Roman family name.
Ventĭto, āre, *a. et n.* to come often.
Ventus, i, *m.* the wind.
Verber, ĕris, *n. used in the sing. only in the gen. and abl., but complete in the plur.*, a scourge; a blow.
Verbĕro, āre, *a.* to beat; to scourge; to molest.
Verbum, i, *n.* a word.
Vērè, *adv.* indeed; truly.
Vĕrēcundia, æ, *f.* respect, modesty.
Vĕrēcundus, a, um, modest.
Vĕreor, ĭtus, ēri, *dep.* to revere; to fear.
Vērĭsĭmĭlis, is, e, probable.
Vērĭtas, ātis, *f.* truth.
Vēro, *conj.* but; *adv.* truly; indeed.
Verres, is, a Roman surname; Caius, the Sicilian prætor, against whom Cicero delivered several of his orations.
Versor, ātus, āri, *dep.* to turn; to be employed about; to dwell.
Verto, ti, sum, tĕre, *a.* to turn; to overturn; to alter.
Vērum, *conj.* but, but yet.
Vĕruntămen *or* vērumtămen, but; however.
Vērus, a, um, true; real.
Vesontio, ōnis, the capital of the Sequani.
Vespa, æ, *f.* a wasp.
Vespasianus, i, one of the Roman emperors.
Vesper, ĕris, *and* vesperus *or* vesper, ĕri, *m.* the evening.
Vester, ra, rum, your *or* yours.
Vestīgium, i, *n.* the print of a foot; a trace.
Vestīgium, i, *n.* a step with the foot, a footstep; the foot.
Vestīmentum, i, *n.* a garment.
Vestis, is, *f.* a garment.
Vĕtĕrānus, a, um, old; *s. m.* a veteran.
Vĕto, ui, ĭtum, āre, *a.* to forbid.
Vĕtus, us, us, ĕris, old, ancient.

Vĕtustas, ātis, *f.* antiquity; old age.
Vexillum, i, *n.* a standard; a banner.
Via, æ, *f.* a way.
Vibillius, *or* Vibullius Rufus, a friend of Pompey's.
Vīcīnus, a, um, neighbouring.
Vīcīnus, i, *m.* a neighbour.
Victōria, æ, *f.* victory.
Victus, ūs, *m.* food; victuals.
Vīcus, i, *m.* a village.
Vīdēlĭcet, *adv.* one may see; certainly; namely.
Vĭdeo, īdi, īsum, ĭdēre, *a.* to see; *pass.* to seem.
Vĭgeo, ui, —, ēre, *n.* to be fresh; to flourish.
Villa, æ, *f.* a farm-house; a villa.
Vincio, nxi, nctum, ncīre, *a.* to bind.
Vinco, īci, ictum, incĕre, *a.* to conquer.
Vincŭlum, i, *n.* a chain; bond.
Vindĭco, āre, *a.* to avenge; to claim; to assert one's liberty.
Vīnea, æ, *f.* a vineyard; a shed used at sieges for protecting the assailants.
Vīnum, i, *n.* wine.
Viŏlo, āre. *a.* to hurt.
Vir, iri, *m.* a man, a husband.
Viridomărus, or Virdumăris, i, a king of the Gauls.
Viridovix, icis, a chief of the Unelli.
Virtus, ūtis, *f.* valour; virtue.
Vīs, vim, vi, *f.* force, violence; *plur.* vires, ium, strength, power.
Vīta, æ, *f.* life.
Vĭtium, i, *n.* vice, a fault.
Vīto, āre, *a.* to shun.
Vĭtŭlus, i, *m.* a young bullock.
Vĭtŭpĕrātio, ōnis, *f.* blaming.
Vīvo, vixi, victum, vivĕre, *n.* to live.
Vīvus, a um, alive; lively.
Vix, *adv.* scarcely, with difficulty.
Vŏcābŭlum, i, *n.* a word; a name.
Vŏcātio, ōnis, *f.* a calling.
Vŏcĭto, āre, *a.* to call often; to call.
Vŏco, āre, *a.* to call; to summon.
Voconii Forum, a place near Marseilles.
Vŏlo, vŏlui, velle, *n. irr.* to be willing, to wish.
Vŏluntas, ātis, *f.* will; pleasure; good-will.
Vŏluptas, ātis, *f.* pleasure.
Volusenus, C. a military tribune.
Vōtum, i, *n.* a vow.
Vŏveo, vōvi, vōtum, vovēre, *a.* to promise; to vow.
Vox, vōcis, *f.* a voice; a word.
Vulcānius, a um, belonging to Vulcan.
Vulcānus, i, the god of fire.
Vulgo, āre, *a.* to make common, to make known, spread abroad, divulge.
Vulgo, *adv.* here and there; generally.
Vulgus, i, *n.* the common people.
Vulnĕro, āre, *a.* to wound; to offend,
Vulnus, ĕris, *n.* a wound.

X

Xĕnocrătes, is, a disciple of Plato.
Xĕnŏphon, ōntis, a disciple of Socrates.
Xerxes, is, king of Persia.

Z

Zēno, ōnis, the founder of the Stoics.

INDEX.

---

* See p. 12.

B

G

H

I

J

L

M

N

O

* Cicero sometimes constructs permitto with the infinitive; in which he is not to be imitated. Cæsar uses always *ut*.

Q

T

THE END.

CPSIA information can be obtained
at www.ICGtesting.com
Printed in the USA
LVHW111636170422
716440LV00006B/588

9 783752 594102